高等院校英语测试指导类公共选修课教材

主审 黄远振 / 主编 林明金 / 编著 黄梅仙 邓敏容

新思路 大学英语

六级实训教程

阅读分册

New Perspective
College English Test:Band 6

● Reading

国防工业出版社
National Defense Industry Press

图书在版编目(CIP)数据

新思路大学英语六级实训教程. 阅读分册/林明金主编. —北京:国防工业出版社,2009.11
ISBN 978-7-118-06544-2

Ⅰ.①新... Ⅱ.①林... Ⅲ.①英语—阅读教学—高等学校—水平考试—自学参考资料 Ⅳ.①H310.42

中国版本图书馆 CIP 数据核字(2009)第 169527 号

※

国防工业出版社出版发行

(北京市海淀区紫竹院南路 23 号 邮政编码 100048)
天利华印刷装订有限公司印刷
新华书店经售

*

开本 880×1230 1/32 印张 10 字数 271 千字
2009 年 11 月第 1 版第 1 次印刷 印数 1—5000 册 定价 19.00 元

(本书如有印装错误,我社负责调换)

国防书店:(010)68428422 发行邮购:(010)68414474
发行传真:(010)68411535 发行业务:(010)68472764

前　言

FOREWORD

2008 年 6 月，教育部高等教育司司长张尧学院士在大学英语四、六级考试改革会议上提出四、六级考试改革的方向和总体思路是："采用以试卷库为基础的计算机网络系统，尽可能在适当时间、适当地点为考生提供以听力测试为主，包含说、读、写、译、测试在内，重点考查英语学习可持续发展能力的计算机考试。"正是基于这一新思路，我们适时编写了这套《新思路大学英语六级实训教程》。

"大学英语"既是一门非英语专业大学生公共必修基础课，也是一门融语言知识、技能运用、交际策略培养和跨文化交际修养培养为一体的综合性课程，它涉及语言知识、语言技能、学习策略、文化意识和情感价值等方面内容。课程目标是帮助学生打下较为扎实的语言基础，掌握良好的外语学习方法，形成良好的学习习惯，增强自主学习能力，提高综合文化素养，使学生具有较强的英语综合应用能力，特别是听说能力，并能用英语进行有效的口头和书面的信息交流，以适应社会发展、经济建设和国际交流的需要。根据语言输入假设理论，语言学得和习得应强调大量的可理解输入。但是"大学英语"课程课时十分有限，为了保证足够的语言输入和实践的量，必须在优化教学设计、扩大语言输入量和输出量方面取得实质性的突破，而开设"大学英语四六级实训"公共选修课就是一个很好的尝试。

"大学英语四六级实训"公共选修课教学的特点是：从"教教材"转变为"用教材教"，在课程内容设计中依托教材但又不拘泥于教材，在显性教材中再生隐性课程，遵循虚实相生、难易结合、动静结合、衔接自然、课外延伸的思路。课程设计依据新颁布的《大学英语课程教学要求》，注重阐释语言技能和应试技巧，以解析四、六级考试真题与经典考点为突破口，强化英语应试思维，阐释英语命题规律与得分秘笈，预测最新考试趋势。课程目标是：帮助考生应对各类考试所要达到的综合语言技能和交际能力；全面掌握大纲所规定的听、说、读、写、译各个方面的技能；帮助学生顺利通过大学英语四、六级考试。

《新思路大学英语六级实训教程》即为配合"大学英语六级实训"公共选修课程而专门编写的系列教材，分《听力分册》、《阅读分册》、《写作分册》、《词汇分册》、《综合分册》五个分册，教材编写注重实用、生动、精细，重基础又善实战，重技巧更重能力。按学生英语能力及需求设计章节，难易适中，循序渐进，力求做到重点突出，系统全面，分项击破，精准预测。

《新思路大学英语六级实训教程·阅读分册》共有六章。其主要特点是：

（1）剖析六级阅读的考点与难点。知己知彼，百战不殆。本书开篇介绍了六级阅读考点分布和题型构成，并通过分析全真试题，归纳阅读考试难点所在，为提高针对性训练的效果创造条件。

（2）传授有效的阅读方法，帮助考生走出阅读理解的误区。不少考生迎考时，特别注意扩大自己的词汇量，学习语法结构知识，也做了不少题目，但成绩总不如意，屡屡败走麦城。究其原因，大都是缺乏正确的阅读方法。常言道：方法得当，事半功倍，人人都能成功；方法失当，事倍功半，强者也会失利。因此，本书以真题为范本，从词—句—段—篇等多层次指导学生如何处理生词、长难句，进而上升为篇章的有效阅读和理解。

（3）破译命题规律，指明解题捷径。根据《大学英语六级考试大纲》的要求，结合对历年考试全真试题的分析，在深入地研究了每种题型的命题手段、考查角度、考点范围之后，本书归纳出各种命题规律及相应的解题技巧。只要掌握这些规律和技巧，考生应试时便能心中有数，胸有成竹，从而提高应试速度和准确率。

（4）真题实战，强化各专项应试能力。本书在每章节的后面，都科学地配有相应数量的真题，供考生演练，巩固所学技巧，提高应试能力。

（5）综合演练，营造临战氛围，检测复习成效。本书的第六章提供4套阅读综合模拟试题，选材新颖，导向性强，专为考生冲刺时量身定制。

（6）答案解析简明扼要，力求实用。本书所有的练习都配有答案解析，篇章阅读练习还配有结构剖析、语境记忆、难句分析和带有题区画线的参考译文，旨在帮助考生知其然，并知其所以然。避免读而不精，做而不思的现象。

本分册编者在编写此书的过程中，参阅了大量的相关书籍和网络文章，在此谨向这些文章的作者们深表谢意！由于学识水平有限，书稿编成难免挂一漏万，真诚欢迎读者、专家和同行提出宝贵意见和建议。

请登陆"金精乐道网站"（www. mingjinonline. com）下载与本系列教材配套的大学英语拓展学习资料。该网站系大学英语课外拓展学习专用平台，提供各类大学英语四六级备考锦囊、教学日志、习作交流、在线测试、音频视频、学习论坛等，助你全面提升英语应用能力、顺利通过大学英语六级测试！

作者

目 录

CONTENTS

第一章　直面六级阅读　　001

第一节　阅读理解概述　　001

第二节　阅读高分攻略　　005

第三节　专项训练　　027

第四节　答案与解析　　033

第二章　快速阅读　　041

第一节　设题特点　　041

第二节　应试技巧　　044

第三节　实战演练　　047

第四节　历年典型真题突破训练　　060

第三章　仔细阅读——短句问答　　084

第一节　设题特点　　084

第二节　应试技巧　　086

第三节　实战演练　　088

第四节　历年典型真题突破训练　　094

第四章　仔细阅读——篇章词汇　　102

第一节　考点揭秘与设题特征　　102

第二节　应试技巧　103

第三节　实战演练　104

第四节　专项训练　108

第五节　答案与解析　110

第五章　仔细阅读——篇章阅读　116

第一节　考点揭秘与设题特征　116

第二节　命题规律　122

第三节　选项的设置规律与选择方法　153

第四节　解题步骤及应试技巧　163

第五节　实战演练　165

第六节　历年典型真题突破训练　170

第七节　答案解析　181

第六章　阅读综合模拟训练　195

Reading Practice 1　195

Reading Practice 1 答案与解析　208

Reading Practice 2　224

Reading Practice 2 答案与解析　237

Reading Practice 3　252

Reading Practice 3 答案与解析　264

Reading Practice 4　281

Reading Practice 4 答案与解析　293

第一章　直面六级阅读

第一节　阅读理解概述

一、明确考纲要求

大学英语六级考试阅读理解部分要求考生"能基本读懂英语国家大众性报刊杂志的一般性题材的文章,阅读速度达到每分钟 70 词～90 词(四级要求每分钟 70 词)。在快速阅读篇幅较长、难度适中的材料时,阅读速度达到每分钟 120 词(四级要求每分钟 100 词)。能就阅读材料进行略读或查读,能阅读所学专业的综述性文献,并能正确理解中心大意,抓住主要事实和有关细节"。

六级阅读理解部分考核的主要技能是:

1. 辨别和理解中心思想和重要细节

(1) 理解明确表达的概念或细节

(2) 理解隐含表达的概念或细节(如总结、判断、推论等),通过判断句子的交际功能(如请求、拒绝、命令等)来理解文章意思

(3) 理解文章的中心思想(如找出能概括全文的要点等)

（4）理解作者的观点和态度

2. 运用语言技能理解文章

（1）理解词语（如根据上下文猜测词和短语的意思）

（2）理解句间关系（如原因、结果、目的、比较等）

（3）理解篇章（如通过词汇及语法承接手段在文章中所起的作用来理解篇章各部分之间的关系）

3. 运用相关的阅读技能

（1）略读文章，获取文章大意

（2）查读文章，获取特定信息

（3）研读相关句子，理解句子的深层意思

二、了解题型结构

大学英语六级考试的试卷构成中，阅读理解占总分的 35％，其中快速阅读部分占 10％，仔细阅读部分占 25％。题型包括 1 篇快速阅读、1 篇篇章词汇和 2 篇篇章阅读。题型结构具体如下：

题型	试卷题号	篇数	时间	文章长度	设 题 类 型
快速阅读	Part II	1	15 分钟	1200 词左右	4 道是非判断题＋6 道句子填空题
仔细阅读	Part IV(A) 简短回答	1	25 分钟	380 词左右	5 道简短回答题（完成句子＋问答）
	Part IV(B) 篇章阅读	2		440 词左右	5 道多项选择题
	篇章词汇 （备选题）	1		280 词左右	文中 10 个空，从 15 个备选词中选填

三、把握六级阅读理解的难度特点

由于四、六级命题者是一致的，所以从解题思路、命题风格、文章

选材而言,四、六级阅读没有很大的区别,但是阅读难度是有区别的。主要体现在:

1. 词汇难度

六级阅读的词汇难度是遵循教学大纲词汇表的要求,一般在5500个单词和1200个词组范围之内。文章中的超纲词通常用汉语注释,而且一般不超过3%。但是,使用词汇的生僻义项以及词汇的活用的情况经常出现,加上考生未能理解词在句中的作用,如副词,连词在句中所体现的某种逻辑关系,这些都可能增加理解的难度。

例1: The manufacturer who increases the unit price of his product by changing his package size to lower the quantity delivered can, without <u>undue</u> hardship, put his product into boxes, bags, and tins that will contain even 4-ounce, 8-ounce, one-pound, two-pound quantities of breakfast foods, cake mixes, etc. (1997年6月 CET – 6,Passage 1)

例2: Too many vulnerable <u>child-free</u> adults are being ruthlessly(无情的) manipulated into <u>parent-hood</u> by their parents, who think that happiness among older people depends on having a grand-child to spoil. We need an organization to help beat down the persistent campaigns of <u>grandchildless parents</u>. It's time to establish Planned Grandparenthood, which would have many global and local benefits. (2005年12月 CET – 6,Passage 1)

例3: <u>As</u> someone paid to serve food to people, I had customers say and do things to me I suspect they'd never say or do to their most casual acquaintances. (2007年1月 CET – 6,Passage 1)

解析:例1中,"undue"通常指"不恰当"的意思,但这里指的是"过渡的"的意思,较生僻,大多考生没能记住这个意思;例2中"child-free","parenthood"和"grandchildless parents"都是简单词汇的活用,阅读时若不留神,就会搞不清它们的指向从而影响理解了;例3中的"As"考生容易错误地理解为"当……的时候"。As作"当……的时

3

候"引导的是一个句子,此句前半句只有一个名词 someone,paid to serve food to peoples 是动词的过去分词作定语,修饰 someone。意为"为他人提供服务而获得报酬的人",所以 As 在此是"作为"的意思。

2. 句子难度

与四级阅读相比,六级阅读文章句子长(18 词~20 词)、句子结构也复杂得多,常出现从句套从句、倒装结构、繁杂的插入语等复杂的语言现象。许多考生反映有时长句、难句中每一个词都能看懂,却因为无法抓住句子的主干部分,而无法把握整个句子的含义。

例 1:I'm now applying to graduate school, which means someday I'll return to a profession where people need to be nice to me in order to get what they want; I think I'll take them to dinner first, and see how they treat someone whose only job is to serve them. (2007 年 12 月 CET - 6,Passage 1)

例 2:"It's an outrage that any American's life expectancy should be shortened simply because the company they worked for went bankrupt and ended health-care coverage," said the former chairman of the International Steel Group. (2007 年 12 月 CET - 6,Passage 2)

例 3: There is considerable sentiment about the "corruption" of women's language—which of course is viewed as part of the loss of feminine ideals and morality—and this sentiment is crystallized by nationwide opinion polls that are regularly carried out by the media. (2007 年 6 月 CET - 6,Passage 2)

这几个句子是从近年来六级试题的阅读部分中挑选出来的,这种长难句六级考试中经常出现。许多考生在考试中碰到这类句子时,对句子的语法结构,尤其是各个句子成分之间的关系弄不清楚,句子理解起来很慢、很吃力,有时根本就看不懂,从而影响阅读效果。

3. 写作深度和知识跨度大

根据教学大纲,大学英语学习具有工具性(instrumental)的特点,其工具性主要体现在两个方面：一是学术性（academic），即用工具进行学术研究，获取学术信息；二是实用性（practical）。六级阅读侧重学术性，这是因为参加六级考试的学生大多是大学高年级学生和研究生，要求具备各方面知识和信息的综合应用能力。所以阅读材料是生活中常见的，多选自学术性较强的报刊杂志，如 Newsweek，New Scientist and Time 等。这类文章知识跨度较大，写作较有深度，不太好理解。

4. 阅读量大

六级阅读测试一直强调速度。六级考纲要求考生在 15 分钟之内快读一篇 1200 词～1300 词的文章并完成文章后的题目；在 25 分钟内以完成三篇阅读，每篇篇幅为 400 词～420 词，这就要求考生 8 分钟就得做完一篇文章。如果不能熟练地运用相关的阅读技巧，许多考生无法在规定时间内完成阅读任务，结果是要么匆忙之下胡乱作答，要么占用后面其他题的解题时间，这样必定影响考试成绩。

第二节　阅读高分攻略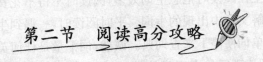

攻破六级，应从阅读入手。那么，怎样提高阅读理解的能力呢？首先，要根据考试要求，学会捕捉、分析相关信息并区别对待，不同层次（如词、句、段、篇章）的阅读重点应给予不同的重视。

进行词汇层次的阅读时，要特别重视实词。因为实词比虚词重要，实词含有实在的意思，而虚词不包含任何实在的意思（但虚词中的连词不可忽视，它常常用来表明词与词或句与句之间的逻辑关系），其他可不必太在意。阅读句子时，要特别注意句子的主干部分或主干部分的谓语，作者经常在这些部分表达主要的内容信息。抓住了句子的主干部分也就抓住了句子的主要信息，这样理清该句与上下文的逻辑关系以及作者的思路就不难了。阅读段落时，要特别注意该段的首尾两句，他们往往是作者概括段落中心意思的主题句，包含着重要信息。

当然，作者偶尔也会将主题句置于段中或不写出来，这就需要考生通过阅读加以归纳，提炼该段大意。阅读含有多段的短文时，短文的首尾两段特别重要，常常包含着重要的信息，议论文和说明文尤其如此。作者往往会在文章的首段开宗明义地告诉读者他想说明什么，或者他想就什么论点进行讨论或分析。在文章的末尾段，作者对所说明的问题或所讨论的论点进行归纳。所以，结论性的内容往往会在末段出现。当然，如果一篇文章只有一段，它的首尾句往往包含重要信息。这样阅读时，应有选择地读，不必按照文章顺序一句一句地从头读到尾，并对每一个词、每个句子或每个段落都给予同等的重视。其次，要掌握必要的阅读技巧和解题方法。下面就按照"词汇－句子－篇章"的顺序介绍一些阅读技巧与解题方法。

一、词汇层次的应试策略

很多考生在阅读时抱怨生词太多，阅读时不得不花费大量的时间和精力去理解文章中出现的生词。平时阅读时，一遇到生词或者不能准确理解的单词便停下来查词典。诚然，词汇量是任何英文阅读的基础。但是，阅读理解的真正目的是 read to learn，即阅读是为了获取解题所需的信息，而不是 learn to read，即为了阅读而阅读。过多注意生词会影响篇章大意的理解和把握，"捡了芝麻，丢了西瓜，得不偿失"。这样的阅读法不仅耗费大量的时间和精力，同时也破坏了思维的连贯性。

其实，对付生词的有效办法是根据合理化原则顺势阅读。也就是当你遇到生词时，如果不影响对语义的理解，就不理它们，顺势读下去；如果该词汇影响到整体语义的理解，就应当根据周围语言环境，根据合理化原则推测出一个合理的含义，继续顺势向下读。具体方法如下：

1. 绕开生词法

我们知道英语文章中不是所有的词的功能都是同等的，有些词担负着传达主要信息的功能,而有些词主要起语法作用,它们所传达的信息和下文的其他信息没有联系。这类词有:表示人名,地名,机构名等专有名词。遇到这些词,只要我们能辨认出它们是专有名词,就能理解文章而不必知道它的意思。比如在下面的句子中:"In fact", says David Dinges, a sleep specialist at the University of Pennsylvania School of Medicine, "there's even a prohibition against admitting we need sleep." 两个引号之间的部分为机构专有名词,可以不必去管它,直接阅读"In fact",..., "there's even a prohibition against admitting we need sleep." 注意主干部分即可。所以,当遇到与答题无关的字、词或短语时,不必慌张,不必为个别晦涩的难词所束缚,冷静地读下去,可以"不求甚解",绕开它们,重点把握与答题相关的句子。

例如: It's often said that only the rich are getting ahead; everyone else is standing still or falling behind. Well, there are many undeserving rich—overpaid chief executives, for instance. But over any meaningful period, most people's incomes are increasing. From 1995 to 2004, inflation-adjusted average family income rose 14.3 percent, to \$43,200. People feel "squeezed" because their rising incomes often don't satisfy their rising wants—for bigger homes, more health care, more education, faster Internet connections. (2007 年 6 月 CET－6,Passage 1)

题目: Why do people feel squeezed when their average income rises considerably?

A. Their material pursuits have gone far ahead of their earnings.

B. Their purchasing power has dropped markedly with inflation.

C. The distribution of wealth is uneven between the rich and the poor.

D. Health care and educational cost have somehow gone out of control. (A)

解析:也许考生不能准确理解上文中划线词的意思。不用着急,可先读题目:为什么人们收入提高了,却依然有"捉襟见肘"之感? 根据题干"feel squeezed"信息,可将答案定位于本段最后一句:People feel "squeezed" because their rising incomes often don't satisfy their rising wants...(……人们收入的增加并不能满足他们不断上涨的需求……),而前面的句子,与本题无关,可以跳过,更不用理会其中的生词了。选项 A"他们对物资的追求超出他们的收入"与 their rising incomes often don't satisfy their rising wants... 是同意转述,故选项 A 为答案。

2. 猜测词义法

上面提到阅读时如果遇到与答题无关的生词可以绕过去,照样可以准确做题。但是,如果遇到与答题有关的生词,或不弄清该词意思就无法理解句子或段落大意时就需要去猜测词义。所谓猜测词义,是指在阅读过程中根据对语篇的信息、逻辑、背景知识及语言结构等的综合理解去猜测或推断某一生词、难词、关键词的词义。具体做法有二:一是根据构词法判断词义。这种方法需要认识大量的词根(常用词根见附录),否则一切猜测都无从谈起;二是根据与上下文的关系推测其词义。根据上下文猜测词义是一种非常有用的阅读技巧,也是六级阅读经常测试的一个方面。

由于考试时间有限,内容多,所以猜词猜测到什么程度是十分关键的。一般情况下考生在根据上下文内容所提供的一些线索进行猜测词意时不必过细,只要充分利用短文中上下句的互释作用,猜出或体会出某种生词的指向范围或大致含义就可以了,如过分苛求,一则不可能做到,二则会影响阅读速度,从而影响答题效果。最常见的根据上下文暗示或线索进行猜词的方法有以下五种:

(1) 相关信息法。即根据生词与全篇文章主题的关系,结合一些基本常识或背景知识来猜测一些生词意思。

例如:The manufacturer who increases the unit price of his product by changing his package size to lower the quantity delivered can, without **undue** hardship, put his product into boxes, bags, and tins that will contain even 4-ounce, 8-ounce, one-pound, two-pound quantities of breakfast foods, cake mixes, etc. (1997 年 6 月 CET - 6,Passage 1)

本文主要论述商品的包装带有极大欺骗性的问题——包装盒变高了,变窄了,食品的分量也减少了,但是价格却没有降低。所以,根据文中相关信息,可推测出"undue"是"过渡的"而不是"不适当的,不相称的"。

(2) 定义法或重释法。在文章中,作者估计某个词、短语或句子一般读者不熟悉,作者会直接给出其定义,或换一种说法,对前面的词、短语或句子重新解释。考生可以根据定义或重释的信号词、标点符号和限制成分来判断生词的词义。(1)常见的定义或重释信号词有:that is, that means, namely, refer to, or, be defined as, in other words 等等。(2)定义或重释的标点符号有:冒号或逗号(引出具体的说明或例子);分号(引出类似的、对应的观点);破折号(引出同位语);(3)用同位语或定语从句来定义或重释被考词。

例 1:Many U. S. companies are **downsizing**—or reducing the number of employees—in order to save money and increase the amount of profit that the companies can make.

解析:此例中 or 后面的短语意为"减少雇员"。是对前面生词 downsizing 的重述,因此我们不难猜出 downsizing 是"裁员"的意思。

例 2:The others questioned the veracity—the truthfulness—of these reports.

解析:此例破折号中的 truthfulness 与前面生词 veracity 是同位关系,因此我们不难猜出 veracity 意为"真诚"。

例 3:Krabacber suffers from SAD, which is short for seasonal affective disorder, a syndrome characterized by severe seasonal mood swings.

解析:根据生词 SAD 后面定语从句 which is short for seasonal affective disorder 和同位语 a syndrome characterized by severe seasonal mood swings,我们可以推断出 SAD 含义,即"季节性情绪紊乱症"。

(3) 对照比较法。作者为了强调事物间的区别和对立,往往用反义词来表述这种对照关系,则要求考生要善于用语言知识和分析能力去领会相关信息之间存在的逻辑关系,利用语句中的对比得到某词、短语或句子的意义。与对照相反,作者为了强调事物的相同之处,往往用比较来表示意义上的相似程度,我们可以利用比较其相似性来领悟不熟悉的词汇。常见的信号词或短语有:unlike, while, but, though, although, however, even though, instead, rather than, nevertheless, on the contrary, or 等。

例 1:And yet there are substantial sectors of the vast U. S. economy—from giant companies like Coca-Cola to **mom-and-pop** restaurant operators in Miami—for which the weak dollar is most excellent news. (2008 年 6 月 CET‑6,Passage 1)

解析:破折号后的 from giant companies like Coca-Cola to mom-and-pop restaurant operators in Miami 是对前面 substantial sectors of the vast U. S. economy 的补充说明,句中 giant 和 mom-and-pop 具有对照的关系,根据 giant(大的)意思,便可推断出 mom-and-pop 是"小的"的意思了。

例 2:Andrew is one of the most **supercilious** men I know. His brother,in contrast,is quite umble and modest.

解析:句中短语 in contrast(相对照的,相对比的),我们可推断 supercilious 和后面词组 humble and modest(谦卑又谦虚)是对比关系后,便能猜出 supercilious 是"目空一切的,傲慢的"之意。

(4) 举例法。作者为了阐明某一种重要观念或者讲清某一抽象

10

概念,往往采取举例的方式对这一观点或概念进行具体的说明和解释,帮助读者理解其具体的含义。表示举例的信号词有 such as, for example, for instance 等等。

例如: Various means of **conveyance**—for example, cars, subways, and ships are used worldwide.

解析:for example 后面的 cars, subways, and ships 是对 conveyance 的解释说明,据悉可推断出 conveyance 指的是"运输设备"。

(5) 构词法。英语单词的构成一般有派生、合成、转化、截短、混合及缩略等。英语中大部分词汇是由具有特定含义的词根和词缀构成的。词根是单词的核心部分,它体现词的基本含义,词缀分为前缀和后缀。了解英语构词法,可以帮助我们了解词性及其构成部分之间的关系,进而猜出该词的基本含义。

例如: But a foreigner might not have the knowledge and sympathy necessary to write the king's biography—not for a *readership* from within the kingdom, at any rate. (1997 年 6 月 CET - 6, Passage 6)

解析:-ship 在名词后面表示"……的状态","……的地位(职位)"和"总数,总体"的意思。如 friendship(友情), professorship (教授的职位), listenership (听众)。句子中 not for a *readership* from within the kingdom, at any rate 前使用了破折号,因此,它是进一步说明前面的一句话,据此可推测,readership 在这里的意思是"读者群",全句的意思是"但是一个外国人则可能缺少为国王写传记所必须具备的知识和心气,至少以他对国王的理解和情感所写的传记在该王国内不会有大量的读者"。

综上所述,利用各种已知信息推测、判断词义是一项重要的阅读技巧。在阅读实践中,我们应灵活地综合运用上面提到的几种猜测技巧,排除生词的障碍,顺利理解文章的思想内容,提高阅读速度和效果。

二、句子层次的应试策略

句子是阅读的关键，是表达语义的基本单位。掌握科学的阅读句子、理解长句和难句的方法，是阅读获得高分的关键所在。

1. 句子层次阅读方法——意群阅读法

所谓意群是指具有一个中心意思的词的群体，即一个句子可根据意思和语法结构分成若干小段，每一小段称之为一个意群。意群可以是一个词、一个词组或短语，也可以是并列句的一个分句或复合句的一个主句、从句等等。意群阅读是以意群而不是单词为最小阅读单位的一种快速阅读方法。它不仅可以提高阅读速度，而且有利于对句子的整体理解，避免死抠字眼、逐词理解的不良阅读习惯。例如："Recent decades have seen the rapid development of information technology. As a result, many electric inventions, including E-books, have found their way into our everyday life and have gained increasing popularity among common people（2008年6月CET-6，Passage 1）"。这个段落共有34个单词，如果逐字阅读，不但速度慢，而且形不成一个完整的意思。但是，如果按8个意群来读：Recent decades / have seen /the rapid development of information technology. / As a result, / many electric inventions, / including E-books, / have found their way into our everyday life/ and have gain-ed increasing popularity among common people. 因为视线是落在每个意群上停留，这样停留次数减少，句子脉络清晰，句意明了，阅读效率也就高了。

2. 长难句理解方法——化繁为简法

英语句子的成分较复杂，阅读时最重要的是化繁为简，抓住句子的主干部分。那么，如何抓住句子的主干部分呢？前面提过，六级文章的长难句都是从句套从句，逻辑结构复杂。其实，英语长句都是在主句的基础上，采用连词进行扩展生成的。连词就像是环扣，将一个或多个从句与主句层层相连,成为一个有机的整体。所以,在阅读时,先要根据连词,定位整个句子的主干成分,即哪个分句是整句话的主句。一旦定位了主干成分,整个句子的结构必然迎刃而解。确定了主句之后,还要进一步分析勾画出主句中的关键成分,即主语、谓语、宾语、表语等。抓住了主干就抓住了句子的中心,不仅能加快阅读速度,而且能够准确的理解句子的意思。

例1: Supporters of the biotech industry have accused an American scientist of misconduct after she testified to the New Zealand government that a genetically modified (GM) bacterium could cause serious if released. (2005 年 6 月 CET - 6,Passage 3)

解析:本句共有 32 个词。要迅速定位此句主干,没有必要从头到尾逐词阅读,只要直接找出所有的连词。在这句话里有三个连词 after,that 和 if ,找出后把这三个连词引导的从句暂时去掉不看,剩下的成分 Supporters … have accused an American scientist of misconduct 就是句子的主干(支持者指责科学家的行为不当)。接着,对从句进行分析。After 引导时间状语从句对主句的谓语进行补充说明,that 引导宾语从句,而 if 引导的是省略条件句: if (it is) released。整句意思是:一位美国科学家向新西兰政府证实,有一种转基因细菌被释放后可能会造成严重破坏。为此,生物技术产业的支持者们指责她行为不当。

例2: Too many vulnerable child-free adults are being ruthlessly(无情的)manipulated into parent-hood by their parents,who think that happiness among older people depends on having a grandchild to spoil.(2005 年 12 月 CET - 6,Passage 1)

解析:该句共有 34 个词,主句是被动句:Too many vulnerable child-free adults are being ruthlessly manipulated into parent-hood by their parents,划线部分分别是主句中的主、谓、宾成分(……成年人在……无情摆布下成为父母),主句后面带有一个由 who 引导的非限制定语从句,修饰主句中的“their parents”,定语从句中又含有一个由

13

that 引导的宾语从句。整个句子框架为：... adults are being ruthlessly manipulated into parent-hood by their parents, who think that.... 理清句子的整体结构，抓住主干部分，整个句子的理解难度就降低了大半。本句大意是：有太多没有子女的易于屈服的成年人在自己父母的无情摆布下成为父母，因为他们的父母认为老年人的快乐就在于含饴弄孙。

例 3：There is considerable sentiment about the "corruption" of women's language—which of course is viewed as part of the loss of feminine ideals and morality—and this sentiment is crystallized by nationwide opinion polls that are regularly carried out by the media.（2007 年 6 月 CET - 6，Passage 2）

　　解析：该句较长，有 42 个词，其主干部分是由 and 连接的两个分句组成：There is considerable sentiment about... and this sentiment is crystallized by...（对于……有很大的意见，这种意见被表现得一清二楚），此句第一个破折号后引导的非限制定语从句，修饰 "corruption" of women's language 这件事；第二个破折号后引导定语从句，修饰 opinion polls。抓住并列主干部分，再把补充说明的次要成分放到相应的位置，整个句子意思就完整了，即：对于女性语言的"腐化"有很大的意见——当然这被视为失去女性规范和道德观念的部分表现——这种意见通过媒体定期进行的全国民意调查表现得一清二楚。

　　从以上的例子中，我们不难发现六级阅读虽然生词长句多，但其实都是在简单句的基础上逐步堆积难词和词组构成的。因此在看到这些难句或生词时，一要充满自信地找出那些熟悉的单词，二要有整体意识，把握句子核心内容，这是最主要的，而不是去搜索记忆，发掘每一个生词的含义。总之，阅读句子时要有整体意识，句子核心概念。平时训练时，只要碰到读不太懂的句子就应该拿出来，具体分析，直到弄懂，从中领会长难句的理解规律，提高英语语感。

14

三 篇章层次的应试策略

1. 把握选材原则及体裁特点

从近几年的试题来看,文章题材的范围比较广泛,但主要还是以这些题材为主:一是社会生活方面的文章。涉及面较为广泛,包括一切与人的生活有直接关系的内容,诸如它们的发展,给人的生活带来的影响等等;二是教育、经济和文化方面的文章。此类文章常反映出社会最新的热点信息。比如2008年6月份六级阅读考试选择若干篇与当前国际热点密切相关的文章;三是科普类的文章。这类文章有两个特点:一是涉及面很广,几乎可以涉及科学技术领域的方方面面,当然涉及的深度不会太深或太专业;另外一个特点是,即使是一般科技领域也多涉及其社会意义,不是完全在科技方面的探讨。了解这些题材的范围是要让我们知道,在做阅读理解题时,除了要具备语言方面的知识以外,还应该有较广泛的知识面,它往往能够帮助我们克服文字上的理解障碍。所以考生可以有意识地加强一下这几个方面的背景知识,但需要强调的是,考生答题时要严格根据文章的内容作答,千万不可根据自己所掌握的背景知识想当然地答题,这是在做阅读题中一定要把握的一点。

一般来说,文章的体裁大致包括议论文(argumentative)、描述文(descriptive)、说明文(expositive)和记叙文(narrative)等。不同体裁的短文有其不同的段落组织方式和脉络层次,也就有不同的阅读理解方式。六级阅读体裁主要是以议论文、说明文和记叙文为主,其中议论文和说明文是较难的两种文体。下面我们以六级阅读真题为例,分析议论文、说明文和记叙文的行文特点,以便在解答问题时更好地做到有的放矢,最大限度地读懂较难的文章。

(1) 议论文

议论文一般由三大部分构成:提出话题+反驳与论证+得出结论。其中占较大比重的是第二部分,但最重要的是第一、三部分,它们

15

往往最能说明作者的主要观点和写作意图。作者的观点态度有时通过论点明述，有时则通过论证或驳论暗示。这种模式特点决定了它的主要题型是作者观点态度题，文章主旨题以及推理判断题。阅读时如果能抓住作者的观点立场及相关的结构，确定各段落主题思想，解答问题就不难了。

例 1： Whether the eyes are "the windows of the soul" is debatable; that they are intensely important in interpersonal communication is a fact. During the first two months of a baby's life, the stimulus that produces a smile is a pair of eyes. The eyes need not be real: a mask with two dots will produce a smile. Significantly, a real human face with eyes covered will not motivate a smile, nor will the sight of only one eye when the face is presented in profile. This attraction to eyes as opposed to the nose or mouth continues as the baby matures. In one study, when American four-year-olds were asked to draw people, 75 percent of them drew people with mouths, but 99 percent of them drew people with eyes. In Japan, however, where babies are carried on their mother's back, infants do not acquire as much attachment to eyes as they do in other cultures. As a result, Japanese adults make little use of the face either to encode (编码) or decode meaning: In fact, Argyle reveals that the "proper place to focus one's gaze during a conversation in Japan is on the neck of one's conversation partner."

The role of eye contact in a conversational exchange between two Americans is well defined: speakers make contact with the eyes of their listener for about one second, then glance away as they talk; in a few moments they re-establish eye contact with the listener or reassure themselves that their audience is still attentive, then shift their gaze away once more. Listeners, meanwhile, keep their eyes on the face of the speaker, allowing themselves to glance away only

16

briefly. It is important that they be looking at the speaker at the precise moment when the speaker re-establishes eye contact: if they are not looking, the speaker assumes that they are disinterested and either will pause until eye contact is resumed or will terminate the conversation. Just how critical this eye maneuvering is to the maintenance of conversational flow becomes evident when two speakers are wearing dark glasses: there may be a sort of traffic jam of words caused by interruption, false starts, and unpredictable pauses. (1997 年 6 月 CET - 6，Passage 4)

解析：

这是一篇明述论点的议论文，文章共包含两个段落。作者在第一段提出了自己的观点：Whether the eyes are "the windows of the soul" is debatable; that they are intensely important in interpersonal communication is a fact.. （眼睛是不是心灵的窗户是个有争议的问题，但是眼睛在人际交往中起着十分重要的作用则是无可争辩的事实）。接着，作者举例说明一双眼睛（无论真假）能逗乐两个月大的婴儿，而把眼睛遮住的面孔或只露出一只眼睛的侧面是不能逗乐婴儿的。第二段，作者通过描述谈话中双方目光接触所体现的不同含义，论述了眼睛在人际交往中的重要性，与文章的第一句相呼应。

例 2：If sustainable competitive advantage depends on work-force skills，American firms have a problem. Human-resource management is not traditionally seen as central to the competitive survival of the firm in the United States. Skill acquisition is considered an individual responsibility. Labour is simply another factor of production to be hired—rented at the lowest possible cost—much as one buys raw materials or equipment.

The lack of importance attached to human-resource management can be seen in the corporation hierarchy. In an American firm the chief financial officer is almost always second in command. The post of head of human-resource management is usually a specialized job, off at the edge of the corporate hierarchy. The executive who holds it is never consulted on major strategic decisions and has no chance to move up to Chief Executive Officer (CEO). By way of contrast, in Japan the head of human-resource management is central—usually the second most important executive, after the CEO, in the firm's hierarchy.

While American firms often talk about the vast amounts spent on training their work forces, in fact they invest less in the skills of their employees than do either Japanese or German firms. The money they do invest is also more highly concentrated on professional and managerial employees. And the limited investments that are made in training workers are also much more narrowly focused on the specific skills necessary to do the next job rather than on the basic background skills that make it possible to absorb new technologies.

As a result, problems emerge when new breakthrough technologies arrive. If American workers, for example, take much longer to learn how to operate new flexible manufacturing stations than workers in Germany (as they do), the effective cost of those stations is lower in Germany than it is in the United States. More time is required before equipment is up and running at capacity, and the need for extensive retraining generates costs and creates bottlenecks that limit the speed with which new equipment can be employed. The result is a slower pace of technological change. And in the end the skills of the bottom half of the population affect the wages of the top half. If the bottom half can't effectively staff the processes that have to be operated, the management and professional jobs that go with these processes will disappear. （1997 年 6 月 CET － 6，Passage 2）

解析：

这是一篇隐含观点的议论文。本文一开始，便提出美国公司向来不重视人力资源管理的问题：Human-resource management is not traditionally seen as central to the competitive survival of the firm in the United States. （按照美国的传统，人力资源管理未被看作是公司在市场竞争中能否生存的一个十分重要的环节）。接着，在第二、三、四段中，作者通过具体两个事例阐明存在的问题：一是在美国公司里人力资源部门不受重视，地位低下；二是有限的培训资金主要用在专业和管理人员的培训上，忽略了工人的基本技术训练，从而影响工人熟悉和掌握新技术，其结果便是减慢了技术改造的速度。作者采用"问题—分析—结论"模式提出自己的见解：美国公司人力资源管理策略影响公司竞争力的问题。

（2）说明文

说明文也是由三部分构成：提出话题（观点或事例）＋用事例说明原因＋得出结论。说明文和议论文有相似之处，他们都是提出一个问题或一种观点为开头部分，最后得出结论而结束全文。他们不同之处在中间部分，议论文主要是反驳与论证，说明文则从几个方面加以说明和阐述。说明文的行文方式有其特点，即主要有比较、对照和分类几种格式，每篇短文以一种为主，有时几种兼用，其语篇模式一般也比较固定、整齐。

例 3：In the 1920s demand for American farm products fell, as European countries began to recover from World War I and instituted austerity（紧缩）programs to reduce their imports. The result was a sharp drop in farm prices. This period was more disastrous for farmers than earlier times had been, because farmers were no longer self-sufficient. They were paying for machinery, seed, and fertilizer, and they were also buying consumer goods. The prices of the items farmers bought remained constant, while prices they received for their

19

products fell. These developments were made worse by the Great Depression, which began in 1929 and extended throughout the 1939s.

In 1929, under President Herbert Hoover, the Federal Farm Board was organized. It established the principle of direct interference with supply and demand, and it represented the first national commitment to provide greater economic stability for farmers.

President Hoover's successor attached even more importance to this problem. One of the first measures proposed by President Franklin D. Roosevelt when he took office in 1933 was the Agricultural Adjustment Act, which was subsequently passed by Congress. This law gave the Secretary of Agriculture the power to reduce production through voluntary agreements with farmers who were paid to take their land out of use. A deliberate scarcity of farm products was planned in an effort to raise prices. This law was declared unconstitutional by the Supreme Court on the grounds that general taxes were being collected to pay one special group of people. However, new laws were passed immediately that achieved the same result of resting soil and providing flood-control measures, but which were based on the principle of soil conservation. The Roosevelt Administration believed that rebuilding the nation's soil was in the national interest and was not simply a plan to help farmers at the expense of other citizens. Later the government guaranteed loans to farmers so that they could buy farm machinery, hybrid (杂交) grain, and fertilizers. (2000 年 6 月 CET - 6, Passage 1)

解析:

这是一篇关于 20 世纪二、三十年代美国农业所面临的困境及美国政府采取的种种措施帮助农业摆脱困境的说明文。全文共三段:第一段是铺垫,提出美国农业面临的困境和原因及其对农民造成的灾难性后果的问题;第二、三段为主体,阐明美国政府振兴农业的措施,尤以第三段为重点,三十年代罗斯福总统执政后采取的通过立法手段恢复农业经济的两个阶段的措施,前一阶段通过 AAA 法案直接减少耕地面积,并给农民有偿补助;第二阶段在 AAA 被最高法院认定为违宪后,通过一系列殊途同归的基于耕地保养原则的削减耕地、洪涝挽救措施。

（3）记叙文

六级阅读中的记叙文主要是记人叙事,重点在叙述人的经历、感受、观察和发现,或叙述事物的发展、变化与过程等。叙述方式大多以时间为线索来进行,或顺序或倒序。单纯的记叙文比较简单、易懂,所以在试题中一般选择夹叙夹议的文章。记叙文的特点决定了该类文章后的阅读理解试题大多是和文章的内容先后顺序一致的细节题。其基本模式是:引入话题——叙述先前的事例及其感悟或发现——作出结论。

例 4：Amitai Etzioni is not surprised by the latest headings about scheming corporate crooks（骗子）. As a visiting professor at the Harvard Business School in 1989, he ended his work there disgusted with his students' overwhelming lust for money. "They're taught that profit is all that matters" he says. "Many school don't even offer ethics（伦理学） courses at all. "

Etzioni expressed his frustration about the interests of his graduate students. "By and large, I clearly had not found a way to help classes full of MBAs see that there is more to life than money, power, fame and self-interest," he wrote at the time. Today he still takes the blame for not educating these "business-leaders-to-be. " "I really feel like I failed them," he says. "If I was a better teacher maybe I could have reached them. "

Etzioni was a respected ethics expert when he arrived at Harvard. He hoped his work at the university would give him insight into how questions of morality could be applied to places where self-interest flourished. What he found wasn't encouraging. Those would-be executives had, says Etzioni, little interest in concept of ethics and morality in the boardroom-and their professor was met with blank stares when he urged his students to see business in new and different ways.

Etzioni sees the experience at Harvard as an eye-opening one and says there's much about business schools that he'd like to change. "A lot of the faculty teaching business are bad news themselves," Etzioni says. From offering classes that teach students how to legally manipulate contracts, to reinforcing the notion of profit over community interests, Etzioni has seen a lot that's left him shaking his head. And because of what he's seen taught in business schools, he's not surprised by the latest rash of corporate scandals. "In many ways things have got a lot worse at business schools. I suspect," says Etzioni.

Etzioni is still teaching the sociology of right and wrong and still calling for ethical business leadership. "People with poor motives will always exist," he says. "Sometimes environments constrain those people and sometimes environments give those people opportunity." Etzioni says the booming economy of the last decade enabled those individuals with poor motives to get rich before getting in trouble. His hope now: that the cries for reform will provide more fertile soil for his long-standing messages about business ethics. (2006 年 12 月 CET‐6, Passage 2)

解析:

这是一篇报道性记叙文。第一段指出阿米泰·伊茨欧对最近的商业欺骗并不感到惊讶是因为他在哈佛商学院担任过客座教授。第二至第四段,记叙了阿米泰·伊茨欧在哈佛商学院的经历:那里的学生只重视金钱,毫不重视商业道德;很多教师也存在这样的问题。第五段记述了阿米泰·伊茨欧仍然坚持不懈地倡导商业道德。文章通过记叙作者在哈佛商学院作访问学者的见闻,反映了现在的商界存在的问题:只重视金钱和利润,不重视伦理道德,也反映了作者对这种问题的忧虑以及对商业道德的呼唤,从而达到了记叙的高潮。

通过研究以上的文章结构特点,我们不难发现,在六级考试阅读理解中无论任何体裁的文章都遵循着这样一个共同的模式:提出话题(观点或事例)——用事例分析原因(或批驳观点)——得出结论。对文章结构特点的把握有助于读者更加自觉地关注文章的开始和结尾,分清观点和事例,从而在六级考试的阅读理解中准确定位,快速答题。

2. 掌握基本的阅读技巧

不少考生认为要想在阅读理解部分获得较高的分数,只要具备丰富的词汇和语法结构知识就够了。不需要什么阅读技巧、解题技巧和方法。这是有一定道理的,因为如果没有一定的词汇量和丰富的语法结构知识作为支撑,奢谈什么技巧或方法都无益。基础是第一位的,而技巧是第二位的。但是如果在具备相当的词汇量和语法结构知识的同时,能够了解并掌握一定的阅读技巧和解题方法,对考生一定会大有好处。尤其是在阅读测试时间紧、阅读量大的情况下,掌握并运用好有效的阅读技巧将取到事半功倍的效果。阅读基本技巧有:略读、查读和研读。

(1) 略读(skimming)

目的:获取文章大意及其谋篇布局

适用题型:主旨题

阅读要领:快读时,精力要集中,速度要快。一般地说,400 字左右的短文要求在五六分钟内看完。快读时,可略去个别生词或难懂的词句,留心文章中反复出现的词语,因为它们往往与文章的主题有关。快读时,还应特别注意文章的首尾两段以及其他段落的段首句和结尾局,因为他们往往是对文章内容的最好概括。掌握并熟练地运用略读法可以使考生在尽可能短的时间内了解整篇文章的整体布局和大概意思,这对后面有关中心思想方面的试题解答很有益,同时还能帮助考生快速确定其他试题的大概位置。

（2）查读（scanning）

目的：快速获取特定信息

适用题型：细节题

阅读要领：查读与略读不同，它不求通篇地了解中心内容，只需了解某一特定的内容。通过查读，仔细地阅读相关部分，了解其内容和理解其深层含义。在回答每篇文章后所附的问题时，就需要运用查读的方法，即先阅读题干，确定关键词，然后在文章中找到并标明与题干相关的句子，与此无关的内容要很快掠过，最后对所提供的四个选项进行判断，确定正确的答案。

（3）研读（Reading for full understanding）

目的：弄清文章中字里行间的潜在意思

适用题型：推断题

阅读要领：找到文章中的有关范围后，要逐句阅读其中句子，特别对关键词、句要仔细琢磨，以便对其有较深刻、较准确的理解。不仅要理解其字面意思，而且要通过推理和判断，弄清文章中"字里行间"的潜在意思。遇到生词、长难句时，要善于运用猜词法和长难句理解方法，如语法手段对其加以分析，以达到透切的理解。

略读、查读和研读在阅读应试中是相辅相承的。完成每篇文章的试题，都必须灵活运用这三种阅读方法。一般说来，可按以下步骤进行篇章阅读：先用快读方法浏览全文，以了解中心思想及大意。在此基础上，可根据题干中的关键词，用查读方法，查到文章中与大体内容有关的范围后用研读方法来确定答案。全部问题回答完之后，若时间允许，可再读一遍全文，核实所确定的答案是否符合文章的中心思想。

俗话说熟能生巧。平时的阅读练习中，应该有意识地加强略读、查读和研读方法的训练，在考试中才能更快、更准地回答问题，从而获得好成绩。

3. 采用有效的解题步骤

在熟练掌握基本的阅读技巧的基础上，应试时，应根据自己的习惯,采用有效的阅读步骤进行解题,方能提高阅读效果。常见的解题方法有三种:一是先看文章,再看题;二是先看题,再看文章;三是读一层意思做一道题,读文章做题交叉进行。这三种方法各有利弊,考生应根据文章的难易程度和自己对文章的理解程度采用合适的阅读方法。阅读难度适宜的文章可采用第一种阅读方法,对比较难懂、生词又多、内容不熟悉的文章可采用第二种阅读方法,对段落较多的文章,阅读速度又较慢的同学可采用第三种阅读方法。但是不管采用哪一种方法,都应该清楚它们的特点,灵活运用阅读的基本技巧。

(1) 先略读再查读和研读——先看文章,再看题

A:应用这种方法做题,一般可以采用以下步骤:

① 第一步用1分钟~2分钟的时间快速浏览全文,大致了解全文中心及每段的侧重点;

② 第二步再用1分钟~2分钟的时间将提出的问题及选项粗略读一遍,大致了解要回答哪些问题和有哪几种题型,同时大致确定一下这些问题在原文中的出处;

③ 第三步用5分钟~6分钟的时间分别细读与这些问题有关的段落和句子(题区),对提出的问题的选项作出判断。

B:应用这种方法做题时应该注意以下几个问题:

① 特别注意有选择地进行阅读段首主题句和段尾结论句,把握文章中心与作者基本观点,即抓大的放小的。

② 注意重要细节的位置,第一遍阅读时在了解主题之后知道某个东西在哪里,胜过你知道它是什么。

③ 注意黑体字、斜体字和关联词(信号词),因为这些字、词具有强调或特殊意义。如表示转折的 but, however, yet, on the contrary 等;表示顺序的 firstly, secondly, last, finally 等;表示递进的 moreover, in addition 等;表示总结的 in short, in brief, to sum up 等。

这种方法的优点在于视野广泛,心中有数,主次分明,整个解题过程步骤清楚,时间容易控制。但是这方法对快速浏览的技能要求较高,必须在短时间内快速地通过关键词找到中心内容,否则会因为反

复查找的次数增多而耽误时间。

（2）先查读和研读再略读——先看题，再看文章

A：应用这种方法一般采取以下步骤：

① 第一步用 1 分钟～2 分钟的时间看提出的问题及选项，将细节题与主旨题分开，先做细节题；

② 第二步是带着这些细节题到原文中快速查读、定位、细读相关的段落或句子，然后作出判断，这个过程大约需要 4 分钟～5 分钟；

③ 第三步是解决往往要通过阅读全文才能回答的 1 个～2 个问题。所以这时再快速地浏览全文，把握总体的内容或观点，做出主旨题的判断。

B：应用这种方法做题时应该注意以下几个问题：

① 查读时，必须具有明确的目的，即带着问题进行阅读以便确定题区；

② 对与问题有关的内容要多看、细看，对于问题无关的内容就跳过去；

③ 根据所需信息的性质，特别注意与其相关的语言特点。如果要了解因果，就要注意 consequently，since，because，as a result 等词，若要了解时间以及数据，便要注意有关的数据；

这种方法的优点是快速、直接，阅读时目的性强，可以减少阅读无关信息的时间。但是解题时全局观念差些，不能够借助中心内容的把握来判断选项的对错。另外孤立地看题比较容易忘记，往往看了文章后还要看题，对记忆的要求较高。

（3）先略读再研读——阅读文章与解题交叉进行

这种方法的解题步骤是每次阅读一小段或者一长段的一半后，看一道题做一道题，直至解答完毕。采用这种方法应注意的事项：一是每次阅读新的内容之前，最好把接下来要回答的问题先看一下，提高阅读指向性；二是阅读速度比第一种阅读方法要稍慢一些，力求弄清本段意思；三是合理安排解题时间。一般来说每篇文章解题时间为 9 分钟，读原文要 5 分钟，解题要 4 分钟。

总之,无论是采用以上提及的哪一种方法,首先都要了解其特点,还要了解自己的能力水平及阅读习惯,通过训练,找到自己最适合的方法,才能取得最佳的效果。

第三节 专项训练

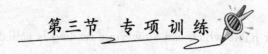

Part I Determine the meaning of the italicized words in the following sentences by using the techniques you have learned.

1. ***Ventilation***, as you know, is a system or means of providing fresh air. It plays a very important part in the field of engineering.

2. A person or thing beyond comparison, a model of excellence, is known as a ***paragon***.

3. He was a ***prestidigitator*** who entertained the children by pulling rabbits out of hats, swallowing fire, and other similar tricks.

4. ***Tornadoes*** (violent and destructive whirl wind) normally occur on hot, ***humid*** (a little wet) day, but not necessarily in the summer.

5. The new tax law ***supersedes***, or replaces, the law that was in effect last year.

6. Mother was tall, fat and middle-aged. The principal of the school was an older woman, almost as ***plump*** as mother, and much shorter.

7. In the past the world seemed to run in an orderly way. Now, however, everything seems to be in ***a state of turmoil***.

8. Defined most broadly, ***folklore*** includes all the customs, belief and tradition that people have handed down from generation to generation.

9. Before the main business of a conference begins the chairman usually makes a short ***preliminary*** (i. e. introductory) speech, or

make a few preliminary remarks. In other words, he says a few things by way of introduction.

10. Since I could not afford to purchase the original painting, I bought a *replica*. An inexperienced eye could not tell the difference.

11. Another habit which can slow your reading is called "*subvocalization*". In this case your lips do not move, but you still "hear" each word in your head as you read silently.

12. When a doctor performs an operation on a patient, he usually gives an *anaesthetic* to make him unconscious, because he does not want his patient to feel pain or to know what is happening to him.

13. If you are capable of working twelve hours a day without a rest, and if you can engage in physical exercise for hours without seeming to get tired, then you are *indefatigable*.

14. My sister is extremely neat in appearance while she is *slovenly* in her housekeeping.

15. Many famous scientists are trying to understand the problems modern people suffer from, but never these *eminent* scholars are confused about what causes them.

Part II　Analyze the following sentences and put them into Chinese

1. This violation of concentration, silence, solitude goes to the very heart of our notion of literacy; this new form of part-reading, of part-perception against background distraction, renders impossible certain essential acts of apprehension and concentration, let alone that most important tribute any human being can pay to a poem or a piece of prose he or she really loves, which is to learn it by heart.（2001 年 6 月）

2. Researchers have begun to piece together an illuminating picture

of the powerful geological and astronomical forces that have combined to change the planet's environment from hot to cold, wet to dry and back again over a time period stretching back hundreds of millions of years. (2006 年 6 月)

3. Bille's lenses are expected to reach the market in the year 2000, and one tentative plan is to use the Internet to transmit information on patients' visual defects from the optician to the manufacturer, who will then produce and mail the contact lenses within a couple of days. (2003 年 6 月)

4. Our enormously productive economy demands that we make consumption our way of life, that we convert the buying and use of goods into ritual, that we seek our spiritual satisfaction, our ego satisfaction, in consumption. (2003 年 1 月)

5. Implementing the new science standards and their math counterparts will be the challenge, he and Schmidt agree, because the decentralized responsibility for education in the United States requires that any reforms be tailored and instituted in one community at a time. (2005 年 1 月)

6. When I think about all the problems of our overpopulated world and look at our boy grabbing at the lamp by the sofa, I wish I could have turned to Planned Grandparenthood when my parents were putting the grandchild squeeze on me. (2005 年 12 月)

7. At the same time, the politicians demand of scientists that they tailor their research to "economic needs", that they award a higher priority to research proposals that are "near the market" and can be translated into the greatest return on investment in the shortest time. (2005 年 12 月)

8. While it's true that we all need a career, it is equally true that our civilization has accumulated an incredible amount of knowledge in

fields far removed from our own and that we are better for our understanding of these other contributions—be they scientific or artistic. (2003 年 1 月)

9. Also on the agenda for next year is a proposal, backed by some influential law-makers, to split the INS into two agencies—a good cop that would tend to service functions like processing citizenship papers and a bad cop that would concentrate on border inspections, deportation and other functions. (2004 年 6 月)

10. For hundreds of millions of years, turtles(海龟)have struggled out of the sea to lay their eggs on sandy beaches, long before there were nature documentaries to celebrate them, or GPS satellites and marine biologists to track them, or volunteers to hand-carry the hatchlings(幼龟)down to the water's edge lest they become disoriented by headlights and crawl towards a motel parking lot instead. (2009 年 6 月)

11. Thus many in the industrial lands have a sense that their world of plenty is somehow hollow—that, misled by a consumerist culture, they have been fruitlessly attempting to satisfy what are essentially social, psychological and spiritual needs with material things. (2003 年 1 月)

12. Now Germany's Nobel Prize winning author Gun ter Grass has revived the memory of the 9,000 dead, including more than 4,000 children—with his latest novel Crab Walk, published last month. (2004 年 6 月)

Part III   Skim the following passage for its main idea and select the best answer to the questions followed.

Passage one

Recently the attack on illiteracy has been stepped up. A world plan has been drawn up by a committee of Unesco experts in Paris, as part of the United Nations Development, and an international conference on the subject has also been held. Unesco stresses that functional literacy is the aim. People must learn the basic skills of responsible citizenship: the ability to read notices, newspapers, timetables, letters, pricelists, to keep simple records and accounts, to sort out the significance of the information gathered, and to fill in forms.

The passage is primarily concerned with _____.

A. the stepped up attack on literacy

B. a world plan by a committee of Unesco experts

C. an international conference on the problem of illiteracy

D. the Unesco's stresses on learning the basic language skills

Passage two

Perhaps the invention of agriculture marked the beginning of a differentiation between men's and women's roles. Men continued to hunt, and women became food gathers and tended the field. Men later became agriculturists as well, when the hunt no longer provided enough sustenance for the community. The biological fact that women bear children, and that each time they give birth they are unable, for a time, fully to play their role in the provision of sustenance and other work for the family, slowly gave rise to more distinct men's and women's roles. Men who are physically stronger took on such 'natural' roles as warriors, and in most cases men became chiefs, commanders, and kings. In the course of history, as matriarchal systems became minorities in many cultures, the roles of men and women in many societies became increasingly gender oriented and differentiated.

The author's discussion centers around _____.

A. the differentiation between men's and women's roles as the fading of matriarchal systems

B. men as hunters and agriculturists

C. women as food gatherers and children raisers

D. the invention of agriculture that marked the beginning of a differentiation between men's and women's roles

Passage three

Whether the eyes are "the windows of the soul" is debatable; that they are intensely important in interpersonal communication is a fact. During the first two months of a baby's life, the stimulus that produces a smile is a pair of eyes. The eyes need not be real: a mask with two dots will produce a smile. Significantly, a real human face with eyes covered will not motivate a smile, nor will the sight of only one eye when the face is presented in profile. This attraction to eyes as opposed to the nose or mouth continues as the baby matures. In one study, when American four-year-olds were asked to draw people, 75 percent of them drew people with mouths, but 99 percent of them drew people with eyes. In Japan, however, where babies are carried on their mother's back, infants do not acquire as much attachment to eyes as they do in other cultures. As a result, Japanese adults make little use of the face either to encode (编码) or decode meaning: In fact, Argyle reveals that the "proper place to focus one's gaze during a conversation in Japan is on the neck of one's conversation partner. "

The role of eye contact in a conversational exchange between two Americans is well defined: speakers make contact with the eyes of their listener for about one second, then glance away as they talk; in a few moments they re-establish eye contact with the listener or reassure themselves that their audience is still attentive, then shift their gaze away once more. Listeners, meanwhile, keep their eyes on the face of the speaker, allowing themselves to glance away only briefly. It is important that they be looking at the speaker at the precise moment when the speaker re-establishes eye contact: if they are not looking, the speaker assumes that they are disinterested and either will pause until eye contact is resumed or will terminate the conversation. Just how critical this eye maneuvering is to the maintenance of conversational flow becomes evident when two speakers are wearing dark glasses: there may be a sort of traffic jam of words caused by interruption, false starts, and unpredictable pauses. (1997 年 6 月 CET - 6, Passage 4)

The author is convinced that the eyes are _____.

A. of extreme importance in expressing feelings and exchanging ideas

B. something through which one can see a person's inner world

C. of considerable significance in making conversations interesting

D. something the value of which is largely a matter of long debate

第四节 答案与解析

Part I Determine the meaning of the italicized words in the following sentences by using the techniques you have learned.

1. 【解析】以 be 动词为线索猜测词义。该句中 ventilation 可能是个生词,但 is 后面是对该词的明确定义。是什么东西或什么手段才能提供新鲜空气呢? 所以不难看出 "ventilation" 这个词的意思是 "通风"。

2. 【解析】以 be known as 为线索猜测词义。该句中 paragon 一词的词义可从句子的主语推测出来:一个人或物是无与伦比的,即优秀

33

的典范,这不就是"模范、优秀的人或物"吗? 显然"be known as"前面的主语给出了后面"paragon"的词义。

3. 【解析】以定语从句为线索猜测词义。该句中的 who 引导的定语从句对生词"prestidigitator"的词义进行定义,根据这一定义,考生就不难猜测出 prestidigitator 的词义。能从帽子里拉出兔子、吞火和玩其他类似的把戏的人不就是变戏法的人吗? 因此,"prestidigitator"一词的词义就应是"变戏法者"。

4. 【解析】以括号作为猜词线索猜出词义。该句中的"tornado"和"humid"两词的词义都在括弧里被清楚地表述出来。"tornado"即一种非常剧烈的、破坏性很大的旋转的风,很明显,这是"旋风、飓风";humid 即有点湿,其词义很清楚是"潮湿的"意思。

5. 【解析】以 or 为线索猜测词义。该句中,作者考虑到"supersede"一词可能是生词,紧接着用 or 引出该词的同义词"replace",此词是一比较常用的词,读者可根据"replace"一词的词义能很容易地推断出"supersede"一词的大概意思来,即"取代,接替"。

6. 【解析】以 as...as 结构为线索猜测词义。此句中,作者把学校的校长和他的母亲相比,有相同之处和不同之处。校长比母亲年纪大些,个子矮些,但有一点是相同的,并用"as...as"结构表示出来。从这一对比中,可以看出 fat 和 plump 是近义词,便可猜出 plump 一词为"肥胖的"意思。

7. 【解析】以信号词 however 为线索猜测词义。该句中,作者用 however 把现在的事情与过去相比,过去是"in an orderly way",而现在是"in a state of turmoil",过去是秩序井然,那么现在则是相反,那就是一片混乱。

8. 【解析】以 include 及常识为线索猜测词义。该句中的 includes 后面的例子具体说明了"folklore"的内容范围,即人们一代传一代的那些风俗、习惯、信仰和传统的东西。这些东西都属于通常所说的"民俗学,民俗传统",这也就是"folklore"一词的基本含义。

9. 【解析】以重述为线索猜测词义。在阅读该句时,如果对"prelimina-

34

ry speech"的意思不是十分清楚,只要接着往下读,意思就会逐渐明朗起来,因为我们发现句中的"or"和"in other words"后面的部分都是对"preliminary speech"的重述,由此可以推断出"preliminary speech"的意思是在开会之前主席所做的一些简单的介绍,即"开场白"的意思。

10. 【解析】以因果关系为线索猜测词义。从信号词 since 以及相关信息,可以看出生词所处的上下文存在很明显的因果关系。since 引出的从句是原因(即因为我买不起那张原画),主句是结果。生词"replica"后一句又进一步解释了另一种原因,即没有经验的人看不出来差别。根据这之间的逻辑关系,就很容易推断:既然不是原画,那么只能是一张"复制品"了。

11. 【解析】以上下文解释或说明为线索猜测词义。根据"subvocalization"一词所在句的下文可推断出它的词义来。因为后面的句子是对"subvocalization"一词的解释。可以想象一下,虽然在阅读时你的嘴唇没有动,但你的脑子仍能听出你在读每一个词,这种阅读不就是我们通常所说的"默读"吗? 由此可以推断出"subvocalization"一词是"默读"的意思。

12. 【解析】根据直接或间接的经验为线索猜测词义。一般具有一点医学常识的人都知道医生在给病人动手术之前,为了减轻病人的痛苦,往往给病人注射麻醉剂使病人失去知觉后再动手术。所以根据这一常识,通过上下文就能比较准确地确定"anaesthetic"一词的意思应该是"麻醉剂"的意思。

13. 【解析】根据逻辑推理推测词义。根据上下文分析,如果一个人能连续工作 12 个小时,能进行体育锻炼数小时而不知疲倦,那么,由此我们可以符合逻辑地推断,这个人一定是一个"不知疲倦的"人。故 *indefatigable* 为"不知疲倦的"的意思。

14. 【解析】以信号词 while 为线索猜测词义。句中 while 表明 slovenly 的意思与 neat 的意思相反。neat 是"整洁的",由此可推出,slovenly 是"不整洁的,邋遢的"的意思。

15.【解析】以同义词为线索推测词义。在句中,为避免重复,"these eminent scholars 替换 many famous scientists,既然 scholars 和 scientists 同义,eminent 也就和 famous 同义,为著名的"。

Part II Analyze the following sentences and put them into Chinese

1.【分析】该句是由分号隔开的并列复合句。分号前的句子是一个简单句,主干是 The violation goes to the heart。分号后句子的结构是 The new form renders impossible essential acts, let alone that most important tribute。特别要注意的是该句中 tribute 由两个定语从句来修饰:一个是省略关系词 that 的 any human being can pay to a poem or a piece of prose he or she really loves;另一个是非限定性定语从句 which is to learn it by heart。

【译文】这种违背集中注意力、安静、独处的方式损害了我们对读写能力的看法,这种新形式在背景有干扰的情形下的半阅读、半感知方式几乎不能做到基本的欣赏和集中注意力,更不用说任何一个人对真正喜爱的一首诗或一篇散文所能表示的最大的赞赏是将其背诵下来。

2.【分析】该句为复合句。句子的框架结构是 Researchers have begun to piece together an illuminating picture。Of the powerful geological and astronomical forces 是介词短语作定语,修饰 picture。that 引导的定语从句修饰 forces,现在分词短语 stretching back hundreds of millions of years 做定语修饰 time period。

【译文】研究人员已经开始着手拼凑一幅具有启示性的画面,以展示过去的数亿年间地质和天文的力量是如何共同作用,使地球环境从热到冷,从湿到干,然后一段时间之后又周而复始。

3.【分析】该句为并列复合句。句中 and 连接两个并列分句,第二个分句中 to use the Internet to transmit information on patients' visual defects from the optician to the manufacturer 是不定式短语作表语。who 引导非限定性定语从句,修饰 manufacturer。

【译文】比尔的眼镜有望在 2000 年上市,一个实验性方案是:利用因特网把患者的视力缺陷资料从眼镜商传给制造商,制造商在之后的两三天将眼镜做好并寄出。

4. 【分析】该句为复合句。demands 后面是三个 that 引导的并列的宾语从句。从句使用了虚拟语气,即"主语+(should)+do+宾语"的结构。遇到 demand, suggest, propose, advise 等词时,它们后面的宾语从句要求用虚拟语气。

【译文】我们庞大的多产经济要求我们把消费作为自己的生活方式,把购买和使用商品变成例行公事,在消费中寻找精神满足、自我满足。

5. 【分析】该句为复合句。he and Schmidt agree 是插入成分,不影响句子的独立。because 引导原因状语从句,从句中包含 that 引导的宾语从句,作 requires 的宾语,宾语从句使用了虚拟语气,即"(should)+动词原形"的结构。

【译文】他和斯奇米德都认同实施新的科学和数学教育标准将是个挑战,因为美国教育权限的不集中要求任何一项改革只能一次一个社区地进行调整和实施。

6. 【分析】该句为多重复合句。句首 when 引导时间状语从句,主句是 I wish I could... squeeze on me。I wish 后面是省略 that 的宾语从句,其中又包含由 when 引导的时间状语从句。Wish 后面的宾语从句表示与现实情况相反的愿望,因此使用了虚拟语气。

【译文】当我想到有关世界人口过剩的所有问题,看着我们的儿子抓沙发的台灯时,就在想如果那时在父母逼着我生孩子的时候,自己能够求助于"有计划地成为祖父母"组织就好了。

7. 【分析】该句为多重复合句。句中前两个 that 引导的宾语从句都作 demand 的宾语,从句中用了虚拟语气,谓语构成为(should)+动词原形。最后一个 that 引导定语从句,修饰 proposals。定语从句中,are "near the market"和 can be translated 是并列谓语。

【译文】同时,政客们要求科学家使其研究适应于经济的需求,也要求他们优先从事那些"靠近市场"并能在最短期内获得最大投资回报的研究提案。

8.【分析】该句为复合句。While 作连词，连接两个并列句子，表示对比关系。it's true that，it is equally true that 是并列结构。it 都是形式主语，真正的主语都是 that 从句。be they scientific or artistic 是倒装句。

【译文】我们都需要有份职业，这是毋庸置疑的；同样毋庸置疑的是，我们的文明在许多我们极其陌生的领域里已经积累了极其丰富的知识，是科技方面的也好，艺术方面的也罢，我们最好还是能懂一些。

9.【分析】该句为复合句。此句第一分句的结构是"表语＋系动词＋主语"，是完全倒装。backed by some influential law-makers 是插入成分，插在中心词 proposal 和定语 to split 之间。两个 that 从句都作定语，分别修饰 good cop 和 bad cop。

【译文】同样在来年的议程上还有一个由一些有影响力的立法人员提出的建议：将移民归化局分成两个机构——一个扮演好警察，主要负责诸如处理公民文件之类的服务性工作；另一个扮演坏警察，负责边境检查、驱逐出境及诸如此类的工作。

10.【分析】该句为复合句。主句是 turtles have struggled out of the sea to lay their eggs on sandy beaches；before 引导时间状语从句，该从句中的 nature documentaries to celebrate them，GPS satellites and marine biologists to track them，volunteers to hand-carry the hatchlings(幼龟)down to the water's，为不定式短语后置做定语修饰前面的名词；lest 引导目的状语从句。

【译文】早在人类有自然纪录片称颂海龟、GPS 卫星和海洋生物学家对其进行追踪或者志愿者用手将幼龟捧到海边以免他们因为桅灯迷失方向而爬向汽车旅馆的停车场之前的数亿年，海龟一直是艰难地爬出海面到沙滩下产卵的。

11.【分析】该句为复合句。句子结构是 many have a sense that... and that...。两个 that 都是引导同位语从句，作 sense 的同位语。

第二个 that 从句中，misled by a consumerist culture 是插入成分。what are essentially social, psychological and spiritual needs 是宾语从句，作 satisfy 的宾语。

【译文】于是，工业国家的许多人感觉到其富足的世界似乎有点空虚——由于受到消费主义文化的误导，他们试图用物质来满足本质上是社会、心理和精神方面的需求，结果徒劳一场。

12.【分析】该句虽然较长，但实际上是简单句。句子主干是 Gun ter Grass has revived the memory。including more than 4,000 children 是插入成分，起补充说明的作用。with his latest novel Crab Walk 是方式状语，published last month 是过去分词短语作定语，修饰 Crab Walk。

【译文】现在，德国作家、诺贝尔奖获得者冈特·格拉斯用其上个月出版的最新小说《蟹行》重新唤起了对那 9000 名遇难者（其中 4000 多是孩子）的记忆。

Part III   Skim the following passage for its main idea and select the best answer to the questions followed.

Passage one

【解析】A．因为全文的主题是世界性的加速扫盲运动，这是主要信息，找到了主要信息，次要信息自然而然就可以确定下来了。上面除了 A 以外的三项选择都涉及次要信息，其中 Unesco 一词是个首字母缩略词，表示"联合国教育科学及文化组织"。

Passage two

【解析】D．因为文章谈论的中心是农业的出现标志着男女的分工，而不是母系氏族制的衰退而产生了男女分工。故选项 D 为答案。

Passage three

【解析】A．本文作者议论的主题是眼睛在人际交往中的重要性。本文共两段，属于"观点—例证—（结论）"模式。第一段作者提出论点并举例说明在不同文化的人群中，人们对眼睛的感情是有差异的；第二段作者论述了谈话时双方目光接触所体现的重要性。题目问及作者对眼睛的看法,考生只要通读全文,弄清本文结构模式后,把握文章第一句话的意思:"眼睛是不是心灵的窗户是个有争议的问题,但是眼睛在人际交往中起着十分重要的作用则是无可争辩的事实",就能容易地判断 A 项为正确答案,即,作者相信"眼睛"在表达情感和相互交流时是非常重要的。选项 A 为答案。

第二章 快速阅读

第一节 设题特点

　　四级快速阅读要求考生在 15 分钟内完成一篇 1000 词～1200 词的文章和后面的 10 道题。前面 7 个题是判断正误(包括 NOT GIVEN)，如果与文章内容相符，就选 Y（for YES）—if the statement agrees with the information given in the passage；不相符则选 N（for NO)—if the statement contradicts the information given in the passage；如果问题中所含的信息在原文中并未提及，则为 NG（for NOT GIVEN)—if the information is not given in the passage。后 3 道是填空题(答案基本都是原文中出现的原词)。而六级快速阅读要求考生在 15 分钟内完成一篇 1000 词～1500 词的文章阅读并做后面的 10 道题。一般情况，前面 4 道题是判断正误(包括 NOT GIVEN)，后 6 道是填空题(答案基本都是原文中出现的原词)。有时也会出现传统的选择题(7 题)和填空题(3 题)。不过，传统的选择题由于常常练习，所以这种题型对大家来说难度不是特别大，因而本文重点仍放在判断正误和填空题这类题型。虽然和新四级相比题型有相似之处，但是六级的快速阅读文章更长，填空题的数量也由 3 个增加到 6 个。同样的时间要完成的量加大，难度也增加。这即符合考纲要求增加对主观题型的考查的趋势，同时也对考生的阅读技巧，阅读能力提出更高的要求。对比而言，六级文章的篇幅和题目的设置都让我们感觉到，在复习阶段考生一定要有意识地培养快速阅读能力，以便有效地应对这个部分的测试。面对六级较长的文章，考生要练习自己搜寻信息的能力，也就是通过略读和寻读法，乃至文章逻辑关系、标点符号等方面的综合运用，实现对随后的题目有效的判断和填写。

做快速阅读的时候，考生只有 15 分钟时间，而阅读量近 1500 个单词，如果通篇阅读下来，每分钟阅读的单词量即接近 100，这几乎是不可能完成的。因此，做题时根据题目在文章中快速定位查找。而定位的技巧在于关键词的使用。一般每个题目中都有一些词——表示时间、地点、数字、名称等的单词，可以以这些词为基础和线索，结合文章的小标题进行范围查找。如果文章没有出现小标题，那么可以仔细阅读每个段落的首句，了解段落大意，这样也可以节省定位时间。同四级一样，六级的快速阅读题也可以基本按顺序原则来推测。

在快速阅读题中，Y、N、NG 这部分，考生对 Y 的判断一般比较有信心，N 次之，而对于 NG 的判断最犹豫。因为有的问题看上去似是而非，让考生大伤脑筋。其实推断题的错误率较高，对比答案就会发现错就错在想得太远了，推断只要想到最直接最简单的就够了。而填空题部分，四级快速阅读中句子填空题的答案都是原文中出现的原词，考生只需找到所需信息相应的地方，然后把它从原文中搬抄下来即可，基本上不需要改动原文信息。其次，所要填写的信息都在题干的最后。六级在这部分则难度增加一些，需要根据题干的关键词找出原文的同义表达。总之，六级在时间上比四级更紧，所以六级更注重的是阅读的技巧。

所谓快速阅读，就是以较快的速度在规定的时间内有目的、有方法、高效率地阅读材料，以便从中准确地获得所需的信息。快速阅读试题的目的就是考察考生在短时间内获取篇章特定信息的能力，对于考生的阅读速度的确有较高的要求，但对于阅读的深度要求则相对较

低。其文章和出题特点如下:

(1) 从样题和 2008 年 6 月的全真题来看,文章长度基本上是 1000 词~1500 词,通常会出现大标题和副标题(如果在今后的考试文章中没有副标题,就可以通过阅读各段的首句和尾句来推测文章某段落可能会涉及的内容),文中的句子结构并不复杂,但词汇量较大。

(2) 文章的选材注重时效性,现实性较强,选自英、美等国家出版的报刊文章和书籍,语言规范,表达生动,涉及最近的社会热点问题,如科普、环境、学术观点、经济、生活、文化等,通常不会涉及到政治、军事、尖端科技等内容。体裁方面,从样题和全真题来看,快速阅读通常是比较客观的介绍或描述,而很少会涉及到作者的态度。可供选择阅读材料的来源有 Time, Newsweek, China Daily, 21st Century 等。平时在阅读这些报刊文章时,应注意选择一般性的题材,这样对应付快速阅读测试会有帮助。

(3) 判断正误题是若干个陈述句组成,要求根据原文所给的信息,判断每个陈述句是对(Yes)、错(No)、还是未提及(Not Given)。试题的题干长度适中,为 20 个词左右,以便于考生在短时间内理解题目,阅读时获取有效信息,迅速找到答案。这种题型的最大难度在于,选项间的混淆程度很深,在 Yes 和 No 之外还有第三种情况:Not Given。所以,必须要把原文中相应的叙述找出来,看哪个选项是对原文的精确改写,是则为正确,否则为错误,但是在很多情况下似乎很难区分 No 和 Not Given(这在后面会加以分析总结),因此考生不能凭印象做题,因为选项间的差异有时候可能就微小到一个介词、连词、冠词、副词或语气词上,更不能完全利用自己的知识背景做出想当然的判断,一切的判断都应以原文为基础。

(4) 后面的 6 个题是根据原文所提供的信息补充完整句子。通过对样卷和真题的分析,这种题型难度不是太大,句子填空题的答案需找到所需信息相应的地方,然后根据原文意思将结构不完整的句子补充成完整的句子。一般用原文中的细节信息,然后用原词或原词的总结性概括,把句子补充完整。空格处要填写的词汇个数不多,一般在 5

个～6个以内。所有需要填写的内容在原文中可以找到。即使需要重新措辞的题目改动也不大。因此,迅速定位找到相关句是最为关键的。

(5) 通过研究和分析样题及全真题,大家可以看出快速阅读的出题规律是——出题的顺序与文章的篇章段落展开的顺序基本是一致的,即题目是按照文章的段落顺序给出的,其答案的顺序当然也是如此,例如第二题的答案在原文中出现的位置应在第一题的答案之后,依次类推。根据这一规律,考生可以快速确定答案的位置,以免重复阅读而浪费时间。

第二节 应 试 技 巧

考生在处理快速阅读时,应该首先明确一个问题,那就是该题型与其他题型的要求不完全一样,其他类型的考题(如详细阅读、完型填空、改错、翻译等)对每句话的要求很高,几乎必须读懂才能做题,而快速阅读考察的是考生在大量材料中的信息搜索能力而非阅读理解能力,它不是以考生对文章的理解来计分,而是以考生答案的对错来计分,因此,考生就没有必要去关注那些对答题没有帮助的内容,那么考生也不必完全掌握整篇文章、了解文章中的每一个细节(其实,考生也没有那么多时间),更不能因为一个不知从何处冒出的难句或生词而彻底放慢速度,跟文章的细节内容纠缠不休。因此,处理该题型时就应采取与其他题型不同的解题思路,遇到生词、词组和结构复杂的句子,要敢于毅然决然地一掠而过,同时可以在心中用合理性原则推知它们的大致含义。另外还应把握一个原则——找原文语言出现的段落和句子。一般而言,题干中的关键词在原文中首次出现的地方通常就是答案所在的位置了。详细的说有以下步骤:

(1) 首先用一分钟左右的时间略读原文,了解文章的大意和结构。主要浏览对象是文章中的标题(Title)和副标题(Subtitle)或段落标题(Section heading)。

例如:在样题中出现的标题是:Rainforests

副标题:What Is A Rainforest?

The Forest for the Trees

Stranglers and Buttresses

All Creatures, Great and Small

Deforestation

从标题中可以推断出这篇文章主要介绍的是雨林。从副标题中可以推测文章将会重点分步介绍热带雨林的组成、生态群落以及各种物种间的竞争与共生关系,同时最后提到砍伐森林带来的后果。这些副标题一方面可以帮助考生迅速合理推测并确定文章的大概内容,避免阅读与问题无关的信息,提高查读的针对性;另一方面,对快速理解和整体把握文章内容以及推测出生词的词义范围有积极的意义。因为英语单词一词多义现象很普遍,一个单词在不同的专业领域往往含有不同的意思,甚至有的单词在同一专业领域在其意义的具体把握上也有细微的差别。另外,当涉及到文章主旨意思时,副标题的综合内容可以帮助考生很快锁定解题范围。在解答题目时,最好先仔细阅读题目,找出题干中的关键词,然后再有目的地在原文中搜索相关信息。将题目中的关键词先定位到原文中的一个段落,进而定位相关句子,需要密切关注的是题干中的关键词在原文中首次出现的地方通常就是答案所在的位置,这将大大缩短解题时间,并提高准确率。最后尤其关键的是出题的顺序与文章的篇章段落展开的顺序是一致的。

(2) 如何确定关键词。这里所说的关键词并不一定是题干中最重要的词,而是特征比较明显,容易识别,具备重要提示功能的词,如表示人名、地点、时间、数字的词语,以及特殊印刷的字体——大写字母、斜体词、粗体词、特殊符号、带下划线的词等。如问题或填空的句子中涉及到人名、地名,则主要寻找首字母大写的单词;有关日期、数目的问题,则主要查找具体数字。而与所要查找的信息无关的内容则可以一掠而过。根据题干中的关键词,迅速确定一个段落,由于答案在该段落中的具体位置是未知的,所以应该从头到尾快速阅读该关键词所处的段落,在原文中找出与题目相关的一句或几句话,通常是一句话。简而言之,快速阅读实际上就是带着明确的目的去看文章,是检索信息,搜索答案,而不是看懂多少内容。

(3) 要注意顺序性,即题目的顺序和原文内容的顺序基本一致。按照问题的顺序,第一题的答案应在文章的前部,第二题的答案应在第一题的答案之后,这个规律也有助于考生确定答案的位置,然后就是根据原文判断正误了。当然有时也会出现不完全依照这一规律的现象,但是总体是有顺序的。

(4) 如何区分错(No)和未提及(Not Given)。这是快速阅读中最难处理的部分。以往的阅读训练中,通常认为没有提到的就是错误的,而在新题型中,"N"指的是和原文的内容完全矛盾或截然相反;而"NG"是指在原文中并没有明确告知,但内容并不与原文相矛盾。

(5) 略读(skimming)与寻读(scanning)相结合,辅以研读,随时调整阅读速度。所谓略读,又称浏览或掠读,是指以尽可能快的速度阅读,如同从飞机上鸟瞰(bird's eye view)地面上的明显标志一样,其目的是迅速获取文章大意或中心思想,换句话说,略读是要求读者有选择地进行阅读,可跳过某些无关紧要的细节或与主题不相干的部分,以求抓住文章的大概,从而加快阅读速度。一般而言,通过标题和副标题就可以推测文章的主题;其次对文章的首段和末段要多加注意,以便发现作者的观点。略读的方法归纳起来就是:去粗取精,不失要点。同略读一样,寻读也是一种快速阅读技巧。寻读(scanning)又称查读,是通过目光扫视,以最快的速度从一篇文章的大量资料中迅速查找出你所期望得到的某一项具体事实或某一项特定信息,如人物、事件、时间、地点、数字等,而对其他无关部分则略去不读的快速阅读方法。运用这种方法,读者就能在最短的时间内掠过尽可能多的材料,找到所需的信息。例如,在车站寻找某次列车或汽车的运行时刻,在机场寻找某次班机的飞行时刻,在图书馆查找书刊的目录,在文献中查找某一日期、人名、地名、数字或号码等,都可以运用这种方法。

在快速阅读中,如果问题或填空的句子中涉及到了人名、地名,则主要寻找首字母大写的单词;有关日期、数字、比率的问题或填空的句子,则主要查找具体数字;有关某个事件、某种观点的题干,就需要寻找与之相关的关键词。在锁定关键词所处的段落或具体到某个句子后,则要刻意放慢速度,认真研读该段落或句子,做到完全理解,然后再与题干相比较,做出正确的判断或填词。

(6) 在试卷上做记号。在阅读过程中,考生不妨在自己认为比较重要的某些句子或词语(主题句、关键词)下面划线,标上记号。一方面做记号可以帮助考生集中注意力,尽快进入做题状态。另一方面,如果发现有不妥之处,做有记号的地方可以方便考生迅速回到对应的选项和原文中查找到所需要的信息,依据文章的意思重新考虑判断,直到合乎逻辑,从而节约时间,将注意力更多地放到解题上面。再者,考生如果对某个选项没有把握或把握不大,最好不要急于做出选择,可以将选项全做完后再做回到做记号的地方重新处理这些选项。切忌因为跟某一道题纠缠而造成更大的损失,考生要充分意识到放弃的背后意味着什么。

第三节　实战演练

Ⅰ Part Ⅱ **Reading Comprehension**（Skimming and Scanning）
（15minutes）

Directions：*In this part，you will have 15 minutes to go over the passage quickly and answer the questions on Answer Sheet Ⅰ.*
For question 1-4，mark

Y（*for* YES）　　　*if the statement agrees with the information given in*
　　　　　　　　　　the passage；

N（*for* NO）　　　*if the statement contradicts the information given in*
　　　　　　　　　　the passage；

NG(for NOT GIVEN) if the information is not given in the passage.
For question 5-10, complete the sentences with the information given
in the passage.

Underdeveloped People

The Indians living on the high plains of the Andes Mountains, in South America, have a background rich in history but rich in little else. These seven million people from the great old Indian nations live in a land of few trees, poor soil, cutting winds and biting cold. Their farms do not give enough food to support them. Their children from the age of three or four must work in the fields. The death rate of their babies is among the highest in the world, their standards of education among the lowest. They live at heights of ten of fifteen thousand feet, where even the air lacks the things necessary for life.

The needs of these Indians, scattered across three countries-Ecuador, Peru and Bolivia are great. Their problems are difficult and their diseases are deeply rooted in an old-fashioned way of life. Probably no single program of help can greatly better their condition. Health programs are no good without farm programs, and farm programs fail where there have been no programs of education.

Five international organizations have combined efforts to seek the answers to the problems of the unfortunate descendants of the Inca Indians. They are working with the governments of Peru, Bolivia and Ecuador on what they call the Andean Mission. Six areas have been formed, one each in Ecuador and Peru, four in Bolivia. Here methods are tested to attack poor education, poor food, poor living conditions and disease all at once.

We passed fields of low corn and thin wheat. Whole villages were at work planting potatoes. The men formed a line and walked slowly backward, beating the soil with sticks. The women, on hands

48

and knees, followed the men, breaking the hard earth with their hands. Their red and orange skirts flashed brightly in the sun. The scene was beautiful, but the land, seeds and crops were all poor.

Upon arriving at a village, we went to visit the school for carpenters. It was in an old building where thirty boys were attending classes. There were two classrooms containing complete sets of tools. I saw more tools there than in any carpenter's shop in Latin America. Most of the boys were cutting boards for practice. They worked steadily and didn't even look up when we entered.

The teacher remarked that the greatest problem at the moment was finding wood, as almost no trees grow on a high plain. Someone remarked that it would not take long for the school to produce too many carpenters in an area without trees, where most of the buildings were of stone or mud. The wood brought from the jungle was too costly for most of the people. The answer was that the original purpose of the school was to train carpenters and mechanics to go to other parts of the country. They would work where the government is developing new villages at the edge of the jungle.

Across from the carpentry-room there was a machine for producing electric power. With it the boys would be taught their first lessons in electricity. Other boys studied car repairing.

In the yard a group of boys surrounded a large tractor. The teacher was showing them how to operate it. No one was sure how many other tractors there were in the area. Guesses ranged from two to ten. If the school turned out more boys to handle them than the farms could use, the rest, it was hoped, would seek a living in the lower villages where more people lived.

The next day, against the cutting winds of the Bolivian mountains, we were going to a village that is the oldest of the four

Bolivian projects of the Andean mission. Behind us, across the valley, rain feel from the black clouds beyond the snowy mountaintops. The wind and rain beat against the car as we traveled across the open fields to come to the yard of an old farm.

My trip had been panned at the last minute. Since the village has no telegraph to telephone services, no one was expecting me. All the driver knew was that I was a visiting "doctor" simply because I was wearing a tie. He showed me into a large room of the farmhouse where some twenty men were watching film. It concerned the problems of a man who could neither read nor write. But in the face of difficulties he managed to start an adult education class in his village. He did this so that he could learn to read and win his girl friend's respect.

From time to time during the film the lights would go on and during these breaks everyone introduced himself. They had been brought together for a three-week course in how to teach, and to add to their own education, which in several cases had not gone beyond the third grade. Though they had not had much training they had the help of great interest and, most important, they knew the native language. When the picture show was over the Bolivian teachers pulled on their wool caps, wrapped their blankets around them, and went off to their beds.

Some of the international teachers went with me to the kitchen, where the cook had heated some food. We talked of the troubles and the progress of the school, until the lights were put out several times. This was a warning that the electric power was about to be shut off for the night.

During the first two years the village project had a difficult time. The Mission had accepted the use of a farm from a large land-

50

owner, and the natives believed that the lands would be returned to the owner after ten years. The Mission began at a time when the Bolivian Government was introducing land-improvement laws. Most of the people believed that the officers of the Mission were working for the owner, who was against the diving up of the land. They had as little to do with the owner as possible. Not until the government took possession of the farm and divided the land did the feeling of the Indians toward the Mission change for the better.

Questions

1. The Andean Indians live in the villages all over South America.

2. The problem of too many carpenters from the training schools would be solved by moving some carpenters to other parts of the country.

3. In the carpentry school the boys were learning to build larger houses.

4. When the writer visited the village of the oldest project the weather there was cold.

5. Some of the Andean teachers had been educated up to only _____ grade.

6. The Indians at first did not like the Mission because they felt that it was in favor of _____.

7. The needs of those Indians in _____ with 4areas formed by the Andean Mission are the greatest among all Indians in the three South American countries.

8. The important advantage the Andean teachers had was that _____.

9. When the Mission started it was on _____.

10. From reading this article you would say that the Andean project had _____.

答案与解析

1. 【答案】(N)

【解析】根据关键词 The Andean Indians 可以定位到第二段第一句 "The needs of these Indians... across three countries" 从而可以得出结论：印第安人分布在 3 个国家，而不是所有南美国家。所以本题陈述错误。

2. 【答案】(Y)

【解析】根据关键词 too many carpenters 可以定位到第六段倒数第二句 "The answer was that... to train carpenters to go to other parts of the country" 从而可以得出结论：本题陈述正确。

3. 【答案】(NG)

【解析】根据关键词 in the carpentry school 以及文章第五段至第七段得出结论：课堂里只有学 electricity，car repairing and how to operate tractors. 没有提到 build larger houses。

4. 【答案】(Y)

【解析】根据关键词 the oldest project 可以定位到第九段 "against the cutting winds ... the oldest of the four... projects 从而可以得出结论：本题陈述正确。

5. 【答案】(the third)

【解析】根据关键词 Andean teachers 可以定位到第十一段第二句 "... which in several cases had not gone beyond the third grade." 从而可以看出老师自身受教育的程度有的不超过三级，所以这里填 the third。

6. 【答案】(rich landowners)

【解析】根据关键词 at first，did not like 可以定位到最后一段倒数第三句 "Most of the people believed that the officers of the Mission were working for the owner..." 句子中的 the owner 就是 the rich landowners。也就是说大多数人认为是有利于富有地主的。从而可以得出结论。

52

7. 【答案】(Bolivia)

【解析】根据关键词 Andean Mission，4 areas 可以定位到第三段 "Six areas have been formed，one each in Ecuador and Peru，four in Bolivia." 从而可以得出结论。

8. 【答案】(they could speak the native language)

【解析】根据关键词 important advantage 可以定位到第十一段第三句"Though they had not had much training they had the help of great interest and，most important，they knew the native language." 从而可以得出结论。

9. 【答案】(borrowed land)

【解析】根据关键词 the Mission 可以定位到最后一段第二句"The Mission had accepted the use of a farm from a large landowner，and the natives believed that the lands would be returned to the owner after ten years."。空格前为介词，所以应该填入名词短语。由单词 the use of 和 returned 确定答案为 borrowed land。

10. 【答案】(some problems but was progressing)

【解析】根据关键词 From reading this article 可以得知本题涉及全文。而一般最后两三段是总结性文字，"We talked of the troubles and the progress of the school..." 从而可以得出结论。

Ⅱ Reading Comprehension (Skimming and Scanning) (15minutes)

Directions：*In this part，you will have 15 minutes to go over the passage quickly and answer the questions on Answer Sheet Ⅰ.*

For question 1-4，mark

Y(*for YES*)　　*if the statement agrees with the information given in the passage；*

N(*for NO*)　　*if the statement contradicts the information given in the passage；*

NG(*for NOT GIVEN*)　　*if the information is not given in the passage.*

For question 5-10 ,complete the sentences with the information given in the passage.

The Nature and Definition of Insurance and Insurance Law

The contract of insurance is basically governed by the rules which form part of the general law of contract, but there is equally no doubt that over the years it has attracted many principles of its own to such an extent that it is perfectly proper to speaker of a law of insurance contract, principally the proposal form and the policy, have long been drafted in a fairly uniform way. In addition, the reasons for many of the principles of the insurance can be found by looking at the history of insurance and of the insurance contract.

History

The origins of the modern insurance contract are to be found in the practices adopted by Italian merchants from the fourteenth century onwards, although there is little doubt that the concept of insuring was known ling before then. Maritime risks, the risk of losing ships and cargoes at sea, instigated the practice of medieval insurance and dominated insurance for many years. The habit spread to London merchants but not, it appears, until the sixteenth century. At first, there were no separate insurers. A group of merchants would agree to bear the risks by each other among themselves.

For a long time, the common law played little or no part in the regulation of disputes concerning insurance. For this purpose merchants in 1601 secured the establishment by statute of a chamber of assurance that was outside the normal legal system. However, with the appointment of Lord Mansfield as Lord Chief Justice in the mid-eighteenth century, the common law courts took an interest in insurance contracts. Lord Mansfield applied principles derived from the law merchant as well as more traditional common law concepts to the

54

solution of disputes over insurance, and by the time of his retirement in 1788, the jurisdiction of the courts over insurance matters had been established.

Maritime insurance retained its prominent position for some considerable time, and from the late seventeenth century onwards was increasingly transacted at a coffeehouse in the city of London owned by a man called Lloyd. There developed the practice that the merchant wishing insurance would pass round to the people willing to provide it, who were gathered there, a slip of paper on which he had written the details of the ship, voyage and cargo etc. The slip was initialed by those willing to accept a proportion of the risk. When the total amount of insurance required was underwritten, the contract was complete. From this practice comes the term "underwriter" which, of course, is still in use today and the name of the owner of the owner coffeehouse attached itself to the institution. Lloyd's of London is now itself a corporation formed with statutory authority, and it has long since ceased to operate from a coffeehouse, but the notable thing is that its members still underwrite the risks personally, putting at risk their entire personal fortunes, and they conduct their business in much the same way as it was done in the coffeehouse. The influence of Lloyd's on insurance and insurance law has been very significant. For example, the standard Lloyd's marine insurance policy was adopted as the statutory form in the Marine Insurance Act 1906. This is not to deny, however, that there have been numerous other companies and associations transacting the business of insurance.

The principles developed in regard to marine insurance have by and large been applied to the other types of insurance subsequently developed. The first of these was fire insurance, its birth was stimulated by the Great Fire of London in 1666. This was followed by life and personal accident insurance, the latter growing rapidly as the railways and industrialization spread rapidly in the nineteenth century. The present century has seen such development that it is now possible to insure almost every conceivable event of thing against the risk of loss or damage. Nevertheless, the law governing all these insurances is basically the same. Marine insurance law was codified in the Marine Insurance Act 1906 and is generally regarded as sui generic. In general, non-marine insurance contracts are still based on case law, but there have been some statutory inroads.

It is suggested that a contract of insurance is any contract whereby one party assumes the risk of an uncertain event, which is not within his control, happening at a future time, in which event the other party has an interest, and under which contract the first party is bound to pay money or provide its equivalent if the uncertain event occurs. It would follow that anyone who regularly enters into such contracts as the party bearing the risks is carrying on insurance business for the purpose of the statute regulating insurance business.

Some Classifications of Insurance

The insurance industry today transacts vast amounts of business, not just in Britain but overseas. The risks that it covers can be classified in several different ways. It is worthwhile explaining two of these classifications because they relate to some important legal distinctions.

First and Third Party Insurance

First, one can distinguish first party insurance, under which one insures one's own life, house, factory or car etc. from third party or liability insurance, that is, insuring against one's potential liability in law to pay damages to another. Of course, first and third party aspects may well be combined in the same policy. The law reflects this difference, first by demanding that some third party insurances should be compulsory and secondly by recognizing that in practice, third party insurance involves the third party as much as the insured person. Often in practice, for example, the victim of a car accident may talk in terms of claiming from the negligent driver's insurer rather than from the driver, which in law is the correct way of expressing the position. The law has deemed that in certain cases the third party should be protected from the strict contractual rights and liabilities between insured and insurer. Although we are not generally concerned with the economics of insurance nor with how efficient it is, it is worth pointing out that in general third party insurance is much more expensive and less efficient than first party insurance. A factor, among others, which has led many people to conclude that in certain areas, especially road and work accidents, involving personal injury or death, the present system of third party insurance backing up a system of liability in tort should be replaced by first party insurance. The latter could be run by private insurers, but more logically should be taken over by the state as part of the social security system. It must be admitted that such a development at present appears highly unlikely.

Life and Other Insurances

A second classification, which is well recognized in law and meaningful in insurance circles, distinguishes between life insurance on the one hand and all other forms of insurance on the other. There is a great variety of forms of life insurance, ranging from pure whole life insurance, an undertaking to pay a certain sum on the death of the life insured whenever this occurs, to endowment policies whereby the insured receives a sum if he survives beyond a certain age, to modern devices which combine an element of life insurance with the more substantial element of investment in securities or properties. Whatever the type of life policy, the uncertainty which, as will be seen shortly, is a necessary feature of all insurances is of a different nature form the uncertainty in other insurances. Death is certain; the uncertainty is as to when it will occur. On the other hand, the property insured against loss by fire may never burn down, the motor insured may never be involved in an accident. Accordingly, contracts of life insurance and related ones such as personal accident insurances are regarded simply as contracts for contingency insurance, in other words, contracts to pay an agreed sum of money when the event insured against occurs. Non-life insurance contracts are, in general, contracts to indemnify the insured only in respect of the loss suffered if it is actually suffered and only to the amount of the loss suffered.

注意:此部分试题请在答题卡 1 上作答。

1. The passage gives a general description of the nature and definition of insurance and insurance law.

2. The common law has always played little or no part in the regulation of disputes concerning insurance.

3. In general, third party insurance is much more expensive and less efficient than first party insurance.

4. First party insurance couldn't be run by private insurers.

5. The slip was initialed by those _____.

6. They conduct their business in _____ as it was done in the coffeehouse.

7. The principles developed in regard to marine insurance have by and large been applied to _____.

8. In general, non-marine insurance contracts are _____.

9. It would follow that anyone who regularly enters into such con-

58

tracts as the party bearing the risks is _____ for the purpose of the stature regulating insurance business.

10. Of course, first and third party aspects may well be _____.

答案与解析

1.【答案】(Y)

【解析】根据关键词 The passage 可以确定本题涉及对文章的理解。从文章标题和小标题可以得出结论：本文大体描述保险与保险法的本质与定义。所以本题陈述正确。

2.【答案】(NG)

【解析】根据关键词 the common law 可以定位到第三段第一句 "For a long time, the common law played little or no part in the regulation of disputes concerning insurance." 对比可知文章中有时间副词，从而可以得出结论：本题陈述未被提及。

3.【答案】(Y)

【解析】根据关键词 third 和 first 可以定位到 First and Third Party Insurance 部分，再由 in general 精确定位到第六句。得出结论：本题陈述正确。

4.【答案】(N)

【解析】根据关键词 First party 可以定位到 First and Third Party Insurance 部分，再由 private insurers 精确定位到倒数第二句。从而可以得出结论：本题陈述不正确。

5.【答案】(willing to accept a proportion of the risk)

【解析】根据关键词 the slip was initialed 可以定位到第四段第三句 "The slip was initialed by those willing to accept a proportion of the risk." 从而可以得出结论。

6.【答案】(much the same way)

【解析】根据关键词 coffeehouse 可以定位到第四段"... they conduct their business in much the same way as it was done in the coffeehouse." 从而可以得出结论。

7. 【答案】(the other types of insurance subsequently developed)

【解析】根据关键词 marine insurance 可以定位到第五段"The principles developed in regard to marine insurance have by and large been applied to the other types of insurance…"从而可以得出结论。

8. 【答案】(still based on case-law)

【解析】根据关键词 In general,non-marine insurance 可以定位到第五段最后一句"In general,non-marine insurance contracts are still based on case law,…"从而可以得出结论。

9. 【答案】(carrying on insurance business)

【解析】根据关键词 such contracts 可以定位到第六段最后一句"It would follow that anyone… bearing the risks is carrying on insurance business for the purpose…"。从而可以得出结论。

10. 【答案】(combined in the same policy)

【解析】根据关键词 Of course,first and third party aspects 可以定位到 First and Third Party Insurance 部分第二句"Of course, first and third party aspects may well be combined in the same policy."从而可以得出结论。

第四节 历年典型真题 突破训练

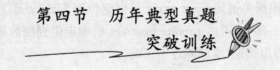

Ⅰ Test One

2008 年 6 月真题

Reading Comprehension(Skimming and Scanning)(15 minutes)

Directions: *In this part,you will have 15 minutes to go over the passage quickly and answer the questions on Answer Sheet 1 For questions 1-7,choose the best answer from the four choices marked A.,B.,C. and D.. For questions 8-10,complete the sentences with* *the information given in the passage.*

What will the world be like in fifty years?

This week some top scientists, including Nobel Prize winners, gave their vision of how the world will look in 2056, from gas-powered cars to extraordinary health advances, John Ingham reports on what the world's finest minds believe our futures will be.

For those of us lucky enough to live that long, 2056 will be a world of almost perpetual youth, where obesity is a remote memory and robots become our companions.

We will be rubbing shoulders with aliens and colonizing outer space. Better still, our descendants might at last live in a world at peace with itself.

The prediction is that we will have found a source of inexhaustible, safe, green energy, and that science will have killed off religion. If they are right we will have removed two of the main causes of war-our dependence on oil and religious prejudice.

Will we really, as today's scientists claim, be able to live for ever or at least cheat the ageing process so that the average person lives to 150?

Of course, all these predictions come with a scientific health warning. Harvard professor Steven Pinker says: "This is an invitation to look foolish, as with the predictions of domed cities and nuclear-powered vacuum cleaners that were made 50 year ago. "

Living longer

Anthony Atala, director of the Wake Forest Institute in North Carolina, believes failing organs will be repaired by injecting cells into the body. They will naturally to straight to the injury and help heal it. A system of injections without needles could also slow the ageing process by using the same process to "tune" cells.

61

Bruce Lahn, professor of human genetics at the University of Chicago, anticipates the ability to produce "unlimited supplies" of transplantable human organs without the needed for human donors. These organs would be grown in animals such as pigs. When a patient needed a new organ, such as kidney, the surgeon would contact a commercial organ producer, give him the patient's immunological profile and would then be sent a kidney with the correct tissue type.

These organs would be entirely composed of human cells, grown by introducing them into animal hosts, and allowing them to develop into and organ in place of the animal's own. But Prof. Lahn believes that farmed brains would be "off limits". He says: "Very few people would want to have their brains replaced by someone else's and we probably don't want to put a human brain in an animal body. "

Richard Miller, a professor at the University of Michigan, thinks scientist could develop "authentic anti-ageing drugs" by working out how cells in larger animals such as whales and human resist many forms of injuries. He says: "It's is now routine, in laboratory mammals, to extend lifespan by about 40%. Turning on the same protective systems in people should, by 2056, create the first class of 100-year-olds who are as vigorous and productive as today's people in their 60s".

Aliens

Colin Pillinger, professor of planetary sciences at the Open University, says: "I fancy that at least we will be able to show that life did start to evolve on Mars well as Earth. " Within 50 years he hopes scientists will prove that alien life came here in Martian meteorites (陨石).

Chris McKay, a planetary scientist at NASA's Ames Research Center, believes that in 50 years we may find evidence of alien life in ancient permanent frost of Mars or on other planets.

He adds: "There is even a chance we will find alien life forms here on Earth. It might be as different as English is to Chinese."

Princeton professor Freeman Dyson thinks it "likely" that life form outer space will be discovered before 2056 because the tools for finding it, such as optical and radio detection and data processing are improving.

He says: "As soon as the first evidence is found, we will know what to look for and additional discoveries are likely to follow quickly. Such discoveries are likely to have revolutionary consequences for biology, astronomy and philosophy. They may change the way we look at ourselves and our place in the universe."

Colonies in space

Richard Gott, professor of astrophysics at Princeton, hopes man will set up a self-sufficient colony on Mars, which would be a "life insurance policy against whatever catastrophes, natural or otherwise, might occur on Earth."

"The real space race is whether we will colonise off Earth on to other worlds before money for the space programme runs out."

Spinal injuries

Ellen Heber-Katz, a professor at the Wistar Institute in Philadelphia, foresees cures for injuries causing paralysis such as the one that afflicted Superman star Christopher Reeve.

She says: "I believe that the day is not far off when we will be able to prescribe drugs that cause severed(断裂的) spinal cords to heal, hearts to regenerate and lost limbs to regrow."

"People will come to expect that injured or diseased organs are meant to be repaired from within, in much the same way that we fix an appliance or automobile: by replacing the damaged part with a manufacturer-certified new part. " She predicts that within 5 to 10 years fingers and toes will be regrown and limbs will start to be regrown a few years later. Repairs to the nervous system will start with optic nerves and, in time, the spinal cord. "Within 50 years whole body replacement will be routine," Prof. Heber-Katz adds.

Obesity

Sydney Brenner, senior distinguished fellow of the Crick-Jacobs Center in California, won the 2002 Nobel Prize for Medicine and says that if there is a global disaster some humans will survive-and evolution will favour small people with bodies large enough to support the required amount of brain power. "Obesity," he says. "will have been solved. "

Robots

Rodney Brooks, professor of robotics at MIT, says the problems of developing artificial intelligence for robots will be at least partly overcome. As a result, "the possibilities for robots working with people will open up immensely".

Energy

Bill Joy, green technology expert in California, says: "The most significant breakthrough would be to have an inexhaustible source of safe, green energy that is substantially cheaper than any existing energy source. "

Ideally, such a source would be safe in that it could not be made into weapons and would not make hazardous or toxic waste or carbon dioxide, the main greenhouse gas blamed for global warming.

Society

Geoffrey Miller, evolutionary psychologist at the University of New Mexico, says: "The US will follow the UK in realizing that religion is nor a prerequisite (前提) for ordinary human decency. "

"Thus, science will kill religion-not by reason challenging faith but by offering a more practical, universal and rewarding moral framework for human interaction. "

He also predicts that "absurdly wasteful" displays of wealth will become unfashionable while the importance of close-knit communities and families will become clearer.

These there changer, he says, will help make us all "brighter, wiser, happier and kinder".

注意：此部分试题请在答题卡 1 上作答。

1. What is John Ingham's report about?

  A. A solution to the global energy crisis.

  B. Extraordinary advances in technology.

  C. The latest developments of medical science.

  D. Scientists' vision of the world in half a century.

2. According to Harvard professor Steven Pinker, predictions about the future _____.

  A. may invite trouble

  B. may not come true

  C. will fool the public

  D. do more harm than good

3. Professor Bruce Lahn of the University of Chicago predicts that _____.

  A. humans won't have to donate organs for transplantation

  B. more people will donate their organs for transplantation

  C. animal organs could be transplanted into human bodies

  D. organ transplantation won't be as scary as it is today

4. According to professor Richard Miller of the University of Michigan, people will _____.

  A. life for as long as they wish

  B. be relieved from all sufferings

C. life to 100 and more with vitality

D. be able to live longer than whales

5. Princeton professor Freeman Dyson thinks that _____.

A. scientists will find alien life similar to ours

B. humans will be able to settle on Mars

C. alien life will likely be discovered

D. life will start to evolve on Mars

6. According to Princeton professor Richard Gott, by setting up a self-sufficient colony on Mars, humans _____.

A. Might survive all catastrophes on earth

B. Might acquire ample natural resources

C. Will be able to travel to Mars freely

D. Will move there to live a better life

7. Ellen Heber-Katz, professor at the Wistar Institute in Philadelphia, predicts that _____.

A. human organs can be manufactured like appliances

B. people will be as strong and dynamic as supermen

C. human nerves can be replaced by optic fibers

D. lost fingers and limbs will be able to regrow

8. Rodney Brooks says that it will be possible for robots to work with humans as a result of the development of _____.

9. The most significant breakthrough predicted by Bill Joy will be an inexhaustible green energy source that can't be used to make _____.

10. According to Geoffrey Miller, science will offer a more practical, universal and rewarding moral framework in place of _____.

答案与解析

1. 【答案】(D)

【解析】根据关键词 John Ingham's report 可以定位到第一段 "John

66

Ingham reports on what the world's first minds believe our futures will be"从而可以得出结论.

2. 【答案】(B)

【解析】根据关键词 Harvard professor Steven Pinker 可以定位到第六段第二句"The answer was that… to train carpenters to go to other parts of the country"从而可以得出结论。

3. 【答案】(A)

【解析】根据关键词 Professor Bruce Lahn of the University of Chicago 可以定位到 Living longer 第二段第一句"Bruce Lahn, … anticipates the ability to produce 'unlimited supplies' of transplantable human organs without the needed for human donors."从而可以得出结论。

4. 【答案】(C)

【解析】根据关键词 Professor Richard Miller 可以定位到 Living longer 第四段"by 2056，create the first class of 100-year-olds who are as vigorous and productive"从而可以得出结论。

5. 【答案】(C)

【解析】根据关键词 Princeton professor Freeman Dyson 可以定位到"Aliens"部分第四段。该部分为 Freeman Dyson 的预测"it 'likely' that life form outer space will be discovered"从而可以得出结论。

6. 【答案】(A)

【解析】根据关键词 Princeton professor Richard Gott 可以定位到 Colonies in space 部分。该部分第一段提到 professor Richard Gott 的预测"man will set up a self-sufficient colony on Mars，which would be a 'life insurance policy against whatever catastrophes …'"从而可以得出结论。

7. 【答案】(D)

【解析】根据关键词 Ellen Heber-katz 可以定位到 Spinal injuries 的

第二段"... lost limbs to regrow"从而可以得出结论。

8.【答案】(artificial intelligence)

【解析】根据关键词 Rodney Brooks 可以定位到 Robots 部分 "says the problems of developing artificial intelligence for robots will be at least partly overcome. As a result，'the possibilities for robots working with people will open up immensely'"题目中空格前的介词表明此处应填入名词或名词短语，从而可以得出结论。

9.【答案】(weapons)

【解析】根据关键词 Bill Joy 可以定位到 Energy 部分"such a source would be safe in that it could not be made into weapons"从而可以得出结论。

10.【答案】(religion)

【解析】根据关键词 Geoffrey Miller 可以定位到 Society 部分"science will kill religion... by offering a more practical, universal and rewarding moral framework for human interaction."其中 kill 与题目中的 in place of 相当。从而可以得出结论。

【参考译文及题区画线】

本周,包括诺贝尔获奖者在内的一些世界顶级科学家将为大家描述从以天然气为动力的汽车到健康技术的巨大进步的 2056 年的世界是什么样子。1)约翰·英格汉为您报道,世界上最伟大的人物对于将来有什么看法。

对于那些能够幸运地活到 2056 年的人来说,2056 年将是一个几乎永远年轻的世界,那时肥胖将成为遥远的记忆,伴随我们的将是机器人。

我们会与外星人摩肩接踵,并移居外空。更为美好的前景是,我们的后代将会生活在一个和平的世界里。

有人预言,到时候,我们会找到一种用之不竭、安全、环保的能源,而且,科学将消除宗教。如果事实确实如此,那么,引发战争的两个主要因素——石油依赖和宗教歧视——就将被我们消除。

我们真的能够像今天的科学家们所说的那样，永远年轻或者至少改变衰老的进程，普通人都能活到150岁吗？

　　当然，所有这些预测都要基于科学的健康征兆。2)哈佛大学教授斯蒂文·平克说："这种预测似乎有点可笑，就像我们在50年前预测现在我们会生活在穹形城市，使用核能发电的真空吸尘器一样。"

寿命更长

　　安东尼·阿塔拉是北加利福尼亚州的维克森林学院的院长，他认为可以通过向体内注射细胞来修复功能衰竭的器官，这些细胞会很自然地直达伤口处，帮助伤口愈合。通过一个无针头的注射系统，使用类似的细胞"更新"，同样可以延缓衰老的进程。

　　3)芝加哥大学的人类遗传学教授布鲁斯·蓝预言，将来无需人类捐赠器官，人类也有能力生产出"能无限供应的"可供移植的人类器官，比如一个肾，那么外科医生就可以与某家商业器官生产商联系，向他们提供病人的免疫资料，然后，生产商便会送来符合条件的肾。

　　这些器官将完全由人体细胞组成，通过将人体细胞植入动物寄主体内，让其生长，在动物体内替代动物原来的相应的器官，以此获得相应的人体器官。但是，蓝教授也相信，大脑的培育可能会被排除在外。他说："很少有人会愿意用别人的大脑来替换自己的大脑，我们可能也不会想要把人类的大脑植入动物的身体"。

　　4)密歇根大学教授理查德·米勒认为，通过研究大型生物如鲸鱼和人类的细胞如何抵抗多种形式的伤痛，科学家可以开发一种"可靠抗衰老药物"。他说："现在，把实验室哺乳动物的寿命延长大约40％是很正常的事。如果将同样的保护系统应用到人类身上，到2056年，将会出现第一代百岁老人，这些老人身体健壮，精神矍铄，能够工作，就像我们现在这个社会里的六十岁老人一样。"

外星人

柯林·匹林格是英国开放大学的行星科学教授,他说:"我想,至少我们能够向人们证明,火星和地球一样,那上面原来确实有过生命的发展迹象。"他希望科学家在未来五十年内能够通过火星的陨石证明外星人来过这里。

克里斯·麦凯是美国国家航空和航天管理局艾姆斯研究中心的行星科学家,他相信在未来五十年内,我们可能会在火星或其他行星上的永久冻层里找到外星生命的证据。

他补充道,"甚至还有这样的可能性,我们会在地球上发现外星球的生命形式。外星球生命(和地球生命的)不同之处就像英语和汉语的不同一样。"

5) 普林斯顿教授弗莱曼·迪森预测:人类"有可能"在 2056 年以前就会发现来自外太空的生命,因为,寻找外太空生命的工具如光学和无线电探测仪、资料处理仪一直在不断改进。

他说:"一旦发现第一证据,我们就会知道要找什么,而另外的证据很可能很快出现。这些发现可能对生物学、天文学和哲学有着革命性的影响。他们也同样可能改变我们对自身及我们在宇宙中地位的认识。"

太空移民

6) 普林斯顿高等研究院教授理查德·戈特希望人类能够在火星上建立一个能够自己自足的移民地,这块移民地将成为一个"生命保险单",以抵抗地球上可能发生的所有灾难,无论是自然灾难还是其他灾难

"现在,真正的太空竞赛是,我们是否能够在太空项目费用花完之前在地球之外的其他世界建立好一个移民地。"

脊椎损伤

7) 美国费城威斯达学院的艾伦·赫柏·凯兹教授预言人类将找到一种方法治疗导致瘫痪的身体损伤。主演《超人》的影星克里斯托弗·里夫患的正是这种疾病。

她说:"我相信,当我们发明出这样的药物,用它来促使断裂的脊椎愈合、心脏再生、以及缺失的肢体重新长出来,这一天也就不会太远了。"

"到时候,人们可以期望受伤的、患病的器官能够从器官内部进行修复,这种修复方式跟我们修理家电或者汽车一样:用通过厂家鉴定的新零件来更换掉坏掉的零件。"她预计在未来五到十年,人类就能让手指和脚趾重新长出来,之后,再过几年,四肢也能重新长出来。神经系统的修复将从视神经开始,然后是脊椎。"未来五十年之内整个身体器官的修复都将是件很平常的事情。"赫柏·凯兹教授补充道。

肥胖

西德尼·布伦纳是加利福尼亚克里克·雅各布计算及理论生物学中心的特聘高级研究员,2002 年诺贝尔医学奖的获得者。他说,如果发生全球性的灾难,一些人类将幸存下来——然后,生物进化将偏好这样的人,他们身材矮小,身体有足够大到能支持脑部所需的能量。"肥胖的问题,"他说,"就会得到解决。"

机器人

麻省理工学院机器人技术教授 8)罗德尼·布鲁克斯称人类在机器人的人工智能发展上的问题至少会得到部分解决。如此一来,"机器人与人类共事的可能性就会大大增加。"他说。

能源

加利福尼亚州绿色技术专家 9)比尔·乔伊说:"最重大的突破是我们将会拥有一种用之不竭、安全、环保的能源,而且,这种能源比现有的能源要便宜很多。"

比较理想化的是,这种能源非常安全,因为它无法被用于制作武器,不会产生危险、不会产生有毒的废物或者二氧化碳,而二氧化碳是温室气体的主要组成部分,这种温室气体会导致全球变暖。

新墨西哥大学进化论心理学家杰弗里·米勒说:"美国将与英国一样,意识到宗教不是普通人行为礼仪的前提。"

10)"因此,科学将消除宗教——不是因为要挑战信仰,而是要给人类的相互行为提供一个更加符合实际的、普遍的、有益的道德框架。"

他还预言。"荒谬的浪费"和炫耀财富将落伍,相反,人们将日益重视保持社区家庭间的密切关系。

他说,这三种变化将有助于我们所有人变得"更聪明、更明智、更快乐、更友善"。

II Test Two

2008 年 12 月真题

Supersize surprise

Ask anyone why there is an obesity epidemic and they will tell you that it's al down to eating too much and burning too few calories. That explanation appeals to common sense and has dominated efforts to get to the root of the obesity epidemic and reverse it/ yet obesity researchers are increasingly dissatisfied with it. Many now believe that something else must have changed in our environment to precipitate(促成) such dramatic rises in obesity over the past 40 years or so. Nobody is saying that the "big two" - reduced physical activity and increased availability of food - are not important contributors to the epidemic, but they cannot explain it all.

Earlier this year a review paper by 20 obesity experts set out the 7 most plausible alternative explanations for the epidemic. Here they are.

1. Not enough sleep

It is widely believed that sleep is for the brain, not the body.

Could a shortage of shut-eye also be helping to make us fat?

Several large-scale studies suggest there may be a link. People who sleep less than 7 hours a night tend to have a higher body mass index than people who sleep more, according to data gathered by the US National Health and Nutrition Examination Survey. Similarly, the US Nurses' Health Study, which tracked 68,000 women for 16 years, found that those who slept an average of 5 hours a night gained more weight during the study period than women who slept 6 hours, who in turn gained more than whose who slept 7.

It's well known that obesity impairs sleep, so perhaps people get fat first and sleep less afterwards. But the nurses' study suggests that it can work in the other direction too: sleep loss may precipitate weight gain.

Although getting figures is difficult, it appears that we really are sleeping less. In 1960 people in the US slept an average of 8.5 hours per night. A 2002 poll by the National Sleep Foundation suggests that the average has fallen to under 7 hours, and the decline is mirrored by the increase in obesity.

2. Climate control

We humans, like all warm-blooded animals, can keep our core body temperatures pretty much constant regardless of what's going on in the world around us. We do this by altering our metabolic(新陈代新的) rate, shivering or sweating. Keeping warm and staying cool take energy unless we are in the "thermo-neutral zone", which is increasingly where we choose to live and work.

There is no denying that ambient temperatures(环境温度) have changed in the past few decades. Between 1970 and 2000, the average British home warmed from a chilly 13C to 18C. In the US, the changes have been at the other end of the thermometer as the proportion of homes with air conditionings rose from 23% to 47% between 1978 and 1997. In the southern states-where obesity rates tend to be highest—the number of houses with air conditioning has shot up to 71% from 37% in 1978.

Could air conditioning in summer and heating in winter really make a difference to our weight?

Sadly, there is some evidence that it does-at least with regard to heating. Studies show that in comfortable temperatures we use less energy.

3. Less smoking

Bad news: smokers really do tend to be thinner than the rest of us, and quitting really does pack on the pounds, though no one is sure why. It probably has something to do with the fact that nicotine is an appetite suppressant and appears to up your metabolic rate.

Katherine Flegal and colleagues at the US National Center for Health Statistics in Hyattsville, Maryland, have calculated that people kicking the habit have been responsible for a small but significant portion of the US epidemic of fatness. From data collected around 1991 by the US National Health and Nutrition Examination Survey, they worked out that people who had quit in the previous decade were much more likely to be overweight than smokers and people who had never smoked. Among men, for example, nearly half of quitters were overweight compared with 37% of non-smokers and only 28% of smokers.

4. Genetic effects

Yours chances of becoming fat may be set, at least in part, before you were even born. Children of obese mothers are much more likely to become obese themselves later in life. Offspring of mice fed a high-fat diet during pregnancy are much more likely to become fat than the offspring of identical mice fed a normal diet. Intriguingly, the effect persists for two or three generations. Grand-children of mice fed a high-fat diet grow up fat even if their own mother is fed normally-so you fate may have been sealed even before you were conceived.

5. A little older...

Some groups of people just happen to be fatter than others. Surveys carried out by the US National Center for Health Statistics found that adults aged 40 to 79 were around three times as likely to be obese as younger people. Non-white females also tend to fall at the fatter end of the spectrum: Mexican-American women are 30% more likely than white women to be obsese, and black women have twice the risk.

In the US, these groups account for an increasing percentage of the population. Between 1970 and 2000 the US population aged 35 to 44 grew by 43%. The proportion of Hispanic-Americans also grew, from under 5% to 12. 5% of the population, while the proportion of black Americans increased from 11% to 12. 3%. These changes may account in part for the increased prevalence of obesity

6. Mature mums

Mothers around the world are getting older. in the UK, the mean age for having a first child is 27. 3, compared with 23. 7 in 1970. mean age at first birth in the US has also increased, rising from 21. 4 in 1970 to 24. 9 in 2000.

This would be neither here nor there if it weren't for the observation that having an older mother seems to be an independent risk factor for obesity. Results from the US National Heart, Lung and Blood Institute's study found that the odds of a child being obese increase 14% for every five extra years of their mother's age, though why this should be so is not entirely clear.

Michael Symonds at the University of Nottingham, UK, found that first-born children have more fat than younger ones. As family size decreases, firstborns account for a greater share of the population. In 1964, British women gave birth to an average of 2. 95 children; by 2005 that figure had fallen to 1. 79. in the US in 1976, 9. 6% of woman in their 40s had only one child; in 2004 it was 17. 4%. this combination of older mothers and more single children could be contributing to the obesity epidemic.

7. Like marrying like

Just as people pair off according to looks, so they do for size. Lean people are more likely to marry lean and fat more likely to marry fat. On its own, like marrying like cannot account for any increase in obesity. But combined with others-particularly the fact that obesity is partly genetic, and that heavier people have more children-it amplifies the increase form other causes.

1. What is the passage mainly about?

   A. Effects of obesity on people's health.

   B. The link between lifestyle an obesity.

   C. New explanations for the obesity epidemic.

   D. Possible ways to combat the obesity epidemic.

2. In the US Nurses' health Study, women who slept an average of 7 hours a night _____.

   A. gained the least weight

   B. were inclined to eat less

   C. found their vigor enhanced

   D. were less susceptible to illness

3. The popular belief about obesity is that _____.

76

A. it makes us sleepy

B. it causes sleep loss

C. it increases our appetite

D. it results from lack of sleep

4. How does indoor heating affect our life?

A. It makes us stay indoors more.

B. It accelerates our metabolic rate.

C. It makes us feel more energetic.

D. It contributes to our weight gain.

5. What does the author say about the effect of nicotine on smokers?

A. It threatens their health.

B. It heightens their spirits.

C. It suppresses their appetite.

D. It slows down their metabolism.

6. Who are most likely to be overweight according to Katherine Flegal's study?

A. Heavy smokers.

B. Passive smokers.

C. Those who never smoke.

D. Those who quit smoking.

7. According to the US National Center for Health Statistics, the increased obesity in the US is a result of _____.

A. the growing number of smokers among young people

B. the rising proportion of minorities in its population

C. the increasing consumption of high-calorie foods

D. the improving living standards of the poor people

8. According to the US National Heart, Lung and Blood Institute, the reason why older mothers' children tend to be obese remains _____.

9. According to Michael Symonds, one factor contributing to the obesity epidemic is decrease of _____.

10. When two heavy people get married, chances of their children getting fat increase, because obesity is _____.

答案与解析

1.【答案】(C)

【解析】根据关键词 the passage 可以得知本题考查全文主旨。由本文的各小标题可以知道本文主要说明导致肥胖流行的七大新理由,从而可以得出结论。

2.【答案】(A)

【解析】根据关键词 US Nurses' health Study 和 7hours a night 可以定位到 1. Not enough sleep 部分第二段最后一句"those who slept an average of 5 hours a night gained more weight during the study period than women who slept 6 hours, who in turn gained more than whose who slept 7." 从而可以得出结论。

3.【答案】(B)

【解析】根据关键词 The popular belief 和 obesity 可以定位到1. Not enough sleep 部分第三段第一句"It's well known that obesity impairs sleep, so perhaps people get fat first and sleep less afterwards." 从而可以得出结论。

4.【答案】(D)

【解析】根据关键词 heating 可以定位到 2. Climate control 部分最后一段最后一句提到"Studies show that in comfortable temperatures we use less energy."而只有 D 答案与肥胖——本文的主题有关,从而可以得出结论。

5.【答案】(C)

【解析】根据关键词 nicotine 可以定位到 3. Less smoking 部分第一段第二句 "It probably has something to do with the fact that nicotine is an appetite suppressant and appears to up your metabolic rate."答案 suppresses their appetite 与原文中的 appetite suppressant 意思一样,从而可以得出结论。

6. 【答案】(D)

【解析】根据关键词 likely to be overweight 和 Katherine Flegal 可以定位到 3. Less smoking 部分第二段的 "they worked out that people who had quit in the previous decade were much more likely to be overweight than smokers and people who had never smoked." 由此可知,戒烟者最容易长胖,从而可以得出结论。

7. 【答案】(B)

【解析】根据关键词 increased obesity,可以定位到 5. A little older... 部分的第二段第二句和第三句"These changes may account in part for the increased prevalence of obesity" 从而可以得出结论。

8. 【答案】(not entirely clear/unclear)

【解析】根据关键词 the US National Heart, Lung and Blood Institute,可以定位到 6. Mature mums 部分第二段最后一句。其中提到,变胖的原因还不清楚,所以可以用原文的 not entirely clear,也可以用自己的语言 unclear。

9. 【答案】(family size)

【解析】根据关键词 Michael Symonds 和 decrease 可以定位到 6. Mature mums 部分"Michael Symonds... found that first-born children have more fat than younger ones. As family size decreases..."从而可以得出结论。

10. 【答案】(partly genetic)

【解析】根据关键词 heavy people, increase 和 obesity 可以定位到 7. Like marrying like 部分,"particularly the fact that obesity is partly genetic,"其中 kill 相当与题目中的 in place of。从而可以得出结论。

超级大惊喜

向任何人问一下：为何肥胖如此流行？他们会告诉你这都是因为吃的太多，而消耗的能量太少。这种解释符合常识，并且一直在人们努力找到肥胖根源、根除肥胖的过程中占主导地位。但是，肥胖研究者对此结果越来越不满。现在很多人相信，在最近的大约四十年里，在我们所处的环境里，一定还有别的东西发生了改变，导致了肥胖的巨增。没有人否认"两大原因"——日益减少的物理运动和不断增加的食物的可获得性——是促成肥胖流行的重要因素，但是他们也并不是全部原因。

今年早些时候，由二十位肥胖专家所做的审查报告，列出了导致这一流行病的七大具有说服力的理由。它们是：

睡眠不足

人们普遍相信，睡眠是针对大脑的，而不是针对身体。难道"闭眼"时间的缩短也会导致我们肥胖吗？

几个大型的研究显示，确实有可能存在联系。根据美国国家健康和营养检测调查所收集的数据显示，一夜睡眠少于七个小时的人与有更多睡眠的人相比，拥有更大的身体质量指数。2) <u>类似情况，根据美国护士健康研究中心十六年来对六万八千名女性的跟踪调查发现，在做调查的这十六年间，那些平均一夜睡眠五个小时的女性比那些一夜平均睡眠六个小时的女性体重增加要多；而这些一夜睡眠六个小时的女性，反过来，比那些平均睡眠七个小时的女性增加的体重又要多些。</u>

3) <u>众所周知，肥胖会消减睡眠，所以或许人们是因为变肥胖才睡眠减少的。</u>但是护士的研究显示，这个过程反过来也可以起作用：睡眠的减少又会导致体重的增加。

尽管得到数据很困难，但是我们的睡眠时间确实在减少。在1960年，美国人的平均睡眠时间为每晚 8.5 个小时；而在 2002 年的

80

一次由国家睡眠基金会组织的测验记录显示,睡眠的平均时间已经减少到了 7 个小时,而伴随这一减少过程的是肥胖的增加。

气候控制

我们人类,就像所有的热血动物一样,可以保持我们的核心身体处在一个恒定的温度,不管我们周围的环境是什么样子。我们是通过新陈代谢速率来达到这一点的,比如发抖和出汗。除非我们是处在中温环境中——其越来越成为我们居住和工作环境的选择——保持温暖或凉爽都会消耗能量。

一个不可否认的事实就是我们周围的环境在过去的几十年里发生了变化。1970 年和 2000 年,英国家庭的温度由寒冷的 13 度上升到了温暖的 18 度。在美国,从 1978 到 1997 年,随着家庭拥有空调的数量从 23％上升到 47％,这些变化已经在温度计的另一端。在南美洲——肥胖率几乎最高——拥有空调的家庭数量由 1978 年的 37％飙升到了现在的 71％。

4）夏天的空调和冬天的暖气真的可以给我们的体重带来什么不同么？不幸的是,确实有证据证实如此——至少暖气是如此。研究结果表明,在舒适的环境里,我们消耗的能量减少。

抽烟少

坏消息:尽管还没有确定到底是什么原因,但是烟民们确实往往比我们要瘦,并且戒烟后很容易发胖。5）很可能与尼古丁抑制食欲的作用有关,而且尼古丁会使你的新陈代谢率升高。

马里兰洲 Hyattsville 美国国家健康数据中心的凯瑟琳·弗莱格和她的同事们发现:戒掉吸烟的习惯是美国流行的肥胖症的一个很小但是非常重要的原因。6）根据在美国国家健康和营养检测调查在 1991 年左右收集的数据,他们发现,在前十年戒掉吸烟习惯的人,往往比现在的烟民以及从未抽过烟的人体重要重。比如,在男人中间,戒烟的男人超过一半都会有体重超重现象,与此相比,非烟民中超重的比例是 37％,而烟民中的超重比例仅仅为 28％。

基因效应

你变肥胖的可能性几乎是在你出生前就已经决定了——至少有一部分是如此。肥胖妈妈生的孩子很有可能在今后的生活中也会有如此现象。在怀孕期间,食用高脂肪食物的母鼠所生的后代,比同一种类但是使用正常食物的母鼠所生的后代,更容易发胖。有趣的是,这种现象会持续两到三代。使用高脂肪食物母鼠的孙子辈都会出现肥胖现象,尽管他们的母亲食用的是正常食物——所以,可能在你母亲怀你之前,你的命运就被决定了。

有一点老了……

有些人群就是比别的人要胖。美国国家健康数据中心所开展的调查发现:四十岁到七十九岁之间的人的发胖几率,将近是年轻人的三倍。非白人妇女往往更容易发胖:美籍墨西哥女性发胖的几率,比白人女性要高出 30%,而黑人女性的几率则是高达白人女性的两倍。

在美国,这些人群的数量在人口中的比例在急速增加。在 1970 年到 2000 年之间,美国人口中 35 岁~40 岁之间的人的数量增加了 43%。7)美籍西班牙人的数量也在增加,从不到人口的 5%增加到了 12.5%,而美国黑人的数量则从 11%增加到了 12.3%。这些变化或许是肥胖不断增加的部分因素。

成熟母亲们

全世界母亲的年龄都在增加。在英国,母亲生第一个孩子的平均年龄是 27.3 岁,而在 1970 年的时候是 23.7 岁。在美国,母亲生第一个孩子时的年龄也在增加,从 1970 年的 21.4 上升到 2000 年的 24.9 岁。

如果不是为了了解大龄母亲可能是肥胖的一个独立因素,那这些都是无所谓的。8)美国国家心肺及血液研究所的研究结果发现:母亲年龄每增加五岁,孩子变肥胖的几率就会增加 14%,尽管还不清楚为什么会这样。

9）英国诺丁汉大学的迈克尔·西蒙斯发现，先生的孩子比后生的孩子更胖。由于家庭规模的减小，先生孩子在人口中的比重越来越大。在 1964 年，英国女性平均每个人生 2.95 个孩子，而到 2005 年，这一数字下降到了 1.79。在美国，1976 年的时候，四十多岁的女性中，9.6％只有一个孩子。到 2004 年，这一比例上升到了 17.4％。高龄母亲以及独生子女这两个因素的结合，也助长了肥胖的流行。

类似的人结婚

就像人们根据长相来配对一样，人们也根据体型来配对。瘦人往往跟瘦人结婚，而肥胖的则通常与肥胖的人结婚。类似的人结婚，本身并不能形成肥胖增加的原因。但是，10）结合到其他因素——特别是肥胖跟基因有关的事实，以及体型重的人往往会生更多孩子——就促使其比其他因素更能成为肥胖流行的原因。

第三章　仔细阅读——短句问答

第 一 节　设 题 特 点

　　六级阅读理解中仔细阅读(Reading in Depth，Section A)即短句问答(Short Answer Questions)和篇章词汇作为二选一题型出现，本章节主要对短句问答进行探讨。短句问答就是原四级经常考察的简答题，六级的仔细阅读要求考生在 10 分钟的时间里读懂一篇 450 字左右长度的文章，用正确简洁的语言(不超过 10 个词)来回答后面的 5 个问题或者是补全句子。考试题型以细节事实题为主，主旨题、词义题为辅。因为简答和快速阅读的出题顺序和作者论证的顺序基本一致，所以考生做题时依然和快速阅读一样应该先读题目，再读文章！短句问答的题目一般不能照搬原文内容，需要对原文句子等做一定的改动。出现的题目和以往相比提问方式有所改变。以前的短句问答题主要是每题提一个问题，然后考生用一个句子或是一个短语来回答。而最近的则更注重考查考生的综合能力，用类似完形填空的方式，给一句话，在这一句子中的某处留出一个空，考生根据自己对原文的理解补全句子。

　　短句问答的评分标准在题目中也有所体现——Then answer the

84

questions or complete the statements in the fewest possible words on the Answer Sheet 2。而根据以往的经验,答案最好不要超过 10 个单词,因为如果超过 10 个单词,很有可能要扣分。考生在答题时要注意一些基本的要求,比如说:句首字母大写,补全对话时注意填入单词的变化和搭配等等。

我们在完成简答题的时候,应该从内容和语言两个方面着手。首先内容方面:a. 回答要与题干范围想吻合,切勿答非所问。b. 尽量简洁。能用单词的不用词组,能用词组的不用句子。用句子一般有三种情况:1)以 why 开头问的问题;2)以 what suggestion/opinion/result 开头问的问题;3)题中要求补全句子的。其次语言方面:1)照搬原则:a. 以词和词组回答的完全照搬。b. 以四个或四个以下词组成句子的可照搬。c. 对于较长句子,可用代词替换名词,动词替换词组 。2)注意一些语言与语法上的错误地方:主谓不一致;时态不对应(问题是什么时态,回答也是什么时态);单词拼写与句法结构。

短句问答(SAQ)原文材料的长度和语言难度一般与阅读理解部分的短文类似。体裁大多属于议论文和说明文。议论文和说明文(特别是议论文)是阅读理解考试的主要体裁,这两种体裁观点鲜明,能够比较全面地考查考生的语言理解能力和运用能力。考生在考试时也可以根据这两种体裁的特点了解文章的主题,快速把握文章的结构,领会作者的意图,在此基础上帮助自己迅速定位找到自己需要的答案依据。然后再用自己的语言重新组织答案。

在做完题目后,考生一定要仔细核查自己的答案是否符合问题的要求,以避免出现语法和语言形式上的错误。在考试中考生常常出现的错误主要包括:主谓不一致、时态混乱、搭配不当、句子结构不完整、用词不当等。常见的语言形式包括:拼写错误、大小写和标点符号错误等。而这些只需要考生回过头再看一遍就可能可以避免。在这里主要讨论答案与原文的转换。1)词与词之间的转换。这类转换指将原文中某个单词根据题目转化为其他词性或是近义词。2)代词的转换。将原文中代替上文中的词汇,短语或是句子的代词转换为其代替的具体内容,既代词具体化。3)词汇、短语与句子之间的转换。4)明否定与暗否定之间的转换。明否定指句子中有明显的否定词(如 no, not, nothing, never 等),暗否定指句子中有含否定意思的词语(如 un-, dis-, -less 等)。5)主语和宾语之间的转换。在回答问题时,由于考查考生对句子的理解程度,句型的改变涉及到(逻辑)主语和(逻辑)宾语的转换。6)there be 句型与其他句型的转换。考生要注意 there be 句型中句子成分之间的内在联系。

第二节　应试技巧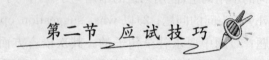

六级 SAQ 属于主观题。它考查的是考生综合应用语言的能力,考查考生是否能够在读懂原文的基础上用文字表达出对原文中各种信息的理解。为了避免或减少在内容错误上失分,考生可以先读懂问题,后浏览全文,并在文中标出问题中的关键词,以保证在做题时答案能更符合要求。对每句话的要求很高,几乎必须读懂才能做题。

SAQ 的评分标准要求答案不能超过 10 个单词,如果超出可能要扣分。因而考生在作答时要注意语言简练,准确,概括性强。在这方面可以采用一些小技巧。比如,可利用缩写,可以把两个词合为一个复合词,可用词或短语代替句子。当然,关键的是考生的语言要具有概括性。

做这类题目考生要增强回答问题的针对性。首先要学会找关键词。文章的关键词是构成语篇的精髓,考生对关键词的把握影响到对文章的理解和回答问题的表达。正确选用关键词比考生用自己的语言组织答案要准确、精练得多。其次要注意提问方式和答案的协调性。不同类型的问题要用不同的方式回答。例如:就原因提问,答案就应当用 because of 短语或 because 从句;就目的提问,答案则用表示目的的用语等等。

SAQ 的常见题型有以下几种。

细节类问题

由于简答题的宗旨在于重点考查语言基本功及概括能力,所以一般而言简答题细节类问题大多可以在原文中找到出处。但是难度在于如何从出处中归纳出问题的答案。因为简答题要求考生用简短的语言回答问题,又无法从原文中照搬,所以这种题目要得满分比较难。

解答这种题目,首先要根据问题中的关键词找到答案在文章中的大体位置,并尽可能的缩小范围,然后再根据要求组织答案。在组织答案的时候要注意以下几方面:

答案的形式要符合提问方式。许多考生在回答时都能正确的定位到文章当中,可是做题时却由于直接照抄原文的句子而不能得到分数或得不到满分。

概括要简洁、准确。由于答案是自己所写而不是直接照抄原文,特别是答案中包含了与问题无关的信息也不能得分。

注意语言表达符合语法。句子填空要求就题干中所缺的关键信息进行补全,所以答案要符合题目句子的成分要求以及要答对关键。

推断类问题

这种类型题目的答案在原文中没有直接对应的句子,考生要根据文章所叙述的细节内容对之进行合理推断才可以得出结论。这类题型一般是针对文中某一细节的推理,因而提问方式与细节类问题的差别不大。但是由于答案不能在文章中直接找到,考生要充分理解原文,根据题目中的关键词在文中定位,然后再挖掘出其中隐含的事实细节。结论要用简洁准确的话语来表述。

主旨类问题

对于此类试题,第一步是找出概括文章中心思想的主题句,当然,主题句原文不能直接作为答案,考生应该对主题句进行重新归纳总结。而且,不是所有的主旨类试题都可以在原文中找到主题句。对于原文中没有提供主题句的主旨题,就要求考生对文章总体理解,再归纳总结答案。

语义类问题

语义题的出题目的在于考查考生转述或解释某个词或语句在特定场合下的特定含义的能力。这类题目要求考生在读懂原文的基础上用自己的语言表达出来。

解答这种题型时，考生可以先找原词在文章中的同义词。如果没有的话，可以注意破折号、同位语从句、插入语等具有解释、说明作用的语言成分。

当然，六级SAQ考生先通读全文，了解主题，把握全文的结构，领会作者的意图。然后根据问题中的关键词到文章的相关部分找答案依据。解答问题时，需要注意引导问题的特殊疑问词来确定问题的性质。而解答句子补充题时要注意根据句子的结构推测出所缺部分的性质和内容。这样在填空时就不会出现所填的词与句子有冲突。

总之，SAQ不太适合粗看一遍原文，再看题目然后带着问题去search的方法，因为有很多细节题型，很可能因为错过一个关键词或关键句而掉入陷阱。相反，应该先看题，再仔细看一遍全文，再解答，时间固然要多花些，但这样的话，你可以仔细地只做一遍，保证正确率，省去检查，众所周知，有时间回头检查的可能性不大，而且检查也有可能把原本选对的改错，所以提倡考生阅读一遍且仅一遍。

第三节　实战演练

Ⅰ **Reading Comprehension（Reading in Depth）（25 minutes）**

Section A

Directions： *In this section, there is a short passage with 5 questions or incomplete statements. Read the passage carefully. Then answer the questions or complete the statements in the fewer possible words on* **Answer Sheet 2.**

Questions 47 to 51 are based on the following passage.

America is a country that now sits atop the cherished myth that work provides rewards, that working people can support their families. It's a myth that has become so divorced from reality that it might as well begin with the words "Once upon a time." Today 1. 6 million New Yorkers suffer from "food insecurity," which is a fancy way of saying they don't have enough to eat. Some are the people who come in at night and clean the skyscrapers that glitter along the river. Some pour coffee and take care of the aged parents of the people who live in those buildings. The American Dream for the well-to-do grows from the bowed backs of the working poor, who too often have to choose between groceries and rent.

In a new book called "The Betrayal of Work", Beth Shulman says that even in the booming 1990s one out of every four Americans workers made less than $ 8. 70 an hour, an income equal to the government's poverty level for a family of four. Many, if not most, of these workers had no health care, sick pay or retirement provisions.

We ease our consciences, Shulman writes, by describing these people as "low skilled," as though they're not important or intelligent enough to deserve more. But low-skilled workers today are better educated than ever before, and they constitute the linchpin of American industry. When politicians crow that happy days are here again because jobs are on the rise, it's these jobs they're really talking about. Five of the ten occupations expected to grow big in the next decade are in the lowest-paying job groups. And before we sit back a decade that's just the way it is, it's instructive to consider the rest of the world. While the bottom 10 percent of American workers earn just 37 percent of our average wage, their counterparts in other industrialized countries earn upwards of 60 percent. And those are countries that provide health care and child care, which eases the economic pinch considerably.

Almost 40 years ago, when Lyndon Johnson declared war on poverty, a family with a car and house in the suburbs felt prosperous. Today that same family may well feel poor, overwhelmed by credit-card debt, a second mortgage and the cost of the stuff that has become the backbone of American life. When the middle class feels poor, the poor have little chance for change, or even recognition.

注意:此部分试题请在答题卡 2 上做答。

47. By saying "it might as well begin with the words 'Once upon a time'" (Line3, Para. 1), the author suggest that the American myth is _____.

48. What is the American Dream of the well-to-do built upon?

49. Some Americans try to make themselves feel less guilty by attributing the poverty of the working people to _____.

50. We learn from the passage that the difference in pay between the lowest paid and the average worker in America is _____ than that in other industrialized countries.

51. According to the author, how would an American family with a car and a house in the suburbs probably feel about themselves today?

答案与解析

47. 【答案】divorced from reality/unrealistic.

   【解析】根据题目提示,考生需要理解该句意思。直接的答案可以用句子中的表达 divorced from reality,也可以根据其意思,用自己的语言表达 unrealistic。

48. 【答案】The backbreaking labor of the working poor. / The bowed backs of the working poor.

   【解析】根据关键词 American Dream 定位到第一段最后一句。所以可以知已获得答案 The bowed backs of the working poor. 或用

90

49. 【答案】(their) lack of skill/(their) low skill.

【解析】根据关键词 feel less guilty, by attributing 定位到第三段第一句,可以得到答案。由于答案需要一个名词性短语放在 attribute to 后,所以将原文 low skilled 转换为 low skill,也可以用自己语言表述(lack of skill)。

50. 【答案】much greater.

【解析】根据关键词 lowest ,average 和 other industrialized countries 定位到第三段倒数第二句,从这句话可以看出美国10%的低收入工人的工资只有平均工资的37%,而在其他工业化国家,低收入工人可以拿到平均工资的60%。所以差异是 much greater。

51. 【答案】Poor.

【解析】根据关键词 a family with a car and house; today 定位到最后一段第一、二句。

Ⅱ Directions: *In this section, there is a short passage with 5 questions or incomplete statements. Read the passage carefully. Then answer the questions or complete the statements in the fewer possible words on* **Answer Sheet 2**.

International Women's Day is an occasion marked by women's groups around the world. This date is also commemorated at the United Nations and is designated in many countries as a national holiday.

The idea of an International Women's Day first arose at the turn of the century, which in the industrialized world was a period of expansion and turbulence, booming population growth and radical ideologies.

In the years before 1910, from the turn of the 20th century, women in industrially developing countries were entering paid work in some numbers. Their jobs were sex segregated, mainly in textiles, manufacturing and domestic services where conditions were wretched and wages worse than depressed. Trade unions were developing and industrial disputes broke out. In Europe, the flames of revolution were being kindled.

Many of the changes taking place in women's lives pushed against the political restrictions surrounding them. Women from all social strata began to campaign for the right to vote. In the United States in 1903, women trade unionists and liberal professional women who were also campaigning for women's voting rights set up the Women's Trade Union League to help organize women in paid work around their political and economic welfare. These were dismal and bitter years for many women with terrible working conditions and home lives driven by poverty and often violence.

In 1908, on the last Sunday in February, socialist women in the United States initiated the first Women's Day when large demonstrations took place calling for the vote and the political and economic rights of women. The notion of international solidarity between the exploited workers of the world had long been established as a socialist principle, though largely an unrealized one.

In 1910, delegates went to the second International Conference of Socialist Women in Copenhagen. The conference of over 100 women from 17 countries, representing unions, socialist parties, working women's clubs, and including the first three women elected to the Finnish parliament came with unanimous approval that women throughout the world should focus on a particular day each year to press for their demands and International Women's Day was the result.

That conference also reasserted the importance of women's right to vote, dissociated itself from voting systems based on property

92

rights and called for universal suffrage-the right to vote for all adult women and men. It also decided to oppose night work as being detrimental to the health of most working women, though Swedish and Danish working women who were present asserted that night work was essential to their livelihood.

注意:此部分试题请在答题卡 2 上做答。

1. What were the general characteristics of industrialized world at the turn of the 20th century?

2. During the first decade of 20th century, women's works were confined to only several kinds of jobs like _____ in industrially developing countries.

3. _____ aroused women's consciousness of fighting against political restrictions for women.

4. It had long been established as a socialist principle for _____.

5. Why were Swedish and Danish working women against the abolishment of night work?

答案与解析

1. 【答案】Expansion and turbulence, booming population growth and radical ideologies.

【解析】根据关键词 at the turning of the 20th century 定位到第二段。所以可以知己获得答案 Expansion and turbulence, booming population growth and radical ideologies。

2. 【答案】textiles, manufacturing and domestic services.

【解析】根据关键词 women's works 定位到第三段第二句 their jobs,可以得到答案。要求举例当时妇女从事的主要工作。

3. 【答案】Many of the changes taking place in women's lives.

【解析】根据关键词 political restrictions 定位到第四段第一句 pushed against-aroused 说明妇女生活上的改变促进了对政治地位的要求。

4. 【答案】the exploited workers of the world.

【解析】根据关键词 established 和 socialist principle 定位到第五段最后一句。

5. 【答案】Because they asserted that night work was essential to their livelihood.

【解析】根据关键词 Swedish and Danish 定位到最后一段最后一句。瑞士和丹麦的妇女认为夜班对她们养家糊口很重要。

第四节　历年典型真题
突破训练

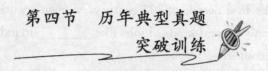

Ⅰ Test One

2008 年 6 月真题

Part IV　Reading Comprehension（Reading in Depth）（25 minutes）

Section A

Directions：*In this section，there is a short passage with 5 questions or incomplete statements. Read the passage carefully. Then answer the questions or complete the statements in the fewest possible words. Please write our answers on Answer Sheet 2*

Questions 47 to 51 are based on the following passage.

　　If movie trailers（预告片）are supposed to cause a reaction，the preview for "United 93" more than succeeds. Featuring no famous actors，it begins with images of a beautiful morning and passengers boarding an airplane. It takes you a minute to realize what the movie's even about. That's when a plane hits the World Trade Center. The effect is visceral（震撼心灵的）. When the trailer played before "Inside Man" last week at a Hollywood theater，audience members began calling out，"Too soon!" In New York City，the response was even more dramatic. The Loews theater in Manhattan took the rare step of pulling the trailer from its screens after several complaints.

"United 93" is the first feature film to deal explicitly with the events of September 11, 2001, and is certain to ignite an emotional debate. Is it too soon? Should the film have been made at all? More to the point, will anyone want to see it? Other 9/11 projects are on the way as the fifth anniversary of the attacks approaches, most notably Oliver Stone's "World Trade Center." but as the forerunner, "United 93"will take most of the heat, whether it deserves it or not.

The real United 93 crashed in a Pennsylvania field after 40 passengers and crew fought back against the terrorists. Writer-director Paul Greengrass has gone to great lengths to be respectful in his depiction of what occurred, proceeding with the film only after securing the approval of every victim's family. "Was I surprised at the agreement? Yes. Very. Usually there're one or two families who're more reluctant," Greengrass writes in an e-mail. "I was surprised at the extraordinary way the United 93 families have welcomed us into their lives and shared their experiences with us." Carole O'Hare, a family member, says, "They were very open and honest with us, and they made us a part of this whole project." Universal, which is releasing the film, plans to donate 10% of its opening weekend gross to the Flight 93 National Memorial Fund. That hasn't stopped criticism that the studio is exploiting a national tragedy. O'Hare thinks that's unfair. "This story has to be told to honor the passengers and crew for what they did," she says. "But more than that, it raises awareness. Our ports aren't secure. Our borders aren't secure. Our airlines still aren't secure, and this is what happens when you're not secure. That's the message I want people to hear."

95

注意:此部分试题请在答题卡 2 上作答

47. The trailer for "United 93" succeeded in _____ when it played in the theaters in Hollywood and New York City.

48. The movie "United 93" is sure to give rise to _____.

49. What did writer-director Paul Greengrass obtain before he proceeded with the movie? _____

50. Universal, which is releasing "United 93", has been criticized for _____.

51. Carole O'Hare thinks that besides honoring the passengers and crew for what they did, the purpose of telling the story is to _____ about security.

答案与解析

47. 【答案】causing a reaction.

【解析】根据关键词 The trailer for "United 93"定位到第一段第一句。题目空格前的介词要求填入的动词改为分词形式。

48. 【答案】an emotional debate.

【解析】根据关键词"United 93"定位到第二段第一句"United 93" is the first feature film to deal explicitly with the events of September 11, 2001, and is certain to ignite an emotional debate. 可以得到答案。其中 is certain to 相当于题目中的 is sure to。

49. 【答案】The approval of every victim's family.

【解析】根据关键词 writer-director Paul Greengrass 定位到第三段第二句"Writer-director Paul Greengrass..., proceeding with the film only after securing the approval of every victim's family."其中 securing 与题目中的 obtain 相当。

50. 【答案】exploiting a national tragedy.

【解析】根据关键词 Universal 和 releasing 定位到最后一段第六、七句。空格前为介词,要求填入 exploit 的分词形式。

51. 【答案】raise the awareness.

96

【解析】根据关键词 Carole O'Hare 定位到最后一段最后两句。题目将这两句话综合。空格前为动词不定式,所以填入动词原形。

【参考译文及题区画线】

47) 如果说电影预告片的目的是为了引起人们的反响,那《93号航班》的预告片收获的不仅仅是成功。该片中的角色由非知名演员担任。影片的开头,一个美丽的早晨,乘客们正在登机。你需要看一会儿,等到看见一架飞机撞上世界贸易中心时,你才会明白影片讲述的是什么故事。影片效果震撼人心。上周,该预告片在好莱坞一个电影院放映《局内人》之前播放时,观众都大呼"拍这种片子为之过早!"在纽约,人们对该片的反应更强烈。曼哈顿的罗尔斯剧院在观众的不断抗议下,停播了该片的预告片。

48)《93号航班》是首部讲述发生在 2001 年 9 月 11 日"9·11事件"的故事片,这必然会引起观众的情感争论。这部片子是不是拍的太早了? 是不是根本就不应该拍摄? 更重要的是,会有人想去看这部片子么? 随着"9·11事件"五周年纪念日的临近,其他与该事件有关的影片也正准备上映,这些影片当中最令人关注的是奥利弗·斯通导演的《世贸中心》。但是,作为打头阵者,《93号航班》无疑会最令人关注,无论它是否值得人们这么做。

关于第 93 号航班,真实的情况是,在四十名乘客和机组成员反抗机上恐怖分子的过程中,飞机坠毁在宾夕法尼亚洲的一块土地上。49)编剧兼导演的保罗·格林格拉斯写这个故事时,竭尽全力地想提高这个故事的可信度,拍电影前还特意征求飞机上每一位遇难者家属的同意。"我对大家的同意是不是感到吃惊呢? 是的,非常吃惊。通常情况下,总会有一两名家庭不太情愿,"保罗·格林格拉斯在一封电子邮件中写道,"但是令我吃惊的是这些遇难者家属不一般的地方,他们欢迎我们进入他们的生活,分享他们的经历。"卡罗尔·奥黑尔是其中一位遇难者的家属,她说,"他们对我们很坦率,很诚实,让我们成为整部影片的一分子"。该片的发行方环球电影公司计划将影片上映第一周票房收入的 10% 捐赠给 93 号航班纪念馆。50)但是,这也没能阻止大家对该公司的批评,大家认为该公司利用了国家的灾难来发财。奥黑尔觉得这不公平。"我们必须讲述这个故事,以此来表达我们对机上乘客和机组成员所做事情的尊敬,"她说,"更重要的是,51)这部片子提高了大家的意识。我们的港口并不安全,我们的边界并不安全,我们的飞机也不安全,如果我们不安全,那么,就会发生那样的惨剧,这是我想让大家知道的事情。"

II Test Two

2008 年 12 月真题

Part IV Reading Comprehension (Reading in Depth) (25 minutes)

Section A

Questions 47 to 51 are based on the following passage.

One of the major producers of athletic footwear, with 2002 sales of over $10 billion, is a company called Nike, with corporate headquarters in Beaverton, Oregon. Forbes magazine identified Nike's president, Philip Knight, as the 53rd-richest man in the world in 2004. But Nike has not always been a large multimillion-dollar organization. In fact, Knight started the company by selling shoes from the back of his car at track meets.

In the late 1950s Philip Knight was a middle-distance runner on the University of Oregon track team, coached by Bill Bowerman. One of the top track coaches in the U. S. , Bowerman was also known for experimenting with the design of running shoes in an attempt to make them lighter and more shock-absorbent. After attending Oregon, Knight moved on to do graduate work at Stanford University; his MBA thesis was on marketing athletic shoes. Once he received his degree, Knight traveled to Japan to contact the Onitsuka Tiger

Company, a manufacturer of athletic shoes. Knight convinced the company's officials of the potential for its product in the U. S. In 1963 he received his first shipment of Tiger shoes, 200 pairs in total.

In 1964, Knight and Bowerman contributed $500 each to from Blue Ribbon Sports, the predecessor of Nike. In the first few years, Knight distributed shoes out of his car at local track meets. The first employees hired by Knight were former college athletes. The company did not have the money to hire "experts", and there was no established athletic footwear industry in North America from which to recruit those knowledgeable in the field. In its early years the organization operated in an unconventional manner that characterized its innovative and entrepreneurial approach to the industry. Communication was informal; people discussed ideas and issues in the hallways, on a run, or over a beer. There was little task differentiation. There were no job descriptions, rigid reporting systems, or detailed rules and regulations. The team spirit and shared values of the athletes on Bowerman's teams carried over and provided the basis for the collegial style of management that characterized the early years of Nikes.

47. While serving as a track coach, Bowerman tried to design running shoes that were _____

48. During his visit to Japan, Knight convinced the officials of the Onitsuka Tiger Company that its product would have _____.

49. Blue Ribbon Sports as unable to hire experts due to the absence of _____ in North America.

50. In the early years of Nike, communication within the company was usually carried out _____

51. What qualities of Bowerman's teams formed the basis of Nike's early management style? _____.

答案与解析

47. **【答案】**lighter and more shock-absorbent.

    【解析】根据关键词 Bowerman 定位到第二段。第二段提到 Bowerman 试着设计跑鞋的特点是 lighter and more shock-absorbent 正好在题中做定语修饰 running shoes。

48. **【答案】**the potentials in the U. S.

    【解析】根据关键词 Onitsuka Tiger Company 定位到第二段倒数第二，三句。从空格可以看出答案应该为名词短语，而题目中已经出现 its product。所以得出答案。

49. **【答案】**established athletic footwear industry.

    【解析】根据关键词 Blue Ribbon Sports 定位到第三段，题目中提到不能雇佣专家的原因可以在本段中找到：The company did not have the money to hire "experts", and there was no established athletic footwear industry... 而题目中空格前的短语 the absence of 对应句子中的 there was no。

50. **【答案】**informally.

    【解析】根据关键词 in the early years of Nike 和 communication 定位到第三段，题目中句子结构较完整，空格跟在动词短语后，应填入副词，所以将原文的 informal 改为 informally。

51. **【答案】**The team spirit and shared valves of the athletes.

    【解析】根据关键词 Bowerman's teams 和 the basis 定位到最后一段最后一句：The team spirit and shared values of the athletes on Bowerman's teams carried over and provided the basis... characterized the early years of Nikes. 而问题中的疑问词 what 决定答案只要回答出名词短语即可。

【参考译文及题区画线】

运动鞋的主要生产商之一，2002 年的销售超过 100 亿美元——是一家叫耐克的公司，其总部在俄勒冈州的比弗顿。《福布斯》杂志在 2004 年将耐克的老总——菲利普·奈特——列为世界财富榜的

100

第五十三位。但是，耐克并非一直都是百万美元的大公司。其实，奈特是通过在各个田径运动会上销售他装在车子后备箱里的鞋子来开始创办公司的。

在 20 世纪 50 年代后期，菲利普·奈特是俄勒冈大学田径队的一个中跑运动员，他的教练是鲍尔曼。47)鲍尔曼是美国顶级的田径教练，同时他也因为试验各种跑鞋设计，以使跑鞋更轻，更减震而闻名。从俄勒冈大学毕业后，奈特前往斯坦福大学读研究生；他的 MBA 论文就是关于营销运动鞋的。在完成学位之后，48)奈特便去了日本，联系运动鞋生产商 Onitsuka Tiger 公司。奈特说服了公司的领导相信自己的产品在美国的潜力。1963 年，他收到了来自 Onitsuka Tiger 公司的第一批货——共 200 双 Tiger 鞋。

1964 年，奈特和鲍尔曼各自出资 500 美元，创建了 49)蓝带运动，也就是耐克的前身。在开始的那些年里，奈特把鞋装在自己车里，到当地各个田径运动会去卖。奈特的第一批雇员是以前大学里的一些运动员。49)公司没有钱去雇佣专家，而且在北美也没有成立运动鞋行业，从而也就无法从这一领域招聘有才能的人。在成立的早期，公司是以非常规的方式运作的，这一方式以其创新及创业方式为特色。50)交流是非正式的；公司人员总是在走廊里，在跑步过程中或者是在喝啤酒的时间来讨论一些想法以及公司的事务。工作几乎没有分工，也就没有职务说明，没有死板的报告体系或者具体的规章制度。51)鲍尔曼队伍的团队精神以及运动员共同的价值观，构成了耐克公司早期的合议风格的管理特色。

第四章 仔细阅读——篇章词汇

仔细阅读部分是考试中的重头戏，它包括 Section A 篇章词汇（或短句回答）和 Section B 篇章阅读（即多项选择）两部分。下面着重介绍篇章词汇的考点、设题特征和答题技巧。

第一节 考点揭秘与设题特征

篇章词汇题（banked cloze）是短句问答（Short Question Answer）的替换题。其测试形式是在一篇 250 词～300 词的文章留出 10 个空格，要求考生从所给的 15 个备选词中选出 10 个填入文中的相应处，使文章语句通顺，表达正确。篇章词汇题虽然是传统完形填空（multiple-choice cloze）的一种形式，但是它更侧重于考查考生在理解全文、宏观掌握篇章结构的基础上对词汇的认知和语法的理解。换句话说，它既要求考生在理解全文的基础上弄清文章的宏观结构，又要求考生具体细化到对每个单词的微观理解。

篇章词汇题的设计者一般遵循以下原则：首句不设空；一句话中不设两空；设空比较均匀，基本覆盖整个段落；设空不影响考生对文章大意的理解；所提供的备选词主要是实词，即能独立担任句子成分的名词、动词、形容词、副词。每个正确选项均有干扰项。试题难度主要有三级：第一级难度是所提供的 15 个备选词的词义互不关联，词性也不同，其中 10 个是正确答案选项，5 个干扰项；第二级难度是备选词中有 2 个左右的一词多性词，2 个左右的一词多义词；第三级难度是存在正确选项之间互相干扰的现象，尤其是语篇层面的题目。

第二节 解题技巧

做选词填空，关键是在保证正确率的前提下解题速度要尽量快。根据篇章词汇的考点及设题特点，考生必须要在通读全文、把握文章结构与大意的前提下，熟悉选项、根据上下文信息进行逻辑推理、分析和对比等手段来确定答案。具体解题步骤及技巧如下：

第一步：浏览全文，把握主旨（1 分钟）

这一步的目的是通过浏览全文了解文章的大致内容，做到心中有数。特别是要仔细看文章的第一句和各段的首句。这是因为西方人写文章惯用演绎法，总是先把自己要说的意思用一句话概括出来，然后再铺陈论证。例如 2008 年 12 月的四级篇章词汇真题就是用演绎法展开的一个典型（六级至今还未出现此类题型）。作者在文章的前两句就点明主题：没有书籍的生活是不完整的生活。书籍影响人们生活的深度和宽度。

第二步：整理选项，词性归类（1 分钟）

纵观历年篇章词汇真题，测试重点主要是实词，即：名词（n.）、动词（v.）、形容词（adj.）和副词（adv.）。建议考生用一分钟时间给短文后的 15 个备选单词标注词性，把 15 个备选单词分成名词、动词、形容词、副词四个类别，这样可以为下一步的正确选择作铺垫。因为 15 个备选单词中一般有三到四个动词，三到四个名词。如果确定某个空格需要一个名词的话，这个时候就变成三选一，四选一。假设下面一个空又需要一个名词的话，你就发觉越到后面越好选择。

辨别词性要注意下面几点：

（1）记不得单词词性时，看单词后缀。英语构词法中，前缀管意思，后缀管词性。所以看一个词的词尾，往往能大致分出词性。一般说来，以-ion, -age, -ness, -ty, -ship, -ace, -ance, -ancy, -ence, -ency, -dom, -itude, -um, -mony 结尾的是名词；以-ize, -ise, -fy 结尾的大都是动词；以-ive, -ent, -ant, -ful, -ous, -able, -ary, -c, -cal, -less 结尾的是大都是形容词；以-ly, -s, -ways, -wise 结尾的大都是副词。

（2）遇到多性词时，一一标注。有的词，如 wrench, relay, patent，即可做名词又可做动词，没有上下文是很难判断的，这时两个词性都要标出来。

（3）动词要两分，那就是谓语和非谓语动词。所谓非谓语动词，就是-ing, -ed, to do 型的，其他的都是谓语动词。但-ed 型的有两种可能性，无法确定的要先打问号。

（4）词性无法确定的词要暂时搁置，不必赌气誓死纠缠，那样可能会把自己缠死。

第三步：语法切入，语义配合（4 分钟）

将选项分类之后，就得从文章中来寻找对应的线索了。选项与文章匹配的因素有两个，第一是词性，第二才是词义。做题时可以遵循语法切入，语义配合的原则，即先从语法角度看，空格需要填什么词性，再根据意思从该词性的几个单词中做出选择。

第四步：复读全文，检查答案（1 分钟）

填空完成后，再复读全文，检查所填入的词是否能将文章合情合理地补全，即，是否使文章连贯、一致，是否符合语法规则。

第三节 实战演练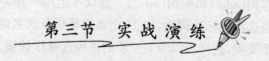

由于六级样题及真题还没有出现过篇章词汇，下面我们以 2008 年 12 月的四级篇章词汇真题为例，对篇章词汇的解题技巧与步骤进行解释。

A bookless life is an incomplete life. Books influence the depth and breadth of life. They meet the natural __47__ for freedom, for expression, for creativity and beauty of life. Learners, therefore, must have books, and the right type of book, for the satisfaction of their need. Readers turn __48__ to books because their curiosity concerning all manners of things, their eagerness to share in the experiences of others and their need to __49__ from their own limited environment lead them to find in books food for the mind and the spirit. Through their reading they find a deeper significance to life as books acquaint them with life in the world as it was and it is now. They are presented with a __50__ of human experiences and come to __51__ other ways of thought and living. And while __52__ their own relationships and responses to life, the readers often find that the __53__ in their stories are going through similar adjustments, which help to clarify and give significance to their own.

Books provide __54__ material for readers' imagination to grow. Imagination is a valuable quality and a motivating power, and stimulates achievement. While enriching their imagination, books __55__ their outlook, develop a fact-finding attitude and train them to use leisure __56__. The social and educational significance of the readers' books cannot be overestimated in an academic library.

A. abundant	B. characters	C. communicating	D. completely
E. derive	F. desire	G. diversity	H. escape
I. establishing	J. narrow	K. naturally	L. personnel
M. properly	N. respect	O. widen	

第一步:浏览全文,把握主旨

本文是一篇议论文。作者在文章的前两句就点明主题:没有书籍的生活是不完整的生活。书籍影响人们生活的深度和宽度。

n.	characters（人物,性格）desire（愿望,要求）diversity（差异,多样性）personnel（人员）respect（尊重）
v.	communicating（交流）derive（起源于）escape（逃脱,避开）establishing（建立）widen（拓宽）respect（尊重）
adj.	abundant（丰富的）narrow（狭窄的）
adv.	completely（完全地）naturally（自然地）properly（适当地）

第三步:语法切入,语义配合,逐题解答

47：【答案】F. desire

【解析】名词辩义题。空格位于形容 natural 之后,同时需要跟后面的 for 搭配。故此处要填名词,根据文义,选项中的另四个名词 B. characters（人物,性格）,G. diversity（差异,多样性）,L. personnel（人员）和 N. respect（尊重）,词义均不符。

48：【答案】K. naturally

【解析】副词辩义题。空格位于 turn 和 to 之间,我们可以判断此处需要添一个副词,三个候选副词中,D. completely（完全地）,M. properly（适当地）不符句意,故排除。

49：【答案】H. escape

【解析】动词辩义题。空格前面是一个动词不定式符号 to,可知此处要填一个动词(原形),再根据后面的介词 from,我们可以将包围圈缩小到 escape,derive 两个词范围,再根据下文意思,应当选"逃离"(他们自己有限的环境)。

50：【答案】G. diversity

【解析】名词辩义题。空格前缺少名词,与前面的冠词 an 和后面的 of 组成短语。选项中的名词 B. characters 是复数形式,可以直接排除,而 L. personnel（人员）和 N. respect（尊重）,均不符合句意。根据意思和搭配,故选择 diversity (a diversity of 许多)。

51：【答案】N. respect

【解析】:动词辩义题。空格后面为名词,此空要选一个及物动词原形。E. derive (起源于)和 O. widen (拓宽)虽然都可以做及物动词,但不符合句意,故选 N。

52：【答案】B. establishing

【解析】:动词辩义题。句子结构完整,空格前为连词 while,这里缺少现在分词作状语。故选 B。

53：【答案】B. characters

【解析】:名词辩义题。空格前是冠词 the,所以是缺少名词。根据从句的谓语动词 are 来判断,此处需要填名词复数形式。故选 B,因为只有"人物"才能"经历各种调整"。

54：【答案】A. abundant

【解析】:形容词辩义题。空格后面是一个名词,此处需要填一个形容词。因为本文的主题是谈书籍对人生的重要作用,因此这里需要填书籍有助于想象力的提高,故选 A。

55：【答案】O. widen

【解析】:动词辩义题。空格缺少动词原形与 develop,train 作并列谓语。根据此空后面名词"眼界"及并列关系来推断,动词 widen 是最佳选择。

56：【答案】M. properly

【解析】:副词辩义题。句子结构完整,空格位于动宾短语 use leisure 后面,故缺少副词。根据文义,故选 M。

透过四级真题演示,我们基本可以合理地推断六级篇章词汇题型的特点,了解其解题思路。不过这里要特别提醒考生的是四级要求的词汇量是 4200 个左右,六级要求的词汇量是 5500 个左右,所以六级重点要掌握的词汇主要是六级比四级多出的 1000 多个单词。对这 1000 个词的词义、词性要了如指掌,方能做好这一题型。

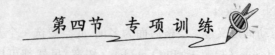

Banked Cloze

Direction: *In this section, there are 5 passages. There are 10 blanks in each passage. You are required to select one word for each blank from a list of choices given in a word blank following the passage. Read the passage through carefully before making your choices. Each choice in the blank is identified by a letter.* **You may not use any of the words in the blank more than once.**

Passage one

It is often claimed that nuclear energy is something we cannot do without. We live in a consumer society where there is an enormous demand for __1__ products of all kinds. Moreover, an increase in industrial production is considered to be one solution to the problem of mass unemployment. Such an increase __2__ an abundant and cheap energy supply. Many people believe that nuclear energy provides an __3__ and economical source of power and that it is therefore essential for an industrially developing society. There are a number of other advantages in the use of nuclear energy. Firstly, nuclear power, except for accidents, is clean. A __4__ advantage is that a nuclear power station can be run and maintained by relatively few technical and administrative staff. The nuclear reactor represents an enormous step in our scientific evolution and, whatever the anti-nuclear group says, it is wrong to expect a return to more __5__ sources of fuel. However, opponents of nuclear energy point out that nuclear power stations bring a direct threat not only to the environment but also to civil liberties. Furthermore, it is questionable whether __6__ nuclear

108

power is a cheap source of energy. There have, for example, been very costly accidents in America, in Britain and, of course, in Russia. The possibility of increases in the cost of uranium (铀) in addition to the cost of greater safety provisions could price nuclear power out of the __7__ In the long run, environmentalists argue, nuclear energy wastes valuable resources and __8__ the ecology to an extent which could bring about the destruction of the human race. Thus if we wish to survive, we cannot afford nuclear energy. In spite of the case against nuclear energy __9__ above, nuclear energy programmes are expanding. Such an expansion assumes a continual growth in industrial production and consumer demands. However, it is doubtful whether this growth will or can continue. Having __10__ up the arguments on both sides, it seems there are good economic and ecological reasons for sources of energy other than nuclear power. (344 words)

A. disturbs	B. ultimately	C. market	D. commercial
E. primitive	F. circulation	G. invariably	H. weighed
I. disposition	J. further	K. awesome	L. presumes
M. inexhaustible	N. conversion	O. outlined	

Passage two

Human vision like that of other *primates* (灵长类动物) has evolved in an *arboreal* (多树的) environinent. In the __1__ complex world of a tropical forest, it is more important to see well than to develop an __2__ sense of smell.

In lhe course of __3__ , members of the primate line have acquired large eyes while the *snout* (长鼻子) has shrunk to give the eye a better view. Of mammals only humans and some primates __4__ color vision.

The red flag is black to the bull. Horses live in a colorless world. Light __5__ to humnan eyes occupies only a very nanow band in the whole electromagnetic spectrum. Ultraviolet rays are invisible to humans though ants and honeybees are __6__ to them.

Humans have no direct __7__ of infrared rays unlike the rattle-snake which has receptors toned into wavelengths longer than 0. 7 *micron* (微米). The world would look strangely different if human eyes were sensitive to infrared __8__. Then instead of the darkness of night, we woukl be able to move easily in a strange shadowless world where objects glowed with __9__ degrees of intensity. But human eyes excel in other ways. They are in fact __10__ discerning in color gradation. The color sensitivity of normal human vision is rarely smpassed even by sophisticated technical devices.

A. perception	B. varying	C. alter	D. radiation
E. evolution	F. expanded	G. dense	H. enjoy
I. sensitive	J. capacity	K. acute	L. visible
M. remarkably	N. transforming	O. unbearable	

第五节　答案与解析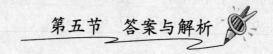

Pasage one

> 结构剖析:议论文。作者对核能的利与弊进行论述后,提出从经济和生态两方面看,我们应该选择使用核能以外的其它能源。

词性归类

n.	Market（市场）circulation（运行,流通,发行量）disposition（性格,性情,倾向）conversion（改变,皈依,折合）

v.	disturbs(妨碍,打扰) market（营销）weighed(称……的重量,权衡) outlined（画出……的轮廓,概述）
adj.	commercial(商业的,商业性的)primitive（原始的,未开化的）awesome（令人敬畏的）inexhaustible（用之不竭的,不倦的）further（更远的,进一步的）
adv.	ultimately(最后,终极地) invariably（不变地,一定地,总是）further（更远地,进一步地）

答案与解析

1. 【答案】D. commercial

【解析】：形容词辨义题。空格后为名词,前为介词,由此推断此处缺少形容词作定语。根据句意"当前的社会是个消费的社会……",选项中 awesome(令人敬畏的), primitive(原始的), inexhaustible(取之不尽的), further(进一步的)都不符合句意。故选 D commercial(商业的)。

2. 【答案】L. presumes

【解析】：动词辨义题。此句主语是单数,缺少谓语,一般现在时。从语法结构上看,选项 A 和 L 都可以,但是只有 L 符合句意,即"这样的增长首先要有一个极为丰富和廉价的能源"。

3. 【答案】M. inexhaustible

【解析】：形容词辨义题。此句空格前是 an,根据空格后 and economical source of power,由此可推断此处需要形容词与 economical 并列作定语,修饰 source of power。综合句意,M 为最佳答案。本句意为"很多人认为核能能提供既经济又取之不尽的电力,因此对发展工业的社会来说是必不可少的"。

4. 【答案】J. further

【解析】：形容词辨义题。从语法上看,此句空格缺形容词修饰主语

advantage,从语义看,选项 J 符合句意。因为上文讲的是核能还有一些其他的优势。之后,作者列举了第一个优势(只要不出问题是不会污染的),本句是对其另一优势的进一步阐述。故选 J。

5. 【答案】E. primitive

【解析】:形容词辨义题。空格前为 more,空格后为 sources,此空格应填形容词。选项中只剩两个形容词 K. awesome(令人敬畏的)和 E. primitive(原始的),只有 E 符合句意" 放弃核能去重新使用更为原始的燃料是十分错误的"。故选 E。

6. 【答案】B. ultimately

【解析】:副词辨义题。句子主谓结构完整,此空格需要一个副词修饰 is。结合上句:反对者认为,核电站不仅对环境,而且对民权构成威胁;后一句进一步说明核能是否是电力的廉价来源还是个问题。E. invariably(总是)不合题意,故选 B。

7. 【答案】C. market

【解析】:名词辨义题。空格前为 the,此处需要填名词,与前面的 out of 构成介词短语。选项中 F. circulation(循环),I. disposition(性情),N. conversion(转化)均不能与谓语动词 price 搭配使用,故选 C。price...out of the market 意为:由于要价过高而失去市场。

8. 【答案】A. disturbs

【解析】:动词辨义题。从语法上看,此处需填动词第三人称与 and 前面的动词 wastes 构成并列谓语。虽然选项 A 与 L 都是动词第三人称,但唯有 A 符合句意,即"从长远看,核能的使用浪费了宝贵的资源,破坏了生态,直至导致了人类的死亡"。

9. 【答案】O. outlined

【解析】:动词辨义题。此空格后是副词,空格前是由 in spite of 引导的介词短语,从而推断此处需要填个动词的过去分词修饰 the case against nuclear power。从语法上看,选项 H 和 O 都可以,但根据句意,O 是最佳答案。本句意为:"尽管有上述反对核能的说法,发展核能的计划还在扩大"。

10. 【答案】H. weighed

【解析】:动词辨义题。此空格前是 Having,说明此处需要动词过去分词,因为空格后是 up,故选 H weighed,与 up 构成动词短语,意为"权衡"。

Passage two

结构剖析:说明文。本文主要讲述了动物视力的进化,指出在哺乳动物中只有人类和其他的一些灵长类动物进化为具有彩色的视力。

词性归类

n.	perception（感知能力）radiation（放射物,放射线,辐射）evolution（进化,发展）capability（能力）
v.	varying（改变,变化）alter（改变,变更）expanded（扩大,扩张,膨胀）enjoy（享有,享受,喜爱）transforming（改革,变换）
adj.	Varying（变化的,不同的）dense（密集的,浓密的,密度大的）sensitive（敏感的）acute（敏锐的,急性的,尖锐的）visible（可见的）transforming（转化的,使变形的）
adv.	Remarkably（引人注目地,非凡地）unbearably（无法容忍地）

答案与解析

1. 【答案】G. dense

【解析】形容词辨义题。空格前为 the,此处应填形容词与空格后的 complex 共同修饰 world。从上文提到 an aboreal environment 和下文提到 a tropical forest 可推知,此处应为描述热带雨林特点的形容词,在形容词词库中,dense 符合句意,故选 G。

113

2. 【答案】K. acute

【解析】形容词辨义题。空格前的 an 空格后是名词，决定了此处应填以元音开头的形容词，在形容词库中，acute 符合句意，故选 K，意为"灵敏的味觉"。

3. 【答案】E. evolution

【解析】名词辨义题。根据首段首句可知本文讨论的是视力的进化，本句说的正是灵长类动物视力的进化，所以，此处应为表示"进化"或"发展"的名词与空格前 In the course... 构成介词短语作状语。在名词词库中，evolution 符合句意，故选 E，意为"在进化的过程中"。

4. 【答案】H. enjoy

【解析】动词辨义题。根据句法知识此处需要动词原形作谓语，而且该动词为及物动词。本文主要讲述的是动物的视力进化，在哺乳动物中只有人类和其他的一些灵长类动物进化为具有彩色的视力。动词词库中，只有 alter 和 enjoy(享有，享受，喜爱)两个动词符合句法要求，但 alter 意为"改变；变更"，不符句意，故选 H. enjoy(享有，享受，喜爱)。

5. 【答案】L. visible

【解析】形容词辨义题。此处需要能够与 to 搭配的形容词作后置定语修饰 light。在词库里的形容词中，sensitive 和 visible 从语法结构上来说都可与 to 搭配，但是从句法及上下文意思方面看，显然此句与下一句为并列转折关系，下句中出现了 invisible，所以此处应该选择 visible 才符合句意。

6. 【答案】I. sensitive

【解析】形容词辨义题。此处需要能够与 to 搭配的形容词。在词库里的剩下形容词中，只有 sensitive 可与 to 搭配，且根据句中的 though 判断，此处的单词应与上文的 invisible 成对比关系，故选 I，句意为虽然蚂蚁和蜜蜂能感受到紫外线的存在人类却不能。

7. 【答案】A. perception

【解析】名词辨义题。空格后为 of,此处需要填入名词,从句中的 unlike 可知,本句要说的是人类与响尾蛇不同,不能直接感受到红外线。在名词词库中,perceptlon 意为"感知,感受",符合题意,故选 A。

8. 【答案】D. radiation

【解析】名词辨义题。处需填入名词,与 infrared 构成短语。在上句中与 infrared 连用的是 rays,因此这里的名词也应该是类似的意思,在名词词库中 radiation 有"光线,射线"的意思,故选 D。

9. 【答案】B. varying

【解析】形容词辨义题。此处需要形容词修饰名词 degrees。而通常修饰 degrees 的词含有为"不同的"的意思。形容词词库中,varying 和 transforming 都具有"变化的"的意思,从句法结构上来说都可以用在此处,但是,transform 通常是指某事物根本性的变化,而本句讲的是光线的强弱度变化,所以只有 varying 符合句意,故选 B。

10. 【答案】M. remarkably

【解析】副词辨义题。此处需要填个副词修饰谓语 are discerning。根据上句可推知本句句意为:人类的眼睛在识别颜色的强弱变化方面具有"非凡的"能力。副词词库中,只有 remarkably,符合句意,故选 M。

第五章 仔细阅读——篇章阅读

第一节 考点揭秘与设题特征

六级考试的篇章阅读理解部分包括两篇 400 字词左右,内容、难度和体裁不同的短文,每篇短文后有 5 道选择题,旨在综合考查学生关于阅读的各种能力:要求能理解个别句子的意义,也能理解上下文的逻辑关系;既能理解字面意思,也能理解隐含意思;既能理解事实和细节,也能理解所读材料的主旨和大意,能对文章的内容进行判断、推理和信息转换。不但要求准确率,也要求有一定的速度。

总结历年六级阅读真题,可以得出阅读题目设置具有以下特点,可以据此指导解题思路。

1. 题目题干都对原文词句进行一定程度的信息转换或概括,增加了根据题干中线索词确定答案所在题区的难度;

例 1: Meanwhile, most children are vulnerable to the enormous influence exerted by grandchildless parents aiming to persuade their kids to produce children. They will take a call from a persistent parent, even if they're loaded with works. In addition, some parents make handsome money offers payable upon the grandchild's birth. Sometimes these gifts not only cover expenses associated with the infant's birth, but extras, too, like a vacation. In any case, cash gifts can weaken the resolve of even the noblest person. (2005 年 12 月 CET - 6，Passage 1)

题目：According to the passage, some couples may eventually choose to have children because _____.

A. they find it hard to resist the carrot-and-stick approach of their parents

B. they have learn from other parents about the joys of having children

C. they feel more and more lonely ad they grow older

D. they have found it irrational to remain childless

解析：题干是对原文相关段落的高度概括，在原文里找不到和题干相同的词，无法根据关键词定位。但是本段句首可以说明，在父母的影响下，许多夫妻还是要了孩子。本段从两个方面反映了父母的影响：一方面是压力，因为即使他们工作很忙，也得接听他们父母催他们要孩子的电话；另一方面是诱惑，因为有些父母为了让子女要孩子，会答应支付抚养孩子的费用等。选项 A 中的 the carrot and stick（胡萝卜加大棒，软硬兼施）形象地描述了上述情况，故 A 是正确答案。

2. 绝大部分的答案需要把握段落层次上的逻辑关系（段落模式）才能得出；

例 2：Kids count more than their colleges. Getting into Yale may signify intelligence, talent and ambition. But it's not the only indicator and, paradoxically, its significance is declining. The reason：so many similar people go elsewhere. Getting into college is not life's only competition. In the next competition—the job market and graduate school—the results may change. Old-boy networks are breaking down. Princeton economist Alan Krueger studied admissions to one top Ph. D. program. High scores

117

on the GRE helped explain who got in; degrees of prestigious universities didn't. （2008 年 12 月 CET - 6，Passage 2）

题目：What does the author mean by "kids count more than their colleges"(Line 1，para. 4)?

A. Continuing education is more important to a person's success.

B. A person's happiness should be valued more than their education.

C. Kids' actual abilities are more important than their college background.

D. What kids learn at college cannot keep up with job market requirements.

解析：题干中 kids count more than their colleges 是本段的主题句,本段为总分结构。作者从两方面对主题进行论述。一是 Getting into Yale may signify intelligence，talent and ambition. But it's not the only indicator(能够进耶鲁大学是才智和抱负的体现,接着转折对此进行了否定:但上大学也不是唯一的指标……)；二是 Princeton economist Alan Krueger studied admissions to one top Ph. D. program. High scores on the GRE helped explain who got in; degrees of prestigious universities didn't.(Krueger 博士的研究结果表明能够有机会被顶级博士项目录取的是能够在 GRE 考试中有优异的成绩,而不是拥有名牌大学学位的人)。从此推断出孩子的实际能力比大学背景更重要。故 C 为答案。

　　3. 题干和答案一起,构成原文词句意义的蕴含意义、同义转述或言外之意；

例3：American tourists, however, shouldn't expect any relief soon. The dollar lost strength the way many marriages break up-slowly, and then all at once. And currencies don't turn on a dime. So if you want to avoid the pain inflicted by the increasingly pathetic dollar, cancel that summer vacation to England and look to New England. There, the dollar is still treated with a little respect. (2008 年 6 月 CET - 6，Passage 1)

题目：What is the author's advice to Americans?

  A. They treat the dollar with a little respect

  B. They try to win in the weak-dollar gamble

  C. They vacation at home rather than abroad

  D. They treasure their marriages all the more.

解析：本段介绍美元贬值对人民生活的影响"美国游客的痛苦不会那么快得到缓解……货币不会很快升值"接着给出合理建议：So if you want to avoid the pain inflicted by the increasingly pathetic dollar，cancel that summer vacation to England and look to New England（如果想避免伤痛，最好取消去英格兰的暑期旅行计划，去新英格兰），言外之意是取消去国外旅行，转而在国内旅行。本题的题干和答案一起，构成原文词句意义的蕴含意义，故答案为 C。

4. 针对已知句子隐含的内容进行提问，而不是针对文章的细节，即句子的结构或者句子里面所强调的关键词以及句子与句子的关系进行提问；

例 4：It's no secret that there's a lot to put up with when waiting tables, and fortunately, much of it can be easily forgotten when you pocket the tips. The service industry, by definition, exists to cater to others' needs. Still, it seemed that many of my customers didn't get the difference between server and servant. (2007 年 12 月 CET - 6，Passage 1)

题目：What does the author imply by saying "... many of my customers didn't get the difference between server and servant"?

  A. Those who cater to others' needs are destined to be looked down upon.

  B. Those working in the service industry shouldn't be treated as servants.

C. Those serving others have to put up with rough treatment to earn a living.

D. The majority of customers tend to look on a servant as a server nowadays.

解析:本段首句提到"做餐饮招待的忍耐许多事情"(受委屈),末句则指出"客人们似乎并不明白服务人员与仆人的区别"说明客人们将餐饮招待当仆人使唤,也就是说作者认为客人们不应将餐饮招待当仆人来对待,故选项 B 为答案。解答这类题时,一定要抓住这句话所在这段的论点句,由这个论点句推断出在本段可能的意思。

5. 与四级篇章阅读相比,六级阅读理解中推理判断题的比重较大,占 40%左右。其中对主题的考查往往与细节相互交织,需综合概括方能得出正确答案。

例 5:When we worry about who might be spying on our private lives, we usually think about the Federal agents. But the private sector outdoes the government every time. It's Linda Tripp, not the FBI, who is facing charges under Maryland's laws against secret telephone taping. It's our banks, not the Internal Revenue Service (IRS), that pass our private financial data to telemarketing firms.

Consumer activists are pressing Congress for better privacy laws without much result so far. The legislators lean toward letting business people track our financial habits virtually at will.

As an example of what's going on, consider U. S. Bancorp, which was recently sued for deceptive practices by the state of Minnesota. According to the lawsuit, the bank supplied a telemarketer called Member Works with sensitive customer data such as names, phone numbers, bank-account and credit-card numbers, Social Security numbers, account balances and credit limits.

With these customer lists in hand, Member Works started dialing for dollars-selling dental plans, videogames, computer software and other products and services. Customers who accepted a "free trial offer" had, 30 days to cancel. If the deadline passed, they were charged automatically through their bank or credit-card accounts. U. S. Bancorp collected a share of the revenues.

Customers were doubly deceived, the lawsuit claims. They. didn't know that the bank was giving account numbers to Member Works. And if customers asked, they were led to think the answer was no.

The state sued Member Works separately for deceptive selling. The company denies that it did anything wrong. For its part, U. S. Bancorp settled without admitting any mistakes. But it agreed to stop exposing its customers to nonfinancial products sold by outside firms. A few top banks decided to do the same. Many other banks will still do business with Member Works and similar firms.

And banks will still be mining data from your account in order to sell you financial products, including things of little value, such as credit insurance and credit-card protection plans.

You have almost no protection from businesses that use your personal accounts for profit. For example, no federal law shields "transaction and experience" information - mainly the details of your bank and credit-card accounts. Social Security numbers are for sale by private firms. They've generally agreed not to sell to the public. But to businesses, the numbers are an open book. Self-regulation doesn't work. A firm might publish a privacy-protection policy, but who enforces it?

Take U. S. Bancorp again. Customers were told, in writing, that "all personal information you supply to us will be considered confidential. " Then it sold your data to Member Works. The bank even claims that it doesn't "sell" your data at all. It merely "shares" it and reaps a profit. Now you know. (2004 年 6 月 CET - 6, Passage 1)

题目: We can infer from the passage that _____ .

A. banks will have to change their ways of doing business

B. privacy protection laws will soon be enforced

C. consumers' privacy will continue to be invaded

D. "free trial" practice will eventually be banned

解析:这是道推断题。文章在第 2 段指出消费者活动家期望政府能出台更好的保护隐私的法律,但至今未果;第 2 段至第 6 段提到美国银行公司将客户的个人资料泄露给一家电话销售公司,二者被告上法庭,一方坚决否认自己有错,一方还没承认错误就结案了。综合这些事实,便可推知,只要不出台相关的法律,消费者的隐私权就会继续受侵犯,从而说明了立法保护消费者隐私权的重要性。故选项 C 为答案。

第二节 命题规律

任何事物都有一定的规律,六级阅读命题也不例外。阅读理解的题目主要由主观性题目和客观性题目,大致可以分为事实细节题、推理判断题、主旨大意题、观点态度题和词义理解题五种。

不同的题目指向是不同的,同时对考生的思维方向的要求也是不同的。比如,考文章大意的题目实际上考的是归纳推理能力,而考细节的题目更多的是考察英语阅读能力。有的题目只需在原文中找到相关定位即可,有的题目则要求对全文或者某一段落的内容全面掌握。了解命题规律,有助于提高解题效率。从历年全真试题的命题情况来看,六级阅读五种题目的命题有以下规律:

1. 事实细节题和推断题的命题规律

事实细节题和推断题在历年考题中所占比例最大。这两类题的提问方式不同,但是命题规律一样,都是针对文章的某句话、某个对象,如文章中的原因、结果、现象、条件、任务,文章结构等重要细节事实。

　　细节题属于客观类题,是根据短文提供的信息和事实进行提问,选择的依据必须是短文本身提供的信息,因此解题时应迅速根据题干所提供的信息准确确定原文相关语句,仔细判断或推断后确定正确答案,千万不可主观臆断而造成错误选择。推断题(推理与判断)属于主观类题,推断是根据文章中阐述的事实或细节,按照逻辑发展的规律,进行分析和概括,并以此为根据得出合乎逻辑的结论,而推理则是以已知的事实为根据,来获得未知的信息。解答推断题时应注意以下几方面:一是正确的答案是推断出的内容,而不是原文中的内容;二是虽然可以以文章提供的事实或内在逻辑为基础进行推理,但切忌推理过头,概括过度;三是切忌妄加评论,把自己的观点当作作者的观点。

事实细节类题常见的提问方式有:

According to the passage, it is... that _____.

The author describes... as... because _____.

What influences... most in... is _____.

According to the passage, the problem of... partly arises from _____.

推理判断题的提问方式有:

It is implied that _____.

It can be inferred from that text that _____.

Speaking of... , the author implied that _____.

We can learn from the... paragraph that _____.

The author thinks that _____.

According to the author,... _____.

The author ends the passage with implication that _____.

Apparently the author suggests that _____.

What conclusion can we draw from the passage?

命题规律 1　列举、并列处常考

列举和并列指的是文章连续提到三个以上的事物,然后要求考生从列举出的内容选出符合题干要求的答案项。列举的典型句式是"First(ly),..., Second(ly),..., Third(ly),...";并列的典型句式为"A, B and C..."。列举、并列处常出题型是"细节事实题"。

例 1: Most rainforest soils are thin and poor because they lack minerals and because the heat and heavy rainfall destroy most organic matter in the soils within four years of it reaching the forest floor. This means topsoil contains few of the ingredients needed for long-term successful farming (2005 年 6 月 CET - 6, Passage 2)

题目: Most rainforest soils are thin and poor because _____.

A. the composition of the topsoil is rather unstable

B. black carbon is washed away by heavy rains

C. organic matter is quickly lost due to heat and rain

D. long-term farming has exhausted the ingredients essential to plant growth

解析:文章首句中的 because... and because... 列举了造成雨林土壤贫瘠的两个原因:一是土壤中缺乏矿物质;二是有机物到达森林地面后,在不到四年的时间里,大部分就会遭到高温和强降水的破坏。题干是原文信息的部分再现,只要仔细将选项和原文作对比,就能判断 C 为正确答案。

命题规律 2　举例与打比喻的地方常考

为了使自己的观点更具有说服力,更加明确,作者常以具体的例子来佐证。因此,考生应对某些引出这些例子或比喻的标志词如 as, such as, for example, for instance, a case in point 等加以注意,因为这些例句或比喻就常常是命题者提问的焦点。还需要注意的是所举例子一般是和文章的中心或段落的中心紧密相关的,常设"推断性问题"和"细节性问题"。做这种题型要注意抓住文章或段落的中心思想,一般符合中心思想的就是正确答案。

例 2: Last year I left a professional position as a small-town reporter and took a job waiting tables. As someone paid to serve food to people, I had customers say and do things to me I suspect they'd never say or do to their most casual acquaintances. One night a man talking on his cell phone waved me away, then beckoned (示意) me back with his finger a minute later, complaining he was ready to order and asking where I'd been. (2007 年 12 月 CET – 6,Passage 1)

题目: What does the author intend to say by the example in the second paragraph?

A. Some customers simply show no respect to those who serve them.

B. People absorbed in a phone conversation tend to be absent-minded.

C. Waitresses are often treated by customers as casual acquaintances.

D. Some customers like to make loud complaints for no reason at all.

解析:本段的例子是为了解释说明第二段第二句的观点。该句指出做着为他人提供餐饮服务而获得报酬的工作,我遇到一些顾客,他们对我说了一些也做了一些我觉得他们从来不会对一般的熟人说过或做过的事情。他们认为我为客人服务是理所当然的,我得招之即来挥之即去,不会为我考虑,说明他们不尊重服务人员,故 A 为答案。

命题规律 3　转折对比处常考

通常说来,转折后的内容常常是语义的重点,命题者常对转折处的内容进行提问。转折一般通过 however,but,yet,in fact 等词语来引导。强调对比常由 like,unlike,until,not so much...as 等词语引

125

导。命题者常对对比的双方属性进行考查。

例 3：Like most people, I've long understood that I will be judged by my occupation, that my profession is a gauge people use to see how smart or talented I am. Recently, however, I was disappointed to see that it also decides how I'm treated as a person. (2007 年 12 月 CET - 6, Passage 1)

题目：The author was disappointed to find that _____ .

    A. one's position is used as a gauge to measure one's intelligence.

    B. talented people like her should fail to get a respectable job

    C. one's occupation affects the way one is treated as a person

    D. professionals tend to look down upon manual workers

    解析：本段第一句指出我一直认为我的职业是人们判断我的聪明才智的标准，但第二句中的 however 表明作者的失望，即职业还是一个人受到何种待遇的标准。故选 C。

命题规律 4　（指示）代词出现处常考

    这类考题常用来考查考生是否真正理解上下文之间的句际关系和意义。

例 4：Raw materials have not run out, and show no sign of doing so. Logically, one day they must: the planet is a finite place. Yet it is also very big, and man is very ingenious. What has happened is that every time a material seems to be running short, the price has risen and, in response, people have looked for new sources of supply, tried to find ways to use less of the material, or looked for a new substitute. For this reason prices for energy and for minerals have fallen in real terms during the century. The same is true for food. Prices fluctuate, in response to harvests, natural disasters and political instability; and when they rise, it takes some time before new sources of supply become available. But they always do, assisted by new farming and crop technology. The long-term trend has been downwards. (2002 年 1 月 CET-6, Passage 1)

题目: One of the reasons why the long-term trend of prices has been downwards is that _____.

A. technological innovation can promote social stability

B. political instability will cause consumption to drop

C. new farming and crop technology can lead to overproduction

D. new sources are always becoming available

解析:根据题干中的 reason 可将答案定位于本段第 5 句 For this reason 后,还得弄清 this reason 指代的是什么。联系上文 people have looked for new sources of supply,.... For this reason prices for energy and for minerals have fallen in real terms ,说明从长远来看,价格处于下降趋势的原因之一应该是总能找到新的能源,故选 D。

命题规律5 因果关系常考

两个事件内在的因果关系常常成为出题人的命题点,一般说来,这种选择题有两种形式:给原因推结果或是给结果找原因。表示因果关系的词、短语和结构由:because of, since, for, as, therefore, consequently, result in/from, originate from, owe... to, attribute... to, arise from, as a result, lead to, thus, hence 等。

例 5: Etzioni sees the experience at Harvard as an eye-opening one and says there's much about business schools that he'd like to change. "A lot of the faculty teaching business are bad news themselves, to reinforcing the notion of profit over community interests, Etzioni has seen a lot that's left him shaking his head. And because of what he's seen taught in business schools, he's not surprised by the latest rash of corporate scandals. "In many ways things have got a lot worse at business schools. I suspect," says Etzioni. (2006 年 1 月 CET-6, Passage 2)

题目：In Etzioni's view, the latest rash of corporate scandals could be attributed to _____.

A. the tendency in business schools to stress self-interest over business ethics

B. the executives' lack of knowledge in legally manipulating contracts

C. the increasingly fierce competition in the modern business world

D. the moral corruption of business school graduates

解析：首先，从题干中的 be attributed to 可得知本题的考点与因果关系有关，然后根据关键词语 be attributed to 定位文中第 4 句 And because of... 为本题题区，找出 what he's seen taught in business schools 指的是第 3 句提到的现在的课堂强调利益观念，便可断定选项 A 为本题答案。

命题规律6 特殊标点符号后的内容常考

特殊标点符号如：破折号、括号和冒号表示解释、说明；感叹号表示作者的情感、态度；引号表示应用某人的观点。由于这些特殊标点符号后的内容常是对前面内容的进一步解释和说明，因此命题者常对标点符号后的内容进行提问。

例6：Many Europeans may view the U. S. as an arrogant superpower that has become hostile to foreigners. But nothing makes people think more warmly of the U. S. than a weak dollar. Through April, the total number of visitors from abroad was up 6.8 percent from last year. Should the trend continue, the number of tourists this year will finally top the 2000 peak? Many Europeans now apparently view the U. S. the way many Americans view Mexico — as a cheap place to vacation, shop and party, all while ignoring the fact that the poorer locals

128

can't afford to join the merrymaking. (2008 年 1 月 CET - 6,
Passage 1)

题目：How do many Europeans feel about the U. S with the devalued
dollar?

A. They feel contemptuous of it

B. They are sympathetic with it.

C. They regard it as a superpower on the decline.

D. They think of it as a good tourist destination.

解析：本题考察的是欧洲人对美元贬值后的美国的看法，从而将
答案定位到上文第 4 句 Many Europeans now apparently view the
U. S. the way many Americans view Mexico—as a cheap place to va-
cation，shop and party...。该句中破折号后的短语是对前面句子的
说明，整句话的意思是现在很多欧洲人看待美国的方式就像美国人看
墨西哥一样——他们将美国当作一个廉价的地方，来这里度假、购物、
开派对。这说明欧洲人认为美国是他们的理想的旅游目的地，故选项
D 为答案。

命题规律 7　最高级及绝对性词汇常考

　　文章中若出现 first、must、all、only、anyone、always、never、none
等绝对性词汇或 most＋形容词(副词)＋est 等最高级词汇，或者 sole、
unique、simply、just 等表示唯一的词汇往往是考题要点，一般会出"细
节性问题"。这是因为它们都有一个共同的特征，那就是概念绝对、答
案唯一。无论是命题还是答题，答案不会产生歧义和疑问，很容易为
命题者所青睐。

例 7：Ask most people how they define the American Dream and
chances are they'll say, "Success. " The dream of individual opportunity has been home in American since Europeans discovered a "new world" in the Western Hemisphere. Early immigrants like Hector St. Jean de Crevecoeur praised highly the
freedom and opportunity to be found in this new land. His

glowing descriptions of a classless society where anyone could attain success through honesty and hard work fired the imaginations of many European readers:... (2005 年 12 月 CET - 6, Passage 1)

题目：What is the essence of the American Dream according to Crevecoeur?

    A. People are free to develop their power of imagination.

    B. People who are honest and work hard can succeed.

    C. People are free from exploitation and oppression.

    D. People can fully enjoy individual freedom.

    <u>解析</u>：本题考察的是 Crevecoeur 眼中美国梦的精华所在。根据题干的 Crevecoeur 将答案定位到上文第 4 句，其中定语从句中的 anyone 指的就是 people 的意思。选项 B 是对该定语从句的同义转述，即人人都能够通过诚实和辛勤工作获得成功。故 B 为答案。

命题规律 8　人物论断处常考

    作者为正确表达自己观点或使论点更有依据，常会引用某些权威人士的论断或采纳其重要发现等。命题者常在此处做文章。

例 8：Kids count more than their colleges. Getting into Yale may signify intelligence, talent and ambition. But it's not the only indicator and, paradoxically, its significance is declining. The reason: so many similar people go elsewhere. Getting into college is not life's only competition. In the next competition—the job market and graduate school—the results may change. Oldboy networks are breaking down. Princeton economist Alan Krueger studied admissions to one top Ph. D. program. High scores on the GRE helped explain who got in; degrees of prestigious universities didn't.

题目：What does Krueger's study tell us?

    A. Getting into Ph. D. programs may be more competitive than getting into college.

B. Degrees of prestigious universities do not guarantee entry to graduate programs.

C. Graduates from prestigious universities do not care much about their GRE scores.

D. Connections built in prestigious universities may be sustained long after graduation.

解析：根据题干中的 Krueger's 可将答案定位到上文最后两句。该句提到博士研究结果：能够有机会被顶级博士项目录取的是能够在 GRE 考试中有优异成绩的，而不是拥有名牌大学学位的人，这一结果进一步证明了作者前面提出的观点，即上大学不是人生的唯一竞争，能上名牌大学并不一定就代表在以后的人生路上处处优越于别人。故选项 B 为答案。

命题规律 9　复杂句常考

复杂句常是命题者出题之处，包括同位语、插入语、定语、长句、从句、不定式等，命题者主要考查考生对句子之间指代关系、文章段落之间关系的理解，常以逻辑推理题型出现，包括少量词汇等题型。解答这类阅读题时，考生一定要注意弄清复杂句的层次逻辑关系。

例 9：The new rich selfishly act on their own unfairly grab the wealth that the country as a whole has produced. The top 1 percent of the population now has wealth equal to the whole bottom 95 percent and they want more. Their selfishness is most shamelessly expressed in downsizing and outsourcing because these business maneuvers don't act to create new jobs as the founders of new industries used to do, but only to cut out jobs while keeping the money value of what those jobs produced for themselves. (2006 年 12 月 CET - 6, Passage 1)

题目：The immediate consequence of the new capitalists' practice is _____.

A. loss of corporate reputation

B. lower pay for the employees

C. a higher rate of unemployment

D. a decline in business transaction

解析：本题考察的是对上文最后一句话的理解。该句是个复合句：Their selfishness is most shamelessly expressed in downsizing and outsourcing because... don't act to..., but only to cut out...。从句中的 downsizing（裁员）、outsourcing(产品外包)、don't act to create new jobs 和 cut out jobs 词语可推断出现在的资本家做法的直接后果就是造成大批工人的失业。故选项 C 为答案。

命题规律10　段落或句群的概括常考

命题者有时要求考生对一个段落、句群进行概括和推断。这种题类似主旨题,解题时必须理解段落或句群中的所有句子才能做出正确的推断。

例10：LeDoux studies the way animals and humans respond to threats to understand how we form memories of significant events in our lives. The amygdala receives input from many parts of the brain, including regions responsible for retrieving memories. Using this information, the amygdala appraises a situation—I think this charging dog wants to bite me—and triggers a response by radiating nerve signals throughout the body. These signals produce the familiar signs of distress：trembling perspiration and fast-moving feet, just to name three. (2006 年 12 月 CET - 6, Passage 1)

题目：From the studies conducted by LeDoux we learn that _____.

A. reactions of humans and animals to dangerous situations are often unpredictable

B. memories of significant events enable people to control

fear and distress

C. people's unpleasant memories are derived from their feelings of fear

D. the amygdala plays a vital part in human and animal responses to potential danger

解析：上文首句提到，LeDoux 动物和人对潜在危险的反应方式，之后又主要指出扁桃核在危险反应机制中的作用。由此可推知，在人类和动物对潜在危险的反应过程中，扁桃核起了非常重要的作用。通过概括所有句子的大意，便可确定选项 D 为答案。

2. 主旨大意题的命题规律

主旨大意题旨在考查考生对文章中心思想或段落的主题的理解能力以及区别主要信息和次要信息的能力。所谓主旨，就是一篇文章或一个段落的核心，是作者写作意图的具体表现，其表现形式应题材和论证方式的不同而有所不同。这就要求考生具备总结、概括和归纳事物的能力。通常来说，文章的中心思想由主题句来体现，这些主题句常位于文章的开头或结尾。但六级阅读考试中有 70% 的文章是没有一个主题句概括，而是贯穿全文，或是用转折的方法提出作者的观点，这就要求考生一要善于综合每一段的信息来归纳主题思想；二要善于抓转折处，因为转折处通常表达作者真实的写作目的或基本观点。

根据问题内容的不同，这类问题可分为主题型、标题型和目的型。主题型顾名思义就是找文章中心（Main Idea）；标题型是为文章选择标题（Title）；目的型就是推断作者的写作意图（Purpose）。文章标题的选择其实就是主题的选择，所不同的是，主题或中心思想的选项一般以句子的形式表达，而标题的选项则以短语形式表达。从选项内容上判断，能够概括全文，内容全面，语气不绝对，符合常识、逻辑的选项一般是答案项，而那些内容片面、单一，概括过度，以偏概全，无关或对立选项是干扰项，应排除。推断作者的写作意图时，除了明白文章的主题外，要特别注意作者的用词和语气，弄清作者对主体的态度，看看作者是带有主观意愿地劝说(persuade),指示(instruct),建议(suggest)等,还是比较客观地呈示(show),说明(illustrate),讨论(discuss)等。

此外,熟悉文章的类型是快速准确确定文章主题的关键。一般说来,文章分为三类:第一类是开门见山型的文章,这种文章的主题和作者观点往往在第一段就有所交待;第二类是靶子型的文章。在靶子型的文章里,第一段里讲述的是一个现象或者一种观点,在第二段里,作者表达出自己的不同看法。所以,这种类型的文章在第二段中才能够看到文章的主题和作者的观点。第三种文章是并行的两条线索,比如说对比美国和日本两国的企业文化差异等,这种类型的文章,主题相对来说稍微难把握一点,因为可能每个段落都散布着主题的一个分支,如果幸运的话,考生也许在最后一段能够看到一个综述,否则的话,要想获得主题,还要将每一个段落的小主题做一个叠加才能够获得一个全面的文章主题。总之,判断文章类型,然后根据文章的类型判断主题会设在什么地方,有助于考生准确定位,快速答题。

常见的提问方式有:

(1) 直白型:

What's the main idea (central idea)?

What's the passage mainly about?

The passage focuses primarily on which of the following _____.

The major point of this passage is _____.

(2) 变相型:

What's the best title?

What's the author's writing purpose?

The primary purpose of the passage is to _____.

The author is primarily concerned with _____.

(3) 隐含型:

The first paragraph talks in detail about _____.

134

This passage gives a general description of _____.

一般来说，一篇文章的中心思想或某一段主题思想往往通过段首、段尾句表达出来。考生迅速找到了这些主题句，就能答题。

例1：Clothes play a critical part in the conclusions we reach by providing clues to who people are, who they are not, and who they would like to be. They tell us a good deal about the wearer's background, personality, status, mood, and social outlook.

Since clothes are such an important source of social information, we can use them to manipulate people's impression of us. Our appearance assumes particular significance in the initial phases of interaction that is likely to occur. An elderly middle-class man or woman may be alienated (疏远) by a young adult who is dressed in an unconventional manner, regardless of the person's education, background, or interests.

People tend to agree on what certain types of clothes mean. Adolescent girls can easily agree on the lifestyles of girls who wear certain outfits (套装), including the number of boyfriends they likely have had and whether they smoke or drink. Newscasters, or the announcers who read the news on TV, are considered to be more convincing, honest, and competent when they are dressed conservatively. And college students who view themselves as taking an active role in their interpersonal relationships say they are concerned about the costumes they must wear to play these roles successfully. Moreover, many of us can relate instances in which the clothing we wore changed the way we felt about ourselves and how we acted. Perhaps you have used clothing to gain confidence when you anticipated a stressful situation, such as a job interview, or a court appearance.

In the workplace, men have long had well-defined precedents

and role models for achieving success. It has been otherwise for women. A good many women in the business world are uncertain about the appropriate mixture of "masculine" and "feminine" attributes they should convey by their professional clothing. The variety of clothing alternatives to women has also been greater than that available for men. Male administrators tend to judge women more favorably for managerial positions when the women display less "feminine" grooming (打扮)—shorter hair, moderate use of make-up, and plain tailored clothing. As one male administrator confessed, "an attractive woman is definitely going to get a longer interview, but she won't get a job." (1997 年 6 月 CET - 6，Passage 2)

题目：What is the passage mainly about?

    A. Dressing for effect.

    B. How to dress appropriately.

    C. Managerial positions and clothing.

    D. Dressing for the occasion.

  解析：本文第 1 段第一句指出人们的穿着在我们判断一个人时起重要的作用，接着阐述我们可以利用着装影响别人对自己的印象以及人们对某些服饰的一致看法。所以，选项 A：穿着会给人某种印象，是本题答案。

命题规律 2　需归纳段落或全文的主题

    有一些文章没有段落主题句，它们的主题思想是隐含在句子与段落之中，这时就要求考生自己概括或归纳隐含的主题思想。解答这类题时，可以从归纳每段段落中心开始，最后将他们集中概括便是该文的中心思想。

例 2：If sustainable competitive advantage depends on work-force skills, American firms have a problem. Human-resource management is not traditionally seen as central to the competitive survival of the firm in the United States. Skill acquisition is considered an indi-

136

vidual responsibility. Labour is simply another factor of production to be hired—rented at the lowest possible cost—much as one buys raw materials or equipment.

The lack of importance attached to human-resource management can be seen in the corporation hierarchy. In an American firm the chief financial officer is almost always second in command. The post of head of human-resource management is usually a specialized job, off at the edge of the corporate hierarchy. The executive who holds it is never consulted on major strategic decisions and has no chance to move up to Chief Executive Officer (CEO). By way of contrast, in Japan the head of human-resource management is central—usually the second most important executive, after the CEO, in the firm's hierarchy.

While American firms often talk about the vast amounts spent on training their work forces, in fact they invest less in the skills of their employees than do either Japanese or German firms. The money they do invest is also more highly concentrated on professional and managerial employees. And the limited investments that are made in training workers are also much more narrowly focused on the specific skills necessary to do the next job rather than on the basic background skills that make it possible to absorb new technologies.

As a result, problems emerge when new breakthrough technologies arrive. If American workers, for example, take much longer to learn how to operate new flexible manufacturing stations than workers in Germany (as they do), the effective cost of those stations is lower in Germany than it is in the United States. More time is required before equipment is up and running at capacity, and the need for extensive retraining generates costs and creates bottlenecks that limit the speed with which new equipment can be employed. The re-

137

sult is a slower pace of technological change. And in the end the skills of the bottom half of the population affect the wages of the top half. If the bottom half can't effectively staff the processes that have to be operated, the management and professional jobs that go with these processes will disappear. （1997 年 6 月 CET - 6，Passage 2）

题目: What is the main idea of the passage?

    A. American firms are different from Japanese and German firms in human-resource management.

    B. Extensive retraining is indispensable to effective human-resource management.

    C. The head of human-resource management must be in the central position in a firm's hierarchy.

    D. The human-resource management strategies of American firms affect their competitive capacity.

解析:本文没有明确的主题句。作者在第 1 段指出,由于美国公司向来不重视人力资源,因此,如果公司想要在竞争保持持续的优势,而这一优势又取决于工人的技术水平,那么美国公司就会面临很大的问题。接着在第 2、3、4 段指出美国公司不重视人力资源部门,忽略了工人基本技术培训,其结果便是减慢了技术改造的速度,而这些势必影响美国公司的竞争力。由此可概括出本文的中心思想是:美国公司的人力资源管理策略影响公司的竞争力。故选项 D 为答案。

命题规律3　注意文章中出现频率较高的词

    有时一篇文章中出现频率较高的词,它们常常是蕴含中心思想的关键词,也可能是文章标题的一部分。命题者常出的题目要么是针对中心思想,要么是针对标题。

例3: There are some earth phenomena you can count on, but the magnetic field, some say, is not one of them. It fluctuates in strength, drifts from its axis, and every few 100,000, years undergoes a dramatic **polarity reversal**—a period when north pole becomes south pole and south pole becomes north pole. But how is the field generated, and why is it so unstable?

Groundbreaking research by two French geophysicists promises to shed some light on the mystery. Using 80 meters of deep sea sediment (沉淀物) core, they have obtained measurements of magnetic-field intensity that span 11 **polarity reversals** and four million years. The analysis reveals that intensity appears to fluctuate with a clear, well-defined rhythm. Although the strength of the magnetic field varies irregularly during the short terra, there seems to be an inevitable long-term decline preceding each polarity reversal. When the poles flip—a process that takes several hundred thousand years—the magnetic field rapidly regains its strength and the cycle is repeated.

The results have caused a stir among geophysicists. The magnetic field is thought to originate from molten (熔化的) iron in the outer core, 3,000 kilometers beneath the earth's surface. By studying mineral grains found in material ranging from rocks to clay articles, previous researchers have already been able to identify **reversals** dating back 170 million years, including the most recent switch 730,000 years ago. How and why they occur, however, has been widely debated. Several theories link polarity flips to external disasters such as meteor (陨星) impacts. But Peter Olson, a geophysicist at the Johns Hopkins University in Baltimore, says this is unlikely if the French researchers are right. In fact, Olson says intensity that predictably declines from one **reversal** to the next contradicts 90 percent of the models currently under study. If the results prove to be valid, geophysicists will have a new theory to guide them in their quest to understand the earth's inner physics. It certainly points the direction for future research. (1999 年 1 月 CET - 6, Passage 2)

题目: Which of the following titles is most appropriate to the passage?

A. Polarity Reversal: A Fantastic Phenomenon of Nature.

B. Measurement of the Earth's Magnetic-Field Intensity.

C. Formation of the Two Poles of the Earth.

D. A New Approach to the Study of Geophysics.

解析：题目问的是这篇文章最合适的标题是什么。浏览文章可以发现一些方面的词不断出现，尤其是 polarity reversals 差不多在每段都有提及，故选项 A 为答案，而 B、C、D 只是涉及细节。

命题规律4　语义转折处常考

命题者常在语义转折处，尤其是段首语义转折处设题。语义转折处常以 but，however，though 等词引导句子，表达作者真实的写作目的或基本观点。

例 4: It used to be that people were proud to work for the same company for the whole of their working lives. They'd get a gold watch at the end of their productive years and a dinner featuring speeches by their bosses praising their loyalty. **But** today's rich capitalists have regressed（倒退）to the "survival of the fittest" ideas and their loyalty extends not to their workers or even to their stockholders but only to themselves. Instead of giving out gold watches worth a hundred or so dollars for forty or so years of work, they grab tens and even hundreds of millions of dollars as they sell for their own profit the company they may have been with for only a few years.

...

The middle class used to be loyal to the free enterprise system. In the past, the people of the middle class mostly thought they'd be rich themselves someday or have a good shot at becoming rich. **But** nowadays income is being distributed more and more unevenly and corporate loyalty is a thing of the past. The middle class may also wake up to forget its loyalty to the so-called free enterprise system altogether and the government which governs only the rest of us while letting the corporations do what they please with our jobs. As things stand, if somebody doesn't wake up, the middle class is on a path to being downsized all the way to the bottom of society. (2006 年 12 月 CET - 6，Passage 2)

题目：What is the author's purpose in writing this passage?

  A. To call on the middle class to remain loyal to the free enterprise system.

  B. To warn the government of the shrinking of the American middle class.

  C. To persuade the government to change its current economic policies.

  D. To urge the middle class to wake up and protect their own interests.

 &boxed;**解析**：文章首尾两段都出现 But 引出作者观点的句子。作者在首段指出现在的资本家和过去的不一样，不值得中产阶级对其效忠一生，尾段有呼吁广大中产阶级尽快觉醒，学会保护自己的利益。故选项 D 最能体现作者的写作意图。

  3. 态度和语气题的命题规律

  态度和语气（Attitude/Tone）是反映作者对所叙述的事件的观点、态度和情绪。通过阅读理解作者是赞成还是反对，是欣赏还是厌恶，是讽刺幽默还是直陈意思，是更深层的阅读理解。

  通常，语篇的 Tone 会在文章的措词、文体和结构中反映出来。解题时，在通读全文，把握了主题思想和主要事实后，还必须注意以下几个方面：

  （1）从文体和内容区分主观情感和客观事态（Subject and Object）

  议论文中，文章的中心句一般都表明了作者的态度，当然在表明作者的态度时，往往会涉及到其他人的或群体的观点，所以需要仔细区分。说明文中，因其体裁客观，所以作者的态度中立。

例 1： Lichens are a group of, flowerless plants growing on rocks and trees. There are thousands of kinds of lichens, which come in a wide variety of colors. They are composed of algae and fungi which unite to satisfy the needs of the lichens.

题目： The tone of the passage can best described as (is)_____.

A. subjective   B. objective

C. positive   D. negative

解析：这是篇说明文，旨在传达信息，大意是地衣是一种生长于岩石与树木上无花的植物，地衣有数千种，颜色千变万化。它们由水藻和真菌组成，共同满足地衣的需求。文章措辞具体、肯定，没有夹杂个人感情，完全从客观事实出发，介绍有关地衣的情况。故选项 B 为答案。

例 2： Christmas is supposed to be a time to express our love and good will towards others, It is supposed to be a time when we perform acts of kindness for people less unfortunate than ourselves. Bud do we think of other people when we sit down to our Christmas dinner? Of course not. We're too busy eating those delicious foods associated with Christmas. We are to busy wondering whether the presents we gave were as nice as or better than the ones we received. We forget to think of the sick and the homeless. The whole idea of Christmas now is completely unchristian. . .

题目： The author's attitude towards the celebration of Christmas might be summarized as one of _____.

A. approving   B. disapproving

C. positive   D. indifferent

解析：这是篇议论文。文中运用许多反映主观情感的词语，如 is supposed to be，but，of course not，too busy eating，completely un-

142

christian 等。这些词反映了作者对如今人们过圣诞节的看法。他认为圣诞节应是表示对他人的爱心和美好祝愿的时候,可是,人们在自己尽情享乐时,却忘记了这一切,整个节日已毫无基督性质可言。所以,他反对圣诞节。故选项是 B 为答案。

(2) 分析文章的表现手法和语言特点

在有些文章中,作者会用轻松、幽默的语言来描述严肃的事,或选用特定的词语来暗示自己对其中某一具体问题所持的态度和观点,这需要考生从语篇的字里行间(read between the line)去捕捉、推断。考生要特别注意文章中的衔接词(如 but,however,on the contrary 等),特殊句式如虚拟语气中的措词以及形容词、副词、情态动词等,这些词往往能体现作者的观点态度。

例 3: Sam and Joe were astronauts. There was once a very dangerous trip and the more experienced astronauts knew there was only a small chance of coming back alive. Sam and Joe, however, thought it would be exciting though a little dangerous. "We're the best men for the job." They said to the boss. "There may be problems, but we can find the answers. "They're the last people I'd trust," thought the boss. But all the other astronauts have refused to go.

Once they were in space. Joe had to go outside to make some repairs. When the repairs were done, he tried to go back inside the spaceship. But the door was locked. He knocked but there was no answer. He knocked again, louder this time, and again no answer came. Then he hit the door as hard as he could and finally a voice said, "Who's there?" "It's me! Who else could it be?" shouted Joe, Sam let him in all right, but you can imagine that Joe never asked to go on a trip with Sam again!

题目: The overall tone of the story is _____.

    A. serious   B. humorous

    C. a matter-of-fact   D. argumentative

解析：这是篇幽默文章，首先我们知道太空实验是一种十分严肃的事，可老板却派两个他认为最不合适的人去做(They are the last people I'd trust, thought the boss)；还有，在如此讲究高度科学态度的场合，竟出现 Joe 多次敲门而 Sam 不应声的情况。其次，我们知道在浩瀚的太空中，除了 Joe 和 Sam 外，四周空旷无人，所以当读者读到，敲门时，Sam 的问话"Who is there?"以及 Joe 的回答"It's me! Who else could it be there"时，不禁哑然失笑。故选项 B 是正确答案。

(3)考生应分清并熟悉选项中的褒义词、贬义词和中性词。

常见的褒义的词有：positive 赞成的，supporting 支持的，approving 赞许的，optimistic 乐观的，admiring 羡慕的，humorous 幽默的，serious 严肃的，enthusiastic 热情的，pleasant 愉快的，concerned 关切的；somber 冷静的，enthusiastic 热情的，sympathetic 同情的，advisable 明智的，objective 客观的，insightful 有洞察力的。

常见的贬义的词有：apprehensive 忧虑的，arbitrary 武断的，biased 有偏见的，偏心的，disgusted 感到恶心的，厌恶的，gloomy 沮丧的，忧愁的，critical 批评的，negative 否定的，subjective 主观的，反对的，suspicious 怀疑的，tolerant 容忍的，忍让的，pessimistic 悲观的，depressed 沮丧的，disappointed 失望的，ironic 讽刺的，sarcastic 挖苦的，bitter 痛苦的，cynical 玩世不恭的，sentimental 感伤的，radical 激进的，极端的，reserved 有保留的，寡言的，内向的，scared 惊恐的，恐慌的，indignant 愤慨的，superficial 肤浅的。

常见的中性的词有：indifferent 冷淡的，不关心的，impassive 冷淡的，不动感情的，ambivalent 情绪矛盾，neutral 中立的，impersonal 不带个人感情的，informative 提供信息的，impartial 不偏袒的，折衷的，apathetic 漠不关心的，matter-of-fact 就事论事的，straightforward 率直的等。

观点态度题提问方式有：

The author's attitude towards... is _____.

144

In the author's opinion, _____.

The author thinks（believes，suggests，argues，deems）that _____.

The author's attitude towards... might be summarized as one of _____.

The tone of the passage can best described as（is）_____.

命题规律 1　作者提出观点处常考

例 1：When I think about all the problems of our overpopulated world and look at our boy grabbing at the lamp by the sofa，I wish I could have turned to Planned Grandparenthood when my parents were putting the grandchild squeeze on me.

If I could have，I might not be in this parenthood predicament （窘境）. But here's the crazy irony，I don't want my child-free life back. Dylan's too much fun.

题目：What does the author really of the idea of having children?

A. It does more harm than good.

B. It contributes to overpopulation.

C. It is troublesome but rewarding.

D. It is a psychological catastrophe

解析：乍一看,作者对要孩子的看法是否定的：I wish I could have...，但是,文章的最后两句作者用转折语气说出了与上文相矛盾的观点,即,"具有讽刺意味的是,我再也不想回到没有孩子的日子",原因是给她带来很多快乐。故只有选项 C 能概括出作者的两面看法。

命题规律 2　文中提及的某人或某个群体的观点常考

例 2：Unfortuately，few of us have much experience dealing with the threat of terrorism，so it's been difficult to get facts about how we should respond. That's why Hallwell believes it was okay for people to indulge some extreme worries last fall by asking doctors for Cipro(抗炭疽菌的药物) and buying gas mask.

题目：In Hallow's view, people's reaction to the terrorist threat last fall was _____.

A. ridiculous   B. understandable

C. over-cautious   D. sensible

解析：作者在上文中提到，我们中间很少有人有过被恐怖主义威胁的经历，所以很难收集到我们应该如何应对这种情况的资料。由此推断，it was okay for people to indulge some extreme worries last fall 说的是人们去年秋天对恐怖主义威胁的反应是"可以理解的"。故选项 B 为答案。

例3：Nowadays, it is commonly observed that young women are not conforming to the feminine linguistic (语言的) ideal. They are using fewer of the very deferential "women's" forms, and even using the few strong forms that are know as "men's." This, of course, attracts considerable attention and has led to an outcry in the Japanese media against the defeminization of women's language. Indeed, we didn't hear about "men's language" until people began to respond to girls' appropriation of forms normally reserved for boys and men. There is considerable sentiment about the "corruption" of women's language—which of course is viewed as part of the loss of feminine ideals and morality—and this sentiment is crystallized by nationwide opinion polls that are regularly carried out by the media. (2005 年 12 月 CET - 6，Passage 2)

题目：How do some people react to women's appropriation of men's language forms as reported in the Japanese media?

A. They call for a campaign to stop the defeminization.

B. The see it as an expression of women's sentiment.

C. They accept it as a modern trend.

D. They express strong disapproval.

146

解析：本段第 3 句（这引起了人们相当大的关注，也导致日本媒体强烈反对女性语言非女性化的现象）及最后一句（对于女性语言"腐化"现象很伤感……）表明了媒体的反对呼声及进行模拟以测验表现出的伤感。由此可推知，人们持强烈的反对意见，故选项 D 为答案。

命题规律3 在篇章层面上设题

例4： The more women and minorities make their way into the ranks of management, the more they seem to want to talk about things formerly judged to be best left unsaid. The newcomers also tend to see office matters with a fresh eye, in the process sometimes coming up with critical analyses of the forces that shape everyone's experience in the organization.

Consider the novel views of Harvey Coleman of Atlanta on the subject of getting ahead. Coleman is black. He spent 11 years with IBM, half of them working in management development, and now serves as a consultant to the likes of AT&T, Coca-Cola, Prudential, and Merch. Coleman says that based on what he's seen at big companies, he weighs the different elements that make for long-term career success as follows: performance counts a mere 10%; image, 30%; and exposure, a full 60%. Coleman concludes that excellent job performance is so common these days that while doing your work well may win you pay increases, it won't secure you the big promotion. He finds that advancement more often depends on how many people know you and your work, and how high up they are.

Ridiculous beliefs? Not to many people, especially many women and members of minority races who, like Coleman, feel that the scales (障眼物) have dropped from their eyes. "Women and blacks in organizations work under false beliefs," says Kaleel Jamison, a New York-based management consultant who helps corporations deal with these issues. "They think that if you work hard, you'll get ahead—

147

that someone in authority will reach down and give you a promotion." She adds, "Most women and blacks are so frightened that people will think they've gotten ahead because of their sex or color that they play down (使……不突出) their visibility." Her advice to those folks: learn the ways that white males have traditionally used to find their way into the spotlight. (2002 年 12 月 CET - 6，Passage 2)

题目： The author is of the opinion that Coleman's beliefs are _____.

    A. biased   B. popular   C. insightful   D. superficial

解析：这道观点题是设在篇章层面上的，考生只有通读本文后，弄清科尔曼的观点，才能推断出作者对科尔曼观点的看法。首先，作者在介绍科尔曼观点时用了 the novel views of 的字眼，novel 是褒义词，"新颖的"的意思；在第 3 段开时，作者肯定了科尔曼的观点不荒唐，而且许多人听到科尔曼的观点后，突然眼睛一亮（the scales have dropped from their eyes），弄清了多年来未明白的问题。这些都说明了科尔曼的观点不仅正确，而且是把问题分析透彻的，因而是有洞察力的。故选项 C 为答案。

4. 词义理解题命题规律

词义理解题主要是测试考生根据上下文判断生词或新短语意义的能力。解此类题时，考生需注意以下两点：一是要结合上下文与字里行间的线索，辨明句与句之间的内在关系，如因果关系，解释关系，对比关系，呼应关系等，后再确定词义；二是要注意新词或短语的引申意义。有些词或短语考生也许见过或认识，但这些词或短语在新的背景或上下中可能与原意不同或者有进一步的引申。这就需要考生具有一定的判断能力才能确定一个词或短语的确切含义。

词汇题的提问方式有：

The word "…" most probably means _____.

The statement "…" probably means _____.

The word "…" stands for "_____".

By saying that "...", the author means _____.

The expression... stands for _____.

The author uses the phrase "..." to illustrate _____.

What does the author probably mean by "..." in... paragraph?

命题规律 1 测意指代题

这类题型一般用双引号标出需考生理解部分。标出部分一般有两种内容：一种属于超纲词汇的推理；另外一种属于大纲词汇的理解，尤其考查一些需要考生通过阅读文章来进行理解的一些简单的一词多意词。解题时，考生应先对于该词、词组或者分句所在句子进行理解，如果无法得出结果，到前句寻找答案。

例 1： In department stores and closets all over the world, they are waiting. Their outward appearance seems rather appealing because they come in a variety of styles, textures, and colors. But they are ultimately the biggest deception that exists in the fashion industry today. What are they? They are high heels—a woman's worst enemy (whether she knows it or not). High heel shoes are the downfall of modern society. Fashion myths have led women to believe that they are more beautiful or sophisticated for wearing heels, but in reality, heels succeed in posing short as well as long term hardships. Women should fight the high heel industry by refusing to use or purchase them in order to save the world from unnecessary physical and psychological suffering.

For the sake of fairness, it must be noted that there is a positive side to high heels. First, heels are excellent for aerating (使通气) lawns. Anyone who has ever worn heels on grass knows what I am talking about. A simple trip around the yard in a pair of **those babies** eliminates all need to call for a lawn care specialist, and provides the perfect-sized holes to give any lawn oxygen without all those messy chunks of dirt lying around. Second, heels are quite functional for defense against oncoming enemies, who can easily be scared away by threatening them with a pair of these sharp, deadly fashion accessories. (2001 年 1 月 CET - 6, Passage 2)

题目: The author uses the expression "those babies" (Line 3, Para. 2) to refer to high heels _____.

    A. to show their fragile characteristics

    B. to indicate their feminine features

    C. to show women's affection for them

    D. to emphasize their small size

   |解析|:本题考查考生对 those babies 含义的理解。题干明确指出 those babies 是 high heels,那么,作者为何要用 baby 呢? 在文章的第 1 段,作者提到 high heels 时用了 rather appealing(颇具吸引力),女人们都相信穿高跟鞋能使她们更漂亮,妻子更优雅,由此可看出女人对高跟鞋的钟爱,再者 baby 一词也包含怜爱的成分,所以作者用 those babies 是说明女人对高跟鞋的钟爱。故选项 C 为答案。

|命题规律 2| 具有指代上下文意义功能的词(照应名词)常考

    常见的照应名词有:approach, belief, classification, doctrine, evaluation, evidence, insight, investigation, illusion, notion, opinion, position, supposition, theory, viewpoint 以及某类人的名词等等。

例 2: The critical point here is causality. The alarmists say they have proved that violent media cause aggression. But the assumptions behind their observations need to be examined. When labeling games as violent or non-violent, should a hero eating a ghost really be counted as a violent event? And when experimenters record the time it takes game players to read "aggressive" or "non-aggressive" words from a list, can we be sure what they are actually measuring? The intent of the new Harvard Center on Media and Child Health to collect and standardize studies of media violence in order to compare their methodologies, assumptions and conclusions is an important step in the right direction.（2006 年 6 月 CET - 6，Passage 1）

题目：The author uses the term "alarmists"(Line 1, Para. 5) to refer to those who _____.

    A. use standardized measurements in the studies of media violence

    B. initiated the debate over the influence of violent media on reality

    C. assert a direct link between violent media and aggressive behavior

    D. use appropriate methodology in examining aggressive behavior

  解析：本段第 2 句提到 alarmists 已经证实 violent media cause aggression，说明 alarmists 认为媒体暴力和现实的暴力有直接联系，故选项 C 为答案。

命题规律3　一词多义处常考

例3：Studies of birds may offer unique insights into sleep. Jerome M. Siegel of the UCLA says he wonders if birds' half brain sleep "is just the tip of the iceberg（冰山）" He speculates that more examples may turn up when we take a closer look at other species.（2001 年 1 月 CET - 6，Passage 1）

题目：By "just the tip of the iceberg"(Line 2, Para. 8), Siegel suggests that _____.

    A. half brain sleep has something to do with icy weather

    B. the mystery of half brain sleep is close to being solved

    C. most birds living in cold regions tend to be half sleepers

    D. half brain sleep is a phenomenon that could exist among other species

解析：the tip of iceberg 字面上是"冰山一角"的意思，但这里指的是它的引申义，必须通过对上下文的理解才能确定其确切含义。根据 just the tip of iceberg 的上下文：Studies of birds may offer unique insights into sleep... He (Siegel) speculates that more examples may turn up when we take closer look at other species. （对鸟类的研究可能提供对睡眠的独特认识。……他推测当我们对其他物种仔细观察时，就会发现更多的例证。）说明 half brain sleep 不仅仅存在于鸟类中，也可能存在于其他物种。因此选项 D 符合段落意思，是本题答案。

命题规律 4　复杂句常考

　　复杂句包括同位语、插入语、定语、长句、从句、不定式等，命题者主要考查考生对句子之间的指代关系和文章段落内容的理解等等。解答这类阅读题时，考生一定要注意弄清复杂句的层次逻辑关系。

例 4：The question of whether war is inevitable is one which has concerned many of the world's great writers. Before considering this question, it will be useful to introduce some related concepts. Conflict, defined as opposition among social entities directed against one another, is distinguished from competition, defined as opposition among social entities independently striving for something which is in inadequate supply. Competitors may not be aware of one another, while the parties to a conflict are. Conflict and competition are both categories of opposition, which has been defined as a process by which social entities function in the disservice of one another. Opposition is thus contrasted with cooperation, the process by which social entities function in the service of one another. These definitions are necessary because it is important to emphasize that competition between individuals or groups is inevitable in a world of limited resources, but conflict is not. Conflict, nevertheless, is very likely to occur, and is probably an essential and desirable element of human societies. (1996 年 6 月 CET - 6, Passage 3)

题目：The phrase "function in the disservice of one another" (Line 11, Para. 1) most probably means _____.

A. betray each other

B. harm one another

C. help to collaborate with each other

D. benefit one another

解析：词组 function in the disservice of one another 所在的句子是一个复合句，其中 which 引出定语从句修饰前面的 opposition，而 by which 引出的定语从句修饰前面的 process，而且这个句子的上下句也都是复合句。理解这个词组关键在于理解上下文的逻辑关系。这个词组的上文指出"战争和竞争属于对抗的不同类别，对抗定义为……"；下文则说"因此对抗与合作形成对比，合作是社会实体相互服务的过程"。由此可推知，本题所考的这一词组与下文的 function in the service of one another 相反，是对比关系。再者，根据构词法，前缀 dis-表示"否定"之意，而 service 的意义则是"服务、帮助"，因此可推出 disservice 是 service 的反义词。故选项 B 为答案。

第三节　选项的设置
规律与选择方法

许多考生在做阅读理解部分时，最大感受就是时间紧、答案选项迷惑性大，因而很难及时而又准确地选出答案。通过研究历年六级阅读理解题，我们发现，在所设置的正确选项和干扰选项中，也有一些普遍性规律可循。如果考生了解、熟悉并掌握了这些规律，他（她）们就可以找到做题时的"第六感觉"，达到超常发挥的水平。

1. 正确选项的特征及设置规律

正确选项的特征：1)符合主题。很多正确选项都是和主题直接或间接相关,所以只要把握好文章的主题,不要进行主观推断或臆断,就能确定正确答案项。2)原文改写。六级当中的正确答案很多时候是原文当中一小段内容的改写,重点是表达改变,实词有所替换。3)选项语气较辨证,不太绝对。如选项中含有 probably, possibly, might, maybe, more or less, relatively, be likely to, not necessarily 语气不十分肯定的词。

设置规律 1　同意替换。

正确选项对原文内容进行了大幅度的改写,即使采用了原文的部分词句,其关键词也一定会换用其他的表达形式,也就是说照抄原文不是答案。最常见的原文改写的方法:一是词性变换,同义词、同义词组的替换,这些变化往往体现了选项文字与原文文字之间的精确对应;二是句式和表达法的转换。

例1: In other words, if middle-class Americans continue to struggle financially as the ultrawealthy grow ever wealthier, it will be increasingly difficult to maintain political support for the free flow of goods, services, and capital across borders. And when the United States places obstacles in the way of foreign investors and foreign goods, it's likely to encourage reciprocal action abroad. For people who buy and sell companies, or who allocate capital to markets all around the world, that's the real nightmare. (2007 年 12 月 CET - 6, Passage 2)

题目: What may happen if the United States places obstacles in the way of foreign investors and foreign goods?

A. The prices of imported goods will inevitably soar beyond control.

B. The investors will have to make great efforts to re-allocate capital.

C. The wealthy will attempt to buy foreign companies across borders.

D. Foreign countries will place the same economic barriers in return.

解析：根据题干中 United States places obstacles 将答案定位在上文第二句 And when the United States places obstacles..., it's likely to encourage reciprocal action abroad. 选项 D 中的 in return 是对上文第二句中的 reciprocal 的同意改写,故选项 D 为答案。

设置规律 2　概括或归纳

正确选项是对原文内容的概括或归纳,即具有概括性、抽象性的选项多半是答案,而具体的则不是答案。

例 2: Part of its mission would be to promote the risks and realities associated with being a grandparent. The staff would include depressed grandparents who would explain how grandkids break lamps, bite, scream and kick. Others would detail how an hour of baby-sitting often turns into a crying marathon. More grandparents would testify that they had to pay for their grandchild's expensive college education. (2005 年 12 月 CET - 6, Passage 1)

题目: Planned Grandparenthood would include depressed grandparents on its staff in order to _____.

A. show them the joys of life grandparents may have in raising grandchildren

B. draw attention to the troubles and difficulties grandchildren may cause

C. share their experience in raising grandchildren in a more scientific way

D. help raise funds to cover the high expense of education for grandchildren

解析：根据题干中 depressed grandparents 将答案定位在上文第二句。本段主题句指出,该组织的一部分任务是要让更多的父母知道作为祖父母的风险和现实,第二句是对主题句的具体论述,由此归纳

155

得出 B 项符合题意,故选项 B 为答案。

设置规律 3 　倒着考或反着考

倒着考,即将文章中的某句话倒过来考。命题模式:文章中 A 导致 B;问题:有 B 这一结果,为何? 答案:因为 A。反着考,即将文章中的某句话反过来考。其命题模式:文章中 A 具有 X 属性,B 与 A 不同;问题:B 有何属性? 答案:非 X 属性。

例3: The weak dollar is a source of humiliation(屈辱),for a nation's self-esteem rests in part on the strength of its currency. It's also a potential economic problem, since a declining dollar makes imported food more expensive and exerts upward pressure on interest rates. And yet there are substantial sectors of the vast U. S. economy-from giant companies like Coca-Cola to mom-and-pop restaurant operators in Miami-for which the weak dollar is most excellent news. (2008 年 6 月 CET - 6,Passage 1)

题目: Why do Americans feel humiliated?

　　A. Their economy is plunging.

　　B. Their currency has slumped.

　　C. They can't afford trips to Europe.

　　D. They have lost half of their assets.

解析:本题考察的是美国人觉得丢脸的原因。根据题干中 humiliation,将答案定位在上文第一句:疲软的美元使美国人感到丢脸……故选项 B 为答案。

例4: Ask most people how they define the American Dream and chances are they'll say, "Success." The dream of individual opportunity has been home in American since Europeans discovered a "new world" in the Western Hemisphere. Early immigrants like Hector St. Jean de Crevecoeur praised highly the freedom and opportunity to be found in this new land. His glowing descriptions of a classless society where anyone could attain success through honesty and hard work fired the imaginations of many European readers: in Letters from an American Farmer (1782) he wrote, "We are all excited at the spirit of an industry which is unfettered（无拘无束的）and unrestrained, because each person works for himself... We have no princes, for whom we toil（干苦力活）, starve, and bleed: we are the most perfect society now existing in the world." The promise of a land where "the rewards of a man's industry follow with equal steps the progress of his labor" drew poor immigrants from Europe and fueled national expansion into the western territories.

（2005 年 12 月 CET - 6，Passage 2）

题目：By saying "the rewards of a man's industry follow with equal steps the progress of his labor" (Line 10, Para. 1), the author means _____.

A. the more diligent one is, the bigger his returns

B. laborious work ensures the growth of an industry

C. a man's business should be developed step by step

D. a company's success depends on its employees' hard work

解析：题干问 the rewards of a man's industry follow with equal steps the progress of his labor 这句话的意义。答案出处在本段末句，此句前后都讲了新大陆是平等自由的，人们依靠努力和诚实劳动获得成功。此句是对这些观点的陈述，一个人的获得是与他的劳动成正比，反过来就是说如果一个人越勤奋，得到的回报就越多。故选项 A 为答案。

设置规律4 关键词

例 5：By day, Bille's contact lenses will focus rays of light so accurately on the retina（视网膜）that the image of a small leaf or the outline of a far distant tree will be formed with a sharpness that surpasses that of conventional vision aids by almost half a *diopter* (屈光度). At night, the lenses have an even greater potential. "Because the new lens— in contrast to the already existing ones—also works when it's dark and the pupil is wide open," says Bille, "lens wearers will be able to identify a face at a distance of 100 meters"—80 meters farther than they would normally be able to see. In his experiments night vision was enhanced by an even greater factor: in semi-darkness, test subjects could see up to 15 times better than without the lenses.

(2003 年 6 月 CET‐6，Passage 4)

题目：According to Bille, with the new lenses the wearer's vision _____.

A. will be far better at night than in the daytime

B. may be broadened about 15 times than without them

C. can be better improved in the daytime than at night

D. will be sharper by a much greater degree at night than in the daytime

解析：上文最后一句对比了新的眼镜对人在白天和夜间视力的影响。四个选项都围绕答案所在句的关键词 enhanced 设问。选项 A 混淆了原文的对比点，错误理解了该句的意思；选项 B 是断章取义，忽略了该句事实上讲的只是在半黑暗的状态下，夜间视力清晰度提高这一点；选项 C 内容与原文相矛盾，故选项 A 为答案。

2. 干扰选项的特征与设置规律

干扰选项的特征：1)无中生有。选项内容本身而言并没有错误，但是和文章内容并无关系；2)混淆本末，主次不分。虽然以文章提供的事实或内在逻辑为基础进行推理，但推理过头、概括过度；3) 直接、间接不分。把文章中明确表达当成推理出来的；4) 因果颠倒。原文的原因变成了选项中的结果，或反之；5) 手段与目的颠倒。原文的手段变成了选项中的目的，或反之；6)和常识一致，却和原文中科学论述

158

相悖;7)选项意义较具体、肤浅;8)语气极端、过于绝对。如项中含有 must, always never, the most, all, merely, only, have to, any, completely, none 等绝对语气词。

设置规律 1 答非所问

选项中有提及相关内容,但逻辑关系不对。

例 1: It's hardly news that the immigration system is a mess. Foreign nationals have long been slipping across the border with fake papers, and visitors who arrive in the U. S. legitimately often overstay their legal welcome without being punished. But since Sept. 11, it's become clear that terrorists have been shrewdly factoring the weaknesses of our system into their plans. In addition to the their mastery of forging passports, at least three of the 19 Sept. 11 hijackers(劫机者)were here on expired visas. That's been a safe bet until now. The Immigration and Naturalization Service(INS)(移民归化局)lacks the resources, and apparently the inclination, to keep track of the estimated 2 million foreigners who have intentionally overstayed their welcome.

But this laxness(马虎) toward immigration fraud may be about to change. Congress has already taken some modest steps. The U. S. A. Patriot Act, passed in the wake of the Sept. 11 tragedy, requires the FBI, the Justice Department, the State Department and the INS to share more data, which will make it easier to stop watchlisted terrorists at the border (2004 年 6 月 CET - 6, Passage 2)

题目: Terrorists have obviously taken advantage of _____.

A. the legal privileges granted to foreigners

B. the excessive hospitality of the American people

C. the irresponsibility of the officials at border checkpoints

D. the low efficiency of the Immigration and Naturalization Service

159

解析：文章中没有涉及到选项 A 和 B 的内容，可直接排除。文章提到了美国要加强边境安全以防恐怖分子的袭击，但是没有指出恐怖分子是利用边境检查官的不负责任而混入美国的，这不符合原文逻辑，所以选项 C 是错误的。而文章首段指出恐怖分子一直在精心利用移民体系的弱点，接着提到移民规划局(INS)的机构状况：既缺乏人力物力，同时也不愿意去追踪大约 200 万故意超过居留期的外国人（其中就有恐怖分子）。综上可知，恐怖分子是利用 INS 办事不力的弱点。故选项 D 为答案。

设置规律 2　曲解题意、偷换概念

选项对原文断章取义或歪曲、偷换原文某些词的意思。

例 2： It's possible that plutocrats(有钱有势的人) are expressing solidarity with the struggling middle class as part of an effort to insulate themselves from confiscatory (没收性的) tax policies. But the prospect that income inequality will lead to higher taxes on the wealthy doesn't keep plutocrats up at night. They can live with that.

No，what they fear was that the political challenges of sustaining support for global economic integration will be more difficult in the United States because of what has happened to the distribution of income and economic insecurity. (2007 年 12 月 CET‐6，Passage 2)

题目： What is the real reason for plutocrats to express solidarity with the middle class?

　　A. They want to protect themselves from confiscatory taxation.

　　B. They know that the middle class contributes most to society.

　　C. They want to gain support for global economic integration.

　　D. They feel increasingly threatened by economic insecurity

解析：上文首段指出这些有钱有势的人表达……的愿望，可能是他们希望免遭没收性税收政策控制的一种努力。但是，紧接着作者用But 否定这一推测，尤其最后一句指出这些有钱有势的人对没收性税收政策是可以忍受的(They can live with that.),上文末段指出他们真正关心的是从全球经济一体化中可以获得的收入分配。因此,选项A显然曲解首段段意,不是答案项;选项B的内容,文中没有提到,可直接排除;选项D属偷换概念,因为他们害怕的是政治上的困难会影响它们的分配和经济安全,而不是害怕 economic insecurity 的威胁,故选项C为答案。

设置规律3 表述肤浅

选项给出的是某关键词的字面意义,表达意义较具体、肤浅。

例3: The cult (推崇) of lecturing dully, like the cult of writing dully, goes back, of course, some years. Edward Shils, professor of sociology, recalls the professors he encountered at the University of Pennsylvania in his youth. They seemed "a priesthood, rather uneven in their merits but uniform in their bearing; they never referred to anything personal. Some read from old lecture notes and then haltingly explained the thumb-worn last lines. Others lectured from cards that had served for years, to judge by the worn edges... The teachers began on time, ended on time, and left the room without saying a word more to their students, very seldom being detained by questioners... The classes were not large, yet there was no discussion. No questions were raised in class, and there were no office hours." (2003 年 6 月 CET - 6, Passage 1)

题目: By saying "They seemed a priesthood, rather uneven in their merits but uniform in their bearing..." (Lines 3-4, Para. 4), the author means that _____.

A. professors are a group of professionals that differ in their academic ability but behave in the same way

B. professors are like priests wearing the same kind of black gown but having different roles to play

C. there is no fundamental difference between professors and priests though they differ in their merits

D. professors at the University of Pennsylvania used to wear black suits which made them look like priests

解析:本题考查的是对"They seemed a priesthood, rather uneven in their merits but uniform in their bearing..."这句话的理解。选项 A、B、C 都含有 priest 一词,都是对句中关键词 priesthood 进行了字面理解,旨在干扰考生的理解。其实理解本句的关键是要弄清 they 和 their 在句中指的是 professors 而不是 priesthood,整句话的意思是:他们看起来像一个牧师,尽管才能各有千秋,但穿着非常统一……,故选项 A 为答案。

设置规律 4 缺乏原文依据或与原文相矛盾

选项与常识相符,但文中并没有提到或意思与原句内容相反。

例 4: When we worry about who might be spying on our private lives, we usually think about the Federal agents. But the private sector outdoes the government every time. It's Linda Tripp, not the FBI, who is facing charges under Maryland's laws against secret telephone taping. It's our banks, not the Internal Revenue Service (IRS), that pass our private financial data to telemarketing firms. (2004 年 6 月 CET - 6, Passage 1)

题目: Contrary to popular belief, the author finds that spying on people's privacy _____.

A. is mainly carried out by means of secret taping

B. has been intensified with the help of the IRS

C. is practiced exclusively by the FBI

D. is more prevalent in business circles

解析:题目问的是作者对偷窥人们的私生活的看法。选项 A 的意思(主要通过秘密录音)符合常规做法,但缺乏原文依据,也不符题干意思;选项 B 与本段末句不符;选项 C 与本段第 3 句矛盾,所以选项

162

A、B 和 C 都是错误的。再者,从作者所举的两个例子(某公司正面临窃听电话的指控;银行把客户的个人信息泄露给电话营销公司)可推知,偷窥我们私生活的主要是商业企业,而不是政府。故选项 D 答案。

3. 选项的阅读与选择

1) 选项缩读:①先纵向扫描选项,若有共同要素,则回去做精确定位;②若无共同要素,看选项是不是句子:若是,则先读(只看)主句;若不是,则只看是名词结构还是动词结构,名词结构看主名词,动词结构则看谓语和宾语。

2) 选项排除:比较典型的排除干扰选项的方法有:①用同性元素来排除;②用错误选项的典型特征排除:A. 所述和原文相反;B. 无中生有;C. 和常识一致,却和文中科学论述相悖;D. 是原文不严谨的改写或推理;E. 违背常理;F. 语气极端,过于绝对。

第四节　解题步骤及应试技巧

仔细阅读一直以来都是以测试对文章主题、逻辑关系、特定细节的理解为主的,充分体现阅读的两大考点"主题"和"定位"。因此考生可以采用"把握中心、确定题型、关键词定位、区域解题"的四步法进行解题。具体步骤如下:

第一步:通读全文,把握中心

重点阅读首段(中心句、核心概念常在第一段,常在首段出题)及其他各段的段首和段尾句。同时,判断该文属何种体裁并用一分半钟时间思考 3 个问题进一步确定中心:1)文章叙述的主要内容是什么? 2)文章中有无提到核心概念? 3)作者的大致态度是什么?

第二步:确定题型,关键定位

前面提过,六级考试阅读部分主要涉及主旨题、态度题、猜词题、细节题和推论题五种题型,解题时,考生首先应该判断考查题型,确定做题方法,然后圈定题干关键词,即题干中名词、大写字母、地名、时间、人物、数字等。

第三步：关键词定位，划定各题区域

借助题干中的关键词通读全文，圈定关键词和逻辑关系词（因果、转折、举例等），依次确定各题区域。在带着题干关键词进行定位时考生务必要注意这样一条原则，即一定要转化，千万不要期望在文章中找到与题干的主要内容一模一样的单词或词组。

第四步：缩读选项，定位正确答案

在第三步的基础上，考生应对选项进行筛选，以确定答案。判断四个选项时，采用缩读方法，即先纵向扫描选项，抓住选项中的关键词，把选项定位到原文的某处比较，重叠选项，选出答案。五道题都做完后，如时间许可，把五个选出的答案连起来看一看，检查一下是否存在明显的逻辑不通或相冲突。如果有，及时订正；如果没有，便可接着解题。

另外，如果解题时间实在不够，不要瞎填答案，只要能熟练掌握正确选项与干扰项的特征，可采用"狗急跳墙"的做法——不读文章只做题目，也可命中一些。应急诀窍如下：

（1）针对主旨大意题只读段首、段尾句。前面提到，一篇文章的中心思想或某一段主题思想往往通过段首、段尾句表达出来，若能迅速找到这些主题句，也能答题。

（2）若是针对某人的言论、特殊符号（如冒号、引号、破折号）后的内容出题，可只读该人言论、符号前后句的内容。

（3）如果题目只是针对某一段内容而提问，可只看该段内容即可答题，而不必等把文章全看完才做，以防到时要交卷，回答问题因时间不足而瞎猜。

（4）针对词汇题，可只看词汇所在句和前后句内容即可答题，因为对单词词义的揣测，一般只通过单词所在句或前后句内容就能猜出。

如果能很好掌握前面提到的阅读理解常考题型及命题规律（常考的考点），就更能提高采用"狗急跳墙"法解题的命中率。

第五节 实战演练

下面我们以 2008 年 6 月六级考试真题中 Passage One 为例说明阅读解题"四步法"的应用。

Imagine waking up and finding the value of your assets has been halved. No, you're not an investor in one of those hedge funds that failed completely. With the dollar slumping to a 26—year low against the pound, already expensive London has become quite unaffordable. A coffee at Starbucks, just as unavoidable in England as it is in the United States, runs about $8.

The once all powerful dollar isn't doing a Titanic against just the pound. It is sitting at a record low against the euro and at a 30-year low against the Canadian dollar. Even the Argentine peso and Brazilian real are thriving against the dollar.

The weak dollar is a source of humiliation, for a nation's self-esteem rests in part on the strength of its currency. It's also a potential economic problem, since a declining dollar makes imported food more expensive and exerts upward pressure on interest rates. And yet there are substantial sectors of the vast U. S. economy-from giant companies like Coca-Cola to mom-and-pop restaurant operators in Miami for which the weak dollar is most excellent news.

Many Europeans may view the U. S. as an arrogant superpower that has become hostile to foreigners. But nothing makes people think more warmly of the U. S. than a weak dollar. Through April, the total number of visitors from abroad was up 6. 8 percent from last year. Should the trend continue, the number of tourists this year will finally top the 2000 peak? Many Europeans now apparently view the U. S. the way many Americans view Mexico-as a cheap place to vacation, shop and party, all while ignoring the fact that the poorer locals can't afford to join the merrymaking.

The money tourists spend helps decrease our chronic trade deficit. So do exports, which thanks in part to the weak dollar, soared 11 percent between May 2006 and May 2007. For first five months of 2007, the trade deficit actually fell 7 percent from 2006.

If you own shares in large American corporations, you're a winner in the weak-dollar gamble. Last week Coca-Cola's stick bubbled to a five-year high after it reported a fantastic quarter. Foreign sales accounted for 65 percent of Coke's beverage business. Other American companies profiting from this trend include McDonald's and IBM.

American tourists, however, shouldn't expect any relief soon. The dollar lost strength the way many marriaqe: break up slowly, and then all at once. And currencies don't turn on a dime. So if you want to avoid the pain inflicted by the increasingly pathetic dollar, cancel that summer vacation to England and look to New England. There, the dollar is still treated with a little respect.

52. Why do Americans feel humiliated?
   A. Their economy is plunging
   B. They can't afford trips to Europe
   C. Their currency has slumped
   D. They have lost half of their assets.

53. How does the current dollar affect the life of ordinary Americans?
   A. They have to cancel their vacations in New England.
   B. They find it unaffordable to dine in mom-and-pop restaurants.

166

C. They have to spend more money when buying imported goods.

D. They might lose their jobs due to potential economic problems.

54. How do many Europeans feel about the u. s. with the devalued dollar?

A. They feel contemptuous of it

B. They are sympathetic with it.

C. They regard it as a superpower on the decline.

D. They think of it as a good tourist destination.

55. What is the author's advice to Americans?

A. They treat the dollar with a little respect

B. They try to win in the weak-dollar gamble

C. They vacation at home rather than abroad

D. They treasure their marriages all the more.

56. What does the author imply by saying "currencies don't turn on a dime"(Line 2,Para 7)

A. The dollar's value will not increase in the short term.

B. The value of a dollar will not be reduced to a dime

C. The dollar's value will drop, but within a small margin.

D. Few Americans will change dollars into other currencies.

第一步:通读全文,把握中心

通读全文可知上文是一篇议论文。文章主要讨论的是美元贬值的问题。第一段与第二段描述了美元开始在世界范围内贬值这一大背景;第三段至倒数第二段介绍了美元贬值对美国经济、美国人的日常生活以及欧洲人的影响;末段作者指出了美国人在美元贬值期间的正确做法。

第二步:确定题型,关键定位

52. Why do Americans feel humiliated? (细节题,关键词是 Ameri-

cans 和 humiliated)

53. How does the current dollar affect the life of ordinary Americans? (细节题,关键词是 affect the life of ordinary Americans)

54. How do many Europeans feel about the u. s. with the devalued dollar? (细节题,关键词是 Europeans)

55. What is the author's advice to Americans? (推断题)

56. What does the author imply by saying "currencies don't turn on a dime" (Line 2, Para 7)? (猜词题,猜测句子隐含含义)

第三步:关键词定位,搜索有效信息

考生可以借助题干中的关键词 Americans, humiliated, affect the life of ordinary Americans, Europeans 等通读全文,画出相关题区域,搜索有效信息。

52 题定位第三段第一句:The weak dollar is a source of humiliation, for a nation's self-esteem rests in part on the strength of its currency.

53 题定位第三段第二句:It's also a potential economic problem, since a declining dollar makes imported food more expensive and exerts upward pressure on interest rates.

54 题定位第四段第五句:Many Europeans now apparently view the U. S. the way many Americans view Mexico-as a cheap place to vacation, shop and party, all while ignoring the fact that the poorer locals can't afford to join the merrymaking.

55 题定位末段倒数两句:So if you want to avoid the pain inflicted by the increasingly pathetic dollar, cancel that summer vacation to England and look to New England. There, the dollar is still treated with a little respect.

56 题定位末段第三句:And currencies don't turn on a dime.

第四步:查读题项,定位正确答案

在第三步的基础上,认真阅读选项,大胆猜测,排除干扰,合理推断答案。

52. 细节题。本题考查美国人觉得丢脸的原因。选项 A 与原文意思相悖。选项 B 内容原文没提到。选项 D 表述的是美元贬值造成的事实之一,但并非美国人感到羞辱的原因。原文 The weak dollar is a source of humiliation,句意是"美元的贬值是屈辱的来源",换句话说,屈辱的原因是美元的贬值,这个意思正好暗合选项 C 的意思(货币暴跌)。故选项 C 为答案。

53. 细节题。本题考查目前美元贬值对美国人日常生活的影响。选项 A 及 D 原文未提及,可排除。选项 B 与第三段末句含义不符,该句说的是以公司巨头到小饭馆老板认为美元贬值对他们来说是个令人兴奋的消息,因为进口食品价格上涨,导致消费者购买本国产品,而不是 B 项描述的人们没钱去小饭馆吃饭。第三段第二句提到美元贬值对经济的两个影响——进口商品价格上涨以及利率压力的不断加大,从而说明美国人需要花更多的钱购买进口商品。故选项 C 为答案。

54. 细节题。本题考查欧洲人对美元贬值后的美国的看法。选项 A 是偷梁换柱型的干扰项,因为原文说的是美国人一直很自傲,瞧不起外国人,并不是说欧洲人瞧不起美国人,故排除。选项 B 和 C 的内容原文未提到,也可排除。第四段末句提到许多欧洲人眼中的美国就像美国眼中的墨西哥一样(墨西哥一直是美国人喜欢度假的地方),这说明了欧洲人认为现在的美国是他们的理想的旅游地方了。故选项 D 为答案。

55. 推断题。本题考查作者给美国人的劝告是什么。选项 A 与原文相悖,末段末句说的是在国内消费美元还会得到一些尊重,并不是说人们看不起美元。选项 B 未提及。选项 D 是对原文 The dollar lost strength the way many marriaqe: break up slowly, and then all at once. 的错误理解。根据末段最后两句:如果想避免伤痛,取消去英格兰的暑期旅游计划,那就去新英格兰吧,即,就在国内旅游吧。故选项 C 为答案。

56. 猜词题。本题主要考查的是对 on a dime 这一短语的理解。dime 意为"便宜的,不值钱的",on a dime 意为"短时间内,立即"。结合本文中心及本词组所在句的上下文:美元失去其强势的过程就跟许多婚姻的破裂过程一样慢慢地进行。所以建议取消国外旅行,转而国内旅行,由此说明美元走弱形势在短期内不会改变。故选项 A 为答案。

　　巧用"四步法"于英语阅读理解中,你会发现原本复杂的事情变简单了,从而轻松克服阅读难关,在英语考试中取得理想成绩。

第六节　历年典型真题

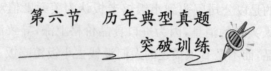

突破训练

Passage one (2008 年 12 月真题)

Sustainable development is applied to just about everything from energy to clean water and economic growth, and as a result it has become difficult to question either the basic assumptions behind it or the way the concept is put to use. This is especially true in agriculture, where sustainable development is often taken as the sole measure of progress without a proper appreciation of historical and cultural perspectives.

To start with, it is important to remember that the nature of agriculture has changed markedly throughout history, and will continue to do so. Medieval agriculture in northern Europe fed, clothed and sheltered a predominantly rural society with a much lower population density than it is today. It had minimal effect on biodiversity, and any pollution it caused was typically localized. in terms of energy use and the nutrients captured in the product it was relatively inefficient.

Contrast this with farming since the start of the industrial revolution. Competition from overseas led farmers to specialize and increase yields. Throughout this period food became cheaper, safe and more reliable. However, these changes have also led to habitat loss and to diminishing biodiversity.

What's more, demand for animal products in developing countries is growing so fast that meeting it will require an extra 300 million tons of grain a year by 2050. Yet the growth of cities and industry is reducing the amount of water available for agriculture in many regions.

All this means that agriculture in the 21st century will have to be very different from how it was in the 20th. This will require radical thinking. for example, we need to move away from the idea that traditional practices are inevitably more sustainable than new ones. We also need to abandon the notion that agriculture can be "zero impact". The key will be to abandon the rather simple and static measures of sustainability, which centre on the need to maintain production without increasing damage.

Instead we need a more dynamic interpretation, one that looks at the pros and cons of all the various way land is used. There are many different ways to measure agricultural performance besides food yield: energy use, environmental costs, water purity, carbon footprint and biodiversity. It is clear, for example, that the carbon of transporting tomatoes from Spain to the UK is less than that of producing them in the UK with additional heating and lighting. But we do not know whether lower carbon footprints will always be better for biodiversity. What is crucial is recognizing that sustainable agriculture is not just about sustainable food production. (428 words)

52. How do people often measure progress in agriculture?

A. By its productivity

B. By its sustainability

C. By its impact on the environment

D. By its contribution to economic growth

53. Specialization and the effort to increase yields have resulted in _____.

A. localised pollution   B. the shrinking of farmland

C. competition from overseas   D. the decrease of biodiversity

54. What does the author think of traditional farming practices?

A. They have remained the same over the centuries

B. They have not kept pace with population growth

C. They are not necessarily sustainable

D. They are environmentally friendly

55. What will agriculture be like in the 21st century?

A. It will go through radical changes

B. It will supply more animal products

C. It will abandon traditional farming practices

D. It will cause zero damage to the environment

56. What is the author's purpose in writing this passage?

A. To remind people of the need of sustainable development

B. To suggest ways of ensuring sustainable food production

C. To advance new criteria for measuring farming progress

D. To urge people to rethink what sustainable agriculture is

Passage two (2008 年 12 月真题)

The percentage of immigrants (including those unlawfully present) in the United states has been creeping upward for years. At 12.6 percent, it is now higher than at any point since the mid 1920s.

We are not about to go back to the days when Congress openly

172

worried about inferior races polluting America's bloodstream. But once again we are wondering whether we have too many of the wrong sort for newcomers. Their loudest critics argue that the new wave of immigrants cannot, and indeed do not want to, fit in as previous generations did.

We now know that these racist views were wrong. In time, Italians, Romanians and members of other so-called inferior races became exemplary Americans and contributed greatly, in ways too numerous to detail, to the building of this magnificent nation. There is no reason why these new immigrants should not have the same success.

Although children of Mexican immigrants do better, in terms of educational and professional attainment, than their parents, UCLA sociologist Edward Telles has found that the gains don't continue. Indeed, the fourth generation is marginally worse off than the third. James Jackson, of the University of Michigan, has found a similar trend among black Caribbean immigrants. Tells fears that Mexican-Americans may be fated to follow in the footsteps of American blacks-that large parts of the community may become mired in a seemingly state of poverty and underachievement. Like African-Americans, Mexican-Americans are increasingly relegated to (降人) segregated, substandard schools, and their dropout rate is the highest for any ethnic group in the country.

We have learned much about the foolish idea of excluding people on the presumption of the ethnic/racial inferiority. But what we have not yet learned is how to make the process of Americanization work for all. I am not talking about requiring people to learn English or to adopt American ways; those things happen pretty much on their own, but as arguments about immigration hear up the campaign

173

trail, we also ought to ask some broader question about assimilation, about how to ensure that people, once outsiders, don't fovever remain marginalized within these shores.

That is a much larger question than what should happen with undocumented workers, or how best to secure the border, and it is one that affects not only newcomers but groups that have been here for generations. It will have more impact on our future than where we decide to set the admissions bar for the latest wave of would-be Americans. And it would be nice if we finally got the answer right. (428 words)

57. How were immigrants viewed by U. S. Congress in early days?

　　A. They were of inferior races.

　　B. They were a Source of political corruption.

　　C. They were a threat to the nation's security.

　　D. They were part of the nation's bloodstream.

58. What does the author think of the new immigrants?

　　A. They will be a dynamic work force in the U. S.

　　B. They can do just as well as their predecessors.

　　C. They will be very disappointed on the new land.

　　D. They may find it hard to fit into the mainstream.

59. What does Edward Telles' research say about Mexican-Americans?

　　A. They may slowly improve from generation to generation.

　　B. They will do better in terms of educational attainment.

　　C. They will melt into the African-American community.

　　D. They may forever remain poor and underachieving.

60. What should be done to help the new immigrants?

　　A. Rid them of their inferiority complex.

　　B. Urge them to adopt American customs.

C. Prevent them from being marginalized.

D. Teach them standard American English.

61. According to the author, the burning issue concerning immigration is _____.

A. how to deal with people entering the U. S. without documents

B. how to help immigrants to better fit into American society

C. how to stop illegal immigrants from crossing the border

D. how to limit the number of immigrants to enter the U. S.

Passage three (2008 年 6 月真题)

In the college-admissions wars, we parents are the true fights. We're pushing our kids to get good grades, take SAT preparatory courses and build resumes so they can get into the college of our first choice. I've twice been to the wars, and as I survey the battlefield, something different is happening. We see our kids' college background as a prize demonstrating how well we've raised them. But we can't acknowledge that our obsession(痴迷) is more about us than them. So we've contrived various justifications that turn out to be half-truths, prejudices or myths. It actually doesn't matter much whether Aaron and Nicole go to Stanford.

We have a full-blown prestige panic; we worry that there won't be enough prizes to go around. Fearful parents urge their children to apply to more schools than ever. Underlying the hysteria(歇斯底里) is the belief that scarce elite degrees must be highly valuable. Their graduates must enjoy more success because they get a better education and develop better contacts. All that is plausible—and mostly wrong. We haven't found any convincing evidence that selectivity or prestige matters. Selective schools don't systematically employ better instructional approaches than less selective schools. On two measures—professors' feedback and the number of essay exams selective schools do slightly worse.

By some studies, selective schools do enhance their graduates' lifetime earnings. The gain is reckoned at 2-4% for every 100-poinnt increase in a school's average SAT scores. But even this advantage is probably a statistical fluke(偶然). A well-known study examined students who got into highly selective schools and then went elsewhere. They earned just as much as graduates from higher-status schools.

Kids count more than their colleges. Getting into Yale may signify intelligence, talent and ambition. But it's not the only indicator and, paradoxically, its significance is declining. The reason: so many similar people go elsewhere. Getting into college is not life's only competition. In the next competition—the job market and graduate school—the results may change. Old-boy networks are breaking down. princeton economist Alan Krueger studied admissions to one top Ph. D. program. High scores on the GRE helped explain who got in; degrees of prestigious universities didn't.

So, parents, lighten up. The stakes have been vastly exaggerated. Up to a point, we can rationalize our pushiness. America is a competitive society; our kids need to adjust to that. But too much pushiness can be destructive. The very ambition we impose on our children may get some into Harvard but may also set them up for disappointment. One study found that, other things being equal, graduates of highly selective schools experienced more job dissatisfaction. They may have been so conditioned to being on top that anything less disappoints. (461 words)

57. Why dose the author say that parents are the true fighters in the

college-admissions wars?

A. They have the final say in which university their children are to attend.

B. They know best which universities are most suitable for their children.

C. They have to carry out intensive surveys of colleges before children make an application.

D. They care more about which college their children go to than the children themselves.

58. Why do parents urge their children to apply to more schools than ever?

A. They want to increase their children's chances of entering a prestigious college.

B. They hope their children can enter a university that offers attractive scholarships.

C. Their children will have a wider choice of which college to go to.

D. Elite universities now enroll fewer student than they used to.

59. What does the author mean by "kids count more than their colleges" Line1, para. 4?

A. Continuing education is more important to a person's success.

B. A person's happiness should be valued more than their education.

C. Kids' actual abilities are more important than their college background.

D. What kids learn at college cannot keep up with job market requirements.

60. What does Krueger's study tell us?

A. Getting into Ph. D. programs may be more competitive than getting into college.

B. Degrees of prestigious universities do not guarantee entry to graduate programs.

C. Graduates from prestigious universities do not care much about their GRE scores.

D. Connections built in prestigious universities may be sustained long after graduation.

61. One possible result of pushing children into elite universities is that _____

A. they earn less than their peers from other institutions

B. they turn out to be less competitive in the job market

C. they experience more job dissatisfaction after graduation

D. they overemphasize their qualifications in job application

Passage four (2006 年 12 月真题)

In a purely biological sense, fear begins with the body's system for reacting to things that can harm us the so-called fight-or-flight response. "An animal that can't detect danger can't stay alive," says Joseph LeDoux. Like animals, humans evolved with an elaborate mechanism for processing information about potential threats. At its core is a cluster of neurons(神经元) deep in the brain known as the amygdala(扁桃核).

LeDoux studies the way animals and humans respond to threats to understand how we form memories of significant events in our lives. The amygdala receives input from many parts of the brain, including regions responsible for retrieving memories. Using this information, the amygdala appraised a situation I think this charging dog wants to bite me and triggers a response by radiating nerve signals throughout the body. These signals produce the familiar signs of dis-

178

tress: trembling, perspiration and fast-moving feet, just to name three.

This fear mechanism is critical to the survival of all animals, but no one can say for sure whether beasts other than humans know they're afraid. That is, as LeDoux says, "if you put that system into a brain that has consciousness, then you get the feeling of fear."

Humans, says Edward M. Hallowell, have the ability to call up images of bad things that happened in the past and to anticipate future events. Combine these higher thought processes with our hard-wired danger-detection systems, and you get a near-universal human phenomenon: worry. That's not necessarily a bad thing, says Hallowell. "When used properly, worry is an incredible device," he says. After all, a little healthy worrying is okay if it leads to constructive action-like having a doctor look at that weird spot on your back.

Hallowell insists, though, that there's a right way to worry. "Never do it alone, get the facts and then make a plan," he says. Most of us have survived a recession, so we're familiar with the belt-tightening strategies needed to survive a slump.

Unfortunately, few of us have much experience dealing with the threat of terrorism, so it's been difficult to get facts about how we should respond. That's why Hallowell believes it was okay for people to indulge some extreme worries last fall by asking doctors for Cipro and buying gas masks.

52. The "so-called fight-or-flight response" (Line2, Para. 1) refers to "_____".

   A. the biological process in which human beings' sense of self-defense evolves

   B. the instinctive fear human beings feel when faced with potential danger

    C. the act of evaluating a dangerous situation and making a quick decision

    D. the elaborate mechanism in the human brain for retrieving information

53. Form the studies conducted by LcDoux we learn that _____.

    A. reactions of humans and animals to dangerous situations are often unpredictable

    B. memories of significant events enable people to control fear and distress

    C. people's unpleasant memories are derived from their feelings of fear

    D. the amygdale plays a vital part in human and animal responses to potential danger

54. Form the passage we know that _____.

    A. a little worry will do us good if handled properly

    B. a little worry will enable us to survive a recession

    C. fear strengthens the human desire to survive danger

    D. fear helps people to anticipate certain future events

55. Which of the following is the best way to deal with your worries according to Hallowell?

    A. Ask for help-from the people around you.

    B. Use the belt-tightening strategies for survival.

    C. Seek professional advice and take action.

    D. Understand the situation and be fully prepared.

56. In Hallowell's view, people's reaction to the terrorist threat last fall was _____.

    A. ridiculous   B. understandable

    C. over-cautious   D. sensible

第七节 答案解析

Passage one

【结构剖析】议论文。本文主要讨论农业的可持续发展问题。文章首段指出,人们忽略了从历史和文化的角度去合理地评价在农业领域的可持续发展,接下来的三段具体分析了人们是如何忽略的,第五段之末端提出现在的农业将与以前的不同,要求人们改变原有的在农业上的可持续发展的思想。

【语境记忆】

1. sustainable [səˈsteinəbl] *adj.* 可以忍受的,足可以支撑的

2. perspective [pəˈpektiv] *n.* 前途,观点,看法

3. assumption [əˈsʌmpʃən] *n.* 假定,设想,假装

4. predominantly [priˈdɔminəntli] *adv.* 主要地,突出地,显著地

5. specialize [ˈspeʃəlaiz] *n.* 专攻,专门研究

6. diminish [diˈminiʃ] *v.* (使)减少,(使)变小

7. contrast... with... 与……对比   8. lead to＋ V-ing 导致

9. radical thinking 激进的思想

【难句分析】

Sustainable development is applied to... everything from... to... and..., and as a result it has become difficult to question.... (L. 1-3, Para. 1)

此句为复合句。介词短语 from... to... grow 在文中修饰 everything; either the basic assumptions... or the way 在文中作 question 的宾语;the concept is put to use 是定语从句,修饰 way。

答案与解析

52. B【定位】第一段末句。

【解析】细节题。本题考查人们通常如何来衡量农业的进步。该段末句提到,在农业领域,可持续发展经常被用作衡量进步的唯一标准。题干中的 measure progress 对应原文的 measure of progress。选项(B)中的 sustainability 是对原文的 sustainable development 的同义转述,故选项 B 为答案。

53. D【定位】第三段。

【解析】细节题。本题考查专业化和人们努力提高产量的结果。该段第二句提到,来自海外的竞争使得农民不得不使农业专业化并提高产量。第四句提到农民这么做的负面结果:导致栖息地的丧失和生物多样化的锐减。题干中的 resulted in 对应原文的 led to,decrease of biodiversity 是对原文的 diminishing biodiversity 的同义转述,故选项 D 为答案。

54. C【定位】第五段。

【解析】细节题。本题考查作者对传统农作方式的看法。该段第三句提到,我们需要摒弃那种认为传统的耕作方式就一定比新方法更具有可持续发展的思想。由此可知,作者认为传统的耕作方式不一定就有可持续发展性,故选项 C 为答案。

55. A【定位】第五段。

【解析】细节题。本题考查 21 世纪的农业会是什么样子。该段前两句提到,所有的这一切都预示着 21 世纪农业将与 20 世纪的极为不同。这就要求有激进的思维。由此可推断知,21 世纪的农业将会发生巨变,故选项 A 为答案。

56. D【定位】全文。

【解析】主旨题。本题考查作者写这篇文章的意图。文章首段提到,在农业领域,可持续发展经常被当作衡量进步的唯一标准,但人们忽略了从历史和文化的角度去合理地评价它,接下来的三段具体分析人们是如何忽略的;第五段与末段提出现在的农业将与以前的极为不同,要求人们改变原有的在农业上的可持续发展思想。综合可知,作者主要是为了让人们重新思考什么是可持续发展的农业,故选项 D 为答案。

【参考译文及题区画线】

几乎每个领域都应用到了可持续发展——从能源到洁净水和经济增长。结果,想质问这一概念背后的基本假设或者这一概念是如何被执行的,变得很困难。52)这一现象在农业领域更是如此。在农业领域,可持续发展经常被当作衡量进步的唯一标准,但人们忽略了从历史和文化的角度去合理地考量。

首先,意识到农业的性质在历史过程中经历了很大变化而且将继续变化是很重要的。北欧中古时期的农业为农业社会的人口提供了主要的衣食住行,那时候的人口密度比现在要小得多。它对生物的多样性的影响甚微,并且它所带来的污染都是典型的、局部化的。从食物中获取的营养和能量是相对不足的。

以此与工业革命后的农业相比。53)来自海外的竞争迫使农民们不得不专业化并提高产量。在这一过程中,事物变得更便宜、更安全、更可靠。然而,这些变化也导致了栖息地的丧失和生物多样化的锐减。

更严重的是,发展中国家对动物制品的需求发展如此之快,以至于到 2050 年,每年要消耗的额外的谷物量将达 3 亿吨。而不断发展的城市和工业,也在不断消减许多地区可获得的农业用水的数量。

54)所有的这一切都预示着 21 世纪的农业将与 20 世纪的有极大的不同。这就要求有激进的思维。比如说:我们需要摒弃那种认为传统的耕作方式就一定比新方式更具有可持续发展的思想;我们必须放弃农业就是"零影响"的想法。55)关键在于摒弃那种简单的、静止的衡量标准可持续性,即那种集中在不增加破坏的同时保持产量的可持续性。

相反,我们需要有更动态的理解——看到土地的各种使用方式的正、反两面。除了食物产量以外,还有很多种不同的方法来衡量农业业绩:能量消耗,环境代价,水的净化,碳质残留物以及生物多样性。比如,很明显,把西红柿从西班牙运送到英国所消耗的炭肯定比在英国通过额外增加温度和光照来生产所消耗的碳少。但是我们不知道耕地的碳质残留物对于生物多样性是否总是更好的。关键是要认识到可持续农业并不仅仅是可持续的食物生产。

Passage two

【结构剖析】议论文。本文主要论述美国的新移民问题。首先指出美国移民数量一直在增加,然后给出对新移民的两种观点,最后说明应当防止新移民边缘化及其重要性。

【语境记忆】

1. creep [kri:p] *vi.* 蹑手蹑脚地走 2. fit in 适应 3. inferior race 劣等族 4. exemplary [igˈzempləri] *a.* 惩戒性的;示范的 5. follow the footsteps of sb. 步某人的后尘 6. be relegated to 被降到 7. assimilation [əˌsimiˈleiʃən] *n.* 吸收;(民族或语音的)同化

【难句分析】

1. Although children of Mexican immigrants do better, in terms of educational and professional attainment, than their parents, UCLA sociologist Edward Telles has found that the gains don't continue. (L. 1-3, Para. 4)

   此句为复合句。Although 引导让步定语从句,in terms...attainment 在句中作插入语,that 引导宾语从句作 find 的宾语。句架:Although...,...Edward Telles has found that...

2. Telles fears that Mexican-Americans may be fated to follow in the footsteps of American blacks—that large parts of the community

may become mired in a seemingly state of poverty and underachievement. (L. 4-6, Para. 4)

此句为复合句。that 引导宾语从句作 fear 的宾语;破折号后的内容对前面的内容进行解释说明,说明美籍墨西哥人步美国黑人后尘的状况。

57. A【定位】第二段。

【解析】细节题。本题考查早期国会对移民的看法。第二段首句提到,我们不必再去追溯国会认为劣等民族会污染美国血统的日子。结合首段首句的 immigrants 可知,这句话中的 inferior races 指的正是移民,由此可推知,以前国会认为移民是劣等民族,故选项 A 为答案。

58. B【定位】第三段。

【解析】细节题。本题考查作者对新移民的看法。第三段第二句提到,意大利人、罗马尼亚人以及其他所谓的劣等民族的人成了模范式的美国人。第三句(双重否定句)指出,没有理由认为为什么这些新的移民就不能成功。综上可推知,作者认为新的移民也能和他们的前辈一样成功,故选项 B 为答案。

59. D【定位】第四段。

【解析】细节题。本题考查泰勒斯研究里涉及的美籍墨西哥人的内容。第四段第四句指出,泰勒斯担心,美籍墨西哥人注定要步美国黑人的后尘,即大部分人都可能陷入看似永久的贫困和不成功。D 中的 may forever remain poor and underachieving 是对原文的 may become mired in a seemingly permanent state of poverty and underachievement 的同义转述,故选项 D 为答案。

60. C【定位】倒数第二段。

【解析】推断题。本题考查帮助新移民应该做些什么。倒数第二段的第二句提到,我们不了解如何使"美国化"的过程对每个人都起作用。第四句提到,我们应该问一些关于同化,关于如何确保那些曾经是外人的美国人不会永远被边缘化之类的问题。由此可推断出,作者认为应思考并寻找方法,避免移民们被边缘化,故选项 C 为答案。

61. B【定位】末段。

【解析】推断题。本题考查作者认为什么是关于移民极其重要的问题。末段首句指出,这是一个更重要的问题。句中 That 为指代词,指的是上段末作者提到的 some broader questions about assimilation, about how to ensure that people, once outsiders, don't forever remain marginalized within these shores. (一些关于同化,关于如何确保那些曾经是外人的美国人不会永远被边缘化之类的更广泛的问题)。题干中的 burning issue 对应原文的 broad question 和 much larger question。选项 B 的内容是对 how to ensure that people, once outsiders, don't forever remain marginalized within these shores 的同义转述,故 B 为答案。

【参考译文及题区画线】

美国移民(包括非法的)的数量多年来一直在悄悄上升。目前的移民人口比例是 12.6%,这比 20 世纪 20 年代以来的任何时候都要高。

57)我们不必再去追溯国会公开担心劣等民族会污染美国血统的日子。但是,我们想再次知道我们是否拥有太多错误种类的新来者。呼声最高的批判是大量涌入的新移民不能——而且也确实不想——像先前几代一样融入美国。

现在我们知道哪些种族主义者的观点是错误的。58)随着时间的推移,意大利人、罗马尼亚人以及其他所谓的劣等民族的人民成了模范式的美国人,并且为这个伟大国家的建设贡献了巨大力量,他们的贡献方式不胜枚举。没有理由认为为什么这些新的移民就不能成功。

尽管墨西哥移民在教育和职业造诣方面比他们的父母做的要好，加利福尼亚大学洛杉矶分校的社会学家爱德华·泰勒斯发现，这种状态不会继续。诚然，第四代移民确实比第三代的情况要稍微差点。密歇根大学的詹姆斯·杰克孙在加勒比黑人移民当中也有类似的发现。59)泰勒斯担心，美籍墨西哥人注定要步美国黑人的后尘——大部分人都可能陷入看似永久的贫困和不成功。像美籍非洲人一样，美籍墨西哥人正急剧地被划分到被隔离的和不符合标准的学校，他们的辍学率在各个少数民族中是最高的。

对于根据民族、种族的劣等性的论断来把人排除在外的愚蠢想法，我们已经了解了很多。60)但是我们所不了解的是如何使"美国化"的过程对每个人都起作用。我不是说人人都学英语或者采取美国的生活方式；这样的事情都是自发的。但是随着有关移民问题的辩论逐渐在竞选活动中愈演愈烈，我们应该问一些更广泛的问题——关于同化，关于如何确保那些曾经是外人的美国人不会永远被边缘化。

61)这是一个更重要的问题，比应该如何处置无证工人或者如何最好地确保边界安全都重要。这个问题不仅对新来者有影响，而且还会对在这里居住了几代的移民有影响。这比我们决定应该为那些准美国人设置什么样的门槛对未来的影响更大。如果我们最终能找到正确答案，那将是非常了不起的。

Passage three

【结构剖析】议论文。文章批驳了美国家长对名校的态度问题。第一、二段指出美国家长对名校的态度：认为上名校是孩子成功的必经之路，便一味地逼孩子上名校。第三、四段作者根据研究结果批驳美国家长的这种态度。文章末段建议给孩子自己选择的权利。

【语境记忆】

1. obsession [əb'seʃən] *n*. 着魔,鬼迷

2. full-blown ['ful'bləun] *a*. 成熟的;完善的

3. plausible ['plɔːzəbl] *a*. 貌似真实的;花言巧语的

4. indicator ['indikeitə] *n*. 指示器

5. paradoxically [ˌpærə'dɔksikəli] *ad*. 似非而是地;反常地

6. pushiness ['puʃinis] *n*. 一意孤行

【难句分析】

We see our kids' college background as a prize demonstrating how well we've raised them. (L. 4, Para. 1)

此句为复合句。see... as... 意为"把……看作……";现在分词 demonstrating 为 prize 的后置定语;how well we've raised them. 为 demonstrating 的宾语从句。

57. D【定位】第一段头两句。

【解析】推断题。本题考查作者为什么认为家长是高考这一战争中的真正战斗者。选项 A(家长对孩子上哪所学校有决定权)和 B(家长最明了哪所大学最适合孩子)曲解了原文的意思。选项 C 未提及。所以 A、B 和 C 是错误的。从第一段的信息词 our first choice,a prize demonstrating how well we raised them 等,可以看出孩子要上家长们首选的大学,并且大学情况如何将表明家长对孩子教育的优劣。最后三句表明家长虽然不承认他们比孩子在上大学问题上更痴迷更在意,但是他们却承认在此基础上所设计的种种理由都是不真实,有偏见和虚幻,不切实际。最后一句更能体现作者的态度,对于他的孩子 Aaron 和 Nicole 而言,是否能上斯坦福大学并不重要。由此可见,更在乎的是父母而不是孩子,选项 D 符合题意。故选项 D 为答案。

58. A【定位】第二段。

【解析】推断题。本题考查家长逼迫孩子申请更多学校的原因。选项 B 和 D 原文没提及,可排除;选项 C 意为孩子们有更多上大学的选择,是对原文的曲解。第二段第一句说家长难以从名牌大学的恐慌中自拔,即担心孩子无法进入名牌大学,由此萌生让学生多申请的想法。第三句紧接着提出名校毕业生的种种优势,如能够接受更好的教育,更有可能成功等。综合可推知,家长们逼迫孩子向更多的大学提出申请是为了保障孩子有更多的机会迈入名校门槛。故选项 A 为答案。

59. C【定位】第四段第一句。

【解析】语义推断题。文中没有涉及到选项 A、B 和 D 的内容,可排除。比较题干与选项 C,我们可以发现题干中的 count 意为"重要",与选项 C 中的 are important 是同义转述;两句中都用了比较级,题干中的 kids 指孩子本身,即除学习以外的各种技能能力,与选项 C 中的 kids' actual abilities 意义相符,而且宾语 their colleges 也和 C 中的 college backgrounds 属同一范畴。故选项 C 为答案。

60. B【定位】第四段最后两句。

【解析】细节题。本题考查的是 Krueger 的研究结果。选项 A 和 C 曲解原文意思。第四段的最后两句话介绍了普林斯顿经济学家 Alan Krueger 的研究结果:能够有机会被这个顶端博士项目录取的是能够在 GRE 考试中有优异成绩的,而不是拥有名牌大学学位的人,说明即使有名牌大学的学位,也无法保证进入研究生院。故选项 B 为答案。

61. C【定位】第五段第六句与第七句。

【解析】细节题。本题考查家长逼迫孩子进入名校的后果。第五段第六句与第七句提到:我们非要强迫孩子考哈佛,正是家长的这种野心,可能会让一些孩子考进哈佛,也可能会把孩子推向失望的绝谷。一项研究表明,在其他条件相同的情况下,名校毕业生会遭受更多的职场失意。选项 C 符合此意,故为答案。

【参考译文及题区画线】

(57)在高考这场战争中,我们这些家长们才是真正的战斗者。我们督促孩子要考高分,催着他们上 SAT(相当于美国高考)考前班,还拼命要他们写简历,以便他们能如愿以偿地进入我们所中意的大学。我经历两次这样的战争了,可是当我现在再回过头来审视当年的战场,心里却有了异样的感觉。我们将孩子们的大学背景看作是对自己辛苦抚养他们的奖品。(58)但是我们不会承认,其实我们对大学的痴迷更多的是考虑自己而不是孩子,所以,我们编造各式各样的理由,而这些理由其实不过是些半真半假的、带有偏见的或虚构的东西。我的两个孩子 Aaron 和 Nicole 上不上斯坦福大学,其实真的没什么大不了。

(59)我们已经难以从出人头地的恐慌中自拔。我们唯恐没有足够到处炫耀的资本,而这种恐慌让家长们逼迫孩子申请学校,越多越好。支撑这种疯狂的是这样一种信念:鹤立鸡群的高分就是高人一等的资本,考高分上名校毕业的学生肯定会更成功,因为他们会获得更好的教育和更广阔的人际关系。这种看法听起来似乎有些道理——但其实不然。我们并没有获得任何可靠的证据说明所谓的尖子或名牌如何重要。系统地讲,名校并不比非名校采用更好的教育方法。根据这两种衡量标准——教授对学生的反馈和作文测验,名校甚至还要稍为逊色一点。

也有一些研究表明,在人的一生中,名校毕业的学生收入确实要高一些,但是,算下来,SAT 平均每高 100 分,收入也就增加2%～10%,而且,即便是这样的优势也极有可能只是一种统计上的偶然而已。听说过这样一项著名的研究,专门研究那些考进名校但是最后去了别的地方的学生。这项研究表明,这些学生挣的并不比更好的学校的学生少。

(60)起决定性作用的因素是孩子本身,而不是他们所上的大学。考上耶鲁大学也许能说明他们的智力水平、天资和雄心,但是这并不是成功的唯一指标,并且,正相反,这个指标的重要性在日渐消退。原因是:很多同样优秀的学生去了别的地方。考大学并非人生中的唯一竞赛。在随后的竞赛中——求职和考研究生——结果可能都会发生改变。旧有的人际关系也会被打破。(61)普林斯顿经济学家艾伦·克鲁格通过研究某个顶级博士项目的录取情况发现,可以用 GRE 高分来解析为什么这些学生能考进这个项目,但是,没有迹象能表明他们的录取跟原来所在大学的名声高低有什么关系。

所以,家长们,把心态放松点吧。我们把高考看得太重了,认识到这一点我们才会理智,不那么一意孤行。(62)美国是一个竞争社会,我们非要强迫孩子考哈佛,正是家长的这种野心,可能会让一些孩子考进哈佛,也可能会把孩子推向失望的绝谷。一项研究表明,在其他条件不变的情况下,重点大学的毕业生会遭受更多的职场失意。他们可能已经对成功习惯了,任何的挫折都会使他们失望。

Passage four

【结构剖析】说明文。文章阐述了约瑟夫·雷杜克提出的恐惧反应机制观点及其原理和爱德华·M·哈洛韦关于忧虑的观点。

【语境记忆】
1. in a sense 从某种意义上说   2. appraise a situation 对情况的估计
3. retrieve memories 检索记忆   4. trigger a response 产生反应
5. fear mechanism 反应机制   6. call up 使人想起
7. hardwired 固有的   8. survive a recession/slum 从萧条中恢复过来

【难句分析】
That's why Hallowell believes it was okay for people to indulge some extreme worries last fall by asking doctors for Cipro and buying gas masks. (L. 2, Last para.)

此句为复合句。句中 why 引导表语从句,表示原因；it was okay for... 是 believe 的宾语从句,it 前省了连接词 that。

答案与解析

52. C【定位】第一段首句。

【解析】语义题。本题考查的是对"so-called fight-or-flight response"的理解。选项 A 意思与原文相悖,因为 self-depense 与题干中 flight 的意思有矛盾。选项 B 理解欠全面,文中 fear 指的是 fight-or-flight response,不单单是 flight response。故 A 和 B 都是错误的。首句中的破折号是对前面的解释归纳,且选项中的 evaluating 和 making a quick decision 正是对该句的解释,故选项 C 为答案。

53. D【定位】第二段第 1、2 句。

【解析】推断题。本题考查的是对雷杜克研究结论的理解。第二段首句指出,雷杜克研究动物和人类对潜在危险的反应形式,紧接着指出扁桃核在危险反应机制中的作用。由此可推知人类和动物对潜在危险反应过程中,扁桃核起着非常重要的作用。故选项 D 为答案。

54. A【定位】全文。

【解析】细节题。本题考查的是对文中细节辨认与理解的能力。从题干上看,似乎是考查对全文的理解,但是根据设题顺序的规律,便可发现本题区位于第四、五段。第五段第二句提到,如果运用得当,忧虑是一种难于置信的手段,且选项 A 中的 do good to 对应文中的 an incredible device,选项 A 是对原文的同义转述,故为答案。选项 B 曲解原文意思,第五段末句说的是从萧条中恢复靠的是节省开支政策。选项 C 文中未提及。选项 D 是对第四段第一句的错误理解。原文提到,Hollowell 认为人类有能力预测将来发生的事情,但并没有提到这是恐惧作用的结果,所以,选项 B、C、D 都是错误的。

55. D【定位】第五段首句。

【解析】细节题。本题考查的是应对恐惧的最好方法。第五段首句提到...there's a right way to worry,接着又指出...get the facts and then make a plan,综上可知应对恐惧最好的方式是要根据事实做出应对计划。选项 D 内容正是此句的同义转述,其中 understand the situation 和 be fully prepared 分别和原文的 get the facts and then make a plan 对应,故选项 D 为答案。

56. B【定位】末段。

【解析】推断题。本题考查的是哈洛韦对人们灾区年秋天的恐怖威胁所做出反应的看法。作者在上文中提到,我们中间很少有人有过对恐怖主义威胁的经历,所以很难收集到我们应该如何应对这种情况的资料。由此推断,it was okay for people to indulge some extreme worries last fall 说的是人们去年秋天对恐怖主义威胁的反应是"可以理解的"。故选项 B 为答案。

【参考译文及题区画线】

　　(52)从纯粹的生物学意义上说,恐惧源自身体系统对于可能伤害到我们的事物做出反应,即所谓的"反抗或逃跑反应"。"不能探查危险的动物不可能生存。"约瑟夫·雷杜克斯说。和动物一样,人类进化出一套复杂精细的结构用以处理有关潜在威胁的信息。该结构的核心是位于大脑深处的称为"扁核桃"的一簇神经元。

　　雷杜克斯研究动物和人类对威胁做出反应的方式,以便了解生活中我们对于有重要意义的事件是如何形成记忆的。(53)扁核桃接受来自大脑多个部位的信息输入,其中包括检索记忆的区域。在使用这条信息的过程中,扁核桃对情况做出评价——"我想这只正冲过来的狗要咬我"——并通过向全身发出神经信号来激发一个反应。这些信号会产生我们熟悉的表示困境迹象:发抖、出汗、步伐加快就是其中的三个表现。

　　这套能做出恐惧反应的机制对于所有动物的生存都是至关重

要的,但是没有人可以肯定地说,除了人类,动物是否知道它们感到害怕。也正如雷杜克斯所说,"如果你把那套机制放进有意识的大脑中,那么就会感到害怕。"爱德华·M·哈洛韦尔说,人类具备能够回忆过去的不幸并预测未来的能力。把这些更高级的思考过程与我们基本的探查危险的系统结合起来,你就会产生几乎全人类共有的现象:忧虑。

(54)哈洛韦尔说,这未必就是件坏事。"若使用得当,忧虑会是不可思议的工具。"毕竟,如果些许的忧虑能使你采取建设性行动的话——比如让医生检查一下你背部的那个奇怪的斑点——那么这种忧虑是有好处的。

(55)尽管如此,哈洛韦尔坚持说,忧虑要用正确的方法。"永远不要只是忧虑,应收集事实,制订计划。"他说。我们大多数人曾经历过经济萧条时期并幸存下来,所以我们很熟悉为了渡过难关所需要的"紧缩"策略。

遗憾的是,(56)我们几乎没有人具备许多经验来处理来自恐怖主义的威胁,所以要获得相关事实来说明我们应该如何做出反应是很困难的。这就解释了为什么哈洛韦尔认为以下现象也属正常:去年秋天人们处在极度忧虑之中,会到医生那里寻求抗炭疽菌的药物并购买防毒面具。

第六章 阅读综合模拟训练

Reading Practice 1

Part I   Reading Comprehension (Skimming and Scanning) (15 minutes)

It's no Laughing Matter

The following interview is Silvia Cardoso's opinion about laugh. He is a behavioral biologist at the State University of Campinas, Brazil.

Why are you interested in laughter?

It's a universal phenomenon, and one of the most common things we do. We laugh many times a day, for many different reasons, but rarely think about it, and seldom consciously control it. We know so little about the different kinds and functions of laughter, and my interest really starts there. Why do we do it? What can laughter teach us about our positive emotions and social behavior? There's so much we don't know about how the brain contributes to emotion and I think we can get at understanding this by studying laughter.

So why do people laugh so much?

Only 10 or 20 percent of laughing is a response to humor. Most of the time it's a message we send to other people—communicating joyful disposition. a willingness to bond and so on. It occupies a special place in social interaction and is a fascinating feature of our biology, with motor, emotional and cognitive components. Scientists study all kinds of emotions and behavior, but few focus on this most basic ingredient. Laughter gives us a clue that we have powerful systems in our brain which respond to pleasure, happiness, and joy. It's also involved in events such as release of fear.

How did you come to research it?

My professional focus has always been on emotional behavior. I spent many years investigating the neural basis of fear in rats, and came to laughter via that route. When I was working with rats, I noticed that when they were alone, in an exposed environment, they were scared and quite uncomfortable. Back in a cage with others, they seemed much happier. It looked as if they played with one another real rough-and-tumble and I wondered whether they were also laughing. The neurobiologist Jaak Panksepp had shown that juvenile rats make short vocalizations, pitched too high for humans to hear, during rough-and-tumble play. He thinks these are similar to laughter. This made me wonder about the roots of laughter.

Do you believe other animals laugh too?

You only have to look at the primates closest to humans to see that laughter is clearly not unique to us. I don't find this too surprising, because we're only one among many social species and there's no reason why we should have a monopoly on laughter as a social tool. The great apes, such as chimpanzees, do something similar to humans. They open their mouths wide, expose their teeth, retract the corners of their lips, and make loud and repetitive vocalizations in situations that tend to evoke human laughter, like when playing with one another or with humans, or when tickled. Laughter may even have evolved long before primates. We know that dogs at play have strange patterns of exhalation(呼气)that differ from other sounds made during passive or aggressive confrontation.

But I think we need to be careful about over interpreting panting behavior in animals at play. It's nice to think of it as homologous(类似的)to human laughter, but it could just be something similar but with entirely different purposes and evolutionary advantages.

So what's it for?

Everything humans do has a function, and laughing is no exception. Its function is surely communication. We need to build social structures in order to live well in our society and evolution has selected laughter as a useful device for promoting social communication. In other words, it must have a survival advantage for the species.

What have scientists found?

The brain scans are usually done while people are responding to humorous material. You see brainwave activity spread from the sensory processing area of the occipital lobe(枕叶), the bit at the back of the brain that processes visual signals, to the brain's frontal lobe. It seems that the frontal lobe is involved in recognizing things as funny. The left side of the frontal lobe analyses the words and structure of jokes while the right side does the intellectual analyses required to "get" jokes. Finally, activity spreads to the motor areas of the brain controlling the physical task of laughing. We also know about these complex pathways involved in laughter from neurological illness and injury. Sometimes after brain damage, tumors, stroke or brain disorder such as Parkinson's disease, people get "stone-faced" syndrome and can't laugh.

How is laughter different in people who are blind or deaf?

The groundbreaking study in this area was conducted by the human ethnologist Irenaus Eibl-Eibsfeldt. He found that laughter and crying patterns are well-developed in such children. He concluded that these expressions evolved through natural selection. Deaf children have different sound patterns in their laughter, as they have in speech. Blind children seem not to display all the facial components of laughter. We're going to study these differences by statistically analyzing the minute variations in laughter between different types of people. We'll video their faces while they laugh in response to various stimuli. Then we'll analyze every millisecond of their facial behavior and vocalization.

Does laughter differ between the sexes?

I'm sure it does, particularly the uses to which the sexes put laughter as asocial tool. For instance, women smile more than laugh, and are particularly adept at smiling and laughing with men as a kind of "social lubricant". It might even be possible that this has a biological origin, because women don't or can't use their physical size as a threat, which men do, even if unconsciously.

Does laughter also differ between cultures?

Cultural differences are certainly part of it. Loud, raucous(粗声的)laughter with exaggerated movements and expressions is considered "unfeminine" in most cultures, and is much more common among men, particularly if they're with other men. In several situations I see laughter used, apparently unconsciously, to help get things as diverse as power, friendship, a lover or truthful behavior from subordinates. For instance, socially dominant individuals, from bosses to tribal chiefs, use laughter to control their subordinates. When the boss laughs, their minions(僚属)laugh too. Laughter might be a form of asserting power by controlling the emotional climate of the group, and it also has a dark side. There are theories that laughter

198

and aggression have common origins, with some kinds of laughter in primates apparently being threatening—just look at the way they bare their teeth. That might explain why being laughed at is so unpleasant.

Is it true that laughing can make us healthier?

It's undoubtedly the best medicine. For one thing, it's exercise. It activates the cardiovascular system, so heart rate and blood pressure increase, then the arteries dilate(舒展), causing blood pressure to fall again. Repeated short, strong contractions of the chest muscles, diaphragm(横隔膜) and abdomen increase blood flow into our internal organs, and forced respiration—the ha! ha! —makes sure that this blood is well oxygenated. Muscle tension decreases, and indeed we may temporarily lose control of our limbs, as in the expression "weak with laughter". It may also release brain endorphins(内啡肽), reducing sensitivity to pain and boosting endurance and pleasurable sensations. Some studies suggest that laughter affects the immune system by reducing the production of hormones associated with stress, and that when you laugh the immune system produce more T-cells. But no rigorously controlled studies have confirmed these effects. Laughter's social role is definitely important. I'm very concerned that today's children may be heading for a whole lot of social ills because their play and leisure time is so isolated and they lose out on lots of chances for laughter.

Why?

Because when children stare at computer screens, rather than laughing with each other, this is at odds with what's natural for them. Natural social behavior in children is playful behavior, and in such situations laughter indicates that make-believe aggression is just fun, not for real, and this is an important way in which children form

199

positive emotional bonds, gain new social skills and generally start to move from childhood to adulthood. I think parents need to be very careful to ensure that their children play in groups, with both peers and adults, and laugh more. (1375 words)

1. Silvia Cardoso considers that we always think about laugh consciously because it is a universal phenomenon.

2. Laugh is a message we send to other people, which may make others feel stupid.

3. Silvis Cardoso's research on laugh resulted from his professional focus on emotional behavior.

4. Animals' panting behavior at play is similar to human laughter in purposes.

5. _____ is surely the function of human laughter.

6. Scientists found that a great role is seemly played by _____ in recognizing things as funny.

7. Irenaus Eibl-Eibsfeldt concluded that well-developed laughter and crying patterns in blind and deaf children was a result of _____ .

8. The difference of laughter between the sexes lies particularly in treating it as _____ .

9. Besides as some kind of lubricant in a group, laughter also has _____ . for example, threatening others.

10. The author shows great _____ about today's children who don't have much time to play and laugh together.

Part II Reading Comprehension (Reading in Depth) (25 minutes)

Section A

Recent stories in the newspapers and magazines suggest that teaching and research contradict each other, that research plays too prominent a part in academic promotions, and that teaching is badly under-emphasized. There is an element of truth in these statements, but they also ignore deeper and more important relationships.

Research experience is an essential element of hiring and promotion at the research university because it is the emphasis on research that distinguishes such a university from an arts college. Some professors, however, neglect teaching for research, and that presents a problem.

Most research universities reward outstanding teaching, but the greatest recognition is usually given for achievements in research. Part of the reason is the difficulty of judging teaching. A highly responsible and tough professor is usually appreciated by top students who want to be challenged, but disliked by those whose record are less impressive. The mild professor gets overall ratings that are usually high, but there is a sense of disappointment on the part of the best students, exactly those for whom the system should present the greatest challenges. Thus, a university trying to promote professors primarily on the basis of teaching qualities would have to confront this confusion.

As modern science moves faster, two forces are exerted on professors: one is the time needed to keep up with the profession; the other is the time needed to teach. The training of new scientists requires outstanding teaching at the research university as well as the arts college. Although scientists are usually "made" in the elementary schools, scientists can be "lost" by poor teaching at the college and graduate school levels. The solution is not to separate teaching and research, but to recognize that the combination is difficult but vital. The title of professor should be given only to those who profess, and it is perhaps time for universities to reserve it for those willing to be an earnest part of the community of scholars. Professors unwilling to teach can be called "distinguished research investigators" or something else.

The pace of modern science makes it increasingly difficult to be a great researcher and great teacher. Yet many are described in just those terms. Those who say we can separate teaching and research simply do not understand the system, but those say the problem will disappear are not fulfilling their responsibilities.

11. According to the author, suggestion in the recent stories mentioned in the first paragraph _____ the relationships between teaching and research.

12. In most researcher universities, the phenomenon that the greatest recognition is usually given for achivenmnet in research is partly due to _____.

13. Why is excellent teaching important for research?

14. Universities should only grant the title professor to those who, first and foremost, do _____.

15. The phrase "the problem" in Line 4, Para. 5 refers to _____.

Section B

Passage one (2007 年 12 月真题)

Like most people, I've long understood that I will be judged by my occupation, that my profession is a gauge people use to see how smart or talented I am. Recently, however, was disappointed to see that it also decides how I'm treated as a person.

Last year I left a professional position as a small-town reporter and took a job waiting tables. As someone paid to serve food to people, I had customers say and do things to me I suspect they'd never say or do to their most casual acquaintances. One night a man talking on his cell phone waved me away, then beckoned (示意) me back with his finger a minute later, complaining he was ready to order and asking where I'd been.

I had waited tables during summers in college and was treated like a peon (勤杂工) by plenty of people. But at 19 years old, I believed I deserved inferior treatment from professional adults. Besides, people responded to me differently after I told them I was in college. Customers would joke that one day I'd be sitting at their table, waiting to be served.

Once I graduated I took a job at a community newspaper. From my first day, I heard a respectful tone from everyone who called me. I assumed this was the way the professional world worked cordially.

I soon found out differently. I sat several feet away from an advertising sales representative with a similar name. Our calls would often get mixed up and someone asking for Kristen would be transferred to Christie. The mistake was immediately evident. Perhaps it was because money was involved, but people used a tone with Kristen that they never used with me.

My job title made people treat me with courtesy. So it was a shock to return to the restaurant industry.

It's no secret that there's a lot to put up with when waiting tables, and fortunately, much of it can be easily forgotten when you pocket the tips. The service industry, by definition, exists to cater to others' needs. Still, it seemed that many of my customers didn't get the difference between server and servant.

I'm now applying to graduate school, which means someday I'll return to a profession where people need to be nice to me in order to get what they want. I think I'll take them to dinner first, and see how they treat someone whose only job is to serve them. (420 words)

16. The author was disappointed to find that _____.

A. one's position is used as a gauge to measure one's intelligence

B. talented people like her should fail to get a respectable job

C. one's occupation affects the way one is treated as a person

D. professionals tend to look down upon manual workers

17. What does the author intend to say by the example in the second paragraph?

   A. Some customers simply show no respect to those who serve them.

   B. People absorbed in a phone conversation tend to be absent-minded.

   C. Waitresses are often treated by customers as casual acquaintances.

   D. Some customers like to make loud complaints for no reason at all.

18. How did the author feel when waiting tables at the age of 19?

   A. She felt it unfair to be treated as a mere servant by professionals.

   B. She felt badly hurt when her customers regarded her as a peon.

   C. She was embarrassed each time her customers joked with her.

   D. She found it natural for professionals to treat her as inferior.

19. What does the author imply by saying ". . . many of my customers didn't get the difference between server and servant" (Line 3, Para. 7)?

   A. Those who cater to others' needs are destined to be looked down upon.

   B. Those working in the service industry shouldn't be treated as servants.

C. Those serving others have to put up with rough treatment to earn a living.

D. The majority of customers tend to look on a servant as server nowadays.

20. The author says she'll one day take her clients to dinner in order to _____.

A. see what kind of person they are

B. experience the feeling of being served

C. show her generosity towards people inferior to her

D. arouse their sympathy for people living a humble life

Passage two（2007 年 12 月真题）

What's hot for 2007 among the very rich? A ＄7. 3 million diamond ring. A trip to Tanzania to hunt wild animals. Oh, and income inequality.

Sure, some leftish billionaires like George Soros have been railing against income inequality for years. But increasingly, centrist and right-wing billionaires are starting to worry about income inequality and the fate of the middle class.

In December, Mortimer Zuckerman wrote a column in U. S. News & World Report, which he owns. "Our nation's core bargain with the middle class is disintegrating,"lamented（哀叹）the 117th-richest man in America. "Most of our economic gains have gone to people at the very top of the income ladder. Average income for a household of people of working age, by contrast, has fallen five years in a row. " He noted that "Tens of millions of Americans live in fear that a major health problem can reduce them to bankruptcy. "

Wilbur Ross Jr. has echoed Zuckerman's anger over the bitter struggles faced by middle-class Americans. "It's an outrage that any American's life expectancy should be shortened simply because the company they worked for went bankrupt and ended health-care coverage," said the former chairman of the International Steel Group.

What's happening? The very rich are just as trendy as you and I, and can be so when it comes to politics and policy. Given the recent change of control in Congress, the popularity of measures like increasing the minimum wage, and efforts by California's governor to offer universal health care, these guys don't need their own personal weathermen to know which way the wind blows.

It's possible that plutocrats(有钱有势的人)are expressing solidarity with the struggling middle class as part of an effort to insulate themselves from confiscatory(没收性的)tax policies. But the prospect that income inequality will lead to higher taxes on the wealthy doesn't keep plutocrats up at night. They can live with that.

No, what they fear was that the political challenges of sustaining support for global economic integration will be more difficult in the United States because of what has happened to the distribution of income and economic insecurity.

In other words, if middle-class Americans continue to struggle financially as the ultrawealthy grow ever wealthier, it will be increasingly difficult to maintain political support for the free flow of goods, services, and capital across borders. And when the United States places obstacles in the way of foreign investors and foreign goods, it's likely to encourage reciprocal action abroad. For people who buy and sell companies, or who allocate capital to markets all around the world, that's the real nightmare.

21. What is the current topic of common interest among the very rich in America?

    A. The fate of the ultrawealthy people.

    B. The disintegration of the middle class.

C. The inequality in the distribution of wealth.

D. The conflict between the left and the right wing.

22. What do we learn from Mortimer Zuckerman's lamentation?

    A. Many middle-income families have failed to make a bargain for better welfare.

    B. The American economic system has caused many companies to go bankrupt.

    C. The American nation is becoming more and more divided despite its wealth.

    D. The majority of Americans benefit little from the natiion's growing wealth.

23. From the fifth paragraph we can learn that _____.

    A. the very rich are fashion-conscious

    B. the very rich are politically sensitive

    C. universal health care is to be implemented throughout America

    D. Congress has gained popularity by increasing the minimum wage

24. What is the real reason for plutocrats to express solidarity with the middle class?

    A. They want to protect themselves from confiscatory taxation.

    B. They know that the middle class contributes most to society.

    C. They want to gain support for global economic integration.

    D. They feel increasingly threatened by economic insecurity.

25. What may happen if the United States places obstacles in the way of foreign investors and foreign goods?

    A. The prices of imported goods will inevitably soar beyond control.

    B. The investors will have to make great efforts to re-allocate capital.

C. The wealthy will attempt to buy foreign companies across borders.

D. Foreign countries will place the same economic barriers in return.

Reading Practice 1 答案与解析

答案

1. N 2. NG 3. Y 4. N 5. Communication 6. the frontal lobe 7. natural selection 8. a social tool 9. a dark side 10. concern 11. simplifies 12. teaching quality 13. Future scientists who research need good training. 14. teaching 15. the separation of teaching from research 16. C 17. A 18. D 19. B 20. A 21. C 22. C 23. B 24. C 25. D

解析

Part 1

【结构剖析】采访性报道记叙文。本文就关于笑的 11 个问题(即文中的小标题)采访巴西 Campinas 州立大学行为生物学家斯尔维亚·卡多佐。

【语境记忆】

1. primate [ˈpraimit] n. 灵长类动物 2. have a monopoly on sth. 独占,为……所特有 3. retract [riˈtrækt] vt. 缩回,缩进
4. evoke [iˈvəuk] vt. 唤起(记忆等),引起 5. groundbreaking [ˈgraundˌbreikiŋ] a. 开创性的 6. be adept at 善于 7. activate [ˈæktiˌveit] vt. 使活动起来 8. cardiovascular system 心血管系统
9. be at odds with 不和,相争,不一致
10. make-believe a. 假装的,装腔作势的

【难句分析】

1. It might even be possible that this has a biological origin, because women don't or can't use their physical size as a threat, which men do, even if unconsciously.

　　此句为复合句。句中的 it 是形式主语,真正的主语是 that 引导的主语从句。主语从句含有一个由 because 引导的原因状语从句;该原因状语从句又包含一个由 which 引导的非限制定语从句,修饰前句话。

2. I'm very concerned that today's children may be heading for a whole lot of social ills because their play and leisure time is so isolated and they lose out on lots of chances for laughter.

　　此句为复合句。that 引导表语从句。从句中包含一个由 because 引导的原因状语从句,该原因状语从句中又包含一个由 and 连接的并列句。整句的句架为:I'm very concerned that... because... and...。

1. 【定位】小标题 Why are you interested in laughter? 小节中的第一、二句。

　　【解析】原文说的是"……不过我们不常(rarely)想到它,也很少(seldom)有意识地加以控制",题干用 always 代替了原文中的 seldom,与原文的说法不符,故答案为 N。

2. 【定位】小标题 So why do people laugh so much? 小节中的第二句。

　　【解析】原文指出笑是我们传递各种信息的方式,如自己快乐的性情,乐于与对方相处之意等,但未提到 proving others stupid 这种情况,故答案为 NG。

3. 【定位】小标题 How did you come to research it? 小节中的第一、二句。

　　【解析】题干是对原文信息的归纳并同义转述。第二句中的 that

route 指的就是第一句中的 professional focus. . . on emotional be-havior，故答案为 Y。

4. 【定位】小标题 Do you believe other animals laugh too? 小节中的第二段。

   【解析】原文提到动物的喘息与人类的笑有相似之处，但它可能仅是类似，而其目的却与人类的笑迥然不同……，即不是相似，故答案为 N。

5. 【定位】小标题 So what's it for? 小节中的第一、二句。

   【解析】原文提到：Everything humans do has a function, and laugh-ing is no exception. Its function is surely communication. 题干对原文进行了简单的句型转换，很明显，Communication 为答案。注意首字母大写。

6. 【定位】小标题 What have scientists found? 小节中的第三句。

   【解析】题干是对原文的同义转述。原文提到：It seems that the frontal lobe is involved in recognizing things as funny. 显然，the frontal lobe 为答案。

7. 【定位】小标题 How is laughter different in people who are blind or deaf? 小节中的前三句。

   【解析】题干是对原文信息的归纳并同义转述。第三句提到：He concluded that these expressions evolved through natural selec-tion. 其中的 these expressions 指代前面的 laughter and crying patterns patterns are well-devoloped insuch children，故 natural selection 为答案。

8. 【定位】小标题 Does laughter differ between the sexes? 小节中的第一句。

   【解析】第一句提到…… the sexes put laughter as asocial tool. 题干是对问题和答案的概括，故 a social tool 为答案。

9. 【定位】小标题 Does laughter also differ between cultures? 小节。

   【解析】题干是对原文信息的归纳并同义转述。原文提到：Laughter

might be a form of asserting power by controlling the emotional climate of the group, and it also has a dark side. 由此推知，作者要表达的是笑的作用的两面性。题干指出笑在一个群体中起的"润滑剂"的作用，这应是对笑的积极作用的总结，所以要求填入的应是其对立的一面，故 a dark side 为答案。

10. 【定位】小标题 Is it true that laughing can make us healthier? 小节中的最后一句。

【解析】【线索】The author shows great _____ about today's children who don't have much time to play and laugh together.

【定位】倒数第二个小标题下，最后一句。

【解析】倒数第二段的最后一句中表明了作者对今天的孩子的态度(very concerned)，关注的原因是他们很少有在一起嬉闹和大笑的时间。将原文中的形容词 concerned 变为名词形式，故 concern 为答案。

【参考译文及题区画线】

不仅仅是笑

本文是对巴西 Campinas 大学(金边大学)行为生物学家斯尔维亚·卡多佐的采访，其主要内容是关于他对笑的看法。

为何对笑感兴趣？

1)笑，是我们所做的一桩极其普通的事，是无处不在的一种现象。我们一天笑好多次，笑的原因也多种多样，不过我们不常想到它，也很少有意识地加以控制。我们对种种的笑及其功能所知甚少，因此，我对它才真正产生了兴趣。我们为什么笑？就积极的情绪和社会行为而言，笑能教给我们什么？在大脑是如何控制情绪的问题上，我们有着许多的未知数。所以我认为，通过对笑的研究我们可以对其有所了解。

那么，人们为什么笑得那么多？

只有 10%到 20%的笑是因幽默而笑;2)大多数时候,笑是我们向他人发出的信息—传达自己快乐的性情,乐于与对方相处之意等。笑在社交互动中占有特殊的地位,是我们生活规律和现象的一种迷人的、带有运动、感情和认知等心理要素的特征。科学家们研究各种各样的感情与行为,但少有人专注于这一最基本的要素。笑给我们的暗示是:我们的大脑中有着种种强有力的机制让我们对快乐、幸福和喜悦做出反应。笑还发生在诸如恐惧消除之类事情后。

您是怎样研究起它来的?

3)我的专业研究重心一向是感情行为。我曾多年研究老鼠害怕时的神经基础,进而我开始研究笑。我在观察老鼠行为的过程中注意到,老鼠独处在无遮蔽的环境里时会十分不安,显得很惊慌;回到鼠笼和别的老鼠相处时,它们就显得快乐得多。它们仿佛在戏耍——打斗翻滚——我想知道它们是不是还在笑。神经生物学家亚克·潘克泽普曾经提出,幼鼠在打斗翻滚时,叫声短促尖利,超出人类听觉范围。他认为这些叫声类似笑声。这使我对笑之源感到好奇。

您认为别的动物也会笑吗?

你只要看一下与人类最接近的灵长目动物,就知道笑并非人类所独有。我认为这并不十分惊奇,因为我们只不过是很多群居物种中的一个,没有理由把作为社交工具的笑视为人类所特有。像黑猩猩这样的大型猿猴,其行为与人类相似。在那些能引起人类发笑的情景中,如和同伴或者人类戏耍,或者被抓挠发痒时,它们同样会张大嘴、露齿、收缩唇角、大声地发出重复的声音。远在灵长目动物之前,笑可能就已经得到进化。我们都知道,狗在戏耍时,呼气发声的模式就很奇特,不同于消极状态或者气势汹汹时发出的声音。

不过,我认为对4)动物嬉戏时喘息的行为在诠释上要谨慎,避免言过其实。将之视为类似人类的笑固然很好,但它可能仅是类似,而其目的却与人类的笑迥然不同,且进化的优势也完全不同。

那么,笑是为了什么?

212

5)人类行事，必有所用，笑，亦不例外。笑的功能无疑是传递信息。为了社会生活和谐，我们需要建立各种社会结构，而在进化过程中，笑被选择为促进社会交流的有用手段。换言之，它必然具备有助于物种生存的优势。

科学家们已有何发现？

我们通常是在人们对幽默的文字做出反应时对他们的大脑进行扫描。你可以看到脑电波的活动从枕叶的感觉处理视觉信号的那一小小的区域，即位于脑后部处理视觉信号的那一小块，扩展到脑的前叶。6)看来，脑前叶是参与识别那些好笑的事物的。前叶左侧分析语言和笑话的结构，同时右侧对笑话做必要的智力分析以"理解"笑话。最后，脑电波活动扩展到脑的运动区，控制发笑的身体动作。我们还知道由神经疾患和损伤引致发笑行为的那些复杂的脑电波传播途径。有时候，在脑受伤、生长肿瘤、中风或患上如帕金森综合症之类的疾病以后，病人会有"石脸"综合症而不能笑。

盲人和聋人的笑如何不同？

这一领城里奠基性的研究是由人种学家 7)埃雷尼厄斯·埃布尔—埃布斯菲尔特进行的。他发现盲聋儿童的哭笑表达模式十分丰富。他的结论是，他们的哭笑表达模式是在自然选择中进化而来的。聋哑儿童笑时的发声模式就如他们说话时的发声模式一样特别。盲童似乎在笑时面部表情并不充分。我们打算通过统计分析不同类型的人发笑时的细微差异来研究这些区别。我们将对他们就各类刺激做出笑的反应时的面部表情进行录相，然后剖析每一毫秒他们的面部表情与发声情况。

男人和女人的笑有区别吗？

8)肯定有，特别是在把笑作为社交工具的应用上。例如，女人微笑多于大笑。在与男人打交道时作为一种"社交润滑剂"，女人更能妙用微笑与大笑。这甚至可能有着生物之源，因为女人不用或不能把她们的体格作为一种威胁，而男人可以，哪怕是不自觉的。

不同的文化之间呢？

文化差异肯定在笑上有所反应。在大多数的文化中，带有夸张的动作与表情的大声而狂放的笑被认为是"非女性的"，而在男人之间则颇为常见，尤其是男人与男人之间。在某些情形下，我认为，笑显然是不自觉地被用来获取诸如权利、友谊、情人或下属的坦诚行为等形形色色的事物的。例如，从老板到部落首领这样的社会统治人物就利用笑控制下属。老板笑，他们的下属也笑。9)<u>笑可能是一种通过掌控群体内的感情气氛来肯定自己权威的一种形式。但笑也有它黑暗的一面。</u>有一些说法认为，笑与挑衅是同源的。灵长目动物中的一些笑显然是在发出威胁——看看它们露齿的样子就知道了。这也许可以说明为什么被人笑是如此令人不悦。

笑有益健康，此说没错吧？

毫无疑问，笑是良药。起码，它是运动，它会激活心血管系统，从而心律和血压增高，继而动脉舒展。使血压又降下来。胸肌、横膈膜与腹部短促而有力的反复收缩增加血流进入内脏各器官，而用力呼吸——哈哈大笑——可确保血液中含氧丰富。肌肉紧张度减弱，我们实际上可能会如所说的"笑得软成一滩泥"而一时四肢失控。笑还可以释放脑部的内啡肽，减少对疼痛的敏感度，增强我们的耐久力和愉悦感。一些研究认为，笑通过减少因压力关系而分泌的荷尔蒙来影响免疫系统，而且笑的时候，免疫系统会产生更多的T细胞。但这些效应尚未得到有着严格控制的研究的证实。笑的社会作用的重要性是确定无疑的了。10)<u>我感到很不安的是，今日的儿童在游戏和闲暇时远离群体，他们失去了许多笑的机会，从而可能染上许许多多的社会疾病。</u>

为什么？

因为儿童只盯着电脑视屏而不再互相嬉笑，是有悖于他们的天性的。儿童天生的社会行为就是嬉戏，这时的笑表明，装腔作势的攻击行为不是动真格儿的，只是找乐儿，而这是儿童形成正面的感情联系、获得新的社交技巧和普遍开始从童年期过渡到成年期的一种重要方式。我认为,做父母的应当常关切地确保他们的孩子多多和同龄人及成年人集体游戏并更多地欢笑。

Part II   Reading in Depth

Section A

【结构剖析】议论文。第一段提出问题:人们没有认清教学与研究之间的关系。第二段讲述一些学校偏重研究的原因。第三段讲述一些学校在教学评定中遇到的困难。第四段阐述教学和研究的关系。第五段对第一段进行呼应。

11.【定位】第一段末句。

【解析】推断题。根据第一段最后一句作者对报纸和杂志上那些文章的评价:they also ignore deeper and more important relationships。题干要求填入的是一个动词,表示"减弱复杂程度,使简化"的意思,便可得答案。问题的主语是 suggestion,回答时应用动词 simplifies 的第三人称单数形式。

12.【定位】第三段末句。

【解析】细节题。从第三段尤其最后一句可知,需要下力气分析学生对教师的评分情况的大学,其晋升制度的主要依据一定是教学质量。故 teaching quality 为答案。

13.【定位】第四段第二句。

【解析】细节题。第四段中讲述了教学和研究之间的紧密联系。其中提到 The training of new scientists requires outstanding teaching at...(优秀的教学工作对于培训新科学家来说都是需要的),也就是说那些将来要做研究的科学家们需要从教学中得到很好的训练。故 Future scientists who research need good training. 为答案。

14.【定位】第四段倒数第二句。

【解析】细节题。第四段倒数第二句中,作者认为,教授的头衔应该只授给 those who profess。profess 的意思在下一句中通过对比的方式给了出来,就是 teach。故 teaching 为答案。

15.【定位】末段末句。

【解析】词汇题。把握文章的主题是解答此题的关键。文章主要讲的就是大学存在的教学和研究工作分离的问题以及理清两者紧密依附关系的重要性。再综合句中 but 前面的部分所给出的提示:前面批判那些认为两者可以分离的人,后面批判的是那些说两者分离问题将会消失的人,因为兼顾两者其实是很难的。故 the separation of teaching from research 为答案。

【参考译文及题区画线】

11)最近的报纸和杂志上有文章说,教学和研究是互相矛盾的,说研究在学术晋升中占的分量重大。而教学的重要性被严重低估了。这些话里有一定的真实性,但是他们也忽略了教学和研究之间更深层次的、更重要的关系。

一个人的研究经历是他能够在一所研究型大学工作及获得晋升的重要因素,因为研究型大学对于研究工作的重视正是它与文科大学的区别所在。不过一些教师因为研究工作而忽略了教学,这就有问题了。

12)大多数的研究型大学都会对教学工作出色的教师给予奖励,但是学校最看重的通常都是教师们在研究工作中的成就。部分原因是教学工作很难评定。一个高度负责、要求苛刻的教师通常会得到那些希望得到考验的学习最好的学生的欣赏,但那些学习成绩不怎么好的学生就不怎么喜欢他了。温和型的教师得到的总评分通常比较高,但是那些最优秀的学生不免有些失望,尤其是那些觉得教学体系应该给他们提供一些伟大挑战的学生。于是,一所主要依据教学质量来晋升教师的大学将不得不面对这种七嘴八舌的混乱局面。

现代科学的发展日益迅猛，教师们受到了两种明显的压力。一种是他们需要时间来跟上专业的发展步伐，另一种是他们需要时间来教学。不管是在研究型大学，还是在文科大学，13)优秀的教学工作对于培训新科学家来说都是需要的。尽管科学家通常都是在小学阶段就定型了，他们却可能在大学和研究生阶段因为教师槽糕的教学而迷失了方向。解决的方法不是要将教学和研究分开，而是要认识到两者的结合很困难但却很重要。14)教授头衔只应该给那些教授学生的人，大学应该将它们为那些愿意成为学者团体中热心的一分子的那些教师保留起来了。不愿意教学的教师可以被称为"卓越的研究调查者"或其他的什么。

现代科学的发展速度日益加大了人们同时成为一个伟大研究者和伟大教师的难度。仍有许多人拥有这两个称谓。15)那些说我们可以将教学和研究分开的人肯定没有理解两者之间的关系，而那些声称问题会消失的人一定没有完全履行他们的职责。

Section B

Passage one

【结构剖析】议论文。作者通过对比自己在大学期间做侍应生的经历和毕业后的工作经历，说明人们因为职业的不同而受到不同的待遇。第一段指出人们因为职业不同而受到不同的待遇；第二段与第三段叙述作者做侍应生的经历；第四段至第六段讲述作者毕业后在报社工作的经历；第七段与第八段得出人们根据职业区别对待人的结论。

【语境记忆】

1. gauge [geidʒ] *n.* 标准；估计（或判断）方法
2. deserve [di'zə:v] *vt.* 应受，该得
3. courtesy ['kə:tisi] *n.* 礼貌；殷勤，好意　4. waiting tables 侍应生
5. job title 职称　6. casual acquaintance 点头之交

7. cordially [ˌkɔːdjəli] *adv.* 热诚地, 诚挚地, 友善地

8. cater to 迎合

【难句分析】

I'm now applying to graduate school, which means someday I'll return to a profession where people need to be nice to me in order to get what they want. ; I think I'll take them to dinner first, and see how they treat someone whose only job is to serve them. (Last para.)

此句是以分号构成的两个分句。第一个分句包含两个定语从句, 其中 which 引导的非限制定语从句修饰先行词 I'm now applying to graduated school 这件事, where 引导的地点定语从句修饰先行词 profession; 第二个分句由两个并列分句组成, 其中 how 引导宾语从句作 see 的宾语, 而该宾语从句中又包含一个由 whose 引导的定语从句, 修饰先行词 someone。

16. C【定位】首段。

【解析】推断题。首段首句指出我一直认为我的职业是人们判断我的聪明才智的标准, 第二句则指出作者的失望: 最近我非常失望地发现, 我的职业也决定了别人把我当成什么样的人来对待。选项 C 表达同样含义, 是该段意思的总结概括, 故为答案。选项 A 虽然是原文的信息, 但不是作者失望的原因; 选项 B 和 D 文中未提及, 故都应排除。

17. A【定位】第二段。

【解析】推断题。第二段的例子是为了论证该段第二句的观点。该句指出: 作为一个拿别人的钱、侍候别人吃饭的人, 有些顾客对我说过一些也做过一些我觉得他们从来不会对一般熟人说或做过的事情, 说明人们是因为我的身份才这样对待我的。选项 A 描述了对人的态度, 符合题意, 故为答案。其他三项都不符合题意。

18. D【定位】第三段第二句。

【解析】细节题。第三段的第二句提到, 在 19 岁时我认为我应当

218

受到成年的职业人士不公正的对待,和 D 选项"她觉得被成人职业人士的不公正的对待是理所当然的"相符合,故 D 为答案。其他选项意思均和原文意思相反,应排除。

19. B【定位】第七段。

【解析】推断题。本题考查的是"many of my customers didn't get the difference betweensever and sevant"所表达的意思。解答此题关键要把握作者的态度。结合上文可知,作者不赞同这些人的态度,即把从事服务业的人当作仆人对待,由此推知,作者认为客人不应该将服务人员当成仆人们使唤。选项 B 符合此意,故为答案。选项 A 观点是错误的;选项 C 是对第七段首句的错误理解;选项 D 与本文的中心不符。

20. A【定位】末段末句。

【解析】推断题。本题考查的是作者把她的客户带去吃饭的目的。文章最后一句话说要看看他们如何对待那些为他们服务的人,联系文章主旨便可知,作者是想看看他们是否属于那种以职业来区别对待别人的那类人,故选项 A 为答案。选项 B 与原文相悖;选项 C 和 D 文中未提及,皆可排除。

【参考译文及题区画线】

　　像大多数人一样,我很久以前就明白,人们会根据我的职业来评价我,我的职业会成为人们衡量我有多聪明或多有才华的标准。然而,16)我非常失望地发现,我的职业也决定了别人把我当成什么样的人来对待。

　　去年,我辞去了小城记者的专业职位,换了一份餐馆招待的工作。17)作为一个拿别人的钱、侍候别人吃饭的人,有些顾客对我说过一些话、做过一些事——我想,哪怕是对最随便的熟人,他们也都不会说出这样的话、做出这样的事。一天晚上,一个顾客用手机通话时,挥手让我走开,一分钟后又用手指示意我回来,并抱怨说他已经准备好点菜了,问我刚才上哪儿去了。

我读大学时暑假做过餐馆招待,那时很多人把我当苦力看待。18)但那时我才 19 岁,我觉得,这些有专业技术的成年人认为我低人一等,也是理所当然的。而且,等我告诉他们我在读大学时,他们对我的态度就不一样了;有顾客开玩笑说,有朝一日我会坐在他们坐的桌子旁,等着别人来侍候我。

我一毕业就在一份社区报纸找了份工作。我发现,从工作的第一天起,每一个给我打电话的人说话都是彬彬有礼的。我想,职业领域里人们就是这样热情友好地相处的。

但不久我发现情况并非如此。我与一位广告销售代表的座位只相距几尺,他的名字和我的相近。我们俩的电话经常弄混淆,找克里斯汀的电话会转给克里斯蒂。一旦转错了,很快就能察觉出来。也许是因为牵涉到钱的问题,但是也因为别人决不会用对克里斯汀讲话的语气和我讲话。

我的职业头衔让别人对我礼待有加,因此重回餐馆工作后让我吃惊不小。

做餐馆招待得忍耐许多事情,这不是什么秘密。好在有小费入账的时候,你会很容易忘掉许多不愉快的事情。19)服务行业,顾名思义,是为了满足他人的需求而存在的。尽管如此,很多顾客似乎没有弄清楚招待与仆人之间的区别。

目前我在申请读研究生,这意味着有朝一日我会重返某个专业职位。在这个职位上,有人为了得到想要的东西而不得不对我以礼相待。20)我想,我会首先带他们去吃饭,看看他们如何对待那些以给他们提供服务为职业的人。

Passage two

【结构剖析】说明文。本文主要阐述了美国富豪们对美国收入不平等,分化严重的看法。文章第一段至第四段描述现象:美国富豪们关注收入不平等的问题。第五段至第八段说明富豪们关注这一问题的原因。

【语境记忆】

1. leftish [ˈleftiʃ] *a.* 左翼的,左派的   2. right-wing 右翼的,右派的

3. billionaire [ˌbiljəˈnɛə] *n.* 亿万富翁

4. disintegrate [disˈintigreit] *vt.* 使碎裂,使瓦解,使崩溃

5. bankruptcy [ˈbæŋkrəptsi] *n.* 破产

6. outrage [ˈautreidʒ] *n.* 恶行,凌辱,愤慨

7. reciprocal [riˈsiprəkəl] *a.* 互惠的,报答的

8. allocate [ˈæləkeit] 分派,分配

9. distribution [ˌdistriˈbjuːʃən] *n.* 分发,分配,分布

【难句分析】

1. "It's an outrage that any American's life expectancy should be shortened simply because the company they worked for went bankrupt and ended health-care coverage," said the former chairman of the International Steel Group. (L. 2,Para. 4)

此句为多重复合句。句中的 it 是形式主语,真正的主语是 that 引导的主语从句。主语从句含有一个由 because 引导的原因状语从句;该原因状语从句又包含一个省略 that 的定语从句(they worked for)修饰先行词 company。

2. What they fear was that the political challenges of sustaining support for global economic integration will be more difficult in the United States because of what has happened to the distribution of income and economic insecurity. (L. 1,Para. 7)

此句为复合句。句中 what they fear 为主语从句, that 引导表语从句。而 because of 后的 what 引导宾语从句,作 because of 的宾语。

21. C【定位】首段。

【解析】细节题。本题考查的是当前美国富豪们的兴趣热点。首段首句提出此问题,该句提到 income inequality,该文后面的篇幅

都是围绕 income inequality 展开的。由此可推知。"财富分配不均"是富人们所关注的话题。选项 C 是原文意义的再现,而选项 A、B 和 D 文中未提及,故选项 C 为答案。

22. C【定位】第三段。

【解析】推断题。本题考查的是从 Mortimer Zuekerman 所哀叹的话中得到什么结论。文章第二段指出:美国的富豪们,不管左翼、右翼还是中间派,都在抨击收入不均现象。第三段引用 Mortimer Zuekerman,显然也是要说明收入不均的问题。该段提到 Our nation's core bargain... is disintegrating,接着解释说 Most of our economic gains have gone to people at the very top of the income ladder. Average income... has fallen...,说明收入差别加大,综合起来推知,选项 C 为答案。选项 A 是对第三段第二句的错误理解,因为原文没提到中产阶级未能争取到更好的福利待遇。选项 B 在文中无据可依。选项 D 与原文不符,原文提到普通家庭平均收入连续 5 年下降,但这并不表明他们没有从国家财富中获得的好处,故选项 A、B 和 D 都应排除。

23. B【定位】第五段。

【解析】段落主旨题。第五段第二句提到:"富豪们就和我们一样紧跟新时尚、新趋势,在政治和政策问题上也不例外。"说明他们对政治非常敏感,选项 B 符合此意,故为答案。选项 A 是对该段第二句的错误理解;选项 C 所指被扩大了,原文第五段是说 California 而不是 throughont America 将实行全民医疗保健;选项 D 中 by increasing the minimum wage 是假设的内容,不是事实。故选项 A、C 和 D 都应排除。

24. C【定位】第六、七段。

【解析】推断题。本题考查本文中心思想。本文第一段至第四段描述出现的现象:富豪们竟然关心中产阶级的命运了。接着在第五段至第八段分析争议现象的原因,原来富豪们想取得中产阶级在政治上的支持(第五段),以达到两个目的:一是可能为了避免惩罚性税收~~...~~；
二是让中产阶级支~~...（六段）~~，但这对他们来说根本不算什么；
济一体化进程中止，他们~~一体化进程（第七段）~~，因为一旦经
干的 real reason 是为了获取~~...~~损失。综合起来便可推知本题
为答案。选项 A 与第六段中心大~~...~~济一体化的支持。故选项C
项 D 为偷换概念，第七段说的是富豪~~们~~的是政治上的困难会
影响他们收入的分配和经济安全，而不是~~...~~economic insecurity 的威胁。故选项 A、B 和 D 都应排除。

25. D【定位】末段倒数第二句。

【解析】推断题。本题考查的是：如果美国对外国投资者和外国货
物设置障碍的话将会发生什么。末段倒数第二句提到 And when
the United States... foreign goods, it's likely to encourage reciprocal action abroad. 即美国对投资者和商品设置障碍时，那就有
可能引发外国设置同样的障碍。选项 D 符合此意，故为答案。选
项 A、B 和 C 文中未提及，故都应排除。

【参考译文及题区画线】

　　15）2007 年富豪们最热门的话题是什么？价值 730 万美元的
钻戒，坦桑尼亚狩猎之旅，对了，16）还有收入不均。

　　当然，像乔治·索罗斯这样的一些左翼亿万富翁多年来一直在
抱怨收入不均的现象。但现在温和派及右翼亿万富翁也开始越来
越多地为收入不均的现象及中产阶级的命运担忧。

　　12 月，莫蒂默·朱克曼在自己拥有的《美国新闻与世界报道》上
发表专栏文章。17）"我们国家与中产阶级之间的契约正在瓦解"。
这位全球富豪排名第 117 位的美国富翁哀叹，17）"我们经济的大部
分收入都归高踞收入榜首的人所有。与此形成鲜明对比的是，工薪
阶层户均收入过去 5 年连续下降。"他指出："数千万美国人担心，一
场重大的疾病就会让他们倾家荡产。"

　　朱克曼对美国中产阶级面临的痛苦挣扎愤怒不已，小威尔伯·

罗斯也表达了同样的看法。这⋯继续支付医疗保健费用就使得仅仅因为自己所在公司破产⋯。"

美国人寿命缩短,这简直⋯⋯们就跟我们一样紧跟新时尚、新趋势,这是怎么回事? 18⋯⋯不例外。 最近国会控制全国发生变更,提高在政治和政策问题上⋯⋯最低工资水平的举⋯备受欢迎,加州州长努力提供全民医疗保健。⋯⋯须私人气象员提醒,这些家伙也知道现在社考虑到这种种情⋯⋯会风向如何。

这些⋯钱有势的人在表达与中产阶级共进退的愿望,这可能是他们希望免遭没收性税收政策的一种努力,但是,收入不均可能导致对富人收税更重的说法并不会让这些有钱有势的人夜不能寐。加重征税他们承受得起。

19)他们真正担心的是,由于收入不均、经济不稳定,继续支持全球经济一体化的政治挑战将会在美国的处境更加艰难。

换言之,如果美国中产阶级继续在经济困境中挣扎,而富豪们更加富裕的话,要想让中产阶级在政治上支持允许商品、服务及资本自由跨国流通的政策,将会是越来越困难的事。20)而一旦美国对外国投资者及外国商品设置障碍,很可能会引发别国相应的行动。对那些买卖公司或在全球市场分配资本的人来说,这才是真正让他们夜不能寐的噩梦。

Reading Practice 2

Part I Reading Comprehension (Skimming and Scanning) (15 minutes)
Yesterday's Papers

"I believe too many of us editors and reporters are out of touch with our readers," Rupert Murdoch, the boss of News Corporation, one of the world's largest media companies, told the American Society of Newspaper Editors last week. No wonder that people, and in particular the young, are abandoning their newspapers. Today's teens, twenty, and thirty, something "don't want to rely on a god-like figure from above to tell them what's important,"Mr. Murdoch said, " and they certainly don't want news presented as gospel. " and yet, he went on, "as an industry, many of us have been remarkably, unaccountably, complacent(得意的). "

The speech—astonishing not so much for what it said as for who said it may go down in history as the day that the stodgy(墨守陈规的)newspaper business officially woke up to the new realities of the internet age. Talking at times more like a pony-media, new-age techno-lover than an old-media god-like figure at his seventies, Mr. Murdoch said that news "providers" such as his own organization had better get web-savvy(了解),stop lecturing their audiences, "become places for conversation" and "destinations" where "bloggers" and "podcasters" congregate to "engage our reporters and editors in more extended discussions". He also criticized editors and reporters who often "think" their readers are stupid.

Mr. Murdoch's argument begins with the fact that newspapers worldwide have been and seem destined to keep on losing readers, and with them advertising revenue. In 1995-2003,says the World Association of Newspapers, circulation fell by 5% in America, 3% in Europe and 2% in Japan. In the 1960s, four out of five Americans read a paper every day; today only half do so. Philip Meyer, author of "*The Vanishing Newspaper*: *Saving Journalism in the Information Age*" (University of Missouri Press),says that if the trend continues, the last newspaper reader will recycle his final paper copy in April 2040.

Broadband and Blogs(博客)

The decline of newspapers,predates the internet. But the second broadband-generation of the internet is not only accelerating it but is also changing the business in a way that the previous rivals to newspapers, radio and TV never did. Older people, whom Mr. Murdoch calls "digital immigrants", may not have noticed, but young "digital natives" increasingly get their news from web doors such as Yahoo! or Google, and from newer web media such as blogs. Short for "web logs", these are online journal entries of thoughts and web links that anybody can post. Whereas 56% of Americans haven't heard of blogs, and only 3% read them daily, among the young they are standard fare, with 44% of online Americans aged 18-29 reading them of often, according to a poll by CNN /USA Today /Gallup.

Other New Media Tools

Blogs, moreover, are but one item on a growing list of new media tools that the internet makes available. Wikis are collaborative web pages that allow readers to edit and contribute. This, to digital immigrants, may sound like a recipe for anarchic chaos, until they visit, for instance, wikipedia. org, an online encyclopedia that is growing dramatically richer by the day through ex-actly this spontaneous (and surprisingly orderly) collaboration among strangers. Photologs are becoming common; videpblogs are just starting. Podcasting (a conjunction of iPod, Apple's iconic audio player, and broadcasting) lets both professionals and amateurs produce audio files that people can download and listen to.

Blog's Roles in the Wider Media Drama

It is tempting, but wrong, for the traditional mainstream media (which includes *The Economists*) to belittle this sort of thing. It is true, for instance, that the vast majority of blogs are not worth reading and, in fact, are not read (although the same is true of much in traditional newspapers). On the other hand, bloggers play an increasingly prominent part in the wider media drama witness their role in America's presidential election last year. The most popular bloggers now get as much traffic individually as the opinion pages of most newspapers. Many bloggers are braggers, but some are world experts in their field. Matthew Hindman, a political scientists at Arizona State University, found that the top bloggers are more likely than top newspaper columnists to have gone to a, top university; and far more likely to have an advanced degree, such as a doctorate.

Another dangerous thought is to consider bloggers intrinsically parasitic on (and thus, ultimately, no threat to) the traditional news business. True, many thrive on disclosing, contradicting or analyzing stories trial originate in the old media. In this sense, the blogosphere is, so far, mostly an expanded op-ed medium. But there is nothing to suggest that bloggers cannot also do original reporting. Glenn Reynolds, whose political blog, Instapundit. com, counts 250,000 readers on a good day, often includes eyewitness accounts for people in Afghanistan or Shanghai, whom he considers "correspondents" in the original sense of the word.

Blog's Challenge to Existing Media

"The basic notion is that if people have the tools to create their own content, they will do that, and that this will result in an emerging global conversation," says Dan Gillmor, founder of Grassroots Media in San Francisco, and the author of *"We the Media"*, a book about, well, grassroots journalism. Take, for instance, Ohmy News in South Korea. Its "main concept is that every citizen can be a reporter," says Oh Yeon Ho, the boss and founder. Five years old, OhmyNews already has 2m readers and over 33,000 "citizen reporters", all of them volunteers who contribute stories that are edited

227

and fact-checked by some 50 permanent staff.

With so many new kinds of journalists joining the old kinds, it is also likely that new business models will rise to challenge existing ones. Some bloggers are allowing Google to place advertising links next to their postings, and thus get paid every time a reader of their blog clicks on them. Other bloggers, just like existing providers of specialist content, may ask for subscriptions to all, or part, of their content. Tip-jar systems, where readers click to make small payments to their favorite writers, are catching on. In one case last year, an OhmyNews article attacking an unpopular court judge got $ 30,000 in tips from readers, though most of the site's revenues come from advertising.

The tone in these new media is radically different. For today's digital natives, says Mr. Gillmor, it is disgusting to be lectured at. Instead, they expect to be informed as part of an online dialogue. They are at once less likely to write a traditional letter to the editor, and more likely to post a response on the web and then to carry on the discussion. A letters page pre-selected by an editor makes no sense to them; spotting the best responses using the spontaneous voting systems of the internet does.

Newspapers' Future

Even if established media groups—such as Mr. Murdoch's start to respond better to these changes, can they profit from them? Mr. Murdoch says that some media firms, at least, will be able to navigate the transition as advertising revenue switches from print-based to electronic media. Indeed, this is one area where news providers can use technology to their advantage, by providing more targeted audiences for advertisers, both by interest group and location. He also thinks that video clips, which his firm can conveniently provide, will be crucial ingredients of online news.

But it remains uncertain what mix of advertising revenue, tips and subscriptions will fund the news providers of the future, and how large a role today's providers will have. What is clear is that the control of news—what constitutes it, how to prioritize it and what is fact is shifting subtly from being the sole area of responsibility of the news provider to the audience itself. Newspapers, Mr. Murdoch implies, must learn to understand their role as providers of news independent of the old medium of distribution, the paper. (1365 words)

1. Mr. Murdoch wondered that newspapers are being abandoned by today's teens.

2. It's a fact that the numbers of newspaper readers worldwide and advertising revenue have been reducing.

3. Radio, TV and magazine have played almost the same role in changing the business of newspapers.

4. Tip-jar systems have helped one OhmyNews article get $30,000 from readers.

5. Wikipedia. org allows readers to edit and contribute, which leads to its dramatic growth in content.

6. Compared with top newspaper columnists, Matthew Hindman found, more top bloggers have gone to a top university and have _____.

7. Instapundit. com tells us that the blogosphere is not simply an _____.

8. Dan Gillmor says that _____ may come into being after people are able to create their own content in media

9. According to Mr. Gillmor, today's digital natives like to get information in the form of an online dialogue rather than a _____.

10. It is a clear and subtle change of the control of news from the news provider to _____.

Part II Reading Comprehension (Reading in Depth) (25 minutes)

Section A

Some personal characteristics play a vital role in the development of one's intelligence. But people fail to realize the importance of cultivating these factors in young people.

The so-called non-intelligence factors include one's feelings, will, motivation, interests and habits. After a 30-year follow-up study of 800 males, American psychologists found out that the main cause of difference in intelligence is not intelligence itself, but non-intelligence factors including the desire to learn, willpower and self-confidence. Though people all know that one should have definite objectives, a strong will and good learning habits, quite a number of teachers and parents don't pay much attention to cultivating these factors. Some parents are greatly worried when their children fail to do well in their studies. They blame either genetic factors, malnutrition, or laziness, but they never take into consideration these non-intelligence factors. At the same time, some teachers don't inquire into these as reasons why students do poorly. They simply give them more courses and exercises, or even rebuke or ridicule them. Gradually, these students lose self-confidence. Some of them just feel defeated and give themselves up as hopeless. Others may go astray because they are sick of learning.

The investigation of more than 1,000 middle school students in Shanghai showed that 46.5 percent of them were afraid of learning, because of examinations; 36.4 percent lack persistence, initiative and conscientiousness and 10.3 percent were sick of learning.

It is clear that the lack of cultivation of non-intelligence factors has been a main obstacle to intelligence development in teenagers.

If we don't start now to strengthen the cultivation of non-intelligence factors, it will not only obstruct the development of the intelligence of teenagers, but also affect the quality of a whole generation. Some experts have put forward proposals about how to cultivate students' non-intelligence factors.

First, parents and teachers should fully understand teenage psychology. On this basis; they can help them to pursue the objective of learning and stimulating their willpower.

The cultivation of non-intelligence factors should also be part of primary education for small children. Parents should attend to these qualities from the very beginning.

Primary and middle schools can open psychology courses to help students overcome the psychological obstacles to their learning, daily lives and recreation. (373 words)

11. According to the author, non-intelligence factors, such as one's feelings, will, self-confidence etc, can greatly facilitate the _____.

12. In the second paragraph, what's the purpose of mentioning the way some teachers and parents treat youngsters?

13. What consequences may the lack of cultivation of non-intelligence factors cause to youngsters according to the author?

14. _____ is the first step to be taken if parents and teachers want to cultivate children and students' non-intelligence factors.

15. In the passage, the author mainly wants to call for our _____.

Section B

Passage one(2006 年 12 月真题)

Each summer, no matter how pressing my work schedule, I

take off one day exclusively for my son. We call it dad-son day. This year our third stop was the amusement park, where he discovered that he was tall enough to ride one of the fastest roller coasters(过山车) in the world. We blasted through face-stretching turns and loops for ninety seconds. Then, as we stepped off the ride, he shrugged and, in a distressingly calm voice, remarked that it was not as exciting as other rides he'd been on. As I listened, I began to sense something seriously out of balance.

Throughout the season, I noticed similar events all around me. Parents seemed hard pressed to find new thrills for indifferent kids. Surrounded by ever-greater stimulation, their young faces wore looking disappointed and bored.

Facing their children's complaints of "nothing to do". Parents were shelling out large numbers of dollars for various forms of entertainment. In many cases the money seemed to do little more than buy transient relief from the terrible moans of their bored children. This set me pondering the obvious question: "How can it be so hard for kids to find something to do when there's never been such a range of stimulating entertainment available to them?"

Why do children immersed in this much excitement seem starved for more? That was, I realized, the point. I discovered during my own reckless adolescence that what creates excitement is not going fast, but going faster. Thrills have less to do with speed than changes in speed.

I'm concerned about the cumulative effect of years at these levels of feverish activity. It is no mystery to me why many teenagers appear apathetic (麻木的) and burned out, with a "been there, done that" air of indifference toward much of life. As increasing numbers of friends' children are prescribed medications-stimulants to deal with

232

inattentiveness at school or anti-depressants to help with the loss of interest and joy in their lives—I question the role of kids boredom in some of the diagnoses.

My own work is focused on the chemical imbalances and biological factors related to behavioral and emotional disorders. These are complex problems. Yet I've been reflecting more and more on how the pace of life and the intensity of stimulation may be contributing to the rising rates of psychiatric problems among children and adolescents in our society. (405 words)

16. The author felt surprised in the amusement park at the face that

_____.

A. his son was not as thrilled by the roller coaster ride as expected

B. his son blasted through the turns and loops with his face stretched

C. his son appeared distressed but calm while riding the roller coaster

D. his son could keep his balance so well on the fast-moving roller coaster

17. According to the author, children are bored _____.

A. unless their parents can find new thrills for them

B. when they don't have any access to stimulating fun games

C. when they are left alone at weekends by their working parents

D. even if they are exposed to more and more kinds of entertainment

18. From his own experience. the author came to the conclusion that children seem to expect _____.

A. a much wider variety of sports facilities

B. activities that require sophisticated

C. ever-changing thrilling forms of recreation

D. physical exercises that are more challenging

19. In Para. 6. the author expresses his doubt about the effectiveness of trying to change children indifference toward much of life by _____.

A. diverting their interest from electronic visual games

B. prescribing medications for their temporary relief

C. creating more stimulating activities for them

D. spending more money on their entertainment

20. In order to alleviate children's boredom, the author would probably suggest _____.

A. adjusting the pace of life and intensity of stimulation

B. promoting the practice of dad-son days

C. consulting a specialist in child psychology

D. balancing school work with extracurricular activities

Passage two(2006 年 12 月真题)

This looks like the year that hard-pressed tenants in California will get relief-not just in the marketplace, where rents have eased, but from the state capital Sacramento.

Two significant tenant reforms stand a good chance of passage. One bill, which will give more time to tenants being evicted (逐出), will soon be heading to the governor's desk. The other, protecting security deposits, faces a vote in the Senate on Monday.

For more than a century, landlords in California have been able to force tenants out with only 30 days' notice. That will now double under SB 1403, which got through the Assembly recently The new protection will apply to renters who have been in an apartment for at least a year.

Even 60 days in a tight housing market won't be long enough for some families to find at apartment near where their kids go to school, But it will be an improvement in cities like San Jose where renters rights groups charge that unscrupulous（不择手段的）landlords have kicked out tenants on short notice to put up rents.

The California Landlords Association argued that landlords shouldn't have to wait 60 days to get rid of problem tenants. But the bill gained support when a Japanese real estate investor sent out 30-day eviction notices to 550 families renting homes in Sacramento and Santa Rosa. The land lords lobby eventually dropped its opposition and instead its forces against AB 2330, regarding security deposits.

Sponsored by Assemblywoman Carole Migden of San Francisco, the bill would establish; procedure and a timetable for tenants to get back security deposits.

Some landlords view security deposits as a free month's rent, theirs for the taking. In most cases, though, there are honest disputes over damages—what constitutes ordinary wear and tear.

AB 2330 would give a tenant the right to request a walk-through with the landlord and to make the repairs before moving out; reputable landlords already do this. It would increase the penalty for failing to return a deposit.

The original bill would have required the landlord to pay interest in the deposit. The landlords lobby protested that it would involve too much paperwork over too little money-less than $10 a year on a $1,000 deposit, at current rates. On Wednesday, the sponsor dropped the interest section to increase the chance of passage.

Even in its amended form, AB 2330 is, like SB 1403, vitally important for tenants and should be made state law. (419 words)

21. We learn form the passage that SB1403 will benefit _____.

    A. long-term real estate investors

    B. short-term tenants in Sacramento

    C. landlords in the State of California

    D. tenants renting a house over a year

22. A 60-day notice before eviction may not be early enough for renters because _____.

    A. moving house is something difficult to arrange

    B. appropriate housing may not be readily available

    C. more time is needed for their kids' school registration

    D. the furnishing of the new house often takes a long time

23. Very often landlords don't return tenants' deposits on the pretext that _____.

    A. their rent has not been paid in time

    B. there has been ordinary wear and tear

    C. tenants have done damage to the house

    D. the 30-day notice for moving out is over

24. Why did the sponsor of the AB 2330 bill finally give in on the interest section?

    A. To put an end to a lengthy argument.

    B. To urge landlords to lobby for its passage.

    C. To cut down the heavy paperwork for its easy passage.

    D. To make it easier for the State Assembly to pass the bill.

25. It can be learned from the passage that _____.

    A. both bills are likely to be made state laws

    B. neither bill will pass through the Assembly

    C. AB 2330 stands a better chance of passage

    D. Sacramento and San Jose support SB 1403

Reading Practice 2 答案与解析

答案

1. N 2. Y 3. NG 4. Y 5. Y 6. an advanced degree

7. expanded op-ed medium 8. a global conversation 9. lecture

10. the audience itself 11. development of one's intelligence

12. To show cultivating non-intelligence factors is neglected by many people. /To show many people neglect cultivating non-intelligence factors. 13. It may obstruct/prevent/hinder teenagers' intelligence development. 14. Understanding teenage psychology

15. attention to the importance of cultivating non-intelligence factors

16. A 17. D 18. C 19. B 20. A 21. D 22. B 23. C

24. D 25. A

解析

Part I Reading Comprehension (Skimming and Scanning)

【结构剖析】说明文。文章主要讲述互联网的发展对报纸行业的冲击。前三段指出报业不景气的现状；然后指出当今的报业正在面对来自网络日志、网络广播和维基百科网页等这些新一代互联网技术的挑战；最后对未来的报业提出期望。

【语境记忆】

bloggers 博客 podcasters 播客 broadband 宽带

web portals 门户网站 web logs 网络日志 windbags 空话连篇的人

columnists ['kɔləmnist] n. 专栏作家 blogosphere 博客世界

op-ed medium 专栏媒介 Grassroots Media 大众媒体

video clips 录音剪辑

1. 【定位】第一段第二句。

   【解析】原文说的是默多克认为美国报纸的许多编辑和记者都脱离了读者,难怪大家尤其是年轻人都丢弃报纸不愿看了,而不是对此感到吃惊。故答案为 N。

2. 【定位】第三段首句。

   【解析】题干是对原文信息的归纳并同意转述,故答案为 Y。

3. 【定位】小标题 Broadband and Blogs 小节中的第二句。

   【解析】该句及全文都未提及杂志对报业的影响,故答案为 NG。

4. 【定位】小标题 Blog's Challenge to Existing Media 小节中的第二段的最后两句。

   【解析】原文提到"小费箱"制度的流行……接着举例说,去年,Ohmy News 上的一篇批评一宗不得人心的法庭判决的文章从读者那里得到了共计 3 万美元的小费收入。题干陈述与原文意思相符,故答案为 Y。特别提醒:阅读命题者偶尔也会不遵循设题顺序规律,解题时务必根据题干中的关键词确定题区。

5. 【定位】小标题 Other New Media Tools 小节中的第二、三句。

   【解析】维基百科由于其读者参与性在内容的丰富性上增长极快(is growing dramatically richer)。根据题干要求将 growing dramatically 转换为名词短语,进行同义转述,故答案为 Y。答案是:dramatic growth。

6. 【定位】小标题 Blog's Roles in the Wider Media Drama 小节中的第一段末句。

   【解析】题干将原文中的 more... than 比较结构进行了句型转换,用 compared with 来对 top bloggers 和 newsapapare columnists 所获得学历情况进行比较。根据原文信息本题答案应填:an advanced degree。

7. 【定位】小标题 Blog's Roles in the Wider Media Drama 小节中的第二段。

   【解析】本段先介绍了一种观点:博客不过是专栏媒介的扩充。接

238

着以 Instapundit. Com 为例进行驳斥。所以答案应填：expanded op-ed medium.

8. 【定位】小标题 Blog's Challenge to Existing Media 小节中的第一段首句。

   【解析】题干中的 come into being 对应原文中的 emerging，所以答案应填：a global conversation.

9. 【定位】小标题 Blog's Challenge to Existing Media 小节中的第三段第二、三句。

   【解析】Mr. Gillmor 认为，数字原居民讨厌听人说教(it is disgusting to be lectured at)。根据题干的语法结构要求将动词 lectured 转换为名词，所以答案应填：lecture.

10. 【定位】小标题 Newspapers' Future 小节中的第二段第二句。

   【解析】题干对原文做了简化。答案应填：the audience itself.

【参考译文及题区画线】

昨日的报纸

上周，世界最大传媒公司之一的"新闻集团"的老板 1)鲁伯特·默多克对美国报纸编辑协会说："我认为我们许多编辑和记者都脱离了读者。"难怪大家，尤其是年轻人，都丢弃报纸不愿意看了。默多克先生说：现在的十多岁、二三十岁的年轻人"不想依靠一个上帝似的人物居高临下地告诉他们什么是重要的，所以当然不希望新闻报道读起来像耶稣的训诫似的。"他接着说，然而"作为一个产业，我们中的许多人却无缘由地特别沾沾自喜。"

这番话让人惊讶。其所以如此，不是因为讲话的内容，而是因为讲话的人。到了墨守成规的报业界真正醒悟过来、面对互联网时代这一新现实时，这番话也将载入史册。默多克先生有时说起话来不像一个七十多岁的旧媒体时代的权威人物，而是像扎着马尾辫的新时代的技术爱好者。他说像他自己公司一样的新闻"提供者"最

239

好通晓网络,停止向他们的受众说教,使新闻公司"成为对话的地方",成为"博客"和"播客"汇集一堂、"与我们的记者和编辑进行更加广泛讨论的目的地。"他还批评了那些经常"认为"读者是愚蠢的编辑和记者。

2)默多克先生的观点基于这样一个事实:世界各地的报纸都在失去读者,而且似乎注定要继续失去读者。随之而来的是广告收入减少。世界报业协会说,从 1995 年至 2003 年,美国的报纸发行量减少了 5%,欧洲减少了 3%,日本减少了 2%。在 20 世纪 60 年代,每 5 个美国人中有 4 人天天读报,现在只有一半人读报。密苏里大学出版社出版的《正在消失的报纸:挽救信息时代的新闻业》一书的作者菲利普·梅耶说,如果这种趋势继续下去,最后一位报纸读者将会在 2040 年 4 月将他的最后一份报纸当废品卖掉。

宽带和博客

报业的衰退先于互联网的出现。3)但是作为第二代互联网技术的宽带的出现不仅正在加速报业的衰退,而且也正在改变这一行业。报纸以前的竞争对手电台和电视从来没有这样改变过报业。那些被默多克先生称为"数字移民"、年岁稍长一些的人也许没有注意到这一点。但是年轻的"数字原居民"越来越多地从 Yahoo 或者 Google 这样的网站以及像博客这样的更新型的网络媒体获取消息。博客(blog)是"网络日志(web log)"的简称,是人们思想的记录,或是每个人都可以发帖的一些网页链接。根据美国有线新闻电视网、《今日美国》、盖洛普三家联合民意调查结果,56% 的美国人还没有听说过博客,只有 3% 的人每天阅读博客。然而对年轻人来说,读博客是家常便饭,44%18 岁~29 岁的美国年轻网民经常阅读博客。

其他的新媒体工具

此外,博客只是网络提供的日益增多的新媒体工具之一。5)维基是允许读者进行编辑和投稿的协作性网页。对于数字移民来说,这听起来像造成无政府混乱状态的因素之一,不过他们一旦访问了比如维基网站（wikipedia. org），就不会这么认为了。该网站是通过陌生人之间的自发性合作而日益丰富的网上百科全书（令人惊讶的是，这种合作井然有序）。摄影博客正变得普遍，录像博客正刚刚兴起。网络广播的播客节目制作（苹果电脑公司的著名产品 iPod 音乐播放器与广播的结合体）允许职业和业余爱好者制作音频文件，供人们下载收听。

博客在更广义的媒体中的作用

传统主流媒体（包括《经济学家》杂志）很容易小瞧这种东西，但这是不对的。例如，多数博客确实不值得一读。事实上，也没有多少人去读（尽管传统报纸的情况也一样）。从另一方面来看，博主在更广义的媒体发展中发挥着日益突出的作用，大家都见过了他们在去年美国总统大选中的重要作用。眼下最受欢迎的博客与多数报纸社论版的读者数量是一样的。虽然许多博客空话连篇，但有些是其研究领域内的世界级专家。亚利桑那州立大学的政治家 6)马修·辛德曼发现，顶级博客比顶级报纸专栏作家更有可能上过顶级大学，而且更有可能拥有高级学位，如博士学位。

有人认为博客本质上是寄生于传统新闻业的（因此，最终对传统新闻业不构成威胁）。这是危险的想法。确实，许多博客是靠揭露旧媒体所刊登的报道文章的失实之处，以及对这些文章进行反驳或分析红火起来的。7)从这个角度讲，博客业务所及至今多数只不过是专栏版媒介的扩充。但是，这并不意味着博客做不了原创性的报道。格伦·雷诺兹的政治日志网（instapundit. com）的访问人数最多的一天可达 25 万人次。这个博客的内容经常包括来自阿富汗或上海的事件目击者发出的报道。他认为这些目击者是真正意义上的"驻外记者"。

博客对现存媒体的挑战

8)丹·捷尔默说："如果人们拥有创造内容的工具，他们就会去做，结果会出现全球性的对话。这是个基本的理念。"捷尔默先生是旧金山 Grassroots Media 网站的发起人,也是《草根媒体》一书的作者。该书主要讲的是基层新闻界的事。以韩国的 Ohmy News 为例,其老板和创始人吴连镐说,它的"主要理念是每位公民都可以成为记者。"创办 5 年之久的 Ohmy News 如今已有 200 万名读者和 3.3 万名"公民记者"。他们都是志愿提供报道文章的人。约有 50 名正式员工对他们提供的文章进行编辑,并负责核实报道的真实性。

正因为有那么多新型记者加入到旧有记者队伍当中,新的商业模式就有可能异军突起挑战现存的模式。一些博主允许 Google 将广告链接放到他们帖子的旁边,阅读其博客的读者每点击一次这些链接,博主们就可以得到报酬。其他博主,就像业已存在的提供专业内容的人一样,会要求人们征订他们的所有内容或部分内容。4)"小费箱"制度也正在流行起来。读者只要付很少一点钱便可点击阅读自己最喜爱的作者的文章。去年,Ohmy News 上的一篇批评一宗不得人心的法庭判决的文章从读者那里得到了共计 3 万美元的小费收入,虽然该网站的大部分收入来自广告。

这些新媒体的基调差异很大。捷尔默先生说,9)对于今天的数字原居民来说,他们非常讨厌听人说教,而是期望作为网上对话的一分子而得到信息。他们不太可能立刻给编辑写一封传统意义上的信,而是更有可能在网站发个回应帖子,然后继续讨论。编辑预选好的读者来信版面对他们来说没有意义;利用网络自发的投票系统来获得最佳回音却是有意义的。

报纸的未来

即使像默多克先生所拥有的那样老牌的新闻集团能够更好地应对这些变化,他们能从中获利吗?默多克先生说,当广告收入从印刷媒体转向电子媒体的时候,至少有些传媒公司能够顺应这一转变。确实,在这一领域新闻提供者可以利用技术来发挥自己的优势,根据兴趣群体和地理位置为广告商提供更多的目标受众。他还认为,他们公司能够非常方便地提供录像片段。将来录像片段会成为网络新闻的重要组成部分。

广告收入、小费和征订费加在一起是否能满足新闻公司未来的
资金需求，今天的新闻公司将发挥多大的作用，这些仍然不确定。
10)所能确定的是，新闻的控制权——新闻是由什么构成的、怎样确
定新闻的重要性、什么是事实——这种新闻提供者独有的权限正在
微妙地转向受众本身。默多克先生的意思是，新闻报纸必须理解，
其作为新闻提供者的角色与旧有的传播媒介——报纸——的角色
是不同的。

Part II   Reading Comprehension（Reading in Depth）

Section A

11. 【定位】首段首句和第二段首句。

【解析】细节题。文中首段指出本文论述的话题 some personal
characteristics，接着在第二段再详细说明这些特点是什么，由此
可推知，non-intelligence factors 与首段中的 some personal characteristics 所指相同；此外，题干中的 greatly facilitate 与首段首
句中的 play a vital role 意思相近，所以本题答案为首段首句中的
development of one's intelligence。句意为：作者认为，非智力因
素，诸如一个人的情绪、意志、自信心等能够极大地促进他的智力
发展。

12. 【定位】第二段第三句。

【解析】推断题。第二段援引了不少家长、老师在面对孩子学习表
现不理想时的做法和态度，为的是支持该段第三句提出的……，
quite a number of teachers and parents don't pay much attention
to cultivating these factors 的观点，即家长和老师们忽视了开发
孩子们的非智力因素对推动其智力发展的重要性，因此第三句末
的主句为本题答案。

13. 【定位】第四段。

【解析】细节题。在文章第四段明确指出缺乏对孩子们非智力因
素的培养是孩子们智力发展的主要障碍，由此可知答案。解题

时,根据提纲句法结构要求要将原文中的 obstacle 表达的意思用动词 obstruct 进行改写,也可用 prevent、hinder 表达。

14. 【定位】根据 first... parents and teachers 查找到倒数第三段首句。

【解析】细节题。文中最后三段提到专家们对于如何开发孩子们的非智力因素提出的建议,倒数第三段开头的 first 表明该句的内容就是本题答案所在。

15. 【定位】全文。

【解析】主旨题。本题考查文章的写作目的。文章首段指出了本文的论题,该段第二句中的 but 表明该句为作者最关注的话题,也就是作者的写作目的。该句表明我们 fail to realize the importance of cultivating these factors in young people,由此可推知,作者写这篇文章的目的就是想让读者知道 the importance of cultivating these factors in young people。

【参考译文及题区画线】

11)人的某些性格对于智力发展起重要的作用,然而人们却未能认识到培养青少年的这些(性格)因素的重要性。

12)所谓的非智力因素包括一个人的情绪、意志、主动性、兴趣和习惯。经过对 800 名男性持续 30 年的跟踪调查,美国的心理学家发现导致智力差异的主要原因并不在智力本身,而是非智力因素,包括学习的欲望、意志力和自信心。虽然人们都清楚,人应该有清晰的目标、坚强的意志和良好的学习习惯,13)但是许多教师和父母却并没有对培养这些因素给予足够的重视。有些父母在孩子学习成绩不好的时候忧心忡忡。他们将此(成绩不好)归咎于遗传基因,营养不良或懒惰,但却从来不考虑这些非智力因素。同时,有些教师也没有深入研究这些导致学生成绩差的因素。他们仅仅是让学生上更多的课,做更多的练习,或者甚至责备或冷嘲热讽。渐渐地,这些学生失去了自信。他们中的一些人深感挫败并自暴自弃地认为自己没希望了。还有人可能会误入歧途,因为他们厌恶学习。

一项对 1000 多名上海中学生的调查表明,有 46.5％因考试而害怕学习,36.4％缺乏毅力、主动性和责任心,还有 10.3％厌恶学习。

14) 显然,缺乏对非智力因素的培养已成为青少年智力发展的一个主要障碍。

如果我们还不开始加强对这些非智力因素的培养,那么不但会阻碍青少年的智力发展,而且还会影响整一代人的素质。一些专家已对如何培养学生的非智力因素提出了建议。

15) 首先,父母和教师应该全面了解青少年心理状况。在此基础上,他们可以帮助学生实现学习目标并增强他们的意志力。

对非智力因素的培养也应列为小学教育的一部分。父母应该在一开始就关注这些素质。

中学和小学可以开设心理学课程以帮助学生克服学习、日常生活和娱乐中的心理障碍。

Section B

Passage one

【结构剖析】议论文。本文作者从自己的亲身体会谈起,指出现在的孩子普遍存在精神情绪方面的问题,并依据自己相关工作经验对这一现象的原因进行了分析。

【语境记忆】

1. turns and loops 不停地转弯和转圈
2. shrug [ʃrʌg] vt. (表示疑惑,蔑视,无奈等)耸(肩)
3. out of balance 失去平衡
4. shell out 付款 (通常不情愿地付大笔钱)
5. feverish activity 狂热行为　6. burn out 不再热衷,失去兴趣、热情

【难句分析】

Yet I've been reflecting more and more on how the pace of life and the intensity of stimulation may be contributing to the rising rates of psychiatric problems among children and adolescents in our society. (Last line，Last para.)

此句为复合句。句中的 how 引导宾语从句作 reflect...on 的宾语。

16.【定位】首段倒数第二句。

【解析】细节题。本题考查的是作者对发生在游乐园的哪件事感到惊讶。首段倒数第二句提到作者出乎作者意料的是,他儿子对刚刚乘坐的极速过山车并没有感觉很兴奋。选项 A 正是对此的同义转述,其中的 thrilled 意为"激动的,兴奋的",与原文中的 exciting 相对应。文中的 face-stretching 是夸张用法,用来形容过山车的惊险刺激,转得脸都拉长了,选项 B 是对该词的错误理解,故排除。选项 C 对 in a distressingly calm voice 的错误理解。选项 D 未提及。故答案为 A。

17.【定位】第二段末句。

【解析】细节题。本题考查的是作者对孩子无聊原因的理解。第二段末句提到,虽然孩子们接触到了更多的刺激事物(ever-greater stimulation),但他们的脸上还是充满了失望和无聊的表情。选项 A 和 B 与原文意思相反。选项 C 文中没有提到。选项 D 与原文意思相符,且句中的 more and more kinds of entertainment 正是对原文 ever-greater stimulation 的转述,故选项 D 为答案。

18.【定位】第五段末句。

【解析】推断题。作者根据自身经历总结出,孩子们渴望的刺激与变化的速度关系最大。由此可推知,孩子们期望娱乐活动能够带来不断变化的刺激形式。选项 C 的表述与此一致,故为答案。选项 A、B 和 D 文中均未提及。

19. 【定位】第六段末句。

【解析】细节题。作者在第六段末句提到,越来越多的他朋友的孩子都在靠吃药（medication）解决问题,如用兴奋剂类药品（stimulants）治疗课堂注意力不集中,或者用抗抑郁药品（anti-depressant）帮他们重新找回生活中的乐趣,紧接着作者用 question... the diagnoses 字眼对这种疗法的效果表示质疑。选项 B 的表述与此一致,故为答案;选项 A 是对第四段中 arousing visuals 的错误理解,选项 C 和 D 在文中未提及,故予排除。

20. 【定位】末段末句。

【解析】推断题。作者在文章最后一句表示,他一直在思考这个问题:"生活节奏和所受刺激强度到底是怎样影响儿童及青少年精神问题患病率的。由此可推知,作者认为调节生活节奏和所受刺激的强度是减轻孩子无聊感的方式。选项 A 符合此义,故为答案。选项 B 是对第一段中的 dad-son day 的错误理解,选项 C 和 D 在文中均未提及,故均可排除。

【参考译文及题区画线】

　　每年夏天,不管工作日程多紧,我都会单独抽出一天时间陪我儿子。我们把这一天叫作"父子日"。今年我们玩的第三个地方是游乐园,当时儿子发现自己长高了,已经可以乘坐世界上速度最快的一种过山车了。在九十秒钟内,我们一阵风似地飞速转了一圈又一圈,转得脸都拉长了。16)当我们从过山车上下来的时候,儿子耸耸肩,用平静但有点不爽的语气说,最快的过山车也不过如此,并不比他以前坐过的更刺激。我听后,开始感到有什么东西很不对劲。

　　整个夏天,我注意到周围有很多类似的情况。家长们似乎竭尽全力为那些对什么都提不起兴趣的孩子们寻找新鲜刺激。17)虽然玩的东西都比以前更刺激,但他们的小脸上还是充满了失望和厌烦的表情。

面对孩子们"无事可做"的抱怨,家长们不惜大把掏钱,让孩子们参加各种各样的娱乐活动。然而很多情况下,对于百无聊赖的孩子们无尽的抱怨,这些钱却似乎只能买来片刻安宁,这使我开始思考这样一个显而易见的问题:"现在刺激的娱乐活动那么多,怎么让孩子们有点事做就那么难呢?"

真正令我担忧的是这些刺激的强度。据我观察,当面对电影里那些色情画面和血腥的特效场面产生的巨大冲击时,我小女儿的表情总是十分专注。

为什么孩子们会沉迷于这些如此刺激的东西却还渴求更多呢?我意识到,这恰恰是问题所在。当自己还是一个鲁莽少年时我就发现,能产生刺激效应的不是速度有多快,而是速度有没有加快。18)激动兴奋与速度本身关系不大,而是与速度的变化存在很大关系。

我担心长年沉迷于此种程度的狂热行为会累积产生怎样的后果。我一点都不奇怪为什么许多青少年表现得麻木不仁、无精打采,对生活抱着一种"都见过了,都经历过了"的无所谓态度。19)越来越多的我朋友的孩子都在进行药物治疗——用兴奋剂类药品治疗课堂注意力不集中,或者用抗抑郁药品帮他重新找回生活中的乐趣——我却很怀疑病情诊断是如何定义孩子们的厌倦状态的。

我自身的工作主要着重于研究与行为失常、精神失常相关的化学物质失衡和生物学因素。这些问题很复杂。20)我开始越来越多地反思:我们的生活节奏和所受刺激的强度是如何导致社会上儿童和青少年精神问题患病率的增长。

Passage two

【结构剖析】说明性报道。本文主要介绍了加州两项与租房改革有关的议案:SB1403 号议案和 AB2330 号议案。第一、二段概括介绍两项议案的内容及意义;第三段至第五段详细说明有关 SB1403 号议案的情况;第六段至第十段详细说明有关 AB2330 号议案的情况。

【语境记忆】

1. stand a good chance of 有很大的可能性;大有希望
2. apply...to... 适用于 3. the landlord lobby 房东联合会
5. deposit [di'pɔzit] n. 保证金,押金,定金
6. wear and tear 磨损

【难句分析】

But it will be an improvement in cities like San Jose where renters rights groups charge that unscrupulous landlords have kicked out tenants on short notice to put up rents. (L. 4, Para. 4)

此句为复合句。句中的 where 引导定语从句,修饰 cities like San Jose;that 引导宾语从句,作 charge 的宾语。

21. 【定位】第三段末句。

【解析】推断题。第三段末句提到,SB1403 号议案只适合那些至少居住一年以上的房客,由此可推知,只有这些人能够受益。选项 D 是对原文的同义转述,句中的 tenants 对应文中的 renters, renting a house over a year 对应 in an apartment for at least a year。选项 A 在原文中未提及,选项 B 和 C 与原文相矛盾,均可排除。故选项 D 为答案。

22. 【定位】第四段首句。

【解析】细节题。第四段首句提到,在紧张的住房市场上,有些家庭即使花 60 天的时间也很难找到离孩子学校较近的地方。由此可推知,提前 60 天的通知对房客们来说依然不够,因为合适的房子不好找。故选项 B 为答案,其他三项文中未提及。

23. 【定位】第七段第二句。

【解析】细节题。第七段提到,然而很多时候房客也会就物品的损坏问题和房东据理力争。因为所谓的“损坏”只不过是一些不可避免的日常磨损而已。再结合前面提到的“有些房东认为押金是白得的一个月房租,就等着自己揣进腰包”的推测,说明房东们经

249

常以房客损坏屋内用品为借口拒绝返还押金。选项 C 符合此意，故为答案。题干中的 on the pretext 是"以……借口或托辞"意思。

24. 【定位】倒数第二段末句。

    【解析】细节题。本题考查的是 AB2330 号议案的发起人放弃利息要求的原因。倒数第二段末句提到，AB2330 号议案的发起人删除了关于扣留押金需支付利息的规定为的是提高议案通过的可能性。选项 D 正表达了此意，是对原文的转述，其中 to make it easier for... to pass the bill 与原文的 increase the chance of passage 对应。选项 A 和 B 文中未提及；选项 C 是依据该段第二句设置的强干扰项；故选项 D 为答案。

25. 【定位】全文。

    【解析】推论题。第三段提到 SB1403 号议案最近已通过众议院的表决，最后一段又提到，AB2330 号议案和 SB1403 号议案一样，都对房客非常重要，因此也该成为州内立法，这表明这两项议案都很可能成为州立法。选项 A 符合此推论；选项 B 与文章末句意思矛盾；选项 C 过于片面；选项 D 是对第五段第二句 But tile bill gained support when Japanese... in Sacramento and San Jose 的错误理解。故选项 A 为答案。

【参考译文及题区画线】

看来今年加州被催逼房租的房客可以放心了——不仅因为市场上房租降低了，从加州首府萨克拉门托传来的消息也让他们感到欣慰。

两项意义重大的租房改革议案很可能获得通过。其中一项决定给那些遭驱逐的房客更多的宽限时间。该议案将很快递交州长审批。另一项则对押金进行保护，议案将于星期一在州参议院被投票。

一个多世纪以来，加州的房东逼房客搬家时都只提前 30 天发出通知。现在根据 B2330,提前通知的天数必须翻倍,这项议案最近刚刚通过众议院的表决。21)这一新的保护措施只对那些至少居住了一年以上的房客适用。

22)在紧张的住房市场上,即使有 60 天的时间,一些家庭也可能找不到离孩子较近的住所。但对于圣何塞这样的城市来说这确实将是一个进步,因为房客权利保护团体指责那些不择手段的房东,说他们为了提高租金,只给房客很短的准备时间就责令其搬走。

加州的房东联合会辩解说,房东不必要等上 60 天再赶走问题房客。但是,当一位日本房地产开发商提前 30 天向 550 户在萨克拉门托和圣罗莎租住的房客发出驱逐通知时,这项议案却得到了支持。房东游说团最终放弃了反对意见,而是转而将矛头指向了与押金有关的 AB2330 号议案。

该议案由来自旧金山的女议员 Carole Migden 发起,意在确立一份保证房客拿回押金的程序和时间表。

一些房东认为押金是白得的一个月房租,就等着他们揣进腰包里。23)然而很多时候房客也会就物品的损坏问题和房东据理力争,因为所谓的损坏只不过是一些不可避免的日常磨损而已。

AB2330 号议案将使房客有权要求和房东一起检查损坏情况,并在搬出去之前进行修补:一些名声好的房东已经这么做了。该议案也将加重因为不返还押金而受到的处罚。

最初的议案是要求房东为收取的押金支付利息的。但是房东游说团反对说,这将会因为一点小钱而增加太多的文书工作——按照现在的利率计算,1000 美元押金每年的利息还不到 10 美元。24)星期三,发起人删除了关于利息部分的规定,以提高议案被通过的可能性。

尽管 AB2330 号议案还处于修订阶段中,但其与 SB1403 号议案一样,都与房客的利益息息相关,也理应被制定为该州的法律。

Reading Practice 3

Part I   Reading Comprehension (Skimming and Scanning) (15 minutes)

Easter

Every year as Easter approaches, the stores are filled with jelly beans, candy eggs, egg-coloring kits, stuffed, real and chocolate bunnies of all types, and baskets for carrying all of this Easter bounty. However, most of us know that Easter isn't simply a commercial spring festival about dyeing and hiding eggs or wearing new spring attire. Easter is the Christian ceremony of the crucifixion(受难)of Jesus Christ and his resurrection(复活)days later. It is the central festival of the Christian church and, after the Sabbath(安息日), it is the oldest Christian observance.

Easter's Date

Unlike festivals such as Christmas, Easter has been celebrated without interruption since New Testament times. The dates of all movable feasts are also calculated around the date of Easter. According to the Encyclopedia Britannica:

...western Christians celebrate Easter on the first Sunday after the full moon (the paschal moon) that occurs on or next after the vernal equinox on March 21. If the paschal moon, which is calculated from a system of golden numbers and epacts and does not necessarily coincide with the astronomical full moon, occurs on a Sunday, Easter is the following Sunday.

The U. S. Naval Observatory's Astronomical Applications Department says that Easter is determined by the "ecclesiastical(教会的)moon" as defined by church-constructed tables to be used permanently for calculating. The phase of the moon. This full moon doesn't necessarily coincide with the astronomical full moon, which means, Navy researchers say, that Easter is not necessarily the very next Sunday after a full moon. It could be the next Sunday after the ecclesiastical moon. This happened in 1876.

These calculations say that Easter can fall between March 22 and April 25. This was decreed by Pope Gregory XIII in 1582 as part of the Gregorian calendar.

During New Testament times, the Christian church celebrated Easter at the same time as the Jews observed Passover(逾越节). (The first of Passover's eight days is Nissan 15 on the Jewish calendar. Passover observes the flight and freedom of the Israelites from slavery in Egypt.) By the middle of the second century, Easter was celebrated on the Sunday after Passover. The Council of Nicaea decided in 325 A. D. that all churches should celebrate it together on a Sunday.

The Eastern Orthodox(东正教)church may celebrate Easter up to a month later, as its calculation of the date is based on the Julian calendar, which is currently 13 days behind the Gregorian calendar. In 1865 and 1963, Easter observance in both Eastern and Western churches coincided.

In some countries, Good Friday and the Monday after Easter are national holidays. In the United States, these two days are not federal holidays and observance varies from state to state.

Easter Sunday

Easter Sunday celebrates Jesus' resurrection. Along with Christmas, Easter is considered one of the oldest and most joyous days on the Christian calendar. Religious services and other Easter celebrations vary throughout the regions of the world and even from country to country. In the United States, many "sunrise services" are held outside on Easter morning. These early services are symbolic of the empty tomb that was found early that Sunday morning and of Jesus' arrival in Jerusalem before sunrise on the Sunday of his resurrection.

"Do not be alarmed," he said. "You are looking for Jesus the Nazarene, who was crucified. He has risen! He is not here. See the place where they laid him. "(Mark 16:6, NIV)

It is important to understand that Easter was not celebrated or mentioned in the Bible. Rather, the three-day period from Good Friday through Easter Sunday has become a traditional observance of when Christians believe that the crucifixion, burial and resurrection of Christ occurred.

Traditions

 • **Easter Eggs**

In addition to the religious celebrations and observances of Easter, many countries also celebrate Easter with sweets and baked goods. Eggs, a traditional symbol of new life, are hard-boiled and dyed. Chocolate candies of all shapes and sizes are bought. Cakes and breads are baked and carefully decorated. And in many homes, families celebrate Easter with a gathering of family for an elaborate Easter dinner. According to the book *Festivals and Celebrations*, eggs were dyed in ancient times by the Egyptians and Persians, who then exchanged them with friends. "It was in Mesopotamia that Christians first gave eggs to their friends at Easter to remind them of the resurrection of Jesus," author Rowland Purton writes.

If *Lent*(大斋期)is observed as it was intended to be, eggs are a forbidden food. Centuries ago, when Lent ended on Easter Sunday, it became a tradition for people to give decorated eggs as presents to their friends and servants. Over time, the tradition of painting or decorating eggs has continued, particularly with the Ukrainians and other eastern Europeans known for their beautiful and intricate designs.

The bejeweled "Easter Egg" created by the artist Peter Carl Faberge in the late 1880s in St. Petersburg, Russia, is the extreme of egg decorating. The lapis lazuli(青金石)egg is a gold, enamel(瓷釉),pearl, diamond and ruby creation that features a hinged, enameled "yolk" that conceals a royal crown. This crown is also hinged and opens to reveal a ruby egg. Though this Easter egg is not documented among the Russian Imperial Eggs, experts say it was probably created for a member of Russian royalty. Visit The Cleveland Museum of Art: Special Exhibitions to view other intricate and bejeweled eggs created by Peter Carl Faberge.

- **Rabbits**

Rabbits are a powerful symbol of fertility and new life, and therefore, of Easter. The Easter Bunny, like Santa Claus, has become a popular children's character. But it may be that the Easter Bunny is something of a historical mistake.

At some point, the hare was replaced by the rabbit (some say that this is because it is difficult to tell hares and rabbits, both long-eared mammals, apart).

- **Hot Cross Buns**

According to the book *Dates and Afearzings of Religious & Other Festivals*, hot cross buns "used to be kept specially for Good Friday with the symbolism of the cross, although it is thought that they originated in pagan times with the bun representing the moon and its four quarters."

The custom of eating hot cross buns goes back to pre-Christian times, when pagans offered their god, Zeus, a cake baked in the form of a bull, with a cross upon it to represent its horns. Throughout the centuries, hot cross buns were made and eaten every Good Friday, and it was thought that they had miraculous curative powers. People hung buns from their kitchen ceilings to protect their households from evil for the year to come. Good Friday bread and buns were said never to decay. This was probably because the buns were baked so hard that there was no moisture left in the mixture for the mold to live on. Hot cross buns and bread baked on Good Friday were used in powdered form to treat all sorts of illnesses.

Easter at the White House

Held for more than 120 years, early egg rolling activities took place on the grounds of the U. S. Capitol. However, under President Rutherford Haves, the event was moved to the South Lawn of the White House, where it is still held.

While the children's games have changed over time, simply rolling a hard-boiled egg across the green lawns is still a high point of the day. Presidents and First Ladies and other celebrities have traditionally greeted the children, who, at the end of the day, receive collectible wooden eggs complete with the signatures of the President and First Lady. If you can't go to Washington, D. C. , you can order your own White House Easter Egg from Guest Services Inc.

Another interesting custom: Some countries have pace egg rolling. Eggs are rolled downhill as a symbol of the stone being rolled away from the tomb where Jesus was laid. This became popular despite scholars' assertion that the stone over the tomb was actually rolled uphill!

1. Which of the following has the longest history of being observed by Christians?

    A. Christmas   B. Sabbath

    C. Easter   D. Thanksgiving

2. Easter once fell on the next Sunday after the ecclesiastical moon in _____.

   A. 1582　　　B. 1865　　　C. 1876　　　D. 1963

3. Easter falls between March 22 and April 25 in the _____ calendar.

   A. Greek　　B. Roman　　　C. Jewish　　　D. Gregorian

4. The calculation of the date of Easter in the Orthodox Church is based on

   A. the Julian calendar　　　B. the Israeli calendar

   C. the New Testament　　　D. the Old Testament

5. It is believed that, on the Sunday of his resurrection, Jesus _____.

   A. summoned his disciples before sunrise

   B. summoned his disciples after sunrise

   C. arrived in Jerusalem before sunrise

   D. arrived in Jerusalem after sunrise

6. People use eggs in their celebration of Easter because _____.

   A. eggs are easy to dye　　　B. eggs symbolize new life

   C. eggs have various sizes　　D. eggs are nutritious

7. The bejeweled eggs created by Peter Carl Faberg6 can be seen in _____.

   A. the Metropolitan Museum of Art

   B. the Cleveland Museum of Art

   C. the British Museum

   D. the Louvre

8. People view rabbits as a symbol of Easter because they represent _____.

9. Hot cross buns eaten on Good Friday were believed to have great power of _____.

10. The White House Easter Eggs are first _____ the First Couple, before they are delivered to your home.

Part II   Reading Comprehension (Reading in Depth) (25 minutes)

Section A

A small piece of fish each day may keep the heart doctor away. That's the finding of an   11   study of Dutch men in which deaths from heart disease were more than 50 percent lower among those who consumed at least an ounce of salt water fish per day than those who never ate fish.

The Dutch research is one of three human studies that give strong scientific   12   to the long held belief that eating fish can provide health benefits,   13   to the heart.

Heart disease is the number-one killer in the United States, with more than 550,000 deaths   14   heart attacks each year. But researchers previously have noticed that the   15   of heart disease is lower in cultures that consume more fish than Americans do. There are fewer heart disease deaths, for example, among the Eskimos of Greenland, who consume about 14 ounces of fish a day, and among the Japanese, whose   16   fish consumption averages more than 3 ounces.

For 20 years, the Dutch study followed 852 middle-aged men, 20 percent of whom ate no fish. At the start of the study, the   17   fish consumption was about two-thirds of an ounce each day with more men eating lean fish than fatty fish. During the next two   18 , 78 of the men died from heart disease. The fewest deaths were among the group who   19   ate fish, even at levels far lower than those of the Japanese or Eskimos. This relationship was true   20   of other factors such as age, high blood pressure, or blood cholesterol levels. (261 words)

258

A. emergence	B. incidence	C. used	D. especially
E. appropriately	F. backing	G. regardless	H. daily
I. average	J. decades	K. extensive	L. causing
M. considerate	N. occurring	O. regularly	

Section B

Passage one（2006 年 6 月真题）

Age has its privileges in America, and one of the more prominent of them is the senior citizen discount. Anyone who has reached a certain age—in some cases as low as 55—is automatically entitled to dazzling array of price reductions at nearly every level of commercial life. Eligibility is determined not by one's need but by the date on one's birth certificate. Practically unheard of a generation ago, the discounts have become a routine part of many businesses—as common as color televisions in motel rooms and free coffee on airliners.

People with gray hair often are given the discounts without even asking for them; yet, millions of Americans above age 60 are healthy and solvent(有支付能力的). Businesses that would never dare offer discounts to college students or anyone under 30 freely offer them to older Americans. The practice is acceptable because of the widespread belief that "elderly" and "needy" are synonymous(同义的). Perhaps that once was true, but today elderly Americans as a group have a lower poverty rate than the rest of the population. To be sure, there is economic diversity within the elderly, and many older Americans are poor. But most of them aren't.

It is impossible to determine the impact of the discounts on individual companies. For many firms, they are a stimulus to revenue. But in other cases the discounts are given at the expense, directly or indirectly, of younger Americans. Moreover, they are a direct irri-

259

tant in what some politicians and scholars see as a coming conflict between the generations.

Generational tensions are being fueled by continuing debate over Social Security benefits, which mostly involves a transfer of resources from the young to the old. Employment is another sore point. Buoyed(支持)by laws and court decisions, more and more older Americans are declining the retirement dinner in favor of staying on the job—thereby lessening employment and promotion opportunities for younger workers.

Far from a kind of charity they once were, senior citizen discounts have become a formidable economic privilege to a group with millions of members who don't need them.

It no longer makes sense to treat the elderly as a single group whose economic needs deserve priority over those of others. Senior citizen discounts only enhance the myth that older people can't take care of themselves and need special treatment; and they threaten the creation of a new myth, that the elderly are ungrateful and taking for themselves at the expense of children and other age groups. Senior citizen discounts are the essence of the very thing older Americans are fighting against—discrimination by age. (452 words)

21. We learn from the first paragraph that _____.

   A. offering senior citizens discounts has become routine commercial practice

   B. senior citizen discounts have enabled many old people to live a decent life

   C. giving senior citizens discounts has boosted the market for the elderly

   D. senior citizens have to show their birth certificates to get a discount

22. What assumption lies behind the practice of senior citizen discounts?

A. Businesses, having made a lot of profits, should do something for society in return.

B. Old people are entitled to special treatment for the contribution they made to society.

C. The elderly, being financially underprivileged, need humane help from society.

D. Senior citizen discounts can make up for the inadequacy of the Social Security system.

23. According to some politicians and scholars, senior citizen discounts will _____.

A. make old people even more dependent on society

B. intensify conflicts between the young and the old

C. have adverse financial impact on business companies

D. bring a marked increase in the companies' revenues

24. How does the author view the Social Security system?

A. It encourages elderly people to retire in time.

B. It opens up broad career prospects for young people.

C. It benefits the old at the expense of the young.

D. It should be reinforced by laws and court decisions.

25. Which of the following best summarizes the author's main argument?

A. Senior citizens should fight hard against age discrimination.

B. The elderly are selfish and taking senior discounts for granted.

C. Priority should be given to the economic needs of senior citizens.

D. Senior citizen discounts may well be a type of age discrimination

Passage two(2006 年 6 月真题)

In 1854 my great-grandfather, Morris Marable, was sold on an auction block in Georgia for $ 500. For his white slave master, the sale was just "business as usual." But to Morris Marable and his heirs, slavery was a crime against our humanity. This pattern of human rights violations against enslaved African-Americans continued under racial segregation for nearly another century.

The fundamental problem of American democracy in the 21st century is the problem of "structural racism": the deep patterns of socio-economic inequality and accumulated disadvantage that are coded by race, and constantly justified in public speeches by both racist stereotypes and white indifference. Do Americans have the capacity and vision to remove these structural barriers that deny democratic rights and opportunities to millions of their fellow citizens?

This country has previously witnessed two great struggles to achieve a truly multicultural democracy.

The First Reconstruction(1954-1877) ended slavery and briefly gave black men voting rights, but gave no meaningful compensation for two centuries of unpaid labor. The promise of "40 acres and a mule(骡子)" was for most blacks a dream deferred(尚未实现的).

The Second Reconstruction (1954-1968), or the modern civil rights movement, ended legal segregation in public accommodations and gave blacks voting rights. But these successes paradoxically obscure the tremendous human costs of historically accumulated disadvantage that remain central to black Americans' lives.

The disproportionate wealth that most whites enjoy today was first constructed from centuries of unpaid black labor. Many white institutions, including some leading universities, insurance companies and banks, profited from slavery. This pattern of white privilege and black inequality continues today.

Demanding reparations(赔偿) is no just about compensation for

slavery and segregation. It is, more important, an educational campaign to highlight the contemporary reality of "racial deficits" of all kinds, the unequal conditions that impact blacks regardless of class. Structural racism's barriers include "equity inequity," the absence of black capital formation that is a direct consequence of America's history. One third of all black households actually have negative net wealth. In 1998 the typical black family's net wealth was $ 16,400, less than one fifth that of white families. Black families are denied home loans at twice the rate of whites.

Blacks remain the last hired and first fired during recessions. During the 1990-91 recession, African-Americans suffered disproportionately. At Coca-Cola, 42 percent of employees who lost their jobs were blacks. At Sears, 54 percent were black. Black have significantly shorter life spans, in part due to racism in the health establishment. Black are statistically less likely than whites to be referred for kidney transplants or early-stage cancer surgery. (453 words)

26. To the author, the auction of his great-grandfather is a typical example of _____.

    A. crime against humanity

    B. unfair business transaction

    C. racial conflicts in Georgia

    D. racial segregation in America

27. The barrier to democracy in 21st century America is _____.

    A. widespread use of racist stereotypes

    B. prejudice against minority groups

    C. deep-rooted socio-economic inequality

    D. denial of legal rights to ordinary blacks

28. What problem remains unsolved in the two Reconstructions?

    A. Differences between races are deliberately obscured.

B. The blacks are not compensated for their unpaid labor.

C. There is no guarantee for blacks to exercise their rights.

D. The interests of blacks are not protected by law.

29. It is clear that the wealth enjoyed by most whites _____.

A. has resulted from business successes over the years

B. has been accompanied by black capital formation

C. has derived from sizable investments in education

D. has been accumulated from generations of slavery

30. What does the author think of the current situation regarding racial discrimination?

A. Racism is not a major obstacle to blacks' employment.

B. Inequality of many kinds remains virtually untouched.

C. A major step has been taken towards reparations.

D. Little has been done to ensure blacks' civil rights.

Reading Practice 3 答案与解析

答案

```
1. B   2. C   3. D   4. A   5. C   6. B   7. B
8. fertility and new life   9. treating/ curing all sorts of diseases
10. signed
11. K   12. F   13. D   14. N   15. B   16. H   17. I   18. J
19. O   20. G   21. A   22. C   23. B   24. C   25. D   26. A
27. C   28. B   29. D   30. B
```

解析

Part I   Reading Comprehension (Skimming and Scanning) (15 minutes)

【结构剖析】说明文。文章主要介绍复活节的由来和复活节蛋、兔子,以及十字包的象征意义。

【语境记忆】

1. observance [əbˈzɜːvəns] *n.* 庆典,仪式
2. crucifixion [ˌkruːsiˈfikʃən] 钉死于十字架
3. resurrection [ˌrezəˈrekʃən] *n.* 复活,复苏
4. paschal [ˈpɑːskəl] *a.* 逾越节的,复活节的
5. coincide with 与……相一致
6. astronomical [æstrəˈnɔmikəl] *a.* 天文学的
7. decreed [diˈkriː] *vt.* 颁布,命令
8. bejewel [biˈdʒuːəl] *vt.* 将……饰以珠宝
9. fertility [fəˈtiliti] *n.* 繁殖力
10. in pagan times 在异教徒时代

1. 【定位】第一段最后一句。

   【解析】本题问的是基督徒最古老的庆典节日。第一段最后一句提到,复活节是基督教继安息日之后的最古老的宗教庆典,也就是说,安息日是最古老的宗教庆典,故 B 为答案。

2. 【定位】小标题 Easter's Date 下的第三段最后两句。

   【解析】本题问的是哪一年的复活节正好是教会的满月后的第一个星期日。根据题干中的关键词 ecclesiastical 确定信息源后,逐一查验选项中的年份四个年份,即可发现选项 C 为答案。

3. 【定位】小标题 Easter's Date 下的第四段。

   【解析】本题问的是在哪国的历法中,复活节可能在 3 月 22 日和 4 月 25 日之间来临。利用关键词定位信息源后,可发现 Easter's Date 下的第四段只提到了选项 D 的历法,其他选项均没有在该段提及。其中,选项 A 和选项 B 在文章其他地方也没有提及,而选项 C 在下一段提及,但该历法与 Easter 无关,只与"逾越节"有关而已。

4. 【定位】小标题 Easter's Date 下的倒数第二段首句。

   【解析】本题问东正教是根据何种历法计算复活节的日子。

265

Easter's Date 下的倒数第二段首句提到：东正教教堂可能晚一个月庆祝复活节，它根据朱利安日历来计算日期。故答案为 A。

5. 【定位】小标题 Easter Sunday 下的第一段末句。

【解析】本题问的是耶稣复活后做了什么事，原文小标题 Easter Sunday 下的第一段末句明确表明他复活后"在日出之前到达耶路撒冷"，故选项 C 为答案。

6. 【定位】小标题 Traditions 下的第一点 Easter Eggs 部分的首段第二句。

【解析】本题问用蛋庆祝复活节的原因。原文提到：蛋一直以来被视为新生命的象征……故选项 B 为答案。

7. 【定位】小标题 Traditions 下的第一点 Easter Eggs 部分的最后一段末句。

【解析】本题问在哪可见彼得·卡尔·法伯格制作的镶饰着珠宝的蛋。根据 bejweled 和 Peter Carl Faberge 大概定位 Easter Eggs 部分的最后一段末句：如果你去参观克利夫兰艺术博物馆，你就可以……精致的镶饰着珠宝的蛋。故选项 B 为答案。

8. 【定位】第三个小标题 Traditions 下的第二点 Rabbits 部分的第一段第一句。

【解析】本题问人们把兔子视为复活节的象征的原因。题目中的 represent 与原文的 a powerful symbol of 表意相同，根据句法要求，空白处需填入名词性短语。故答案为 fertility and new life。

9. 【定位】小标题 Traditions 下的第三点 Hot Cross Buns 部分的第二段第二句和最后一句。

【解析】本题问人们认为耶稣受难日吃的十字包具有何种力量。空白处需填入名词，与 of 一起作 power 的定语，表明十字包具有的作用。题目中的 believed 与原文中的 thought 为同义表达，great power 与原文的 marvelous... power 同义，因此，空白处的名词应表达 curative 的意思，结合本段末句，可知此处应填写 curing/treating all sorts of diseases。

10. 【定位】小标题 Easter at the White House 部分的第二段第二句后半部分及末句。

【解析】空白处需填入动词的过去分词,与 are 和 by 构成被动句的谓语成分。原文该段末句提到:孩子们会得到可供收藏的木制的蛋,蛋上还有总统和第一夫人的签名。题干中的 White House Easter Eggs 指的就是此句中的 collectible wooden eggs,故本题答案为 signed。

【参考译文画线点评】

复活节

　　每年要到复活节的时候,商店里就会摆满了软糖、糖果蛋、给蛋染色的工具,形象逼真的各种各样的巧克力兔子,还有用来装这些复活节礼物的篮子。但是,我们中大多数人都知道复活节不仅仅是关于给蛋染色、藏彩蛋或者穿新装的一个商业性的春季节日。复活节是基督教纪念耶稣在十字架受刑死后又复活的节日,1)是基督教堂的主要节日,也是基督教继安息日之后的最古老的宗教庆典。

复活节的日期

　　与圣诞那样的节日不同,人们从新约时期起对复活节的庆祝就从没有中断过。全部非固定节日的日期也都根据复活节的日期而定。据大英百科全书所载:

　　……西方基督教在 3 月 21 日春分或春分之后的第一次月圆(逾越节的月圆)后的第一个星期日庆祝复活节。由 golden numbers 和 epacts 系统计算出来的逾越节的月圆不一定与天文的满月相吻合,如果月圆出现在星期日,那么复活节就推迟一周到下星期日。

　　美国海军天文台的天文应用部指出复活节是由"教会的满月"决定的。教堂编制了可以永久使用的计算月相的时间表,并据此定义"满月"。这样计算出的满月不一定与天文学计算出的满月吻合。

海军研究人员指出,这意味着复活节不一定刚好就是满月后的第一个星期日。2)有可能是教会的满月后的第一个星期日。1876年就是这样的。

3)这些计算说明复活节可能在3月22日和4月25日之间来临。1582年罗马教皇格里高利十三世对此做了规定,将这个日期定为格里历的一部分。

在新约时期,基督教教堂是在犹太人庆祝逾越节的同时庆祝复活节的。(逾越节要庆祝8天,第1天是犹太历尼散月的15号。逾越节主要是庆祝以色列人逃离埃及摆脱奴隶的身份获得自由的节日。)到2世纪中叶,人们开始在逾越节之后的星期日庆祝复活节公元325年召开的尼西亚会议决定,所有教堂都应该在星期日一起庆祝复活节。

4)东正教教堂可能晚一个月庆祝复活节,它根据朱利安日历来计算日期。目前朱利安日历比格里历晚13天。在1865年和1963年,东正教和罗马教会刚好在相同的时间庆祝复活节。

在一些国家,耶稣受难日和复活节后的星期一都是法定假日。但在美国,这两天不是全国法定假日,每个州庆祝节日的方式也各不相同。

复活节

复活节是为了庆祝耶稣的复活而设的节日。连同圣诞节,复活节被认为是在基督教月历中最古老和最快乐的节日之一。对于复活节,世界上不同地区、不同国家的宗教庆典和其他庆祝活动都有所不同。在美国,在复活节早上人们会在户外举行很多的"朝阳礼拜"。5)这些早礼拜象征着在星期日清早发现空坟墓,以及耶稣在他复活的那个星期日的日出之前到达耶路撒冷。

"不要惊慌! 你们寻找那钉在十字架的拿撒勒人耶稣,他不在这里,已经复活了! 请看他们安放他的地方。"(马可16:6,NIV)

有一点我们应该理解,即复活节并没有出现在圣经里。相反,从耶稣受难日到复活节这三天的时间早已经成为一种传统的宗教仪式,基督教徒相信这三天就是耶稣受难、被埋葬然后复活的时间。

传统

· 复活节蛋

除宗教庆典和宗教仪式之外,很多国家也用甜食和烘烤的食物来庆祝复活节。6)蛋一直以来被视为新生命的象征,到了复活节,人们会把蛋煮老一点儿,然后染上色。人们也会买上各种各样的巧克力糖果,烤出蛋糕和面包,再装饰得漂漂亮亮的。在很多人家,一家人会聚在一起共享一顿精心制作的复活节晚餐。根据《节日和庆典》一书的记载,在古代,埃及人和波斯人就有了给蛋染色的习俗了,他们将蛋染好色后与朋友互换。"在美索不达米亚,基督教徒首次在复活节将蛋送给他们的朋友以提醒他们耶稣的复活。"作者罗兰·珀顿这样写道。

如果正逢大斋期,按大斋期的规定,蛋是禁止食用的。几个世纪以前,当大斋期在复活节结束时,将经过装饰的蛋作为礼物送给朋友和仆人就成了一种传统。随着时间的流逝,给蛋染色或进行装饰的传统流传下来,特别是在因美丽而又错综复杂的彩蛋设计而闻名的乌克兰和其他东欧地区。

19世纪80年代后期在俄罗斯圣彼得堡,由艺术家彼得·卡尔·法伯格制作的缀满珠宝的"复活节蛋",则将对蛋的装饰推上了极致。青金石蛋镶饰着黄金、瓷釉、珍珠、钻石和红宝石,其一大特色是它用铰链将涂上瓷釉的"蛋黄"固定在里面,蛋黄里面藏着一顶王冠。王冠也用铰链固定着,打开王冠还可看到一个红宝石蛋。虽然这个复活节蛋在有关"俄帝国的蛋"的文献中没有记载,专家估计它可能是为一名俄国王室成员制作的。7)如果你去参观克利夫兰艺术博物馆,你就可以到特色展区去看看彼得·卡尔·法伯格制作的其他精致的镶饰着珠宝的蛋。

· 兔子

8)兔子有极强的繁殖能力,是新的生命和兴旺发达的象征,因此,也是复活节的象征。复活节兔子,像圣诞老人一样,在孩子当中非常受欢迎。但是对于复活节兔子的说法,可能存在一点历史上的错误。

不知在什么时候,家兔代替了野兔(有人说这是因为很难区分野兔和家兔,它们都是有着长长的耳朵的哺乳动物)。

· 十字包

《宗教和其他节日的日期和意义》一书提到,十字包"象征着十字架,过去常常是在耶稣受难日的时候食用,虽然人们认为十字包是起源于异教徒时代,代表月亮和它的四个月相"。

吃十字包的风俗可以追溯到前基督时代,当异教徒向他们的神宙斯献祭品时,他们将蛋糕烤成公牛状,在上面刻上十字架代表它的角。9)几个世纪以来,人们都在耶稣受难日做十字包吃。并且认为它们有着神奇的治疗疾病的力量。人们把十字包挂在他们厨房的天花板上,以保护家人来年不受邪恶力量的伤害。据说耶稣受难日面包和十字包永远都不会腐烂。这或许是因为十字包被烤得很干以至于里面没有任何可以让霉菌得以生长的水分。在耶稣受难日烤的十字包和面包还被碾成粉末状来治疗各种疾病。

白宫的复活节

早期的滚蛋活动是在美国国会大厦的草地上举行的,这种情况持续了 120 多年。不过,在拉瑟福德·海斯当上总统后,这个活动被移到白宫的南草坪举行,到现在也是如此。

虽然孩子们的比赛随着时间的流逝已经有些改变,但将一个煮熟的蛋滚过绿色的草坪仍然是一天的亮点。总统和第一夫人以及其他名人会按传统欢迎孩子们的到来,10)在一天结束的时候,孩子们会得到可供收藏的木制的蛋,蛋上还有总统和第一夫人的签名。如果你不能去华盛顿。你可以通过客服股份有限公司给你自己预定白宫复活节蛋。

另外还有一个有趣的风俗:一些国家还有快步滚蛋的活动(复活节的一种活动)。将蛋滚下山象征着滚走埋耶稣的坟墓的石头。尽管学者坚持坟墓上的石头实际上是朝上滚的,但这项活动还是深受人们的欢迎。

Part II　Reading Comprehension（Reading in Depth）（25 minutes）
Section A

结构剖析:说明文。本文主要根据荷兰人的研究结果,阐明每天适量吃鱼有益健康,尤其有助于降低心脏病的发病率。

词性归类

n.	emergence 出现;显露　incidence 发生率　backing 支持　average 平均数,平均　decades 十年(复数)
v.	used 使用　backing 支持;使后退　average 平均　causing 引起　occurring 发生,出现
adj.	daily 每天的　average 平均的;平常的　extensive 广大的;广泛的　considerate 体贴的,体谅的　regardless 不重视的
adv.	especially 特别,尤其　appropriately 适当地　regardless 不顾后果地　regularly 有规律地;经常地

11.【答案】K. extensive
　　【解析】形容词辨义题。根据前面的冠词 an 和后面的 study,可知此处需要填入以元音开头的形容词,词库中符合此条件的词有 average 和 extensive。从句子意思上判断,此类研究为了更科学地体现结果,应该是广泛的研究而不是一般的研究,故选 K。

12.【答案】F. backing
　　【解析】名词辨义题。此处需填入名词,作 give 的宾语。根据句意,backing 为最佳选择,表明该研究对与人们的想法提供科学上的"支持",故选 F。

13. 【答案】D. especially

【解析】副词辨义题。此处应填入副词,对上文起强调作用。在词库里的副词中,只有 especially 可表示递进或强周,故选 D。

14. 【答案】N. occurring

【解析】动词辨义题。此处需要动词的现在分词,与 with... from 构成短语作状语,意为这些人"死于"心脏病。在词库中,剩下 occurring 和 causing 两个词符合此条件,其中 occurring 可与 from 搭配,而 causing 一般与 by 连用,故选 N。

15. 【答案】B. incidence

【解析】名词辨义题。空格前的 the 和后面的 of 表明此处需要填名词。从本句的比较点可以推断本句的话题是心脏病的"发病率",词库中,incidence(发生率)符合此意。故选 B。

16. 【答案】H. daily

【解析】形容词辨义题。此处需要形容词,修饰 fish consumption。根据本句的结构可知这个词的意思接近前半句的 a day,意为"每日鱼消费量",故选 H。

17. 【答案】I. average

【解析】形容词辨义题。此处需要形容词,修饰 fish consumption。词库中,剩下 average 和 considerate 两形容词,根据上下文,只有 average 符合句意,意为"鱼的平均消费量",故选 I。

18. 【答案】J. decades

【解析】名词辨义题。此处需要填人名词,与上句开头的 at the start 表明在荷兰所作研究的不同阶段的情况,由此推知,该词应表示时间。结合本段开头三句的时间状语可以知道此处的时间指的就是本段开头提到的 20 years。故选 J。two decades 意为"20年"。

19. 【答案】O. regularly

【解析】副词辨义题。此处需要副词修饰动词 ate。本文讨论的是吃鱼多少对健康的影响,没有讨论吃鱼的正确方法,因此,虽然词库中的 appropriately 和 regularly 两副词在语法上都可行,但从语义看,只有 regularly 符合本文的论题,意为"经常吃鱼",故选 O。

20.【答案】G. regardless

【解析】形容辨义题。此处需要形容词,且可与 of 搭配使用。词库中,剩下 considerate 和 regardless 两个形容词,从语法结构上说,二者都可与 of 搭配,但 considerate 通常用于形容人的品质,意为"体谅的",根据该词所在的上下文,只有 regardless 较符合句意,故选 G。

Section B

Passage one

【解构剖析】议论文。本文讲述美国社会老龄化问题,作者认为美国社会为老龄人群提供的许多优惠和福利事实上并不科学。本文分为三部分。第一段提出现象:老年人在美国现有一种重要的特权——老年折扣。第二段解释现象和原因:给老人打折扣成为惯例"是因为人们普遍认为老年人大多比较贫困,但事实并非如此。第三段至第六段分析这种现象带来的消极影响:老年人折扣引起了年轻一代和老一代之间关系的紧张,造成两代人之间的隔阂。

【语境记忆】

1. be entitled to sth. (对于某事)有……资格,有……权利
2. eligibility [ˌelidʒəˈbiliti] *n.* 适合,合格
3. stimulus [ˈstimjuləs] *n.* 刺激,刺激品,兴奋剂
4. irritant [ˈiritənt] *a.* 刺激的
5. in favor of 赞成……,支持……,有利于……
6. far from 完全不
7. formidable [ˈfɔːmidəbəl] *a.* 可怕的;难对付的,巨大的
8. privilege [ˈprivilidʒ] *n.* 特权,优特

Senior citizen discounts only enhance the myth that older people can't take care of themselves and need special treatment; and they threaten the creation of a new myth, that the elderly are ungrateful and taking for themselves at the expense of children and other age groups. (L. 2, last Para.)

本句为并列复合句。第一个分句含有一个由 that 引导的同位语从句,对 myth 进行补充说明,该同位语从句又含有一个由 and 连接的并列句;第二个分句也含有一个由 that 引导的同位语从句,对 myth 进行补充说明。本句句架为:Senior citizen discounts only enhance the myth that...; and they threaten... a new myth, that...

21.【定位】第一段。

【解析】细节题。本题考查的是对第一段相关细节的理解。首段末句提到:..., the discounts have become the discounts have become a routine part of many businesses,选项 A 正是对该句的同义阐述;其中 a routine commercial practice 对应文中的 a routine part of many businesses,意为"商业惯例"。选项 B 和 C 文中未提及;选项 D 是对首段第三句的错误理解。故选项 A 为答案。

22.【定位】第二段第三句。

【解析】细节题。本题考查的是推行老年人折扣这一做法的原因。第二段第三句提到:The practice is acceptable because of the widespread belief that "elderly" and "needy" are synonymous. 由此可推知,人们之所以推行老年人折扣是因为人们认为老年人的经济状况差,需要社会的帮助。选项 C 符合此意,其意为"生活水平现有的权利比别人低的"。选项 A 和 B 文中未提及,选项 D 是对第四段首句的错误理解。故选项 C 为答案。

23.【定位】第三段末句。

【解析】细节题。本文考查的是一些政客和学者对推行老年人折扣的看法。第三段末句提到：Moreover they are a direct irritant in what some politicians and scholars see as a coming conflict between the generations. 意为"一些政客和学者们更是把它们看作是导致未来两代人之间冲突的直接因素"。选项 B 正是对此意的同义转述，其中 intensify conflicts 对应文中 are a direct irritant in…a coming conflict；between the young and the old 对应文中 between generations。选项 A 文中未提及；选项 C 与原文第三段首句矛盾；选项 D 是对第三段第二句的错误理解。故选项 B 为答案。

24. 【定位】第四段第一句。

【解析】细节题。本题考查的是作者对社会保险体系的看法。第四段第一句提到：… continuing debate over Social Security benefits, which mostly involves a transfer of resources from the young to the old. 说明作者认为社会保险体系是以牺牲年轻人的利益换取老年人的福利，选项 C 符合此意；选项 A 与第四段末句的前半句矛盾；选项 B 与第四段末句的后半句矛盾；选项 D 偷换概念，因为 law and court decision 支持的是老年人拒绝退休一事而不是 social security system。故选项 C 为答案。

25. 【定位】全文。

【解析】推断题。本题考查的是作者对推行老年人折扣的观点。选项 A 是对文章末句的错误理解：原文说老年人目前正在与这种年龄歧视做斗争，并非说明作者认同这种做法。选项 B 文中未提及。选项 C 与第六段首句矛盾。纵观全文可知，作者多次表示其实许多老年人根本不需要价格折扣优惠，再结合末段第二句及末句 Senior citizen discounts only enhance the myth that older people can't take care of themselves and need special treatment;… Senior citizen discounts are the essence of the very thing older Americans are fighting against—discrimination by age，便可推知作者认为推行老年人折扣做法可能会造成年龄歧视现象。故选项 D 为答案。

【参考译文及题区画线】

老年人在美国享有特权,其中一种比较重要的特权就是老年人折扣。任何达到一定年龄的人——有时只需达到 55 岁——都可以在几乎所有的商业活动中自然地享有一系列种类繁多的打折优惠。是否有资格享有这些优惠不是取决于个人的需要而是由其出生证明上的日期决定。实际上,在我们这一代还没有听说过以前,21)这种针对老年人的折扣就已经成为许多行业的惯例行为了——就和房间里的彩电和飞机上的免费咖啡一样普通。

头发花白的老人甚至都无需要求就会经常得到折扣,但是实际上,美国有数以百万计的 60 岁以上的老年人都是非常健康并具备相当的支付能力的。那些从来都不敢向大学士或任何低于 30 岁的人提供折扣的商家却随意地将折扣提供给老年人。22)这种惯例被普遍接受,是因为人们大都认为"年老"是"贫穷"的代名词。或许曾经是那样,但是现在,与其他群体相比,美国老年群体的贫困率却要更低。当然,老年人的经济层次也各不相同,在美国也有许多老年人非常贫困,但是大多数老年人却并非如此。

要确定老年人折扣对单个的公司产生什么样的影响是不可能的,不过对于许多公司来说,折扣确实刺激了收入的增长。但在其他情况下,这种折扣却直接或间接地让年轻一代的美国人付出了代价。23)而且,一些政客和学者们更是把它们看作是导致未来两代人之间冲突的直接因素。

24)关于社会保险福利的持续辩论正在使两代人之间的关系更加趋于紧张。辩论主要是围绕从年轻人到老年人的资源转移问题展开。就业问题是另外一个焦点。在法律和法庭判决的支持下,越来越多的美国老年人正在拒绝依靠退休金生活而宁愿选择继续工作——因此减少了年轻人的就业和提升机会。老年人折扣已经不再像过去那样是一种福利,而是已经变成了一种令享受它们的群体感到局促不安的经济特权,这个群体中有数百万人实际上并不需要它们。

认为老年人的经济需要应该优先于其他群体的经济需要的看法已经不再有意义。25) 老年人折扣只是加强了这样一种观念，即认为老年人不能照顾自己而需要特殊对待；并且它们也阻碍一种新观念的形成，即老年人实际并不感谢这种特殊对待，并且认为自己是在牺牲孩子和其他年龄群体的利益，而老年人折扣恰恰体现了他们斗争的实质——年龄歧视。

Passage two

【结构剖析】议论文。本文讲述美国黑人争取现实生活中平等公民权的斗争，虽取得一些成就，但依然任重而道远。文章第一、二段引出问题：通过祖父被作为奴隶拍卖一事引出美国黑人人权问题，指出美国民主的根本问题是"结构种族主义"。第三段至第五段讲述历史上对该问题的解决：两次争取黑人平等民权的斗争取得了一定成果，但没有从根本上解决问题。第六段至第八段指出问题的现状：在诸多方面，美国黑人仍然遭受着不平等待遇。

【语境记忆】

1. an auction block 拍卖场　　2. racial segregation 种族隔离

3. deferred [di'fə:d] a. 搁置的

4. justify ['dʒʌstifai] vt. 证明……是正当的

5. obscure [əb'skjuə] a. 朦胧的，模糊的

6. disproportionate [ˌdisprə'pɔ:ʃnit] a. 不均衡的，不相称的

【难句分析】

1. Do Americans have the capacity and vision to remove these structural barriers that deny democratic rights and opportunities to millions of their fellow citizens? (L. 4-5, Para. 2)

此句为复合句。本句是一般疑问句型。that 引导定语从句，修饰 barriers。that 在从句中作主语。to remove these structural barriers 是不定式短语作定语，修饰 capacity and vision。

2. The First Reconstruction(1954-1877)ended slavery and briefly gave black men voting rights, but gave no meaningful compensation for two centuries of unpaid labor. (L. 1-2,Para. 4)

此句为简单句。全句有一个主语, 即 The First Reconstruction;三个为动词, 即 ended、gave 和 gave,分别由 and 和 but 连接。

3. It is, more important, an educational campaign to highlight the contemporary reality of "racial deficits" of all kinds, the unequal conditions that impact blacks regardless of class. (L. 1-3, Para. 7)

此句为复合句。more important 是插入成分。to highlight...是不定式短语作定语,修饰 campaign。that 引导定语从句,修饰 conditions。

26. 【定位】第一段第三句。

【解析】细节题。文中第一段第三句提到:But to...his heirs,slavery was a crime against our humanity. 题干中的 To the author 对应文中的 to...his heirs(对他的后代来说),即对于他的后代之一的作者来说,其祖父被拍卖正是奴隶制的恶果,选项 A 符合此意。选项 B 是对原文第二段中 socio-economic inequality 的错误理解;选项 C 文中未提及;由首段末句可知,racial segregation 是新时期美国人权问题的表现形式,选项 D 的 racial segregation 不属于奴隶制时期的产物,它是新时期美国人权问题的表现形式。故选项 A 为答案。

27. 【定位】第二段第一句。

【解析】细节题。文章第二段第一句提到 The fundamental problem of American democracy in the 21st century is the problem of "structural racism": the deep patterns of socio-economic inequality,选项 C 正是对此意的同义转述,其中的 deep-rooted 对应文中的 deep patterns。选项 A 和 D 是对文章第二段第一句中的

the deep patterns of...constantly...by both racist stereotype 和末句中...barriers that deny democratic rights and opportunities 的错误理解;选项 B 中的 minority groups 所指代的范围与本文所讲的黑人平等权利范围不同。故选项 C 为答案。

28. 【定位】第四段和第五段。

【解析】细节题。由文章第四段第一句中 but 后的内容可知,选项 B 为 The First Reconstruction 留而未解决的问题;再从第五段第二句中 but 后的内容可知,在 The Second Reconstruction 中该问题仍未得到解决,故选项 B 符合题意,是正确答案。选项 A 文中未提及;而选项 C 和 D 与第四段中的 The First Reconstruction...briefly gave black men voting rights 和第五段中的 The Second Reconstruction...ended legal segregation in public accommodations and gave blacks voting rights 内容矛盾,皆可排除。

29. 【定位】第六段第一、二句。

【解析】推断题。文章第六段第一句提到:The disproportionate wealth that most whites enjoy today was first constructed from centuries of unpaid black labor. 再结合该段第二句中的 profited from slavery 可推知,大多数白人享有的财富都是几代黑人用血汗劳动积累而来的。故选项 D 为答案。

30. 【定位】第六段末句。

【解析】推断题。根据题干中的 racial discrimination 将题区定位于第六段末句,该句提到:This pattern of white privilege and black inequality continues today. 文章接下来的两段列举了很多黑人所遭受的不平等待遇,即对第六段末句的观点进行论证。选项 B 中的 remains virtually untouched 其实就是对原文 continues today 转述,故选项 B 为答案。选项 A 与末段内容矛盾;选项 C 与作者的观点相反,其中 reparations 意为"赔偿金";选项 D 概括不够全面。故选项 A、C 和 D 都是错误的。

【参考译文及题区画线】

1854 年,我的曾祖父,Morris Marable,曾在佐治亚州的一个拍卖场上以 500 美元被卖掉。对于他的白人奴隶主来说,这种买卖不过是"平常交易",26)但是对于 Morris Marable 和我们这些后人来说,奴隶制则是对人权的犯罪。这种对美国非洲奴隶的人权侵犯在种族隔离制度下又持续了将近一个世纪。

27)21 世纪美国民主的根本问题是"结构种族主义",即社会经济不平等和长期积累不利条件的深层次模式。这种模式以种族为标志并时常在公众演讲中被典型的种族主义者的行为模式和白人的冷漠态度所证实的。美国人真的有能力和远见可以将这些剥夺了他们的数百万公民的民族权利的结构性障碍根除吗?

美国之前已经经历了两次为获得真正的多元文化民主而进行的伟大战斗。

第一次重构(1865—1877)结束了奴隶制并简单地赋予了黑人男性选举权。28. a)但是却没有对两个世纪以来黑人的无偿劳动给予有意义的补偿。"40 亩土地和一头骡子"的承诺对大多数黑人来说都还是一个尚未实现的梦。

第二次重构(1954—1968)也叫做现代民权运动,使公共住宅区内的合法隔离不复存在,并使所有黑人都获得了选举权。28. b)但与此矛盾的是,这些成功却掩盖了由于历史长期积累的不利因素而使黑人付出的巨大代价,而这种不利因素在美国黑人生活中仍然处于中心地位。

29)大多数白人今天所享有的巨大财富最初是通过几个世纪以来黑人的无偿劳动聚积起来的。许多白人机构,包括一些重要的大学、保险公司和银行,都曾经从奴隶制中受益。30)这种白人享有特权、黑人遭遇不平等的情况一直持续至今。

要求赔偿的绝不仅仅是奴隶制和种族隔离制度两方面。更重要的是要开展教育运动,使人们重视各个时期出现的各种"种族赤字",也就是要重视影响各阶层黑人的不平等条件结构种族主义的障碍包括"公平的不平等",黑人资本积累的缺乏是美国历史直接导致的结果。所有的黑人家庭中有三分之一的净资产都为负。1998年典型的黑人家庭的净资产是 16400 美元,还不到白人家庭净资产的五分之一。黑人家庭被拒绝家庭贷款的比率是白人家庭的两倍。

在经济衰退时期,黑人一直是最后被雇佣而又最先被解雇的。1990 年至 1991 年的经济衰退中,非洲裔美国黑人遭受了非常不平等的待遇。在可口可乐公司,失业员工中有 42% 是黑人,而在希尔斯公司,这一比例更是高达 54%。黑人的寿命也在很大程度上短于白人,部分原因就在于医疗机构中存在种族主义。黑人被提供肾脏移植手术或是早期癌症手术的可能性要远远低于白人。

Reading Practice 4

Part I   Reading Comprehension (Skimming and Scanning) (15 minutes)

Safety on Corporation's information

It never rains but it pours. Just as bosses and boards have finally sorted out their worst accounting and compliance troubles, and improved their feeble corporation governance, a new problem threatens to earn them-especially in America-the sort of nasty headlines that inevitably lead to heads rolling in the executive suite: data insecurity. Left, until now, to odd, low level IT staff to put right, Kand seen as a concern only of data rich industries such as banking, telecoms and air travel, information protection is now high on the boss's agenda in businesses of every variety.

Several massive leakages of customer and employee data this year-from organizations as diverse as Time Warner, the American defense contractor Science Applications International Corp and even the University of California, Berkeley-have left managers hurriedly peering into their intricate IT systems and business processes in search of potential vulnerabilities.

"Data is becoming an asset which needs to be guarded as much as any other assets", says Haim Mendelson of Stanford University's business school. "The ability to guard customer data is the key to market value, which the board is responsible for on behalf of shareholders." Indeed, just as there is the concept of Generally Accepted Accounting Principles(GAAP), perhaps it is time for GASP, Generally Accepted Security Practices, suggested Eli Noam of New York's Columbia Business School. "Setting the proper investment level for security, redundancy, and recovery is a management issue, not a technical one," he says.

The mystery is that this should come as a surprise to any boss. Surely it should be obvious to the dimmest executive that trust, that most valuable of economic assets, is easily destroyed and hugely expensive to restore-and that few things are more likely to destroy trust than a company letting sensitive personal data get into the wrong hands.

Such complacency(安心) may have been encouraged-though not justified-by the lack of legal penalty(in America, but not Europe)for data leakage. Until California recently passed a law, American firms did not have to tell anyone, even the victim, when data went astray. That may change fast: lots of proposed data security legislation is now doing the rounds in Washington, D.C. Meanwhile, the theft of information about some 40 million credit card accounts in America, disclosed on June 17th, overshadowed a hugely important decision a day earlier by America's Federal Trade Commission(FTC) that puts corporate America on notice that regulators will act if firms fail to provide adequate data security.

282

The FTC decided to settle with BJ's Wholesale Club, a retailer whose loose data-protection practices the agency said constituted an "unfair practice that violated federal law." The firm collected too much data, kept it too long, did not encrypt (加密) it, lacked password protections and left its wireless network open. This in turn, enable criminals to produce counterfeit credit and debit cards using stolen customer data and collect millions of dollars in fraudulent charges. The firm has agreed to fix these problems and undero information-security audits for 20 years. This settlement represents a big step for the FTC, which had settled various other cases concerning sloppy data management since 2001 including against Eli Lilly, clothing designer Guess, Tower Records and Microsoft but did not on narrow technical ground. For instance, in several cases, the FTC applied the doctrine of "Deceptive practice" to firms that failed to live up to their data-security claims.

In its settlement with BJ's, the FTC used its broad "fairness authority" to penalized bad information-security management. For the FTC to act, this requires evidence both of substantial consumer harm and that the firm did not have reasonable grounds for failing to implement certain practices. The BJ's case, said FTC chair Deborah Platt Majoras, signaled the regulator's "intention to challenge companies that failed to protect adequately consumers' sensitive information".

"Boards should pay as much attention to these IT operational risks as they do to other operational risks in the firm," argued George Westernman of the MIT Sloan School of Management. After all, boards have audit committees and compensation committees. It may be time for a data-protection committee, he argues. Bosses must ensure that there are effective data risk-management processes in

283

place, be aware of their greatest vulnerabilities and promote a corporate culture that acknowledges data risks rather than hides them.

But the problem is often a lack of understanding by senior managers not just of technology but of business process, says Thomas Parenty, author of *Digital Defense*: "what you should know about protecting your company's assets (Harvard Business School Press, 2004)". "No one in the organization bothers to look at the value of what data they hold, the consequences if something bad happens to it, and the appropriate mechanisms to prevent that from happening." he says.

So, what should a boss do? Accountancy firms and consultants are already spotting a chance to profit by conducting an independent security and privacy audit and for many firms, their (no doubt) huge fee will probably be worth the money. The auditors inspect technology systems, data flow and the control on access to data within an organization and with its business partners.

A wise boss will also appoint a senior executive to be responsible for data security and not just to have a convenient scapegoat(替罪羊) the event of a leak. Diana Glassman, a data protection expert, says that a useful first step would be for the boss to write to all employees reminding them of the risks and potential cost of data leakage, and asking them before passing data to anyone else, to question wether that person truly needs, or is entitled to, it.

Many of the worst recent data leakages resulted from failure of the most basic kind. The data-processing firm that suffered the breach that exposed 40 million credit-card accounts was not in compliance with the security standards of Visa and Master Card which may now find themselves liable for negligence. If nothing else gets bosses to focus on data security, surely the prospect of ending up in cout will.

1. The statement "It never rains but it pours" is used to introduce
   _____.
   A. the fierce business competition.
   B. the feeble boss board relations.
   C. the threat from news reports.
   D. the severity of data leakage.

2. According to Paragraph 2, some organizations check their systems
   to find out _____.
   A. whether there is any weak point.
   B. what sort of data has been stolen.
   C. who is responsible for the leakage.
   D. how the potential spies can be located.

3. Haim Mendelson regards customer data as _____.
   A. a special market value   B. an asset
   C. a technology problem   D. an investment

4. American bosses are reluctant to follow Mendelson's idea because
   they don't think _____.
   A. trust is the most valuable asset
   B. customer data leakage destroys trust
   C. trust can be easily destroyed
   D. they will suffer legal penalty for data leakage

5. How did FTC settle Eli Lilly's sloppy data management problem?
   A. By charging it for violation of the law
   B. By imposing information-security audits.
   C. On narrown technical grounds
   D. By the doctrine of " Deceptive practices".

6. The FTC intends to penalize bad information-security management since _____.

A. 2001   B. the BJ's case

C. June 17th   D. the establishment of GASP

7. What does George Westenman sussgest for the boards to do for data protection?

A. Enhance the awareness of data protection of the company.

B. Appoint a senior executive to manage data security.

C. Establish data risk-management processes.

D. Set up a data- protection committee.

8. An obstacle for bosses to to set up effective data risk-management processes is that they often know little about _____.

9. Companies can get services from _____ to independently inspect the data process withing and without.

10. _____ should be responsible for the leakage of 40m credit-card accounts data.

Part II   Reading Comprehension (Reading in Depth) (25 minutes)

Section A

Last week, investors were sending a simple but important message: The future has become a whole lot more uncertain.

That reflects a change that has been developing through this year. We've entered a new Age of Uncertainty in global __11__ markets. The NASDAQ composite is the best barometer of how people feel about the future. It's no accident that it __12__ so sharply last week. The Dow industrial average was off more than 9 per cent for the year.

The Nasdaq's fall is just one sign of a broader anxiety that has been spreading across global financial markets for most of this year. In Asia, there have been growing signs of a new financia __13__ : Japan's Nikkei index is off more than 24 per cent for the year; Korea's Kopsi index __14__ more than 49 per cent. The impact ex-

286

tends to Europe especially in the tech-sector. The "Easdaq" index is off 43 per cent for the year, and the Euro NM index of newmarket companies is down more than 23 per cent.

The investment binges have been replaced by simple human prudence not an attractive quality normally, but one with ___15___ implications for the financial markets.

Last year Wall Street still ___16___ of a U. S. market that was "priced for perfection", and in nearly every direction there seemed to be good news. A surging U. S. economy was pulling the rest of the world along with it: the technology boom was continuing to accelerate: oil prices were ___17___ low. What a difference a few months make. Now, in nearly every direction, there's bad news. The U. S. economy is slowing; tech companies are caught in a new downward ___18___ of declining investment spending.

Uncertainty has some obvious ___19___ for the world economy: First and most important, it makes the future "shorter". Investors shorten the time horizon over which they're willing to project future profitability. The companies are making the same products and even making the same profits. But the predictability of those profits is less because the future is more ___20___.

A. uncertain	B. unfortunately	C. consequences	D. squeeze
E. spiral	F. prune	G. commodity	H. profound
I. boasted	J. relatively	K. prosperous	L. tumbled
M. resemblance	N. slumps	O. financial	

Section B

Passage one（2005 年 12 月真题）

Public distrust of scientists stems in part from the blurring of boundaries between science and technology, between discovery and manufacture. Most government, perhaps all governments, justify public expenditure on scientific research in terms of the economic benefits the scientific enterprise ha brought in the past and will bring in the future. Politicians remind their voters of the splendid machines 'our scientists' have invented, the new drugs to relieve old ailments (病痛), and the new surgical equipment and techniques by which previously intractable (难治疗的) conditions may now be treated and lives saved. At the same time, the politicians demand of scientists that they tailor their research to 'economics needs', that they award a higher priority to research proposals that are 'near the market' and can be translated into the greatest return on investment in the shortest time. Dependent, as they are, on politicians for much of their funding, scientists have little choice but to comply. Like the rest of us, they are members of a society that rates the creation of wealth as the greatest possible good. Many have reservations, but keep them to themselves in what they perceive as a climate hostile to the pursuit of understanding for its own sake and the idea of an inquiring, creative spirit.

In such circumstances no one should be too hard on people who are suspicious of conflicts of interest. When we learn that the distinguished professor assuring us of the safety of a particular product holds a consultancy with the company making it, we cannot be blamed for wondering whether his fee might conceivably cloud his professional judgment. Even if the professor holds no consultancy with any firm, some people many still distrust him because of his association with those who do, or at least wonder about the source of some his research funding.

This attitude can have damaging effects. It questions the integrity of individuals working in a profession that prizes intellectual honesty as the supreme virtue, and plays into the hands of those who would like to discredit scientists by representing then a venal（可以收买的）. This makes it easier to dismiss all scientific pronouncements, but especially those made by the scientists who present themselves as 'experts'. The scientist most likely to understand the safety of a nuclear reactor, for example, is a nuclear engineer declares that a reactor is unsafe, we believe him, because clearly it is not to his advantage to lie about it. If he tells us it is safe, on the other hand, we distrust him, because he may well be protecting the employer who pays his salary. (445 words)

21. What is the chief concern of most governments when it comes to scientific research?

    A. Support from the votes.

    B. The reduction of public expenditure.

    C. Quick economics returns.

    D. The budget for a research project.

22. Scientist have to adapt their research to 'economic needs' in order to _____.

    A. impress the public with their achievements

    B. pursue knowledge for knowledge's sake

    C. obtain funding from the government

    D. translate knowledge into wealth

23. Why won't scientists complain about the government's policy concerning scientific research?

    A. They think they work in an environment hostile to the free pursuit of knowledge.

    B. They are accustomed to keeping their opinions to themselves.

    C. They know it takes patience to win support from the public.

    D. They think compliance with government policy is in the interests of the public.

24. According to the author, people are suspicious of the professional judgment of scientists because _____.

A. their pronouncements often turn out to be wrong

B. sometimes they hide the source of their research funding

C. some of them do not give priority to intellectual honesty

D. they could be influenced by their association with the project concerned

25. Why does the author say that public distrust of scientists can have damaging effects?

A. It makes things difficult for scientists seeking research funds.

B. People would not believe scientists even when they tell the truth.

C. It may dampen the enthusiasm of scientists for independent research.

D. Scientists themselves may doubt the value of their research findings

Passage two（2005 年 12 月真题）

In many ways, today's business environment has changed qualitatively since the late 1980s. The end of the Cold War radically altered the very nature of the world's politics and economics. In just a few short years, globalization has started a variety of trends with profound consequences: the opening of markets, true global competition, widespread deregulation（解除政府对⋯⋯的控制） of industry, and an abundance of accessible capital. We have experienced both the benefits and risks of a truly global economy, with both Wall Street and Main Street（平民百姓） feeling the pains of economic disorder half a world away.

At the same time, we have fully entered the Information Age.

Startling breakthroughs in information technology have irreversibly altered the ability to conduct business unconstrained by the traditional limitations of time or space. Today, it's almost impossible to imagine a world without intranets, e-mail, and portable computers. With stunning speed, the Internet is profoundly changing the way we work, shop, do business, and communicate.

As a consequence, we have truly entered the Post-Industrial economy. We are rapidly shifting from an economy based on manufacturing and commodities to one that places the greatest value on information, services, support, and distribution. That shift, in turn, place an unprecedented premium on "knowledge workers," a new class of wealthy, educated, and mobile people who view themselves as free agents in a seller's market.

Beyond the realm of information technology, the accelerated pace of technological change in virtually every industry has created entirely new business, wiped out others, and produced a pervasive (广泛的) demand for continuous innovation. New product, process, and distribution technologies provide powerful levers for creating competitive value. More companies are learning the importance of destructive technologies—innovations that hold the potential to make a product line, or even an entire business segment, virtually outdated.

Another major trend has been the fragmentation of consumer and business markets. There's a growing appreciation that superficially similar groups of customers may have very different preferences in terms of what they want to buy and how they want to buy it. Now, new technology makes it easier, faster, and cheaper to identify and serve targeted micro-markets in ways that were physically impossible or prohibitively expensive in the past. Moreover, the trend

291

feeds on itself, a business's ability to serve sub-markets fuels customers' appetites for more and more specialized offerings. (405 words)

26. According to the first paragraph, the chances in the business environment in the past decades can be attributed to _____.

A. technological advances

B. worldwide economic disorder

C. the fierce competition in industry

D. the globalization of economy

27. What idea does the author want to convey in the second paragraph ?

A. The rapid development of information technology has taken businessmen by surprise

B. Information technology has removed the restrictions of time and space in business transactions

C. The Internet, intranets, e-mail, and portable computers have penetrated every corner of the world.

D. The way we do business today has brought about startling breakthroughs in information technology.

28. If a business wants to thrive in the Post-Industrial economy _____.

A. it has to invest more capital in the training of free agents to operate in a seller's market

B. it should try its best to satisfy the increasing demands of mobile knowledgeable people

C. it should not overlook the importance of information, services, support, and distribution

D. it has to provide each of its employees with the latest information about the changing market

29. In the author's view, destructive technologies are innovations which _____.

A. can eliminate an entire business segment

B. demand a radical change in providing services

C. may destroy the potential of a company to make any profit

D. call for continuous improvement in ways of doing business

30. With the fragmentation of consumer and business markets _____.

A. an increasing number of companies have disintegrated

B. manufacturers must focus on one special product to remain competitive in the market

C. it is physically impossible and prohibitively expensive to do business in the old way

D. businesses have to meet individual customers' specific needs in order to succeed

Reading Practice 4 答案与解析

答案

1. D 2. A 3. B 4. D 5. C 6. B 7. D

8. technology and business processes

9. accountancy firms and consultants 10. A data-processing firm

11. O 12. L 13. D 14. N 15. H 16. I 17. J 18. E

19. C 20. A 21. B 22. C 23. A 24. D 25. B 26. D

27. B 28. C 29. A 30. D

解析

Part I Reading Comprehension (Skimming and Scanning) (15 minutes)

【结构剖析】议论文。文章通过信息泄漏的事例来阐释信息保护的重要性,批判有些公司未曾意识这些,并建议对信息保护立法。

【语境记忆】

1. agenda [əˈdʒendə] n. 议事日程,记事册

2. comply [kəmˈplai] v. 遵照,照做,顺从,服从

3. diverse [daiˈvə:s] a. 多种多样的

4. executive [igˈzekjutiv] n. 总经理,行政负责人

5. govern [ˈgʌvən] v. 统治,管理,支配

6. intricate [ˈintrikit] a. 复杂的,错综的,难以理解的

7. justify [ˈdʒʌstifai] v. 证明……正当

8. penalty [ˈpenəlti] n. 刑罚,处罚

9. redundant [riˈdʌndənt] a. 多余的,过剩的

10. regulate [ˈregjuˌleit] vi. 管制,控制,调整

11. vulnerability [ˌvʌlnərəˈbiliti] n. 易受攻击的地方,易受攻击性

12. corporate culture 企业文化

13. in compliance with 按照,已从

【难句分析】

1. Left, until now, to odd, low level IT staff to put right, and seen as a concern only of data rich industries such as banking, telecoms and air travel, information protection is now high on the boss's agenda in businesses of every variety. (L. 3-5, Para. 1)

此句为简单句。主干是"... information protection is now high on the boss's agenda...";句子的前面是两个过去分词结构 left... to... 与 seen as a concern..., 作状语。句意:此前,信息保护工作一直被留给临时的、低层次的信息技术人员承担,并且只被看成是信息资源丰富产业所关注的一个问题,比如银行业、电信业以及航空等行业。如今,信息保护已成为各行各业老板的头等大事。

2. Surely it should be obvious to the dimmest executive that trust, that most valuable of economic assets, is easily destroyed and hugely expensive to restore and that few things are more likely to destroy trust than a company letting sensitive personal data get into the wrong hands. (L. 1-3, Para. 4)

此句为复合句。主干是"…it should be obious…that…and that…",其中 it 是形式主语,两个 that 引导的两个从句是真正的主语。在第一个从句中,that most valuable of economic assets 作主语 trust 的同位语,其中 that 表示强调;在第二个从句中现在分词结构 letting sensitive personal data…作 company 的定语。句意:当然,对于最迟钝的管理人员也应清楚,显而易见的应该是,诚信这种最有价值的经济财产很容易遭到破坏,而要恢复诚信却代价高昂,此外,没有什么比让公司敏感的个人资料落入不妥当的人之手更可能破坏诚信的了。

3. Meanwhile, the theft of information about some 40 million credit card accounts in America, disclosed on June 17th, overshadowed a hugely important decision a day earlier by America's Federal Trade Commission(FTC)that puts corporate America on notice that regulators will act if firms fail to provide adequate data security. (L. 4-6, Para. 5)

此句多重复合句。主干是"…the theft of information… overshadowed a hugely important decision…",其中主语中的 information 带有两个定语:about…disclosed….;宾语 decision 带有 that 引导的定语从句 that puts corporate America on notice…,其中 notice(通知)后的 that 引导一个同位语从句 that regulators will act if…,说明 notice 的内容。句意:同时,6 月 17 日有关偷窃大约 4000 万信用卡账户信息这种事件的披露使得一天前美国商务委员会的一个重要决定蒙上了阴影,该决定提请全美国注意,如果公司没有提供适当的信息安全保护措施,那么监管结构就会采取行动。

1. 【定位】首段第一句。

【解析】首段首先提到,不雨则已,一雨倾盆,随后引出了人们面临的一个新问题——数字风险,接着具体介绍了这个问题。这说明,这个句子被用来介绍信息不安全的问题。故选项 A 为答案。

2. 【定位】第二段。

【解析】文章第二段提到,几起重大的员工和客户数据泄漏事件的影响:许多管理者赶紧检查其复杂的信息技术系统和办公程序,以便寻找潜在的薄弱环节。这说明,这些机构检查系统的目的是为了查明系统是否有弱点。故选项 A 为答案。

3. 【定位】第三段首句。

【解析】第三段首句 Haim Mendelson 指出:Data is becoming an asset which needs to be guarded as much as any other assets(数据正在成为一种需要像保护其他资产一样而保护的资产)。故选项 B 为答案。

4. 【定位】第五段首句。

【解析】第四段首句指出:公司老板对上段中 Haim Mendelson 提到的投资与客户信息安全建议感到非常惊讶。第五段首句指出:尽管不能成为理由,但相关法律惩罚的缺失(在美国,不是在欧洲)也许的确对目前信息泄漏的局面起了推波助澜的作用。故选项 D 为答案。

5. 【定位】第六段第五句。

【解析】第六段第五句提到:. . . the FTC, which had settled various other cases. . . including against Eli Lilly. . . but did not on narrow technical ground. 由此可知,FTC 以前处理公司信息管理松散的方式是在狭窄的技术层面上。故选项 C 为答案。

6. 【定位】第七段末句。

【解析】第七段末句提到:The BJ's case. . . signaled the regulator's "intention to challenge companies that failed to protect adequately consumers' sentive information". 即 BJ 案例标志这 FTC 着手追

296

究那些未能充分保护客户敏感信息的公司。故选项 B 为答案。

7. 【定位】第八段倒数第二、三句。

【解析】第八段是关于 George Westerman 对信息安全的建议。倒数第二、三句提到：除审计委员会和赔偿委员会外，还应建立信息安全委员会。故选项 D 为答案。

8. 【定位】第九段首句。

【解析】第九段首句提到：But the problem is often a lack of understanding by senior managers not just of technology but of business process... 即高管们不仅在技术层面上缺乏对数据安全的了解，在交易环节上也是如此。题干中的 knowlittle 对应原文 a lack of understanding。故答案为 technology and business process。

9. 【定位】第十段第二句。

【解析】第十段第二句提到：会计公司和咨询公司已经通过建立独立的安全隐私的审计部门，抓住机会进行盈利。故答案为 accountancy firms and consultants。

10. 【定位】末段第二句。

【解析】末段第二句提到：这起涉及到 4000 万份信用卡账户信息泄漏案的原因是因为那家数据处理公司没有遵守维萨卡和万事达卡的安全准则。故答案为 A data-process firm。

【参考译文及题区画线】

企业信息的安全问题

1)不雨则已，一雨倾盆。就在老板和董事最终解决其最严重的会计账目和相关问题、改善其岌岌可危的公司管理之际，一个新问题可能会使他们——尤其是在美国——成为最可怕的头条新闻，这些头条新闻不可避免地使他们在行政套房里的位置不保。这个问题就是数字风险。此前，信息保护工作一直被留给临时的、低层次的信息技术人员承担，并且只被看成是信息资源丰富产业所关注的一个问题,比如银行业、电信业以及航空等行业。如今,信息保护已成为各行各业老板的头等大事。

今年从时代华纳到美国国防部承包人国际科学应用公司甚至加州大学伯克利分校这样的不同机构,发生过好几次的客户和员工资料的大规模泄漏的事件,2)这几起重大泄密事件使得管理人员匆忙检查其复杂的信息技术系统和办公程序,以便寻找潜在的薄弱环节。

3)"数据正在成为一种需要像保护其他资产一样而保护的资产。"斯坦福大学商学院的海姆·门德尔森说。"保护客户资料的能力是市场价值的关键因素,这是董事会应该为了股东的利益而承担的责任。"纽约哥伦比亚商学院的埃尼·诺姆提议说,"实际上,正如存在公认的会计原则观念一样,现在可能是采取公认的安全措施的时候了。"他还说:"为安全、备份以及恢复确定适当的投资标准是一个管理问题,不是技术问题。"

令人费解的是,这个问题竟会让老板们猝不及防。当然,对于最迟钝的管理人员也应清楚,显而易见的应该是,诚信这种最有价值的经济财产很容易遭到破坏,而要恢复诚信却代价高昂,此外,没有什么比让公司敏感的个人资料落入不妥当的人之手更可能破坏诚信的了。

4)尽管不能成为理由,但相关法律惩罚的缺失(在美国,不是在欧洲)也许的确对目前信息泄漏的局面起了推波助澜的作用。最近,加利福尼亚通过了一项法律,而此前美国的公司不必把资料泄漏的事情告知包括受害者在内的任何人。这种情况可能会迅速改变:如今,许多与数据安全有关的立法提案正在华盛顿的各部门间流传。同时,6月17日有关偷窃大约4000万信用卡账户信息这种事件的披露使得一天前美国商务委员会的一个重要决定蒙上了阴影,该决定提请全美国注意,如果公司没有提供适当的信息安全保护措施,那么监管机构就会采取行动。

FTC 决定处理折价零售商 BJ's Wholesale Club 信息安全管理不善的问题。FTC 认为该公司"不公平的做法，违反了联邦法律"。该公司收集太多信息，保存时间太长，且没有加密，任其无线网络开着，这使得罪犯能够通过使用盗来的客户资料伪造信用卡和借记卡，并诈骗获得数百万美元。该公司已同意解决这些问题并进行信息安全审计 20 年。对 FTC 来说，这种处理方式是一大进步。5)自 2001 年以来，FTC 处理各种公司信息管理松散的问题，包括伊莱利公司的服装设计师 Guess，Tower Records 唱片公司和微软，但都是在狭窄的技术层面上进行处理。例如，在一些案例中，FTC 对那些未达到信息安全管理要求的公司，实施"欺骗性做法"政策。

在处理 BJ's 案件时，FTC 采用其"公正权威"，来惩罚不良的信息安全管理。FTC 采取行动得需要大量的证据表明消费者受到损害和该公司无法提供不作为的合理理由。6)FTC 主席 Deborah Platt Majoras 说"Eli Lilly 公司的案例标志着 FTC 准备追究那些未能充分保护客户敏感信息的公司"。

麻省理工学院斯隆管理学院的 GeorgeWesterman 说到："如同重视做其他业务的风险一样，公司董事会应多注意这些资讯科技业务风险。"7)他说，毕竟，董事会已有审计委员会和赔偿委员会，也许该是建立信息安全委员会的时候了。老板必须确保实施有效的数据风险管理程序，意识到自己的最大弱点并推行承认数据的风险，而不是隐瞒其风险的企业文化。

8)但问题往往是高级管理人员不仅在技术层面上缺乏对数据安全的了解，在业务流程方面也是如此。《数字防御》（哈佛商学院出版社，2004 年）一书 的作者 Thomas Parenty 说："你应该知道如何保护你的公司的资产。""公司里没有人费心去看看他们所持信息的价值、如有不测会有什么后果、以及有何适当的机制来防止这种情况发生。"

那么,老板应该怎么做呢? 9)会计公司和咨询公司已经通过建立独立的安全隐私的审计部门,抓住机会去创造利润。对许多企业来说,它们(毫无疑问)巨大的费用很可能会物有所值。审计师们检查技术系统、信息流、该企业内部或与商业合作伙伴之间信息存取的控制。

聪明的老板也将任命一名高级行政人员,负责信息的安全性,而不是为了信息泄漏时找个替罪羊。信息保护专家 Diana Glassamn 说:最要紧的是老板们要书面告知全体员工,提醒他们信息泄漏的风险和潜在的代价,发送信息前,要求他们问清对方是否确实需要,或是否有权得到该信息。

近来,许多严重的信息泄漏都是因为缺乏基本的防范而发生的。10)那家信息处理公司因没有遵守维萨卡和万事达卡的安全准则,泄漏了 4000 万份信用卡账户信息,现在得他们自己来承担过失。如果没有其他能让老板们重视信息的安全性的话,立法必定行。

Part II   Reading Comprehension (Reading in Depth) (25 minutes)

Section A

结构剖析:说明文。本文主要阐述了世界各大股指下跌引发全球金融市场进入一个新的不确定期以及不确定性给世界经济带来的影响。

词性归类

n.	consequences 结果,后果 squeeze 紧缺,经济困难 spiral 螺旋式的上升(或下降)commodity 商品,货物 resemblance 类似之处
v.	squeeze 挤,压榨 spiral 连续上升(或下降) prune 修整,删除 boasted 自夸,夸耀 tumbled(价格等)暴跌[过去式或分词] slumps 大幅度下降[第三人称单数]
adj.	uncertain 不确定的 spiral 螺旋的 profound 深刻的,深奥的 prosperous 繁荣的,兴旺的 financial 财政的,金融的
adv.	unfortunately 不幸地 relatively 有关地,相关地

11. 【答案】O. financial。

【解析】形容词辩义题。此题涉及文章的主题。全文主题是：人们对未来没有信心，全球金融市场动荡。下段首句中也直接提到 global financial markets。故选 O。

12. 【答案】L. tumbled。

【解析】动词辩义题。空格前的 it 指代的是 Nasdaq composite，由下句中的...was off...可知此处的动词要含有 off 之意，句子时态为过去时。故选 L。

13. 【答案】D. squeeze。

【解析】名词辩义题。本句中的冒号后的内容是用来举例说明冒号前的内容的。亚洲和欧洲金融指数的下降意味着新的经济困难，而不能说意味着新的下降，故排除 N，选 D。

14. 【答案】N. slumps。

【解析】动词辩义题。根据句中的并列关系，选与 is off 同义的现在时，故选 N。

15. 【答案】H. profound。

【解析】形容词辩义题。句中的 but 表转折，but 之前的部分表否定意义，因此此处的形容词应该表示积极含义。prosperous 与 implications 上下文语义不搭配，故选 H。

16. 【答案】I. boasted。

【解析】动词辩义题。从本段倒数第三句中的 a difference 可知下文所指出的情况与其前面的内容所指的情况完全不同，感叹句后是 bad news，那么前面就应该是好消息。故选 I。

17. 【答案】J. relatively。

【解析】副词辩义题。根据上题的分析可知在 what a difference...之前的内容都是讲好的一面，因此可排除选项 B，选 J。

18. 【答案】E. spiral。

【解析】名词辩义题。空格前的 downward 限制了此处名词可以表示一定的趋势。故选 E。

19.【答案】C. consequences。

【解析】名词辩义题。由冒号后的 it makes the future "shorter"可知此处讲的是 it(uncertainty)带来的后果。故选 C。

20.【答案】A. uncertain。

【解析】形容词辩义题。分析此段可知是 uncertainty 导致了无法对利润进行预测。第一段末句也指出了 the future has become... uncertain.尾段是对第一段的呼应。故选 A。

【参考译文】

上周,投资者们发出了一个简单但却重要的信息:未来将会变得更加不确定。

这反映了一个今年一直在发展中的变化趋势。全球金融市场进入了一个新的不确定时期。纳斯达克股市是反映人们对未来预期的最佳晴雨表。上周股市的急剧下跌不是偶然的。今年道·琼斯指数下降了至少 9%。

纳斯达克股市的下跌只是今年大部分时间里更多的人们对全球金融市场更为担忧的征兆之一。在亚洲,出现了很多新财政困难的征兆:日本的东京证券交易所指数今年下降了至少 24%,韩国综合股票价格指数下降了至少 49%。这个影响扩散到了欧洲,尤其是其高科技板块。欧洲高科技企业基金指数今年下降了 43%,欧洲新市场指数下降了至少 23%。

人们不再进行狂热的投资,而是进行谨慎的思考——这种品质平常没多少人会欣赏。但它却深深地影响了金融市场。

去年,华尔街还在鼓吹美国的市场是尽善尽美的,而且看起来几乎在每个方面都是好消息。他们说,美国经济高涨的浪潮同时带动着世界其他地方随之发展,科技繁荣在持续加速,石油价格则相对下降。但几个月之后情况就大不一样了。现在,几乎每个方面都出现了坏消息。美国经济发展在减慢,高科技公司陷于新投资连续下降的窘境。

不确定性给世界经济带来的影响显而易见。首先，也是最重要的，它使得未来变得更加"短暂"。投资者缩短了他们规划未来投资效益的时间。公司在生产同样的产品，甚至获得同样的利润。但是这些利润的可预测性变小了，因为未来变得更加不确定了。

Section B

Passage one

【结构剖析】议论文。本文探讨了公众对于科学家的不信任。第一段分析公众不信任科学家的原因：政府把科研和经济利益挂钩，科学家们不得不按照经济需求来进行研究。第二段提到公众对于科学家持不信任的态度，认为他们是为了经济利益而作出某些不正确的判断和言论。第三段指出对科学家的不信任可能导致的后果。

【语境记忆】

1. distrust of 对某人不信任
2. in terms of 按照，从……方面来说
3. award a higher priority to 对……给予优先考虑
4. be suspicious of 对……表示怀疑
5. discredit [dis'kredit] vt. 败坏名誉
6. stem from 源于，因……而发生
7. tailor sth. to sth. 使……适应……
8. rate... as... 认为……是……
9. blame sb for doing sth. 责备某人做某事
10. play into the hands of sb. 为……提供可乘之机
11. return on... 的回报　　12. be hostile to 对……有敌意
13. cloud [klaud] vt. 使蒙蔽
14. have little/no choice but to do sth. (几乎)没有别的选择

【难句分析】

1. Politicians remind their voters of the splendid machines 'our scientists' have invented, the new drugs to relieve old ailments （病痛）, and the new surgical equipment and techniques by which previously intractable （难治疗的）conditions may now be treated and lives saved. (L. 4, Para. 1)

此句为复合句。三个名词性短语 the splendid machines, the new drugs 和 the new surgical equipment and techniques 是平行结构,都作 remind... of 的宾语。"our scientists" have invented 是省略 that 的定语从句,修饰 machines; which 引导定语从句,修饰先行词 the new surgical equipment and techniques, by 与先行词构成搭配,所以,which 前面要加 by。两词中间省略了 may now be。

2. At the same time, the politicians demand of scientists that they tailor their research to "economics needs", that they award a higher priority to research proposals that are "near the market" and can be translated into the greatest return on investment in the shortest time. (L. 7, Para. 1)

此句为并列复合句。句中的前两个 that 引导两个并列的宾语从句,作 demand 的宾语;第三个 that 引导定语从句,修饰先行词 proposals。

21. 【定位】首段。

【解析】推断题。本题考查的是在科学研究方面,大部分政府的主要关注点是什么? 首段第二句指出:大多数政府都以项目带来的收益来确定在科研上的投入是否值得。第二句又提到:政客们要求科学家的研究切合"经济需要",优先考虑能在短时间内获得最大收益的研究方案。由此可推知,政府最关心的是科研能否带来快速的经济回报,故选项 B 为答案。选项 A 与题干不符,答非所问;选项 C 和 D 文中未提及。故选项 A、C、D 应排除。

22. 【定位】首段第五句。

   【解析】细节题。本题考查的是为什么科学家的研究要适应市场的需要。首段第五句指出：Dependent，as they are，on politicians for much of their funding，scientists have little choice but to comply. 可见为了获得资金，科学家别无他法。故选项 C 为答案。选项 A 和 B 文中未提及。选项 D 是对首段末句的错误理解。故 A，B，D 都应排除。

23. 【定位】首段末句。

   【解析】细节题。题干考查的是在科学研究方面，为什么科学家不投诉政府的政策。作者在首段末句提到：许多科学家有保留意见，但是并不公开，因为对他们而言，他们的工作环境是不利于对真理自由的追求，也不接受彻底的、创新的思想。题干及选项 A 基本上是对此意的转述：题干中的 not compain about 对应文中的 keep them to themselves；选项中的 think 对应文中的 perceive；environment 对应文中的 climate；the free pursuit of knowledge 对应文中的 the pursuit of understanding for its own sake。故选项 A 为答案。

24. 【定位】第二段。

   【解析】推断题。本题考查的是人们对科学家的专业判断持怀疑态度的原因何在。作者在第二段提到了人们为什么不信任科学家判断的原因。从所列举的三个原因可推知，人们怀疑科学家的专业判断是因为科学家或多或少都会受为他们提供科研经费的单位的影响。选项 A、B、C 文中未提及，故选项 D 为答案。

25. 【定位】末段。

   【解析】推断题。题干问的是作者为何说公众对科学家的不信任会有危害。作者在末段第三句提到：This makes it easier to dismiss all scientific pronouncements，but especially those made by the scientists who present themselves as "experts"，其中 this 指代前面提到的 attitude，这种态度会导致公众对所有的科学论断

都一概不信的结果,即使这些论断是真的。故选项 B 为答案。选项 A 是对本文中心大意的错误理解;选项 C 和 D 文中未提及。故选项 A、C、D 都应排除。

【参考译文及题区画线】

公众不信任科学家的部分原因是科学和技术、发现和生产之间的界限模糊不清。大多数政府,16) 也许是所有的政府都根据科研机构在过去已经带来以及未来即将带来的经济效益来确定他们在科研方面的公共开支是值得的。政客们使他们的选民想起"我们的科学家"所发明的绝妙的机器、缓解旧疾的新药以及可以治疗先前的疑难杂症、挽救生命的新的外科手术设备和技术。同时,政客们要求科学家把研究和经济需求挂钩,16)要求他们从事那些"贴近市场"并能在最短期内获得最大投资回报的研究提案。17)由于科学家的许多研究基金取决于这些政客,他们没有别的选择,只能妥协。和我们其他人一样,他们也是社会的成员,而这个社会把创造财富视为最大的善举。18)许多人认为,当下的风气不利于对知识本身的追求和探索创造的精神,他们不认同这种风气,但都把这种看法埋在心里。

在这种情况下,任何人都不应该对怀疑利益冲突的人太刻薄。19)当获知向我们保证某件产品的安全性能的著名教授其实是该产品生产企业的顾问时,我们会想知道他所得到的酬金是否可能会蒙蔽他的专业判断,而这样想是毫无指责的。即使那个教授不是任何一家公司的顾问,有些人仍然可能会因为他和那些担当顾问的人有交往而不信任他,或者至少会想知道他研究基金的来源。

这种态度会导致破坏性的后果。它质疑了在将学术诚信视为最高美德的行业里工作的人们的品格,为那些认为科学家可以收买从而败坏其名誉的人提供了可乘之机。20)这样就更容易摒弃所有的科学声明了,尤其是那些宣称自己是"专家"的科学家所作的声明。例如,对核反应堆安全性能最为了解的科学家是核工程师。而核工程师最有可能成为核企业的员工。如果一位核工程师宣称某个反应堆是危险的,我们相信他,因为很显然撒谎对他不利。而反之,如果他告诉我们反应堆是安全的,我们则不会相信他,因为他很可能是在保护付他薪水的雇主。

Passage two

【结构剖析】议论文。本文围绕当今商业环境的变化展开议论,属于 G(General)-S(Speclhc) 型文章。第一段总论:全球化是如今一个总趋势以及经济全球化引发了几种新的趋势;第二段至第五段分别从四个方面对论点进行论证。

【语境记忆】

1. deregulation [di'regju,leiʃən] *n.* 撤销管制规定
2. accessible [æk'sesəbl] *a.* 可(或易)使用的
3. irreversibly [,iri'və:səbli] *ad.* 不可挽回地
4. as a consequence 结果　5. place/put a premium on 很重视
6. realm [relm] *n.* 王国,领域,范围
7. preference ['prefərəns] *n.* 偏爱的事物(或人)
8. feed on 以……为生、为主食,以……为能源

【难句分析】

1. In just a few short years, globalization has started a variety of trends with profound consequences: the opening of markets, true global competition, widespread deregulation (解除政府对……的控制) of industry, and an abundance of accessible capital. (L. 2 Para. 1)

　　此句虽然较长,但其实是个简单句。主干是 globalization has started a variety of trends。冒号后的四个平行名词短语是对 a variety of trends 的解释和说明。

2. Beyond the realm of information technology, the accelerated pace of technological change in virtually every industry has created entirely new business, wiped out others, and produced a pervasive(广泛的) demand for continuous innovation. (L. 1 Para. 4)

此句看起来复杂,实际上也是个简单句。该句有一个主语 the accelerated pace;有三个平行谓语 has created、wiped out 和 produced,其中后两个谓语省掉了 has。

26.【定位】第一段。

【解析】推断题。本题考查的是在过去几十年间商业环境变化的原因。文章第一段提到:当今的商业环境发生了重大的改变。而就在短短的几年中,globalization 已经开创了 a variety of trends,接下来就是对 globalization 进行了具体的描述,比如说市场开放,真正的全球竞争,所以全球化就是中心。因此可以推断,商业环境的变化应该归因于 globalazation,故选项 D 为答案。其他三个选项均不符合题意。

27.【定位】第二段。

【解析】推断题。本题考查的是作者想在第二段表达什么样的想法。第二段作者着重描写了 information age 和 technology,第一句话是介绍,第二句则强调了中心 breakthroughs in information technology have irreversibly altered the ability to conduct business unconstrained by the traditional limitations of time or space。随后作者用了 intranets, e-mail, and portable computers 和 Internet 作为例子说明 information technology 的重要性,即信息技术上取得的惊人突破,使得商业不再像过去那样受时间和空间的限制。选项 B 表达的意思与此相符,为答案。选项 A 是对该句中的 startling breakthroughs in informatlon techllology 的错误理解;选项 C 中的 every corner 过于绝对;而选项 D 所表达的因

果关系与原文的相反。故选项 A、C 和 D 都应排除。

28. 【定位】第三段。

【解析】细节题。本题考查的是如果一个企业想在后工业经济中大步前进所必须做的事情。文章第三段第二句中提到：We are rapidly shifting from...to one that places the greatest values on information, services, support, and distributlon. 从结构上判断，上句中的 one 指的是 a new economv, 即后工业经济模式。由此可推知一个企业要想在后工业经济模式下繁荣起来，就得重视上述四个方面。选项 C 正说明这点，故为答案。其他三个选项文中均未提及，应排除。

29. 【定位】第四段。

【解析】细节题。本题问的是作者认为破坏性科技是对于什么的创新。文章第四段最后一句提到 More companies are learning the importance of destructive technologies—innovations that hold the potential to make a product line, or even an entire business segment, virtually outdated. 其中破折号后的内容是对前面 destructive technologies 的解释。选项 A 正是对此部分的同义转述，其中 eliminate 对应原文的 make...outdated, 故为答案。选项 B 和 D 文中未提及，可排除；选项 C 与原文矛盾。所以，选项 B、D 和 C 应排除。

30. 【定位】末段。

【解析】细节题。本题问的是随着顾客和商业市场的细分会有什么样的现象出现。文章末段第二句提到 superficially similar groups of customers may have very different preferences in terms of what they want to buy and how they want to buy it, 文章最后一句还提到 Moreover, the trend feeds on itself, a business's ability to serve sub-markets fuels customers' appetites for more and more specialized offerings. 由此可推知，要成功的话，就要抓住这些顾客的心理，制定特定的顾客偏好方案，满足消费者越来

越多的特殊需求。选项 D 正是对原文意思的转述,其中的 meet one's needs 对应原文的 fuels one's appetites,succeed 对应原文的 feed on,故为答案。选项 A 和 B 文中未提及;选项 C 是对末段第三句的错误理解。故选项 A、B 和 C 是错误的,应排除。

【参考译文及题区画线】

自 20 世纪 80 年代后期以来,商业环境在很多方面都发生了质的变化。冷战的结束从根本上改变了世界政治和经济的性质。在短短的几年里,全球化就引发了多种趋势,并带来深远的影响:市场开放、真正的全球竞争、解除政府对工业的广泛控制以及大量的可获得资本的出现。我们从真正的全球经济中获得了好处,同时也经历了风险。不管是华尔街的人还是平民百姓都能感受到远离他们的另外一个半球的经济混乱所带来的伤痛。

同时,我们完全进入了信息时代。信息技术上取得的惊人突破不可逆转地改变了企业的经营能力,使其不再像以往那样受时间和空间的限制。如今已几乎很难想象一个没有企业内部互联网、电子邮件和手提电脑的世界。互联网正在以惊人的速度从深层次上改变着我们的工作、购物、经商和联系的方式。

由此我们真正步入了后工业经济。我们正从以生产和商品为基础的经济迅速转向到极其重视信息、服务、支持和分配的经济。这种转变反过来使得"知识型工人"获得了前所未有的重视。这是一个新的阶层,他们富裕、受过教育、易变通,并认为自己是卖方市场的自由代理人。

除了信息技术领域,几乎每个产业的技术变化的加速发展都创造了全新的产业,淘汰了其他一些产业,并对持续创新提出了广泛的需求。新的产品、加工和分配技术为创造有竞争力的价值提供了有力的手段。更多的公司开始意识到破坏性技术的重要性。这是一种使一条生产线,甚至是整个商业部门都被淘汰的潜在创新。

另一个主要的趋势是消费者和企业（目标）市场的分化。表面上看起来相似的顾客群其实在购物和购物方式方面有不同的偏好，人们正逐渐了解到这一点。如今新的技术使得识别和服务与目标性微观市场变得更简单、更迅速、更便宜。而所采用的方式是在过去不可能发生或是因为费用太高而根本无法实行的。<u>而且，这种趋向可以以自己为依托，一个企业为子市场服务的能力会加大顾客对更多的专业性服务的需求。</u>

内容简介

　　本书全面分析大学英语六级阅读全真试题，破译命题规律，指明解题捷径，归纳阅读考点，传授有效的阅读方法，从词—句—段—篇等多层次指导学生如何处理生词、长难句，进而上升为篇章的有效阅读和理解，并通过真题实战和综合演练，强化各专项应试能力，巩固所学技巧，提高应试能力，营造临战氛围，检测复习成效。本书所有的练习都配有答案解析，旨在帮助考生知其然，并知其所以然。